SHATTERING

GLASS

NANCY-GAY ROTSTEIN

SHATTERING

GLASS

M&S

Canadian Cataloguing in Publication Data

Rotstein, Nancy-Gay
  Shattering glass

ISBN 0-7710-7589-8

I. Title.

PS8585.0845S5 1996   C813'.54   C95-933085-2
PR9199.3.R67S5 1996

The publishers acknowledge the support of the Canada Council and the Ontario Arts Council for their publishing program.

Published simultaneously in the United States of America by Farrar, Straus and Giroux, New York

Printed and bound in the United States of America

McClelland & Stewart Inc.
The Canadian Publishers
481 University Avenue
Toronto, Ontario
M5G 2E9

1 2 3 4 5   00 99 98 97 96

For Tracy, Stephen and Marci
I carry you with me
as a heartbeat . . .

Contents

JUDY

She had been more effective in London than even Alan Lewis had expected, she thought, as the plane lifted off the runway and moved out over the English Channel en route to Milan. Removing her planner from the briefcase she had placed under the seat in front of her, she reviewed yesterday's entries. She'd been able to accomplish everything listed there, except reaching Shane. Once the plane had attained cruising altitude, she released her seat belt from around the tailored suit she had worn during the intense two days of bargaining and, after putting away the planner, reclined her chair. Business class, with its spacious, comfortable seats, still seemed a luxury to her. Through an unblemished sky the craggy coastline of France became visible.

This was the first time she had been able to relax since Alan had informed her over lunch in Washington that she was expected to board British Airways the following evening.

"The only way we're going to take this deal down, Judy," her chief executive officer had instructed before sending her to represent Bancorp on its pending European acquisition, "is to put you on that flight tomorrow with a banker's draft to buy them out fast. Real fast. . . . Knowing how capable you are, you should be able to wrap things up in a week."

And she had bettered his estimate. The share purchase she had charge of had been a rarity: it was completed ahead of schedule. The other side insisted the initial meeting take place at her hotel. The Berkeley had been strategically picked by her Washington-based conglomerate as "the proper London address" for her stay. Its air-conditioned lounge area was subtly arranged into conversation groupings. Disguised with its fine leather wing chairs and cushioned sofas as an elegant salon, it easily lent itself to use as a high-powered deal-clinching site and was often the de facto office for American firms headquartered in the city. The sellers had not tried to change the purchase price. Of course, there had been the dramatic tactical choreography and the usual feints—the last-minute exculpatory clauses and addenda placed on the boardroom table after 9 p.m. on the night preceding the tentatively scheduled 9:30 a.m. closing. But Judy had learned to expect these and put in her customary deal-making all-nighter.

"You'll know you've got yourself a deal," Alan had said, concluding his directions to her, "when you see the big boys fly in from France and Germany. Once they've come to London, they're only there to sign and settle the menu for the closing luncheon."

Then yesterday morning the last of them, the president of Dyfax, had come over by corporate jet from Paris. The signing of the transaction was a mere formality, exactly as Alan had predicted. It ran like clockwork.

"Everything stands as agreed between the parties as of last evening," Atkins-Brown, the pedantic solicitor who represented the vendors, had announced, presiding over the proceedings in his firm's Trafalgar-motif Signing Room. His closely clipped nails tapped the stack of documents before him, each opened to the signature page. "Mrs. Kruger will be executing the agreement for the acquiring company, Mid-Atlantic Bancorp. The transfer will be executed on behalf of the vendors by their respective chairmen, Monsieur Dufresne of Dyfax, Herr Vertlonger of West Deutschlander Bank and Mr. Symonds of the Eagle Star Trust here in the city. Would you be so kind as to take your pen in hand, and begin signing the documents beside your initials, rotating as you go."

Fifteen minutes later, the Taittinger was uncorked, beluga caviar and fresh Scottish salmon were circulated. With much to do before the obligatory lunch traditionally hosted by the vendors, she excused herself from the principals in the minimum time dictated by politeness and returned by cab to the white marble steps of the Berkeley.

Once back in her suite, she changed into the bathing suit she had not previously had time to take out of her suitcase. She took the elevator to the penthouse floor and, walking up a winding stairwell, entered a neo-classical solarium and swim area. Stout columns were joined together by demi-arcs, plaster Roman figurines balanced on broken bases, their cast gaze looked down through thick windows upon the Victorian chimneys of Knightsbridge.

Judy sank into the turquoise liquid, the pool's sole occupant. She enjoyed the cool sensation and the sun that bore upon her shoulders through the porthole of the sliding roof. As she repeatedly spanned the pool's five-stroke length, her mind churned with the details of the transaction, refusing to acknowledge its completion until these pressures, pitted against that of the water, dissipated. She felt the tension begin to ease, as it always did. The cobwebs of her sleepless nights were swept away.

Focused and refreshed from exercising, she decided it was still too early to call Alan, reconsidering his instructions to report to him regardless of the hour. Six a.m. in Washington might not qualify as an acceptable time in spite of the enthusiasm transmitted in his last fax. She'd wait until she could get him at the office.

Briefly she considered telephoning Shane, but he always slept with the earphones of his Walkman in and wouldn't hear the phone ringing. At least, she hoped he was home and asleep. She put out of her mind the possibility that he wasn't; after all, hadn't the court-appointed counselor promised to look in on him while she was away? She must concentrate on what she had to do at the closing lunch. Mr. Lewis was sure to question her about Lord Duffield. And she had yet to meet him.

Wanting a more conciliatory image for this afternoon than the red linen gave her, she put on a camel suit, softening its look further with a cream open-neck shirt, the muted colors she found to be less obtrusive in the financial world. With the sureness of one used to managing her own appearance, she swept back her shoulder-length hair into a French roll, securing it with a tortoiseshell comb and, for this celebratory occasion, framed her oval face with wisps of her auburn hair. She added a dash of eye makeup, blush and a light lipstick, careful to ameliorate the inroads that strain had etched onto her features.

She turned the ornate brass doorknob of Mr. Symonds' club in Knightsbridge on schedule. A butler, attired in morning suit, circumvented her entrance into the foyer.

"May I ask whose guest you are?"

"Mr. Symonds'."

"Very good, madam. This way, please." The firmness inherent in his "please" ensured his authority was not to be disputed. He steered her across an adjoining thin margin of lawn and up an ancient stone path to a side door marked with a polished brass plaque inset with the words "Ladies' Entrance."

"Madam, I'm sure you wish to put away your case," he stated definitively as soon as he had brought her inside. "May I show you to the cloakroom?" He led her past the main floor's vast coat area with its double-width portico displaying the words "Members' Lounge," and up a flight of stairs to a slender door decorated with an Edwardian lady holding a parasol. She set her briefcase beneath her raincoat. Momentarily, she reconsidered this decision, not altogether comfortable being even temporarily separated from her folio. When Judy exited, she found this gentleman still in attendance.

"Might I take you to join the others? . . . Madam, if you please, follow me." His voice held the undisguised joy reserved for the completion of a delicate duty.

"Has Lord Duffield arrived?" she asked as he conducted her along the royal-blue hallway, its walls displaying muted canvases of historic vessels locked in battle.

"You will find his lordship in mid-room," he imparted discreetly, as they entered the salon.

The dining room and demi-bar area in which she found herself was imposing. Tall paneled mahogany doorframes reached toward dark coffered vaulted ceilings. Burnished anteroom chairs circled a bar set with vintage liquor bottles, its leather toned to match the walnut serving stand. A mahogany table stretched behind, its surface extended for thirty-five. The only brightness in the suite came from the silver sporting cups—trophies from cricket and rugby. Otherwise the room was unblemished by color. Judy recognized the major players and suspected the unfamiliar faces must belong to the host company's senior executives. No other woman appeared to have been invited.

"Mr. Graves," she said, greeting the wiry man with metal bifocals who approached her. Despite the day's humidity, he wore a worsted three-piece suit. "How nice to see you. I appreciated your help in taking me through the adjusting entries prior to closing."

"In all my practice I've never had occasion to have a woman representing one of our major clients. It's been a most pleasurable experience."

"Mr. Lewis would like your firm to continue in your capacity as auditors for the corporation."

"Delighted to do so. We've acted for Wydel since the war. . . . Is Mr. Kruger over here with you?"

"I would appreciate receiving a copy of your account so I can report to our chairman on our closing costs," she replied, turning aside his personal inquiry and handing him her embossed business card. "Could you please fax your statement to my private machine. It's the bottom number on the right-hand side."

"I'll attend to that myself. Would you like to be introduced to some of our senior partners?"

"Thank you, that's not necessary. But if you would be so kind, would you introduce me to Lord Duffield?"

"It would be my honor."

He led her to a gentleman of distinguished bearing who was removing his whiskey from the steward's silver tray. His public school tie and the delicate gold chain which looped between the twin pouches of his waist-coat overlay a corpulent chest.

"Lord Duffield, may I present Mrs. Judith Kruger, senior vice president of Bancorp International, who has come over from America to help us close this transaction."

"Judith, right. . . . Alan's new protégé. How good to meet you."

"If you'll excuse me." Mr. Graves moved off, leaving them alone.

He towered over her as he spoke. Barely five foot four, she strained to make eye contact. "My sources tell me you were very tough but fair. My congratulations to you. And to Alan for sending such a capable and charm-ing emissary."

"Thank you, Lord Duffield. I'm sure Alan won't forget the role you played in this matter."

"Is Alan planning to expand operations into other countries in the EC?" He swished around his tumbler as he spoke. "He has that right, you know, under the treaty."

"Our chairman is excited about the potential of the new Europe."

"First class. . . . There are several other interesting situations Alan and I should chat about on his next visit. Do tell me, how did you come to work for my old friend?"

"A fortuitous meeting some years back."

"Awfully clever of Alan to have someone as backup for Brian. I'm sure we shall be seeing more of you over here."

As Lord Duffield turned to the next person awaiting him, James Ingram, the thin, middle-aged solicitor who had been her liaison in London, tapped Judy on the shoulder.

"I'd like you to meet Douglas Boswell, our senior solicitor responsible for Bancorp's European holdings," he said of the stout cherubic-faced gentleman beside him.

"You're in for a treat, Mrs. Kruger. The chef here was recruited from the Dorchester. And the wine cellar is reputed to be among the finest in London. Did you know that Gladstone was a member here?" Boswell's eyes panned the location approvingly.

"Judy was quite impressive in not losing her self-control when Atkins-Brown tried to foist those addenda and undertakings on us at the eleventh hour. I especially liked that line she used. What was it you said, Judy?" James drew his forefinger across his line of mustache. "Right. . . . 'If your plan is to terminate the transaction, please do so quickly. I'd like to save three hundred pounds on my hotel bill.' "

"Actually, I didn't have much need for a hotel. I spent most of my nights in your firm's boardroom."

"Quite." James chuckled. "I can vouch for that."

"If you're staying on in London, Mrs. Kruger," Mr. Boswell said, "my wife would be delighted to show you around."

"Thank you, but I'll be leaving fairly soon."

"I suppose you're anxious to get back to your family," commented James. "Judy, you never did say what it was your husband does in America."

"Should you come to Washington, I'd like to reciprocate your hospitality and I'll do my best not to confine it to our boardroom," she responded, graciously sidestepping his curiosity.

"I trust you're speaking well of me," interjected David Atkins-Brown. Transferring his martini to his left hand, the plaid-bow-tied, balding adversary acknowledged each of his rivals with a handshake. With this maneuver, he cozied up to Judy.

"Can't say that we are," James said drolly. "Actually, we were chatting about Washington."

"I gather that's headquarters for you, Judy?" Atkins-Brown went on undeterred.

"Yes. International Square."

"How awfully interesting. . . . Do you and Mr. Kruger live in Washington proper or in the country?"

"I understand you commute into London, don't you?" She substituted her question for his.

"My wife and I rather enjoy the Devon coast. Takes an hour and a half from Paddington. Awfully good spot for the youngsters." He sipped the contents of his drink.

"What ages are your children, Judy?" James asked.

"I have a son. Seventeen."

"What sports does he play?" Mr. Boswell tossed in.

"He's a team swimmer."

Atkins-Brown gave a swirl to the remaining liquid in the tulip glass and, after popping the olive into his mouth, downed his martini. "I must say, it wasn't exactly sporting of your people to send a woman over here to negotiate. A ploy to get more concessions?" he added testily.

"David, you don't really mean that."

"I do indeed," he continued, refusing to be placated. "Your husband must have an awfully difficult time negotiating with you."

She thought herself impervious by now to personal questions and adept at handling cocktail chatter, but the directness of this unnecessary, hostile remark evoked an unexpected reflex in memory, too vivid to ignore. "If you'll excuse me," she said, and moved off to talk to Wydel's new chief financial officer.

Immediately after Mr. Symonds had completed the customary after-dinner thank-yous on behalf of the former owners, Judy extended her goodbyes to her contacts. She retrieved her case from The Ladies' and exited the club via the side entrance, avoiding the stewardship of the afternoon butler. It was now 1:30.

From her room at the Berkeley, a quarter hour later, she called Alan on his private line. Her CEO picked it up on the first ring.

"Did it close?"

"It's closed and lunched," she reported. Then she reviewed with him her closing notes, including the highlights of Atkins-Brown's ploys.

"Couldn't have gone better." Alan Lewis' resonant voice boomed through the new fiber-optic telephone technology. "Sounds like you got us all we wanted. And without giving anything away. How did Duffield treat you?"

"No problem there. He's looking ahead to future business with Bancorp International."

"Excellent. . . . You did a fine job, Judy."

"I'm glad you're pleased, Mr. Lewis."

He continued as if her comment had not reached Washington. "How are you feeling anyway, still jet-lagged?"

"I haven't had time to get jet-lagged." Fatigue must have entered her voice.

"I had a hunch everything over there depended on speed. You took the deal down in three working days. You've earned yourself a vacation. What plans have you made for the rest of the week?"

"None. Actually, I intended—"

He cut her off. "Figured as much. Fortunately, I have. Tomorrow morning, I want you to go to the British Airways counter at Heathrow, Terminal 1. They've a ticket for you on flight 564, leaving at seven-fifteen for Linate. Take the train from Milan to Como. That's a small village on a lake in northern Italy. Make sure you get off the train quickly at Como. Schedule I have says it only stops for two minutes. And Europeans take their trains seriously. You've got a reservation there at a world-class spa called Itaro. Write the name down. I'll spell it. I-t-a-r-o. Better take their number too. It's 39-31-4391."

"Mr. Lewis, thank you, but I can't possibly—"

"Of course you can. The company's paying for it. I like my senior executives well rested when they return from Europe. Everyone needs a little R and R. I want you to enjoy yourself, Judy, even if it is expensed as business. I don't want to see you in these offices until Monday."

"I appreciate your offer, but I really would like to return home as soon as possible."

"That deal wasn't slated to close until the end of the week. Nothing can be that pressing over here that you can't take some time off. And don't think of it as a vacation. It's a corporate necessity."

How could she risk telling him that for personal reasons she couldn't stay away any longer? It would be easier to go along with him. She would still be back for her son on the day she had promised.

"Did you catch that name?" he said, interrupting her thoughts. "That's Itaro. I-t-a-r-o. Phone Mrs. Fleet if you run into any problems. But you won't. I've arranged everything myself."

Without taking the time to charge the next call to her corporate AT&T card, she dialed her apartment in Crystal City. It connected instantly. No answer. Five rings and still no answer. Why wasn't Shane picking up the phone? Where was he? Her son couldn't have left for school already.

"I hope I'm not disturbing you," she said minutes later to the counselor Judge Arkin had assigned to her son's case. "But I phoned Shane to tell him when I was coming home and he wasn't there."

"Mrs. Kruger, I had a session with your son yesterday and he's fine."

"Would you please give him the message that I will be home on the day I said I would? But I've a change in telephone number. Starting tomorrow, I'll be at Country Code 39, 31-4391. If there's the slightest problem, let me know immediately."

∽

The plane gave a hard bump. Then another. How long were they going to go through this turbulence? From her window, the sky still looked innocent; wisps of clouds hung below the aircraft, tiny islands floating in a sea of blue.

That rude lawyer hadn't been able to resist irritating her at the closing lunch by making one final, nasty comment about the negotiation. Recalling Atkins-Brown's invasive remark broke her barrier of memory, exposing the feelings she had conditioned herself to block, making her vulnerable once again. Overstimulated and short on sleep, she had become more susceptible to these recollections. As the plane settled into the comforting monotony of a smooth flight, unwillingly her mind went back eight years to an earlier negotiation.

∽

Judy was placed at one end of the oak boardroom table across from her husband of almost ten years and three months' duration. The table gaped alienatingly between them, its shiny surface unmarked by its intimate contact with life. More than three dozen chairs, each with armrests, were positioned alongside its massive thirty-foot extension. A platter filled with Oreos had been set in front of Judy, their store-bought indifference in apparent contradiction to the exclusivity of the Limoges on which they were presented. A pot of coffee sat on a credenza, along with two matched thermoses, evidence that this was anticipated to be a long meeting and one allowing no interruptions.

Her husband, in his favorite winter teaching attire of V-neck over the obligatory shirt and tie, rough Harris tweed jacket and gray flannels, looked awkward beside his more substantially turned-out professionals. This retinue, Judy assumed, was purchased through the resources of her husband's affluent family. The eldest of the four, the one with peppered gray hair on both sides of a balding head, wore an immaculate chalk-stripe charcoal suit. A gold watch was set off by the gleaming cuff links on his crisp starched shirt. He sat directly beside Bob. With one arm balanced on the table, his back obstructing her view of his words, in a conspiratorial tone he kept up an ongoing, modulated monologue to her husband. Adjacent to him and along the breadth of the table sat a younger man, stacks of Cerlox tomes and a legal pad before his poised writing hand. Two others sat on Bob's other side, a printing calculator shared between them.

Judy brought a hand uncertainly from her lap and brushed a random auburn strand of pageboy off her cheek, then rearranged the skirt of her rust gabardine, the one Bob had selected the last time they had gone shopping together—fluffing its fullness self-consciously over her knees— and drew her heavy chair reassuringly closer to the comparatively rumpled, unpretentious man who had always handled her legal affairs. They had little choice but to agree to the location of this meeting. The conference area in his modest Alexandria office from which he and his partner ran their eclectic general practice for more than thirty years was insufficient to hold all those presently in attendance.

The two-hour trip had taken its toll. She should have accepted Mr. Scott's offer to drive her to Philadelphia. But she felt the need of the independence the Volvo afforded her, ensuring that she could leave whenever she pleased. It preserved the notion that she still had a semblance of control. She could force the events of today to an abrupt conclusion at any time she willed, shed Philadelphia's chaotic downtown core for the normalcy of Alexandria and be home in time to pick up Shane from swim practice.

"Mrs. Kruger, I'm John Irwin, senior counsel of Higgins, Stuart and Ross," said the man beside Bob. "Your husband has retained my firm to act on his behalf. Mrs. Kruger, before we commence, may I offer you some coffee?" She declined wordlessly. "Tom, how do you take yours?" he asked her attorney.

"None, thank you."

"Well, it's here if anyone changes his mind." He gestured to the young man beside him. "Josh Stevens is my associate. And Ted Hancock and Matthew Watson are partners in the accounting firm of Harris and Partners." Each of the gentlemen rose when introduced and extended a hand to Judy and her counsel. "I have been told by my client that you and he have come to an amicable arrangement," resumed Mr. Irwin. "The advantage of a negotiated settlement such as you and Mr. Kruger are entering into today is that it keeps everyone out of court. Formalizing the understanding you and your husband have reached should not be a tedious matter. We may even be out of here by lunch. Shall we aim for that?"

Judy's mind had snagged on Mr. Irwin's first operative sentence. "Amicable" was the word Judy had also chosen in describing her impending divorce to her friends. After all these years together, there had been no rancor. Her marriage was dissolving noiselessly.

Perhaps she should have known it might end this way, with the ease with which it had begun. Her father's death in May of her freshman year at Swarthmore and her mother's remarriage two years later had left her shaken and bereft. She rarely heard from her mother, who had since moved South and was preoccupied with her new life. Some of her friends had already married and were issuing daily fresh bulletins of happiness.

Only months after she received word that she had been one of the few women accepted at Georgetown University Law Center, Bob emerged on the scene. She felt apprehensive about the great commitment ahead of her, unsettled by the words of the noted woman attorney whom she had consulted. "You better understand, Judy, this is primarily a male-dominated profession—an all-boys club," Mrs. Belmont had said. "You'll have to work twice as hard as any of them to prove yourself. Are you prepared to give up friends, vacations, a private life of your own?"

Bob seemed to discourage her further, agreeing with Mrs. Belmont. "What's the point, Judy? Why put yourself through that?" He had been serious about their relationship right from the start. "Don't you want to marry someday, have a husband, a family? Law's a tough profession, I'd hate to see you out there in the rat race."

She married Bob a week after graduating from college. He was everything she hoped she might someday find in a husband. He possessed an intellect she admired, a composite of solid, scholarly features, a pedigree unencumbered by any desire to work in the family business, and he shared her enthusiasm for life beyond the boundaries of a large city. Although she intended to be an attorney, Bob had been offered a postdoctoral fellowship at the University of Michigan, and she wanted to be with him. Reluctantly, she turned down her law school acceptance.

Bob had chosen teaching after finishing his year at Ann Arbor, preferring the academic life over commerce, and had encouraged Judy to use her elementary school training. The birth of Shane a year into marriage curtailed even this career. With their twenty-year-old wood house with floor-to-ceiling windows and treed lot on the outskirts of Alexandria demanding as much attention as her son, the years slipped by. But the close, loving relationship she had believed she had found with Bob eluded her.

She found herself becoming increasingly restless as she approached thirty, her days unfulfilled. Marriage cemented into responsibility. Dreams you have at twenty-one, you do not willingly forsake at twenty-nine, aware that with the passage of the years the opportunity to realize them becomes more remote. But even though her world wasn't as perfect as she had imagined it would be, she felt grateful for the warmth and security of family life.

"I don't like the way our marriage is going," Bob announced one morning at breakfast immediately after Shane had left to meet the boys he always walked with to school. "I certainly don't want to spend my life like this. Do you?" These statements and the forcefulness with which Bob made them took her by surprise. This past month or so he had been more attentive to her than usual, bringing her bouquets of carnations or irises, not being content until he coaxed from her expansive details about her day. And he had become more aggressively loving.

As he spoke, he was fidgeting with the outer edge of his newspaper, which today remained unopened on the glass table beside his coffee mug. "Let's face it, Judy, how many times did I have to ask you to marry me? A dozen maybe, or more? When we met, you were headed into law. You've so much potential you've never had a chance to fulfill. You had barely begun to teach when Shane came along."

"I have no regrets about Shane," she said.

"That's true. I only wish you could say the same for me."

"But I don't regret marrying you."

"I know you don't feel about me the way you used to. I've felt this for some time now." He stood up and a moment later sat down, moving his chair closer to her.

"What are you trying to say?" she asked, attempting to figure out where he was leading. Her stomach knotted up as it always did when something terrible and beyond her control was about to happen. "Are you saying you don't love me anymore?"

"I've always loved you, Judy. But how do you think it makes me feel that you're unhappy? I know things haven't been what they should be between us."

The steady hum of the refrigerator seemed to fill the room.

"Is there someone else?" she asked softly, not really wanting to hear his answer. Her heart had suspended its rhythm.

"You should know me better than that. It's just that you've given up too much already for this marriage. I've been thinking it might be better for you if we were living apart. . . . You deserve more out of life."

Through the sudden silence that dropped between them came the whirl of the washing machine finishing the laundry she had put in before she made breakfast.

"I don't know what I'd even do with myself," she heard herself say.

"You could go back to teaching. Or else become a lawyer. It's not too late to pick up where you left off. This is a much better time for you to enter law. Remember, years ago, the way Mrs. Belmont warned you what it meant for a woman to be an attorney? Well, it's a different world today. And you won't have to worry about money, whatever you decide to do. I promise you I'll take care of you and Shane until you're able to support yourself. . . . You have your whole life ahead of you."

She was stunned and hurt. This was all so unbelievable to her. However, she felt with time and Bob's love for Shane, they would get through this crisis. But Bob repeated these ideas week after week in a collage of remarks. He seemed convinced his solution was best for both of them. Demoralized, she agreed to a divorce. Had Bob not pressed for this, she would never have considered such a radical step. For what was happy? A quotient with no absolute measurement possible.

As events began to move inescapably toward a parting, she became more uncertain of her decision. Bob might not have been the best husband for her but he was a good man—consistent, dependable, her source of security. And a good father to Shane. Maybe there would be no one else better out there, ever. How was she going to handle being single again? Marrying so young, she'd lived such a protected life. Even though she had sometimes felt lonely when she was living with Bob, she had never really been on her own before. She wasn't prepared for a career. She was used to being a full-time mother. How difficult was it going to be for her as a single parent, raising a nine-year-old boy? And the ten years she and Bob had been together and the memories they shared, could these all come down to nothing? Had her expectations of him and of herself been unreasonable?

But once they had discussed the general framework for a settlement and Bob went to a lawyer and recommended that she do the same, it had become impossible to turn back. The mechanics of the divorce took on a momentum of their own.

"Now on the issue of alimony"—Judy caught up to Mr. Irwin's agenda at this point—"I'm sure you are aware that my client's salary as an associate professor at George Mason University is a fixed one. Mr. Watson, would you be so good as to show Tom Mr. Kruger's most recent income tax return?"

"Mr. Kruger's paycheck is not in dispute," blustered Mr. Scott, running his hand through his thatch of gray hair.

"Good, we can move directly to your client's entitlement, which as dictated under the statutes in this state, as well as your own, is determined by need as ascertained by expenses and a spouse's ability to pay," the senior counsel said. "Mr. Hancock and Mr. Watson have before them the canceled checks covering a six-year period from the parties' joint bank account. These are inclusive of the allowance Mr. Kruger gives his wife for management of the household. Fortunately, he has retained these, along with his credit card statements, for tax purposes. Mr. Hancock and Mr. Watson have gone through the process of organizing them for us today. Each pile is one year of receipts, divided monthly, and is marked with the appropriate year. They have then further broken them out for the purpose of this meeting into heads of expenses. I believe, Mr. Hancock, you have divided them into shelter, clothes, medical and dental, food, education, entertainment and leisure. A summary of their findings has been prepared for your convenience and appears as Schedule A in the top binder already before you."

Judy opened the maroon book. The document marked Schedule A was, as the senior counsel had stated, at the front of the first of five of these color-coded materials.

Numbers were charted into categories and groupings with subtotals and totals underneath. Theirs were not the rough figures that Mr. Scott had requested of her—they were set out to the penny. And the dollars allocated beside each were dramatically lower than those she had estimated. Also their figures didn't make sense. Her clothing for all of last year must have been more than $1,050.95. Her dress for the dean's party alone had been $350 and Bob had certainly reminded her of it often enough. How could their entertainment have been only ten dollars in November and twelve dollars in December? They had driven into Washington two weeks in a row sometime around that period, once for a concert at the Kennedy Center and then the following week for Susan Simpson's birthday at the Columbia Restaurant. And where was the record of the cash that Bob would often hand her?

Across the expanse of polished oak she looked over at her husband, hoping he would note the inaccuracies. But he had not bothered to open his set of documents.

She felt the color which earlier she had uncharacteristically applied, wanting for the last time she would be in her husband's company to look her best, drain from her cheeks, leaving her wan and unprotected.

"These aren't correct," she whispered to Mr. Scott.

She felt his hand on her arm, restraining further comment.

"Let me handle this, Judy." Putting his elbows precipitously on the table, her lawyer leaned toward the group. "My client and I have also gone through these items. These numbers do not come near our understanding of the expenses. Based on our calculations, your figures are grossly inadequate."

"I assume you brought your tabulations. May we see them?"

"With pleasure." Five copies of the single page which Mr. Scott had asked her to provide him and they had reviewed cursorily yesterday were passed about the table, each participant removing one until the sheet reached Mr. Irwin.

"Mr. Scott, you have presented our client with a gross amount under each category. You have not itemized these numbers. I presume you can produce copies of the invoices to support your client's claim?"

"There's no need for them. My client has been running the household for ten years and knows precisely what those costs regularly are, as well as her own and the child's."

Why was her husband so silent and detached, as though he were not part of the proceedings? Surely he knew she would not misrepresent her expenses, that the ones she had produced were accurate.

"You can't expect our client to agree to such an extravagant sum without some backup. With all due respect, Tom, the sheet you tabled is tantamount to a wish list."

"Why didn't you tell me you needed receipts? I have most of my personal ones. And the others that are necessary, I could have arranged to get hold of . . . I still can," she said, modulating her voice so only her counsel could hear.

"It isn't necessary. We have all the information we need to get you a good settlement. Leave everything to me," and elevating his voice, he replied aggressively, "These figures are my client's current expenses and her minimum requirements with which she is prepared to leave the marriage."

"There's no need to take that attitude, Mr. Scott. . . . May I suggest that we begin by working with the figures that Mr. Hancock and Mr. Watson have brought together in the binders? And let's see how far apart we really are. These gentlemen can answer any questions you or your client might have. . . . Why don't we start with utilities? That's a straightforward area. I see you have put it under Household Expenses. Harris and Partners lists it on page five under Shelter. If you care to turn there, you will see they have set out each month's accounts for telephone, electricity, heating oil and water. As you can see, in no month did the aggregate approach the figure you submitted for your client. . . . Mr. Hancock here has the specific invoices if you care to examine them."

There was the snap of a series of elastic bands as this accountant pulled from each of the piles a clipped cache of receipts and walked them around to Mr. Scott. Her attorney glanced through them; he rippled the collection as if it were a deck of playing cards.

In all the years of their association, Judy had only seen her lawyer in the casual setting of his Alexandria office. He always seemed in control, relaxed amid a clutter of documents on his desk. But here, he seemed disorganized and misplaced.

"These seem in order," he mumbled. "Judy, any other points?"

Judy reapplied herself to the maroon binder. Bob did the accounting and banking and she knew how precise he was. Why didn't these figures correspond with her own? "There seem to be things missing from this schedule," she said, alerting Mr. Scott to her concerns. "I don't see the water heater we had to install two years ago. And they don't have the air-conditioning units in the bedrooms. They're not here either."

"My client deserves an explanation as to why the air conditioners and water heater do not appear on this list," he said gruffly, relaying these omissions.

"Mrs. Kruger is quite right," replied the accountant. "There have been capital outlays in the past. We have brought these nonrecurring expenses together under Contingencies. You will find that heading forms the final entry in every category. I trust that satisfies your client's question."

"Judy, I think we're okay. They've dealt with your concern."

"But look under Leisure. I don't see Hilton Head or Tanglewood."

Mr. Scott privatized their conversation. He backed off his elbows and angled his considerable bulk between Judy and the others. "Let me explain this to you," he said with exaggerated patience. "It's important you understand what they were saying just now. In each of the categories, they've taken into consideration the one-time expenses and built in a miscellaneous item called Contingencies. That will cover you for those things that you've been asking about. If you accept their records as complete, they're being quite evenhanded."

"Tom, is there anything further on these sheets you or your client would like to pursue?" inquired Mr. Irwin, cutting their conference short.

"No. We're satisfied at this point," Mr. Scott replied, reclining in his chair. Judy looked down the length of the table at Bob. He was impassive, his face unrevealing of information.

"Then, according to Harris and Partners, that places Mrs. Kruger's justifiable expenses at twelve hundred a month, or fourteen thousand and four hundred dollars annually. And it is on the basis of this amount that support is to be calculated. That is the amount on which any court in this state would base an order. There has been no question here of what a court calls a marital fault—adultery, cruelty—committed by either party to this divorce agreement. No extenuating circumstances that might lead a court to alter entitlement.

"Tom, I'm sure you've advised your client she has no claim on her husband's parents' sizable holdings. During the entire duration of the marriage her husband has demonstrated a disregard for his family's assets, supporting his wife and son entirely from his salary as an associate professor at George Mason University. Notwithstanding the law, Mr. Kruger, Sr., has asked his son to request a release from your client, as understandably, for people in their position, it could prove an unnecessary embarrassment were she to pursue such a vexatious action. We all know Mrs. Kruger would never entertain such litigation; therefore I'm certain she has no objection to executing a release in favor of Mr. Kruger's parents. You will notice, in the document marked Settlement, that clause ten covers this release. If you'll turn to the blue folder . . ."

Judy's mind blurred. They were discussing everything except the matter most important to her: Shane. Mr. Scott had told her that custody of her son could swing in either direction. As her lawyer shuffled the pages in the folder, she said, "Why haven't they brought up custody? I insist that Shane remain in my—"

"I'll deal with it. . . . John, my client is prepared to sign the release on condition that all other terms can be worked out to her satisfaction."

"Very well," said Mr. Irwin. "Shall we turn to ownership of the house?"

"I suggest we tackle custody first."

"As you wish, Tom. We all know it is impossible to predict with certainty how a judge would decide custody in this instance. Courts are not bound by a single rule but decide by a series of factors brought together under the rubric of what is in the best interests of the child. The tender-age doctrine forms one of these criteria. It usually awards custody of a child that falls within that age to the mother. But the party in question is nine and, therefore, at the high end of the range to which the doctrine applies. Another consideration which would mitigate against the tender-age doctrine being applicable here is that the child in question is a boy, a factor recently tending in the courts to strengthen the father's claim. . . . My client could contest custody, and possibly succeed."

Her eyes groped for those of her husband, but they were unattainable; he held them fixed scrupulously upon his lawyer.

"My client respects the strong feelings his wife holds on the matter of custody. Moreover, he does not want to put his son, whom he loves deeply, through the emotional turmoil guaranteed by a lengthy custody battle. Therefore, he has agreed to give his wife custody, with visitation rights, of course, on every second weekend and on holidays."

She felt limp, overcome with relief.

"Now, John, you wanted to talk about the house?"

"Yes, I do, Tom. My client has given a great deal of consideration to this issue. Your client may be unaware that their home in Fairfax County, Virginia, is registered in Mr. Kruger's sole name as owner and is not marital property. As such, it is his asset to do with entirely as he pleases. However, he has instructed me to give his wife the house. Notwithstanding the dissolution of their marriage, he continues to have strong feelings for his wife and wants her to remain, if she so chooses, in the home they shared together. Furthermore, he is concerned about the welfare of his son and does not want to uproot him. Of course, it will be up to Mrs. Kruger to maintain the expenses, the mortgage payments, repairs and the like. I am sure, Tom, you will agree this is a generous gesture by my client."

Mr. Scott nodded concurrence.

Spontaneously, she looked again in Bob's direction. His shoulders were slouched, his eyes lowered. He appeared to be suffering as acutely as she.

"That brings us to the only remaining issue to be resolved today. A housekeeping matter, so to speak. Your client's preferred method for receiving her support."

Her energies depleted from tension, her mind wandered as Mr. Irwin launched into another recitation of the law. She had gotten what she was most concerned about. She had sole custody of Shane. And her lawyer seemed satisfied with the financial terms—he considered it "even-handed." She had even ended up with the house. Of course, it would be difficult starting over, but she would manage. She was going to make a good life for herself and Shane.

This lapse in concentration was ended by a pair of staccato phrases.

"Lump sum or monthly allowance. What's it to be, Tom?"

"My client hasn't instructed me as to her preference. . . . Judy, what do you want me to tell him?" Her lawyer's inquiry thrust her into the midst of yet another issue.

"I'm awfully sorry. Could Mr. Irwin possibly go over that again?"

"John, my client would like you to restate your position."

"We have no position. Your client has the freedom to choose between monthly allowance or lump sum. I was merely outlining the considerations inherent in both. The monthly allowance is, I believe, closest to my understanding of how the parties presently deal with household expenses. This form of payment renders one dependent on a monthly check. Some women have reason to worry about the punctuality of their check each month or whether indeed it will arrive at all. Mrs. Kruger need not concern herself with this point, considering the integrity of my client. But bear in mind that should Mrs. Kruger at any future time decide to remarry, the monthly allowance will automatically terminate.

"As to the other option—the lump sum—it is a one-time payment. The amount is determined by the same expenses we ascertained earlier, but is paid at one time and, in your case, will be a very sizable sum. That gives you freedom. Many women, even those who never plan to remarry, find the lump sum attractive. It gives them, often for the first time, the opportunity to make their own investments or, if they prefer, the security of knowing they have money in the bank. It facilitates long-term budgeting. They are freed from the dependency on their former husband. Moreover, it does not preclude the possibility of remarriage at some later date. With the one payment, you have already taken the full benefit of your entitlement. The disadvantage of the lump sum arises if you do not feel you have the ability to handle your own finances and you are, therefore, concerned about making improvident investments. It is up to you, Mrs. Kruger, with your attorney's guidance to examine the contingencies and expectations in your life. This is only a summary of your options. I am sure Mr. Scott has gone over this with you in fuller detail."

"What do you think I should do?" she conferenced with Mr. Scott.

"He's really said everything I would have told you if the judge hadn't dragged out the Jones probate an extra two days. It comes down to a judgment call. Only you can decide this one."

"Tom, have you anything you would like to toss into the hopper on this one?"

"I believe you have covered it all. As I was advising my client, this decision is ultimately a personal one."

Five heads stared down the table at her.

Judy had information overload. Up to this meeting, her preoccupation had been getting custody of Shane. She had thought of little else. Her son was everything to her and she had no intention of letting Bob take him from her. On this, her husband knew she was firm. But one payment over another? She had not even turned her mind to this before. Mr. Irwin made it all sound so simple. Door A or Door B. One type of wallpaper or another. Why hadn't Mr. Scott familiarized her with these payment alternatives before she arrived here? And Bob had never mentioned it, merely assuring her that she would have no financial worries.

She stumbled. "I'm sorry, I just can't continue." Her voice trembled and, despite her efforts to contain it, became decibels louder.

"Okay, Judy, you're the client," he said tête-à-tête. "But I don't recommend putting it over to another meeting like this. You're giving them an opportunity to renegotiate the whole settlement."

"I really can't make a decision on this now."

"It's up to you." He took his planner from a stained leather satchel and, opening it with its crimson ribbon, began to turn its pages. "First appointment I can give you in the office is two weeks Wednesday. I'm back in probate until then. And"—still flipping its weeks—"it would have to be another three after that before I can put away a full day to come up here again. But I'm telling you now, I'm not going to alter what I have said here: you're the only one who can make this decision."

Mr. Irwin, who with the others awaited this interaction, broke the etiquette of his profession. He did not wait to have her instructions conveyed to him through her counsel, and when he spoke, he addressed her directly. "Mrs. Kruger, I realize this meeting has been a strain on you, as I can assure you it has been for my client. It really would be better if we can settle this one remaining matter between you and Mr. Kruger now. How you decide to take your alimony really is, as your own lawyer himself said, merely a personal decision. Only you know your intended circumstances, and I am certain you know it as well today as you will a month from now. This is nothing to be fussed about. . . . You have your attorney available to you today. We really should complete everything at this time. And then all the outstanding matters between you and your husband will have been disposed of. I'm sure you would like to see that happen as much as we would. We have all the necessary papers prepared, pending your decision on this final matter."

Judy felt totally alone in a way she had never known before.

As through a heavy screen, Judy heard a voice, gentle and reassuring.

"Judy, would it help if we spoke in private?"

She nodded assent.

"Mr. Irwin, my wife and I would like to have some time to discuss this in private."

"As you wish, Mr. Kruger." The senior counsel withdrew, taking with him his three colleagues.

Only her lawyer remained behind. "I'll sit in on this," he said.

"I'd prefer to speak to my husband alone, if you don't mind."

As Mr. Scott vacated the chair beside Judy, Bob sat into it, heavily. Judy felt an arm brush against her length of curl and encircle her shoulders. His warmth was a welcome relaxant, his touch a trigger of memory. She wanted to take shelter within his arms, refuge from what was transpiring, desperate to return to what might have been. She had not anticipated this roller coaster of emotion. She had not expected these feelings to flood in on her, to be so affected by the events of the day, in this, the formality of what was already passed. For the longest moment he said nothing, just held her like this, and when he spoke it was with compassion.

"Judy, I don't like to see you so troubled. I'm sure you'll make the right decision."

"Bob, it seems so strange being here. It's horrible having our life dissected by all these people. Even now, I can't believe it's really over."

"I know what you mean because I feel the same way. . . . Judy, the reason I gave you the house is that I want you to feel as secure as possible. My lawyers told me that it wasn't necessary. They said the most I should give you was the right to live there. But I know how you and Shane love that old place. . . . Judy, I don't want anyone to pressure you but I really think it would be better to try to make your decision today. I can see how stressful this has been for you. I don't want you to go through this a second time."

"I just don't know, Bob. I'm not sure what to do."

"Well, over the years you have wanted to become more involved in our personal finances and how I invested our money."

"You mean take the lump-sum payment?" She sought to decipher his suggestion. This intimacy made her receptive to his advice.

"That's the one that will give you the most control over your financial security. But only go that way if this is something you would feel comfortable with."

Judy felt reassured by his words and the arm that still lingered on her shoulders. She did not pull away from him. It seemed to her a long time before Bob spoke again.

"Should I ask them to come in now?" A formal quality had returned to his voice.

She felt calmer, able to continue. Bob was right. It would be best to conclude everything today.

"Yes, I'm ready."

Bob invited them to return.

Mr. Scott was pulling out the chair beside Judy when she said to him, "I'll take the one-time lump sum."

The divorce settlement was executed within the half hour, witnessed and placed in the firm's vault by four o'clock that April afternoon.

∽

"Beautiful day, isn't it, Judy?" called Susan Simpson from across the breadth of the parking lot of the Hollin Hills Community Association swimming pool when Judy arrived along with those in the area whose children were enrolled in the 11 a.m. Saturday lesson. They had joined as a family when Shane was a toddler. Judy let the Volvo idle, her window rolled down, as Shane scrambled out of the back and ran to catch up with Susan's son, Mike. The scent of pine from the surrounding wooded area filled the warm Saturday June morning.

"Sure is."

"Aren't you going to stay for the boys' lesson?"

"Wish I could. I've got some errands to do," Judy replied above the clamor of exuberant youngsters.

"I understand. . . . Mike and I go right by your place anyway. I can drop Shane off, if you like, when their class is over."

"Thanks for offering. But that's not necessary."

Coming closer to her, Susan continued. "Must be embarrassing to see Bob's marriage announcement in the paper."

"Bob's marriage announcement? . . . What are you talking about?" she asked stiffly.

"I'm awfully sorry. I guess I shouldn't have said anything."

"When did it come out? What did it say?"

"It was in the *Alexandria Journal.* Friday's edition. Didn't you read it?"

"No."

"Well, according to the paper, Bob has remarried and entered some business. I think it said a clothing chain. I had no idea you didn't know. I feel terrible mentioning it to you like this."

"Excuse me, I really have to be going." Judy ground her engine into gear and, turning her car toward the pitched incline of the subdivision, went directly home.

She retrieved the *Alexandria Journal* from the garbage. Opening the paper to the section on engagements and weddings, she found herself staring at a photo of Bob beside a girl in a traditional bridal gown, above the caption "Walker-Kruger."

Suzanne Carole Walker, daughter of Dr. and Mrs. Mark Walker of Alexandria County, was married Wednesday to Robert Arnold Kruger, formerly of Alexandria County.

Judge Allister Rowland performed the garden ceremony at the Main Line estate of the groom's parents, Mr. and Mrs. Jack Kruger of Philadelphia. The bride, 22, attended T. C. Williams High School and graduated from George Mason University, where she is currently enrolled in a master's program in economics.

The groom, 34, a graduate of Temple University, received a Ph.D. from Swarthmore College and until recently has been an associate professor of economics at George Mason University.

Scanning through the description of the gown of candlelight chiffon, the miniature carnations and white sweetheart roses, she read on:

After a Bermuda honeymoon, the groom will take up a position as president and chief executive officer of Kruger Clothing Industries, a regionally based retail clothing chain and member of the Kruger Enterprises group of companies. The couple will reside in Philadelphia.

How could Bob have done this to her? If their marriage had one consistent component, it had been trust. And she had believed him. Every contrivance, rationalization and manipulation. Every altruistic reason he gave for wanting a divorce.

Her mind involuntarily spun with his fabrications. His words came at her again and again. She was powerless to stop its replay, to end the words she had naively believed.

"I've always loved you, Judy. But how do you think it makes me feel that you're unhappy? . . . You've given up too much already for this marriage. . . . It might be better for you if we were living apart. And you won't have to worry about money. I promise you I'll take care of you until you're able to support yourself. . . . You deserve more out of life."

How could she have been so foolish, so self-absorbed and foolish? How could he have been cheating on her and she not sensed it? The girl he married was probably one of his students. Everyone must have known about the affair. Everyone apparently, but her. Alexandria was really such a small community when you came down to it. He had embarrassed her, defiled what good there had been in their marriage. Separation and divorce was one thing, but humiliation quite another.

And she had continued to trust him right through the divorce. Mr. Irwin stated there had been no question of a marital fault—adultery, cruelty—committed by either party to the divorce agreement. Had he kept the existence of a girlfriend secret from his own lawyers too? Were they, like her, his dupe? Was that why his family insisted on using a Philadelphia firm rather than a local Alexandria one—a firm removed by unimpeachable credentials as well as physical distance from the gossip generated in the smaller inbred city? Or was this firm of exquisite reputation, used exclusively through two generations of Krugers for all the family's acquisitions and transactions, also part of the charade? Did that explain Mr. Irwin's insistence on speed to complete the divorce settlement that day, speed at all cost?

Her husband's unexpected offer not to contest custody of Shane: was it done, as his lawyer had said, out of respect for her wishes, and not to emotionally traumatize his son by forcing him to appear in court? Or was it done for a darker reason—to ensure the divorce would not be held up by a lengthy custody battle, the evidence of which might expose his adultery and, this in turn, force him to pay significantly more in support? Her husband knew his scenario and directed it perfectly. She had trusted him from opening act to curtain. How could she have been so gullible, so gullible and foolish?

∾

Judy dealt daily with the realities of her divorce—the loneliness that engulfed her and the bouts of anger that beset her unexpectedly. And the everyday decisions which seemed to weigh more heavily upon her now that they were hers alone to make, a responsibility never again to be shared. She knew her marriage was a loss society did not permit her to mourn. But to these difficult adjustments she was experiencing was added the trauma of betrayal, one deepened and exacerbated by the continuing reports and commiserations from well-intentioned friends.

"Did you know she's expecting?" Susan reported at their next encounter. "Helen saw them in Old Town yesterday. She says she looks about seven months."

"My husband talked to Bob when he came by for his things at the university." Diane caught Judy while she was clipping their common hedge. "He told Steve he's making well into six figures."

"I sure hope Tom Scott didn't let them get away with minimizing your expenses," commented Elaine. "He may be honest, but he's not the smartest, you know, though he's been at it a long time."

Bob had said it would be an uncomplicated agreement. Trusting him, she felt no need to drain her resources to hire high-priced talent. How could she have expected an overworked attorney with a general practice to be a match for the sophisticated team her husband had assembled.

"Look. You're okay." Adele, herself recently divorced, evaluated Judy's situation as they watched their sons shoot baskets on the mini-court beside Rippen Road. "You have clear custody and the house. Monthly support pegged to an inflation clause—"

"An inflation clause?"

"Yeah. Indexes alimony to the Consumer Price Index. When you're on a fixed income, like we are, it's the only way to keep up with rising prices.

Inflation's an economic fact of life. No one signs a contract today without putting in that clause. . . . I'm sure your lawyer covered you for it."

"I didn't see it there."

"You're still okay. It's not fatal. You've got a fail-safe. With the mega-dollars they say Bob's making now, if you find you need more, just get that lawyer of yours to go back to court and have the agreement changed. No judge in this state would call Bob's tremendous salary hike less than two months after the divorce anything but a material change in circum-stance. . . . You can do that, you know, when you're on an allowance."

"I got a lump sum."

"But that's final. You can't go back to court. . . . What would have possessed you to do something like that?"

Was that what was behind Bob's gift of the house? Was his gesture the ultimate confidence game? Had his lawyers advised him to do this to lower her defenses and reestablish her trust, in order to sell her on the one-time lump-sum payment? And had he told his lawyers to leave him alone with his wife if she resisted this subtle inducement, certain he knew exactly what words and body language were needed to convince her to do what was best for him? Had he carefully written both their lines and she, in turn, on cue, naively read hers? By her ignorance of the law, she had put him irrevocably beyond the reach of the courts.

"I'm sorry, I should never have said that," Adele went on when Judy did not volunteer an explanation. "Of course, no one could have guessed Bob would do a complete career change and end up making so much money."

These encounters left her feeling foolish, depressed and angry. Though she did not doubt her friends' sincerity, increasingly she withdrew from contact with them and moved toward the person with whom she had the greatest affinity. The circumstances of her divorce brought her and her son even closer. They needed each other more: they both had been betrayed.

"Why isn't Daddy picking me up on weekends anymore?" Shane averted his eyes as he asked this question. He poked despondently at his cereal.

At the beginning Bob had adhered to the settlement, coming for Shane every second weekend. But within a few months, the arrangement began to falter. There were last-minute changes and excuses. These left Shane hurt and bewildered.

"What did I do wrong, Mommy? . . . Doesn't Daddy love me anymore?"

Setting down her coffee, she took her son's small hands between hers, encouraging him to look up at her. "Darling, of course Daddy loves you, just as I do. But you know he lives in Philadelphia now, so he can't come to see you as much as he wants to."

"Mike says he has a new Jaguar and a new wife. Why didn't you tell me?"

"You remember we discussed that Daddy had remarried," she said gently. "Now the Jaguar part, I didn't know about. Anyhow, I thought you and Mike liked sports cars—the time the two of you had so much fun working together on his Porsche model. . . . " She was trying to take his mind off his disappointment, turning the conversation to one of his favorite topics.

How do you explain to a ten-year-old that he was not the one who had been rejected, but you? That his father preferred another woman instead of his mother, and so they both had been left? She wanted to tell him it was not his fault that his father had stopped seeing him. It was nothing Shane had done or said, but rather he had been replaced in his father's affection by the arrival of a new son. One that presently was less demanding.

Judy could not tell Shane these things—they still created too much anguish for her to speak about them. She answered him instead by unqualifiedly pouring into him the strength of all her love.

One clear summer night, the Friday of yet another aborted weekend that Shane was to have spent with his father, Judy found her son tossing restlessly in bed. She gathered him up in his pajamas and, taking a flashlight, set off down the incline of their driveway toward Paul Spring Park, a few blocks away. Crickets pulsed from their hiding places in the deep grass. Shane refused to speak but burrowed his hand deep inside the pocket of hers and was unresponsive to her chatter. His mind seemed distanced in thought.

They sat in a clearing overlooking the high brush bordering the dry bed of the creek. Fireflies hovered, their soft tails flickering on and off, minute beacons lighting up the dark night.

"Look at that. There must be thousands of them." Shane broke his silence. "How many do you think there are, Mommy?" he asked incredulously. Happiness had returned to his voice.

Together they counted the fragile creatures until her son, content, was overcome with the heaviness of sleep.

From that night on, she planned every weekend to be an adventure for Shane. She did not want him to have another disappointment.

She renewed their membership at the Hollin Hills Community Association swimming pool. How thin his body looked freed from its disguise of jeans and sweatshirt, his chest and shoulders not yet grown into manhood—thin and vulnerable. Early mornings, he would ply the Olympic pool with her, pacing her stroke for stroke. With the arrival of the boys with whom he had grown up, he would dash away to race lengths. After his day at the club, he was more relaxed and easier to manage.

In the fall, they took the Metro to the National Zoo in Washington. Shane's favorite was the hippopotamus. He would jump up and down, run his fingers over the protective grating and dissolve into laughter as the giant mammal hidden in his cool, murky bath would slowly emerge, thick mud oozing sloppily down his enormous slippery hide.

In the winter, they went to the Smithsonian. He would hurry down the ramp to line up for the space exhibit. When he peered inside the tiny capsule in which the astronauts had flown to reach the moon, his eyes would widen with delight, his mind transported on his own voyage of discovery.

And always there were the Sunday afternoon movies. Shane, involved in the latest extraterrestrial installment or adventure saga, would bounce up and down on the theater's collapsible seats. He would wrap one arm around her neck and, unable to suppress his excitement another moment, reassure her of the hero's triumph by whispering all the details, frame by frame, with which his friends had prepared him.

In the intervening hours when Shane was at school, she sought to keep herself busy in an effort to forestall reliving the past and the depression and sense of worthlessness it inevitably spawned. She put her name in as a substitute teacher for the remainder of the year with the elementary school boards within a half-hour drive from Hollin Hills.

Despite Adele's warnings about inflation, Judy was not feeling any financial strain. She had invested her funds in the asset mix recommended by her financial planner, dividing her $150,000 into three categories with yields corresponding to their level of risk. She struck a balance between conservative investments with lower interest and marginally more aggressive ones with a higher rate of return. A third of her funds went into certificates guaranteed by the government. Another third went into mutual funds, which fluctuated but had the potential for greater yield. She used her remaining $50,000 to purchase a one-half interest in a rental property, a duplex about one mile from her home, an opportunity which came up through her family physician, Dr. Norman. During her annual checkup, he mentioned he was seeking a partner for this property and offered her participation.

But midway through the second year of her divorce, she found that she had to budget more closely. Inflation started to affect her finances. It was eroding in real purchasing power any pretense of a lifestyle. At first, she had been able to save her income from part-time work but she increasingly had to rely on this for her basic expenses. She was determined not to touch her capital.

Teaching, which had begun as a pleasant diversion, a therapy to occupy a mind with excess time, had now taken on the urgency of an economic necessity. She no longer waited passively for the morning call offering her a day's employment. Daily she contacted each board with whom she was registered, pressing for work until she sensed she was becoming a nuisance. She extended her search of where she would work to outlying school districts. By six-thirty, she was dressed and ready to leave the instant a request came through for her services. Despite her efforts, she never could count on working more than three days a week.

Life had become an elimination of luxury.

Clothing became tightly budgeted. No longer could she purchase stylish clothes for herself. By adjusting a hemline, she was able to minimize the dating of her apparel. But soon more was required. As Shane outgrew his clothes, she could not afford to replace them with the brand names he and his friends talked about. Nor any other new clothes for that matter. She and Shane only entered secondhand stores, Once Is Not Enough or the Thrift Shop, often purchasing for him the less fashionable items that in better times she used to put in the Goodwill box.

"How come we're going to these places?" Shane asked as she tried to talk him into a green turtleneck sweater. "I don't like the things here. Why should I wear someone else's clothes?"

Always after such a purchase, she obsessively wrung the dirt out of these garments, again and again, before placing them on Shane's bureau for the morning. These clothes were discards. The pickings left over from other people's lives were now recycled into the fabric of their existence.

She continued to buy from the specialty bread shop where the same staff in plaid aprons and hairnets pinned beneath matched caps had served her since her arrival in Alexandria. But now instead of lining up with the other customers for the freshly baked goods she chose instead from the metal rack marked "Yesterday's Baking."

"Mom," Shane said one morning as she was leaving for work, "don't forget my chocolate cupcakes tonight."

When Judy reached Pastries Galore at five-thirty, the basket yielded no cupcakes. Judy took a number for service and stood at the counter serving freshly baked products.

"Number fifty-nine?" the chunky server shouted, simultaneously boxing and twining the choice of the previous customer. Her back was to the counter. "Who has number fifty-nine?" She pivoted and professionally scanned through the two-row thickness of rush-hour customers before her. Judy passed her the card.

"Dearie, you don't have to wait in the lineup. The day-old bread is over there, where it always is. Didn't you see it? Number sixty. Ready to serve sixty," she bellowed, and bypassed Judy without slacking pace.

When did this rotund woman who had served her for twelve years decide she no longer belonged to the group of ladies called "astute shoppers," those with unlimited money who prided themselves on saving? Those who would routinely buy from Yesterday's Baking but only, of course, if it squeezed fresh. When had she displaced her from this esteemed category and shunted her into the other: the impoverished, the unemployed and unemployable, those who accepted the staleness of the bin or bought nothing at all?

The sweet aroma of fresh rising dough caught in her throat and soured. Her stomach knotted with nausea.

Each week her one hundred dollars seemed to buy less. The first thing to be sacrificed was expensive meats. A tougher cut was substituted for sirloin. She abandoned ground steak for the fattier and cheaper chuck; even this she could barely afford for a further two months unless purchased in a smaller quantity and stretched with Hamburger Helper. Wings and thighs replaced the whole chickens she used to buy. When even these prices became too steep, she was forced to supplement with sections previously never served to Shane.

At one dinner she concealed chicken gizzards with gravy. He cut at the sinewy portion, then asked suspiciously, "What's this, Mommy? It tastes awful."

"You said you were getting tired of hamburgers, so I thought we'd try something new."

"Do I really have to eat this?" His questions twisted into her, a dagger of shame.

"Of course not. Not if you don't want to." She swiftly removed the plate. "How's macaroni and cheese?" she asked casually, taking down the package reserved for tomorrow's dinner. At all costs she was determined to keep from him her mounting fear.

Her approach to grocery shopping had undergone a radical change. No-name brands in detergents, canned vegetables and soda pop replaced the trade products; similarly, dented tins from the half-off catchall replaced the full-price ones she used to indiscriminately toss into her cart without regard for cost. Fresh fruits and vegetables became a delicacy of the past. Eggs, which she liked to give Shane on harsh winter mornings, their yolks large and juicy, which he always requested sunny-side up, she could buy only every second week now, and then only in the least expensive size and in broken lots of six. Dinners abbreviated into chunky soups or pasta. But despite these measures there came a point when she could no longer cut or substitute further.

She knew to the penny the cost of each item she required. Weekly, she stood rooted in terror beside the cashier at checkout. She would concentrate as each number was relentlessly recorded, watch the tape as it dispassionately disgorged its total. Her purse held only the exact change, with not a penny for error. A miscalculation, an increase on an item that had slipped by her unnoticed, meant she would have to strip another staple from Shane's and her diet.

By the third anniversary of her divorce, she had no recourse but to retreat into savings. She began to cash in her certificates of deposit, aware that with every certificate she broke, there would be less income for the following months.

Judy was relieved when their twenty-year-old wood house made no more than its normal groaning to accommodate the changes in weather. With only a fixed amount allocated weekly for all dwelling-related expenses and most of that earmarked for monthly utilities, there was no surplus. Shane handled the grass cutting and the snow removal, pleased to be permitted these indicia of manhood. But by February of that year, her realty taxes skyrocketed. There was no warning. Just a number transposition on the card which the computer spat out—an increase of twenty percent. An increase she could not absorb. The accompanying circular from the city clerk explained that Alexandria required expanded services for its growth and that the civic unions had insisted on inflationary adjustments.

But the most devastating was a letter from her husband's Credit Union concerning her mortgage. It informed her that since Bob was no longer employed by the university, their mortgage, which had been placed with the Union, was fully due and payable on May 15, after the sixty-day notice period, in accordance with clause five of the mortgage document. The payment that Bob had told her was fixed for another twenty-two years. That left her with less than fifty-two days to come up with $25,000 or lose her house. She had never considered such an eventuality. Where would she raise the funds?

She made an appointment with the branch manager where her and Bob's joint account and now her personal account and certificates of deposit were kept. Mr. Devorno assured her that he would expedite her application. The bank's decision came back two weeks later and was conveyed to her with tact and compassion.

"Mrs. Kruger, I'm sorry. I truly am," Mr. Devorno said. "But our mortgage department has had to deny your application. Their calculations tell them there is not enough income stream presently to support the monthly payments. I'm sure you must appreciate we have to follow bank policy. Now, if you have any other income or sources of income you neglected to list on your financial statement, we would be only too glad to recalculate our figures. Do you feel the numbers you have given us can be increased in any way?" He paused appropriately, then concluded their telephone call with "We would be pleased to approve this mortgage if you could prove to us you have the necessary cash flow."

Other major banks returned the same answer to her application for a mortgage but were not as gentle. Their response was typically delivered via a two-paragraph form letter, the second paragraph of which reminded her that the twenty-dollar inspection fee she had been required to post to have the matter considered was nonrefundable.

Left no other recourse, she approached a local mortgage company. They seemed indifferent to her ability to meet the payments, confining their concern to the equity in her Hollin Hills residence. First Virginia Financial Corporation gave her a mortgage at nine percent, which was two percent or a five-hundred-dollar increase per year above what she had been paying to the Credit Union.

She understood both the conditions stated in their forms and those left undocumented. That they did not expect her to be able to meet her monthly payments but would wait, as predators, for the first show of weakness. With that first monthly default that put her into arrears, they would unhesitatingly exercise their legal rights. They would force her to sell her home to recover their principal; or worse, might foreclose her out, thereby making a profit they could not have made through receipt of her regular monthly installments. She understood this and accepted their terms. Fully aware of the implications of the arrangement whereby she could lose her house if she missed a payment, she signed their papers. She had to find that extra five hundred dollars a year somewhere.

The spring and winter of that third year she often lay awake. She listened to the sounds the house made: the cracking of wood in the walls, the hiss of water bubbling through the pipes, the swish of plumbing after Shane's midnight use. Had Shane been rough with the handle when flushing, breaking it again? That had cost her twenty dollars last month, one-fifth of her weekly house budget. That season she had already spent three hundred dollars to replace an electric pump for the furnace. But they had to have heat, there had been no choice.

All her expenses seemed to come down to no choice. No alternative. No exit. No way out of the poverty that seemed to encircle her. Every envelope she opened contained an overdue invoice.

Sounds that once brought her pleasure now carried other emotions. The drop of letters through her mail slot—no longer with the anticipation of an invitation, only the likelihood that more bills had accumulated. A persistent door chime—no longer the welcoming arrival of companionship, but the determination of someone who refused to leave—the hand delivery of yet another registered letter demanding payment. The jangle of the phone—no longer the expectation of a pleasant conversation, rather the intimidation of a bill collector: a warning of more harassment to follow.

Each bringing closer the bill that could not be put off. That could only be satisfied by the collection agency going to a school board where she was registered with a court order garnisheeing her wages. One further degradation and one that could lead a self-righteous school board to cut her from their supply list and another source of income.

Their high-profile residential district had become the silent adversary, pressing her as surely as the belligerence of the bill collectors. It was painful to be poor among the impoverished; it was devastating to be so among the well-to-do. Hollin Hills was reserved for the upwardly mobile, and she had constant reminders of this from Shane.

"Jimmy's going to Miami for Christmas, Dave's off to Arizona for March break," Shane would report. The names and locales rotated with the holiday, as did the content of his flash bulletins. "Dave's got a ten-speed bike. It sure beats my old one-speed." "Mike's father just got a Firebird. They took me for a ride in it. It can do eighty. It's sure faster than our old car." "You know, Joe gets anything he wants for an allowance. His mother never asks him, 'Do you really need it?' The guys like to hang out at McDonald's. Sure would like to join them, at least sometimes."

His communiqué that spring after she had told him she would not be renewing his membership in the Hollin Hills Community Association—the most gut-wrenching of her budget cuts—worried her.

"The guys keep asking me why I dropped out of the swim club. I still can't believe you did that to me."

His unspoken accusations of the past year had now been replaced by what Judy found more alarming: resentment toward her.

Then, in May, the debilitating assault on their finances came unexpectedly with a late-evening call from Dr. Norman. "We have trouble," her partner in the duplex said. "The police just phoned. They're holding the tenant from 2-B for malicious damage and vandalism. You'd better meet me there."

Twenty minutes later, Judy witnessed the debris of her $50,000 real estate investment. The toilet, bathtub and washbasin had all been methodically smashed. Plate glass splintered on chipped tiles. The new appliances in the kitchen were ruined. The door of the refrigerator hung ajar, its handle torn; the face of the microwave was split with deep, irreversible cracks. Wires lay exposed, torn from their sockets. Four windows had been ripped from their casements, the fifth and only remaining one, smashed beyond repair, dangled from its upper hinge. The walls of the common stairwell had been defaced by red paint, large unidentifiable blotches resembling a giant Rorschach test. Cigarette holes had been burned deep and deliberately into the bedroom's broadloom. The stench of liquor permeated the fabric. Empty bottles were everywhere, in the bathtub, the living room, the kitchen sink. Judy's stomach heaved. She ran to the bathroom to rid herself of its poison. On her return to the living room, Dr. Norman was shaking his head in disbelief.

"What type of person would do such a thing?" he said with indignation.

She could not reply. She no longer had the capacity to be objective. When she did garner the strength to speak, it was ever so softly, and her words were meant for herself. They were words of defeat: "It's no use anymore. Nothing is of any use."

The adjustor came the next day and confirmed what Judy had already suspected. He was sorry, but there was nothing his company could do. Tenant vandalism was definitely not covered by their policy. Apparently the duplex was insured against all the natural causes—fire, flood, tornadoes—the vagaries of nature, but not the vagaries of man.

Dr. Norman offered to put up the full $8,000 repair cost, a figure for which Judy could not even begin to pay her half. In exchange, he insisted she assign to him the next twelve months' rent. This meant that on her $50,000 investment—one-third of all her original capital—she would not receive any money for a full year, and would be plummeted into the depths of official statistical poverty.

Through this period, how was she ever going to be able to look after Shane properly? And if she had to ask her son to give up anything more, it could permanently alter his feelings for her. She would never forget the way he spoke to her when she didn't renew his swim club membership. Whom could she turn to for assistance over this rough spot? Her mother's contact with her since her remarriage was reduced to an obligatory card on birthdays and holidays. Even after her divorce, she had not bothered to come up and offer support. And she had never shown any real interest in Shane.

There was no other option: she would have to see Bob in spite of the animosity she felt toward him.

"Hello, Bob," she said when his secretary put her through to him. "How are things with you?"

"Fine, thank you," he said crisply. "Is there a problem with Shane?" She detected apprehension.

"No, he's managing fairly well under the circumstances."

"I haven't been able to get down to see him as much as I would have liked."

"I'm phoning to see when it would be possible for us to meet."

"Why? Do you have something to discuss?"

"Yes, but I don't think we can talk about it over the phone."

"Well, that's the way I'd prefer to deal with it. What exactly is it you want from me, Judy?" she heard him ask guardedly.

"I really need to talk to you in person."

"What's this all about, Judy?" He was becoming irritated.

His refusal to meet fanned the anger she felt she had brought under control before she made the call. She had an urge to hang up, but thought better of it. He had made it clear her only access to him would be now or not at all. She began to tell him about their financial difficulties and their effect on Shane.

"Why are you telling me all this, Judy?" he asked, abrasively cutting her off. "You got more than enough money from the settlement. It's not my responsibility if you've mismanaged it."

"Look, Bob, it's very difficult for me to ask you to help us. I wouldn't be doing this if it wasn't absolutely necessary."

"I have no further legal obligation to you. You signed the agreement and it's final. You're not my responsibility anymore."

"But what about Shane?"

"Judy, I'm not going to discuss this any further. And don't ever contact me about this again. Do you understand?"

A dial tone buzzed in her ear.

She was shaken by the way Bob had treated her. Furious with his lack of concern about his son. And critical of herself for having provided him with the opportunity to humiliate her once again.

A week later, she forced herself up the fourth-floor walk-up and into the offices of the Department of Public Welfare. The room with its off-green walls and shabby linoleum was a place she never in her bleakest despair imagined herself entering. She was entitled to food stamps with an income under $10,000, just as at age sixty-five she would be entitled to social security. At least that was how she had rationalized it.

"Where do I go to apply for food coupons?" she asked the black man with a clipboard.

"There's no special place for food stamps. You wait with everybody else here—unemployment insurance, workmen's comp, child welfare benefits. . . . " She felt him appraise her cursorily. "What do you think this is, lady, a specialty store?"

She stood that day among those who were applying for any form of social assistance—in the ranks of the forsaken of society. And was required to return one further time to satisfy the questions of the eligibility worker, a process that robbed her of any remaining pretense of privacy. Betrayal, humiliation and anger had long passed; these had been superseded by a more basic emotion: the passion for survival.

That June, Judy found herself in another equally unmoving lineup. She had substitute-taught in Washington the previous day and, caught in the bureaucratic traffic escaping from the city for the weekend, had arrived home after seven. Not wishing to keep Shane waiting longer, she postponed her regular shopping, a decision she presently regretted. She now stood behind eight large orders. A flash heat announcing summer had brought into the store more than its usual traffic as enthusiastic early-season cottagers, identified easily by their carts of mops, disinfectants and Raid, prepared to head for more remote areas. These travelers augmented Safeway's usual Saturday morning working-class clientele.

Shoppers vied for carts. Ten cash registers clicked continuously. Forty-five minutes later, Judy began to place her purchases on the carousel. Her right hand unloaded the powdered milk, chicken wings, macaroni, meat bones, bologna and no-name peaches. Her left hand clutched her booklet of food stamps.

"Is that how you're going to pay for these?" The veteran cashier had spotted the coupons. Judy nodded, her face reddening. "Sorry. Can't take those in this lineup. Can't make change," she said while simultaneously tossing the scant items to the discard section of her counter, then slapped on one further sentence. "Try that line over there. They're just opening up, so they should have sufficient food-stamp dollars."

Everything in Judy's life now was restricted by conditions, and one of the myriad on food stamps was that change over a dollar could only be returned in like specie. This rule, she was told, was to protect the type of people who routinely used food stamps, so that they would not receive regular negotiable currency and squander their food allowance on liquor. Judy had accepted this humiliating rationale and blocked it, along with all her other present constraints.

She made her way through the counter's narrow passage. She hastily secured another cart and retrieved her few selections from the discard catchall. She had to act swiftly before these disappeared into the sorter's hands to be returned to the appropriate shelves, necessitating yet another hour's search through the mammoth store to again collect them. It was frustrating to have to go through another lengthy checkout line. She did not want to add further to her time away from Shane.

It was now eleven. The row of shoppers she had recently joined stretched halfway down the detergent aisle, toward the meat counter, the rump of the store. Twenty minutes later, she stood beside Cup-a-Soup. Three other carts were behind her.

"Judy, I haven't seen you in ages. Where have you been keeping yourself?"

Judy had been so flustered by the incident at the checkout that she had been unaware of Susan Simpson's cart clattering down the aisle toward her. It was too late to turn her head toward the shelves in the guise of shopping and thereby avoid her gossipy friend, a defensive ploy she often had assumed in the last two years to avoid potentially embarrassing encounters with meddling former acquaintances.

"You wouldn't mind if I slipped in ahead of you? Mike and Alan are sitting in the car and I just need a few things for the weekend." Without ceasing her patter, she assessed the contents of Judy's cart. "I see you got caught in the same bind."

By the completion of her interjection, she had deftly eased her cart into position in front of Judy, a method by which she effectively circumvented the wrath she knew would follow from others had she executed this maneuver behind Judy. "Is Shane with you?"

Judy shook her head. She had to figure out how to extricate herself from this situation. How could she use her food stamps if Susan was there? But what could she do? She was more than halfway to the cashier. How could she remove herself from the line and not look foolish? Even if she abandoned her place on some pretext or other, it could take her another hour until she reached this position again. Shane was expecting her home. She had already been in the store much too long. Nothing could be done now. She felt trapped. Susan said her son and husband were waiting in the car. That meant she would leave the store quickly. She had to hope Susan would leave aisle four before she had to pass her food-stamp booklet to the cashier.

"Too bad," went on the voice. "I have Mike with me, like I said. It would have given the boys a nice chance to talk." The line continued to inch forward. "Mike said only yesterday how much he and his friends miss Shane at the swim club. Shane's specialty is the butterfly, isn't it?"

Susan talked incessantly, as if her conversation were payment for usurping the other's position. A conversation whose content was increasingly upsetting Judy and, with its thrust of questions, required deflecting answers. It busied her mind, making it harder for her to formulate a contingency plan. The line moved forward relentlessly.

Thirty minutes later, Judy started to remove her products from the cart onto the counter. Susan's purchases had been rung through and, Judy noticed, paid with two crisp twenties. She lingered at the end of the counter, packing her groceries, still within hearing range.

Judy delayed. She unloaded her items from the cart with deliberate slowness, pausing between each transfer. Each product was inspected on some pretext prior to relinquishing it to the cashier. The milk she screened for its expiration date; the bologna she squeezed for freshness; the macaroni checked as to serving quantity; the no-name peaches reconsidered and put through with reluctance; and the meat bones examined as if an alien package had inadvertently been placed in her cart. The cashier rang through the items as soon as Judy released them. As the last of these was placed on the counter, the total was displayed.

"That's fifteen dollars and ninety cents, ma'am."

"Thank you . . ." Judy stalled. She dared not bring out her food-stamp booklet until after Susan left. "Would you mind checking the total? I think you forgot to charge me for the macaroni."

The young cashier studied her tape. A few seconds lapsed. "Thirty-seven cents—it's here. That's fifteen dollars and ninety cents, ma'am."

Susan was now packaging her produce. She reached for the small plastic fruit bag in which to insert her Granny Smith apples. She had freed one from its sheet roll, but its thin cellophane sides clung stubbornly together.

She kept rolling her thumb and forefinger, trying to pull it apart, its resistance making her all the more determined.

"Is it the milk you forgot then?" Judy asked the cashier. "I'm quite sure you forgot to ring up something."

"No, ma'am. That's the first thing I rang up."

Judy opened her purse, grateful she had brought the one holding the greatest debris. Sighing, she began a methodical analysis of its contents.

"Ma'am, I'm sorry to rush you, but, you know, it's Saturday. I'm getting awfully behind."

Susan had completed her parceling. She waved a farewell and headed to the exit.

Judy's tension dissipated. She was safe again. With extreme graciousness she said, "I'm sorry, miss. Here it is." From her purse she took the assortment of food stamps and extended the ten-dollar and five-dollar booklets toward the cashier. It was mandatory that food-stamp dollars be torn off by a store employee and presented along with ID.

"What are you giving me that for?"

"These are food stamps. That's all I have," Judy said softly.

"I don't know anything about this. I just started on cash." She bellowed in a voice meant to be heard above nine clicking registers, "Jean, this lady here says she has food stamps. What am I supposed to do with them?"

"Yeah, I know all about it," the other hollered back over three aisles. "She came here first. I sent her to you. I didn't have any food-stamp dollars left to give her as change. Check your till. See if you got any."

Judy spotted Susan at the exit door. It sprang open in preparation to release her. She paused on its threshold. Then she took a few steps back toward the counter she had just left and rooted there.

Judy saw Susan watching. It seemed that everyone in the store was watching. Judy was powerless to interrupt the employees' dialogue. Her face felt flushed, her hands were saturated with perspiration.

"I don't know. What's it look like?"

"Funny money. Smaller than real money. Tens are red, fives are brown, ones are green. Got any?"

"Nope. Don't have anything," she shouted back.

"Serena, you got any food stamps in your till?" The veteran cashier was even more adept at making herself heard over the clamor. Her other assets included a flawless memory. "There's a woman at checkout four who says that's the only way she can pay."

Judy thought she heard another cash register snap open.

"None here," came back the shrill reply.

"What about you, counter five? Any food stamps?" The roll call seemed endless. Four registers had now effectively ceased functioning. Half of the checkout counters were silenced.

Judy watched helplessly as the woman called Jean left her station. She was heading for the microphone. "Cashiers"—Judy heard with horror the now familiar voice resonate through the entire store—"if you have food-stamp dollars, take them immediately to counter four. Customer over there requires them."

Judy had become this hour's advertised special. She felt eyes rivet on her. Among them the eyes of Susan. All stared with the safety of the spectator, not daring to come too close lest they also become tainted with poverty.

Judy's heart pounded. A sound, she felt, as audible as that of the cashier's words; its pressure enough to burst the cavity of her chest. Blood bruised her temples. Her forehead blazed heat. Faces blurred into one. Even Susan grew distant.

Store sounds jangled together—the canned music over the PA, the squeak of unlubed carts, laughter—all became indistinguishable.

She had to escape from here, from what had become of her life. She forced one leg numbly in front of the other. She left her items circling on the black counter. She did not stop for the bewildered voice of the novice cashier—"Don't you want these things after all?"—and brushed past the outstretched hand returning to her four one-dollar food stamps and a dime in change.

She walked through the door and away from her shame. What she most desperately needed was self-respect and that could not be obtained with food stamps.

She did not listen to the sounds of the house that night. Indecision tormented her. How could she best protect herself and Shane? Whatever decision she reached would have to be right this time. She couldn't afford another dead end. She was thirty-three, she could no longer dissipate the vital years of unbridled energy and health. Even if she met someone, remarriage was not a panacea. It provided no certainty of security. She had learned that too well. The solution had to lie within herself and with her own capabilities.

She had an elementary teacher's certificate, but a permanent position

was not a possibility. The school boards were not hiring. They were elim-
inating their existing staff by declaring them redundant. Substitute teaching was leading nowhere. It yawned before her in perpetuity. She would
have to retrain herself. But to become what? What would give her the
income she needed, an income sufficient to free her from fear of unpaid
bills, to render her immune to humiliation and return to her a sense of
self-worth. An income high enough to ensure she would never have to
deny Shane any request, no matter how frivolous, or observe the hurt of
poverty in his face.

What would give her the knowledge she needed? Knowledge to be freed
from the phrase that condemned her and a generation of women to silent
dependence: "Let me explain this to you." Knowledge to make her confident in her own judgment, and if advice was warranted, to be able to
synthesize its content and assess its merit. Never as she had in her divorce
settlement to be again undermined by incompetency or be vulnerable to
the stirrings of her heart. Someday she might love again, but she would
never allow herself to become reliant. That part of her innocence was
gone forever.

Whatever career she chose, she would have to start at the beginning.

She recalled the meeting with Mrs. Belmont during her senior year at
Swarthmore. The scene returned to her unclouded by the years. She was
twenty-one again, one of a handful of women accepted at Georgetown
Law Center. Imbued with idealism, she had sought out this attorney, one
of the first women in the state to have reached the echelon of partner in
a prestigious firm.

Dusk had already removed from the corner glass office the last vestige
of natural light when Mrs. Belmont, engrossed in her papers, motioned
Judy into the client chair. The meticulously coiffured, wiry matron worked
beneath the intensity of two metallic desk lamps. A thin envelope of pearls
circled her neck. "How can I be of service?" Her raspy voice rebounded
from the surface of her documents. Its directness disarmed Judy.

"I'm planning to go to law school at Georgetown this fall," Judy said.

"Good." Judy now had the woman's full attention. Mrs. Belmont ignored the files before her. "How much do you want it?"

Judy thought perhaps Mrs. Belmont had not understood. She reworded
her opening sentence for clarity. "I've already been accepted there."

"That's not what I asked. I asked you something quite different: How
much do you want to be a lawyer?"

"I want it, of course."

"But how much? Enough to sacrifice for it?"

"You mean how hard am I prepared to work in the next three years to become one?"

"No. That's a very different matter. If you were smart enough to get into law school, I'm sure you've already considered that. That's expected. It's what begins after law school that I'm talking about. Passing the bar exams is only the start."

She paused and repeated her original question. "How much are you prepared to give up to be a lawyer?"

Mrs. Belmont forfeited the emotional neutrality of her desk for a more intimate posture. She shifted into the client's seat beside Judy, angling it to face her directly.

"Are you prepared to give up the luxury of close friends? Friends take aeons of unbillable hours to cultivate. They require constant nurturing. . . . Are you prepared to cancel a vacation booked months ahead for a corporate restructuring, deny yourself birthdays, Thanksgiving and Christmas with your family?"

"You don't live like that."

"Don't I? You only see, Judy, what I have—the glamour in the word 'lawyer,' this office—not what I have given up. The hard choices I have had to make along the way. I don't have any children, but that's another matter. Even if I had, what type of mother would I have been? A shoddy one at best. I don't see how I could have given more of myself than that. By the time I get home, I barely have enough energy to look after myself."

"But your husband . . . " Judy drew upon the public information known about the Belmonts.

"He's equally busy. He keeps even longer hours than I do. He understands and shares my dedication to work. If he didn't, there wouldn't be a marriage. He happens to be exceptional, and I don't delude myself otherwise. Most men wouldn't tolerate my schedule.

"For a woman, law demands commitment. You better understand, Judy, this is primarily a male-dominated profession—an all-boys club— that you have chosen to break into. And they don't take gate-crashers lightly. You will have to work twice as hard as any of them to prove yourself, to overcome the unspoken prejudice."

The hour was late. The nine o'clock cleaning staff had already looked into and bypassed the room.

Mrs. Belmont paused, and like the master lawyer she was reputed to be, capsulized all her preceding remarks: "For a woman, law is not a job alternative. It's a life's work. I have sacrificed for it. Are you prepared to do the same?"

Why should she confront life within the framework of sacrifice? Judy thought. Her world was too full of possibilities to be restricted by such an arduous concept.

In the wake of this encounter, she had changed course and chosen teaching, an occupation that traditionally fit within the corners of a marriage.

Now, in the early hours, it all came together for her. Self-reliance and income, and the knowledge necessary to achieve both. There was a way through which she could protect her son and herself, even without Bob's help. She wouldn't let her divorce destroy their lives. As dawn etched its way into her room, she made her commitment. The very same one she had been hesitant to make thirteen years earlier.

"Yes, I am," she responded to Mrs. Belmont's question from across the expanse of memory, the question that she had left unanswered. "I do want to be a lawyer. And I am prepared for whatever sacrifices must accompany it."

The inquiry phone call Judy made to Georgetown Law Center did not go as planned.

"You said you were accepted here thirteen years ago? Yes, our records go back that far. But I really think you should speak to one of the registrars."

A male voice replaced the female one. "Davis speaking."

"I was accepted to the law school thirteen years ago. Could you please tell me what I need to do to be readmitted."

"Submit an application, like sixty-nine hundred other people."

"But I was already accepted."

"Do you think we keep spots open for life? Do you know how long ago that was? You're even barred by the statute of limitations," he said, sounding pleased with his legal witticism. "Do you have any idea what the competition is like to get into Georgetown today?" He did not wait for her to reply, but used his interrogatories as a preamble. "Do you realize you are talking about being admitted into one of the top five law schools in the nation? Let me tell you, out of sixty-nine hundred applicants last year, we accepted only five hundred." His voice firmed behind the security of statistics. "One in thirteen. Twenty-five hundred we didn't even look at twice. Page one on the application has your GPA and LSAT scores. Without a GPA of three point four and an LSAT of six hundred, you're wasting your postage."

"Are extenuating circumstances considered?"

"Sure. On page two of the application there are 'Disadvantages in Your Life' you feel the committee should know about, along with why you want to go to law school. But this section is irrelevant if you don't meet the objective criteria on page one. No one will even bother to turn the page to find out what you had to say. You didn't really expect to get in here because of a previous acceptance, did you?"

"Can you have a personal interview to explain your situation?" she asked, undeterred.

"You're allowed an informational interview. That's not for you to give us information, only for you to receive it."

"Would it make any difference that I was accepted here before?"

"A quaint historical footnote."

"What if someone is divorced and has a child to support?"

"These things come under 'Disadvantages in Your Life.' But I don't think I've made myself clear. If you have a GPA of three point zero and an LSAT of five hundred, it wouldn't make a bit of difference that Ronald Reagan had given you the Medal of Honor and you had worked with Mother Teresa for five years. You still wouldn't get in here. Forget it. Those factors only weigh in if you're still alive at round two. Do you still want an application?" He paused as if assessing the damage wrought by his information.

"Of course." Forfeit was inconceivable. Her words, immediate and firm, concealed her uneasiness. Getting back into Georgetown was going to be difficult. She had thought all she needed to do was make the decision to apply and she would automatically be in.

That conversation provoked her own process of weighing. Should she tell Shane her plans to go back to law school? Would it be better to tell him now, make her application and LSAT exams another adventure to be shared? Or would it only burden him with her concerns? She had tried to keep the gravity of their financial position from him; should this also be withheld? She did not want her tensions over acceptance into law school mirrored in him. In the past year he never mentioned his father, as if by denying him an existence, he also denied the hurt of abandonment. But he was becoming harder to handle and more irritable. And the marks his teacher sent home, requesting that Judy acknowledge with her signature, documented a continuing slippage in his performance. Her son had enough to contend with. It would be best, she concluded, to delay telling him her plans until she could do so with certainty.

Judy widened her net of applications to include other law schools. But it was Georgetown she needed: the same reason that made it difficult to gain entrance made achieving it essential. If she could graduate in the top one-third, it virtually guaranteed her entry into any major firm in the United States and was the fast track to bridge those lost thirteen years.

By day she substitute-taught, and at night, while Shane slept, she studied for the LSAT. The entrance exam was new to her. She learned the art of writing the computerized test, with its emphasis on speed and reflex answers, and the new math that was integral to it.

Four months later she sat for her LSAT in a lecture hall at Georgetown. Every seat in this room and the four others was filled with candidates a generation younger than herself. The young man beside her placed a stopwatch in front of him. In the next seat, a girl moved five sharpened pencils from a red case and set them to her right. The person two rows ahead reset his watch to coincide with the official clock on the wall. She was competing with more than the legal aptitude of those around her, something much more terrifying. Her opponent was youth with its accompanying mental agility.

She was spooked. Involuntarily, her eyes jumped back and forth among them. The boy beside her recentered his stopwatch. The girl readied one of her pencils in one hand and with her other teased the corner of the exam booklet before her.

Judy had to block these kids from her mind. She had tenacity and determination on her side. That, she said to herself, should just about even things out.

"Begin," came the monitor's instruction.

৵

Shane was less than pleased when presented with the news the following spring that his mother was entering law school. He was scraping the residue of macaroni from their dinner plates. Judy was steadily scouring off the hardened cheese that had become crusted on the pot. They were locked in the comradeship of cleanup. Now almost thirteen, Shane stood only a half-head distance below her. His sandy hair, like most of his friends', was layered into a neatly cut shag.

"Shane, I have good news," Judy paused, "and more good news."

"You mean something different from 'I have good news and then I have bad news, which do you want first?' " He was teasing her in his casual, flip manner.

"You've got it. It's all good news today. Feel like it now?"

"Sure, anytime, Mom."

Judy abandoned her pot in the sink, unmindful of its half-scoured condition. She sat on a kitchen chair and beckoned for her son to do the same. He pressed the palm of his hand against the side of the table and tipped back his chair to his preferred listening position. It balanced on its two hind legs.

"First, good news. I'm going back to school this fall, like you. Law school. Georgetown in Washington accepted me. I got in there once before, long before you were born, and now I'm going to resume my education. And more good news. We're moving into a brand-new development called Crystal City. It's only fifteen minutes on the Metro from there to law school, so I won't lose two hours a day traveling. I'll be able to spend more time with you."

She studied her son's face, assessing the effect of this proposed change on him. He appeared distraught. She hoped she was presenting this properly. "The buildings there are shiny and tall. They're made of large sheets of glass. And each has a huge indoor pool. There's lots of beautiful parkland, the kind you like, and it stretches right down to the Potomac. The area even has a shopping mall. It's really a small city that's been built from scratch, so everyone there will be new, just like us."

He digested the information. "Is that what you call good news?"

"Yes, I think it is. In three years I'll be a lawyer. Georgetown is one of the top law schools in the country, and if I do well, it will make a big difference to us. We'll be able to live like we did before."

"What's wrong with how we live? I don't want to move from here. This is my home. All my friends live here. You have no right to do this to me."

Judy reached to comfort her son. He jerked his body away from her touch. She pretended not to notice his rejection. She had successfully kept from him the level of their economic distress, despite his relative deprivations. Perhaps too successfully, she thought. It had been best not to tell him before. There was nothing she could have done to alter it. But now there was. It was time to confront the reality they both had been living.

"Shane, we can't afford this house anymore. You know the repairs we've had to make—the furnace that broke, the plugged drains, the endless expenses. We would have to sell it even if I didn't go to law school."

"My father gave the house to me. He told me it was mine. He promised me. He told me that before he went away." Shane made the conversation sound as if it had taken place last week.

"Shane, your father may have given us the house, but we still have to pay the bills. And the taxes and the mortgage—they've all gone up."

"You could keep the house if you wanted to. If it was important to you. You just want to move to be closer to that school of yours."

"Shane, listen." She tried to impose some order. To explain it from the beginning, perhaps in a manner to which he could more easily relate. Then maybe he would understand. "You've noticed how we've cut back on food. And that we only shop in secondhand stores. And that I've started teaching—"

"You only do that because you want to," he interrupted.

"No, Shane, that's not true." She did not let his outburst stop her. "We need the money. Shane, these last few years have not been easy for either of us," she said gently. "We've both had to give up things. You've given up the swim club—"

"I don't want you to go back to school," he blurted, then fixed his eyes somewhere beyond the reach of hers. "I want a real mother like Jimmy and David have. A mother who takes care of me."

"Shane, I have no choice. I have to work at something to support us."

"No, you don't. You work because you want to get away from me."

"That's ridiculous. You know that's not true."

"I don't know anything. I just know you're not a good mother. You don't care about me." He pushed the rest of the words from his mouth: "I hate you."

She tried to reason with him, to ignore the cut of his words. "Shane, I'll only be away the hours you're at school. When you come home, I'll be here. I'll be home now more than when I was teaching. It's only three short years until I'm a lawyer. It's the only way to guarantee our future."

"You mean to guarantee your future. . . . Why don't you tell me the truth? You're going to leave me. Like Daddy did." He turned his back on her. He returned to the sink and scrubbed at a clean serving dish obsessively.

"No, Shane, I am never going to leave you. Nothing's going to change between us. Things are only going to get better. I can't help what your father did to you . . . to both of us. But I'll never do that. You're my life. You're all I have. You're the reason I'm going back to school, so we can have a better life together."

"You're lying, just like my father lied to me. He promised nothing would change. And I haven't seen him in three years."

She yearned to comfort him. She had underestimated the depth of Bob's damage. Shane's silence during the past year did not mean he had forgotten his father. Rather it was an anguish embedded deep beneath the surface, an anguish hardened by the cruelty of three years of abandonment. It had not abated with time, as she had imagined, but formed the hard crust of insecurity that now confused his reasoning.

She left her chair and went to him. She put her arms around her son and tried to turn him toward her. She felt his body tense. He scrunched beneath her grasp, prying loose. Deliberately, he dropped the heirloom Wedgwood platter he was holding. It splattered across the kitchen floor. He turned defiantly upon her.

"You're going to leave me anyway. Why don't you do it now?" he shouted accusingly and ran from the room.

She heard the outside door slam. Then all was still.

Shane would come around eventually, she reasoned as she picked up the porcelain pieces. He just needed reassurance and time. When he calmly thought it all out, he would understand.

The "For Sale" sign was speared into their lawn on the second Friday in July. Judy had been apartment hunting in Crystal City that day and came home around seven. Shane was not there. The blue nylon knapsack he always carried was uncharacteristically dumped in the front hall. Otherwise, the house was undisturbed; it bore no indication of his presence.

Judy looked outside. The grass was untended, a chore Shane took pride in completing before the weekend's official start. Its rough green fringe made the realtor's placard look even more ominous.

Judy suppressed her uneasiness. She busied herself with detail. She set the kitchen table, readied the hamburgers and salad and removed Shane's knapsack to his room. She then turned on the TV, appreciative of its diversion in the empty house.

At eight-thirty she put on the porch lights. Dusk was swiftly settling into night. And still no sign of her son. He had obviously come home from his job as a gardener's assistant and gone out again. But where? It was too late to work outside.

She found Shane's tattered notebook in the pouch of his knapsack. In his still immature hand were written the names and numbers of his friends and the gardener for whom he worked. Judy delayed another half hour before making use of this information, not wishing the fallout which a violation of his privacy might bring.

Mr. Arnak's wife called her husband to the phone. Shane had left him at four-thirty, the usual Friday quitting time. Was anything wrong? Could he expect him on Monday? "Of course," was Judy's offhand reply. Her calls to Jimmy, Dave and the Simpson boy only elevated her apprehension. All gave her similar reports. Shane wasn't there tonight. And no, they had no idea where he could be. Jimmy gratuitously added he had not seen him since term finished three weeks ago.

Something was wrong. Terribly wrong. It was ten o'clock. She walked into the blackness of the night and stared in both directions down the silent street. For endless seconds, she strained for the sound of his light, fast steps. Then she reentered the house and hurried upstairs to his bedroom. She dug through his knapsack again. His wallet was there, and in it his school ID. He had left behind his sole means of identification.

He may have been hit by a car. He always walked on the road, never on the sidewalk, no matter how often she cautioned him. And no one could contact her. No one would even know his name.

She must call the hospitals. She dialed Alexandria Hospital first, then Jefferson, Fairfax and even the National Orthopedic in Arlington. "No, ma'am," came back the response from each. "No boy of that description has been brought into Emerg tonight." By her third round of calls, one attendant asked matter-of-factly, "Have you notified the police?"

Judy held back until 2 a.m. before she made that telephone call. Her first inquiry was cut short with "We can't help you. This is the general police emergency number. Call the Criminal Investigation Unit."

She was put through two more switchboards and preliminary interrogations. Why were they doing this to her? Didn't anyone care? Frustration intensified her anxiety. Eventually, she was connected to her correct destination.

Minutes later a patrol car pulled up in front of her home. The officer identified himself as being from the Criminal Investigation Division. He progressed through a seemingly memorized routine.

"Has there been a divorce?" . . . "Name, address and phone please of the father?" . . . "Name and phone please of two friends?" . . . "Do you have a recent photo of your son?" . . . "Can you give a full description of the missing child?" Each question was more probing than the other and each heightened her fear. "Any identifying marks, moles or scars?" . . . "Has your child ever been in trouble with the police?" . . . "Would you agree to enter your child's name in the FBI's computerized files with all the other missing children from across the United States?"

She gave her written consent to search Shane's room. For clothes and clues, the officer said. But she saw him extract Shane's Crest from his night table and press out its turquoise paste; open his unfinished tetracycline prescription and split apart each capsule to examine its red and black grains.

"It's not like that," she heard herself defend her absent son.

"An investigator at this number will be in touch" were his parting words. He handed her a card and closed his black pad.

Judy kept her vigil beside the phone that night and through another fifty-three hours. She remained in her street clothes. She did not have the strength to undress.

The phone rang at seven-thirty on the third day. It was Mr. Arnak. Was Shane coming in today? No, she said, and offered no explanation. She had forgotten it was Monday.

At 9 a.m. she initiated a call to the investigator, then again at one o'clock. "No new information" was the curt reply. By her third call of the day, the receptionist recognized her voice and intercepted: "Are you aware that Detective Melon handles two hundred runaways a month? When he has something to report, he'll contact you."

Around eight in the evening, she received a call from a man whose name Judy could not place.

"Mrs. Kruger? This is Dr. Wooling. I'm the Residential Counselor of Alternative House. A boy who says he is your son has been brought in here by the Fairfax County police. He slept for two nights on park benches in the Old Town section of Alexandria. When it became cooler, he looked for shelter. He was spotted sleeping in a store entrance and picked up by the Alexandria police early this morning. On search, they found a ticket stub from a school play in the Fairfax school district. The Alexandria police took him to the Fairfax Police Runaway Division. Fairfax questioned him and brought him to our hostel. We've given him a full assessment. He told the intake worker his house was sold and he had nowhere to live." His voice was crisp, as if reading from a file.

"Is he all right?" Judy interjected.

"As well as can be expected after three nights on the street," he responded coldly. He then resumed his former tone. "He says he's willing to go home with you. Alternative House is an eight-bed facility run by the Department of Social Services. We're located at Tyson's Corner. I suggest you come here as soon as convenient. And Mrs. Kruger"—the clinical voice delayed her departure—"a runaway child is a serious business. The police have a right to charge your son as a juvenile offender."

Judy had heard all that concerned her before that legal postscript. Shane was alive and he wanted to come home. Nothing else mattered.

She drove the half-hour distance to Gallows Road and Twenty-eighth Street in under twenty minutes. Down the road from the glittering sprawl of the shopping mall was an innocuous two-story white clapboard house.

She found Shane sitting on a cot in a four-bed room, alone. His hair was matted, his face smudged with dirt, his eyes puffed and sunken from lack of sleep. He barely acknowledged her entrance. She walked across the room, bent down and without words stroked his head, her gesture speaking her love. Suddenly his arms broke around her; his body trembled with sobs. She held him fiercely for a long time.

She took his hand into hers as she had on another July night almost three years ago. This time, instead of setting off toward the fields of fireflies, she led him from that room, downstairs, onto the porch and away from the halfway house.

Neither of them spoke of the incident. But from then on, there were subtle changes in their relationship. The insecurity now became Judy's. Her conversation was punctuated with continuous apologies. They slipped from her lips before she could edit them. "I'm sorry" became the phrase that concluded most of Judy's statements. It attached to information on the hour Shane could expect her home; instructions when the precooked dinner should be placed in the oven; a request to change the smoke detector's batteries, to turn off the porch lights, to lower the rock music. These words arose not from concern over alienating her son but, Judy suspected, from loving him too much.

She made sure she involved him in all the plans for their new life together. She let him choose which of the high-rise buildings within the Crystal City complex they would rent in and pick the color of paint for their apartment. She took him to Georgetown Law Center and showed him the lecture halls where her classes would be held. She introduced him to the secretarial staff as her son and, in front of Shane, received the assurance that if he phoned, someone would locate her immediately.

She did all these things to reassure Shane of his importance in her life. Her entry into law school and their move to Crystal City had altered nothing between them. He could rely on her, as always.

Judy crammed happiness into their finite days in Hollin Hills: surprise picnics by the Potomac, a Sunday sail, twilight walks. A return to those earlier, simpler times together. Reminders of her constancy.

The July incident was closed. She tried not to let it worry her. It had been a one-time episode. Something that could never occur again.

O rientation barbecue was held on a perfect Sunday—a rare day for a Washington August, clear and temperate. Auspicious, Judy thought, as she strolled across the lawn in front of the Healy Building to meet those with whom she would share the next three years.

She found her identification tag among all those set out on the acrylic table. In addition to containing her name, she noticed it also read "Section C"—the subgroup of 125 with whom she would have all her first-year classes. Judy pressed on the identifying label.

She surveyed the gathering, noticing a significant number of women. There would be others with whom she would have common interests. The atmosphere was casual. It seemed like a highly organized outdoor floating singles bar. All wore jeans or shorts, colorful tops and varieties of sneakers.

Despite the festive air, Judy hung back. She felt hesitant to initiate conversation, unlike the others, who seemed to circulate with ease. But her reticence did not matter; others approached her. Talk centered on the same topics.

"I got my acceptance last month. When did you hear from Georgetown?"

"Where did you do your undergraduate?"

"I'm sure you had a hard time deciding among the schools like I did. Which law schools did it finally come down to?"

"How many times did you take the LSAT?"

As they chatted, Judy made an effort to remember each student. She glanced at their badges. All who approached her had the same section letter as she did. Most stayed only a few minutes. Once the person had exhausted these items of mutual experience, he would move back into the crowd and, adept at socializing, reappear with another.

Judy enjoyed the afternoon. The barbecue was Texas style with an open charcoal grill. There was an abundance of hot dogs and hamburgers, mounds of coleslaw and potato salad. Long picnic tables were scattered convivially across the lawn.

Law school began in earnest the following day. Judy's mind was disciplined into analyzing cases under the five headings of fact, issue, reasoning, decision and comment. Professors were explicit as to their expectations, each assigning a minimum of one hundred pages to be briefed daily. Both the property and tort men felt it fit to mention at the outset that their course would be the one from which this year's Law Review problem would most likely be drawn.

One noon hour at the end of her first week, Judy sought a spot outdoors in which to have the lunch she had brought from home. She pushed open the Law Center's heavy main door and paused in its entrance; her eyes immobilized by the sun, her body absorbing its warmth. On the upper concourse, she turned to the right and descended the granite steps into a sunken concrete patio, a boxed patch of fresh air adjacent to the basement of the building.

"May I join you?" Judy asked the only other occupant, a face familiar from her law section.

"Sure."

Judy shared a slab stair with the younger woman. She untwisted the neck of her brown bag, withdrawing a bologna sandwich and a Coke. She placed her lunch on the tread above, using it as a table.

"I'm Judy Kruger. We're in the same section."

"I'm Jennifer. . . . I know who you are. You're the one with the kid."

Judy tried not to show her surprise with this unorthodox categorization. "Did you enjoy the barbecue last week?"

"Enjoy is hardly the word. It served its purpose."

"I didn't meet anyone who wasn't in Section C."

"Why would you possibly want to? No one wastes time talking to someone not in their own section. There's no point." She paused and reassessed Judy quizzically. "What do you think was happening on Sunday? It wasn't a church barbecue, you know. That was sizing-up day—a preview of the competition. And we're into it now." Her words sharpened into a question: "Who's in your study group?"

"What study group? I didn't sign up for one."

"No. It's not a school thing. A group of students get together and divide up the work. You have to be asked . . . I'm with Arthur, Jean, Lionel and Joanne."

"No one asked me."

"Guess you didn't size up too well . . . too bad. That's how you survive around here. No one can get through all the material they throw us each night by themselves. Let alone digest it. The profs expect us to divvy it up. It's the only way." The girl bit fiercely into a McIntosh. "Maybe you can do it yourself," she continued after an ardent swallow, "but you'll burn out by Christmas."

Judy knocked over her Coke, saw it drain helplessly down the concrete and form a stagnant puddle at the base of the steps.

She had a sinking feeling and grasped for a change of subject. "From the way the professors talk about Law Review, it certainly seems important around here."

"That? Forget it. It doesn't concern you."

"But how exactly do you get onto Law Review?"

"If you really want to know, it's by invitation. There are only two ways to get it. When the grades come out, find yourself in the top four percent, which even the best of us can't count on. Or do the Write-on. That's a competition that follows directly after finals, before the marks come out. Another handful are added from there. . . . But, as I said, Law Review is not meant for someone like you."

"Why is everyone so concerned about it?" Judy persisted.

"Look." Judy detected impatience. "The ostensible purpose of the competition is to make the panel for next year's Law Review. *Georgetown Law Journal* is the most prestigious, but any of the other three will do the trick. . . . And don't get the idea that everyone around here is literary. The real reason everyone wants Law Review is for their résumé that's filed in the Careers Office. The only thing the firms' recruiters have to go on for hiring for that crucial second-year summer job is that piece of paper. If you're in the top one-third and your résumé reads *Georgetown Law Journal*, you're golden. You're on the fast track to the large firms and the big money. Law Review is the door opener." She punctuated this last phrase with a poke of her finger through the yogurt's tinsel, and with a plastic spoon began to scoop out its contents. She looked at Judy with incredulity.

"You still don't get it, do you? After first-year finals, everything is over. Your future's decided. The big cut has been made—those in the top one-third with Law Review, those in the top one-third without Law Review but on the Dean's List, and everyone else. And those people just blew it. They may as well have gone to Wyoming U. for as far as they are going to get professionally."

"I appreciate the tip."

"Why shouldn't I tell you? You're not my competition. . . . Look—I walked out on my husband. Left him out West. Did it a month before the term began. Now I have no responsibility, no distractions. I've nothing to do but study. I'll make the top one-third and Law Review too."

With that, Jennifer rose and tossed her apple core, yogurt container and crumpled lunch bag into a nearby disposal.

Judy remained fixed as if part of the granite. Her palms were covered in sweat, her body chilled. She pulled her thin cardigan around her.

"What do you need that for? It's blazing hot today," Jennifer said, oblivious to the devastation her words had caused. "Come on. We'll be late for Contracts."

The thought of all the assets she had pledged at First Virginia Financial Corporation in order to come to Georgetown flashed across her mind. And with it the bank manager's formidable warning: "Mrs. Kruger, you have assigned all your collateral to us as security for a personal loan. We have great confidence in your future prospects. But if things don't work out as planned, I want you to be fully aware of our policy. If you are not in a position to pay off your debt in three years, we will automatically dispose of your property. Since we understand the CDs and stocks you pledged to us represent the last of your assets, you will not get any further credit from this bank."

Judy forced herself to her feet. She disappeared into the cold glass superstructure.

Judy's naiveté was gone. She approached her studies tenaciously. She set an austere regime. Minutes were not to be squandered. Lunch became a solitary meal. At an empty table in the cafeteria, she would absent-mindedly consume a sandwich. Her left elbow wedged open the taut binding of a casebook, her right hand highlighted its key passages and penciled notations in the margin.

The instant her three o'clock lecture was over, she would leave the building. When cooler weather set in, she carried her cloth coat and boots between classes rather than sacrifice the time necessary to gather them from her basement footlocker. Every night, she brought all her casebooks from school. She did not work at the library; she wanted to be home for Shane. She read en route to and from Crystal City, unmindful of the train's lurches, the jab of rush-hour elbows and the interruption of switching lines.

She never noticed others in her apartment elevator, only the panel lights illuminated by their fingers' warmth. She watched these luminous cubes, with their enforced stops, impatient with the delay they inflicted on her schedule.

Entering her apartment, she would toss the keys onto the kitchen counter, shake off her coat, put a frozen dinner in the oven, close her bedroom door and continue her reading. She paused from her task only when Shane entered her room and, then, only long enough to hug him distractedly. She returned to work, usually too engrossed to have thought of asking about his day.

She never broke for dinner at a consistent hour, only when she could no longer absorb the material. Shane always waited for this interval with his mother. During these respites her anxiety abated, enabling her to resume, temporarily, her role as mother.

"How did it go today?" she usually would ask belatedly.

"Fine."

"How is the swim team going?"

"No problem."

She accepted his abbreviations. She dared not push beyond the superficial. She no longer had time to cope with problems.

"How are the other boys treating you?"

"Everything's real cool."

She never suggested he bring his friends home. The apartment was small and she needed it quiet.

She ate hurriedly, gulping down her meal, keen to return to work. She would leave Shane at the kitchenette still eating dinner with some variation of "Sorry about the dishes, Shane."

"It's okay, Mom. It really is," he would say reluctantly.

Judy rarely heard the last phrase completed. She was already in her room, her door closed.

Judy worked long after their apartment was stilled and even the noise from Apartment 5B was silenced. Weekends were reserved for summarizing the previous week's material, organizing it into a digestible study format and catching up on the casebook reading she had been unable to finish by her 1 a.m. deadline.

As September locked into October, she was plagued with lack of sleep as well as the volume of work. Throughout the night, her mind was filled with legal concepts, fear of unfinished work, nagged by self-doubt. She would frantically watch the face of her clock radio as its hands rotated, her panic increasing with each restless hour.

By Sunday midnight, she was almost caught up. Then came Monday and, with it, a new cycle of work. Like the mythological Sisyphus condemned for eternity to roll a boulder up a cliff, the peak sighted at last only to have the weight bear down upon him again, she felt that her tasks loomed endlessly, interminably before her, offering no respite. And she had other responsibilities: Shane, groceries, the apartment, and bills.

At the barbecue they had pegged her as a loser and wanted nothing to do with her. Jennifer had told her as much last August. Maybe they were right—she wouldn't be able to do it.

The structure and location of the Law Center increased her sense of isolation. It stood on top of a pyramid of steps, a stark, angry black-and-white enigma; a formidable alienating edifice. It was in an inhospitable neighborhood. Its entrance on Washington Boulevard looked down onto a three-block stretch of bulldozed unkempt land temporarily being used as an ad hoc unsupervised parking lot, where a mugger might lurk behind any vehicle. Beside these abandoned blocks and deeply recessed from the road stood the skeletons of partially demolished buildings, their exposed sides scarred by their violent separation from the adjoining structures.

Kitty-corner to the ground-level side entrance, the one Judy and most of the others used, was a dilapidated Salvation Army thrift store. Its sign hung shabby and uninviting. Adjacent to it was the alcohol rehabilitation center. It competed for clientele with that of a nearby liquor store rumored to be run by two retired policemen. Above this flotsam, the white dome of the Capitol loomed too distant to be anything more than an ideal.

The area offered nowhere to walk safely. There was no opportunity for her to escape the tension that encircled the building as her courses moved ominously to year-end finals. She felt marooned on an island of anxiety.

All courses built to May. Her only feedback came from the one half-year course which had an exam before Christmas. Judy dismissed her above-average mark in Litigation as an aberration. The major question closely paralleled the issues in a supplementary legal writing assignment that she had thoroughly researched. It had been a fortuitous break and one unlikely to recur in May. She drove herself harder, thinking of nothing else.

∞

Around March, Judy noticed that her clothes had become too large for her. Pants sagged; skirts slid over her waist. The scale recorded a twelve-pound weight loss. She felt constantly exhausted: everything seemed somewhat distant from her as if she were a participant in a dream. And on her back and around the right-hand side of her chest toward the stomach area an inflamed, swollen, painful rash was erupting.

"Shingles," Dr. Arfus diagnosed. "See those welts? You have two bands of them." He was still poking at her. "And it looks as if you're developing the same over here on the left side." He balanced on the squat stool, his examination over. "You're abusing yourself, Judy. Exhaustion, bad diet, stress. You're not a teenager anymore and you can't treat your body as if you were. At minimum, you've got yourself a three-month virus. All you can do is wait it out. Treat yourself properly for a change. Plenty of sleep, reduce stress, good food."

Jennifer's prediction was being fulfilled, she was burning herself out. She also said she wouldn't last until May. How could she? Her body was breaking down.

A few days later an assistant dean stopped Judy in the hall. He seemed agitated. "Are you Judy Kruger?"

"Yes, sir."

"The office had an inquiry today from a neurologist about filing a medical certificate in advance of the final exams. He identified himself as your doctor. The call was referred to me. Is Dr. Arfus your doctor?" he cross-examined. The assistant dean's specialty was trial technique.

"Yes, sir." Judy was flustered. The call had been made without her authorization.

"Medical excuses are unacceptable, Mrs. Kruger, and will not change your grades at Georgetown Law Center. If you are not well enough, you should withdraw. If you insist on writing the exams, you do so without any special consideration. We do not permit safety nets here. Furthermore, you should know an absence of over ten days is deemed a withdrawal."

As suspected by Dr. Arfus, another rash appeared. It ran from the spine around to the left side of her chest.

The virus racked her body. She twitched and burned with itchiness. The welts became raised and blistered open into pustules. Sleep became even more elusive; the concentration essential for study, harder to maintain.

In the apartment, she worked on her casebooks with her upper torso bare. Wads of calamine-soaked cotton adhered to her back and stomach. The lotion's pink plaster caked, tugging at the exposed rawness; dried cotton snagged the open sores, further intensifying her discomfort. In order not to miss her lectures at Georgetown, she swathed her upper back with strips of calamine gauze and taped them with lengths of adhesive. The assistant dean was not going to have cause to force her to withdraw.

Her resolve increased as her physical health deteriorated. She no longer had energy to expend on self-doubt. She had to succeed if she were to have control of her life.

Judy sat for her final exams in May in the same hall where she had taken her LSAT. She was fifteen pounds weaker, her body raw with blisters and patched with bandages. But she had five sharpened pencils, a Swatch whose second hand was synchronized with that of the official clock, and a memory indexed with cases and cross-referenced to legal reasoning.

She completed Property, the last of her six three-and-a-half-hour exams, on Friday in the third week of May at four-thirty. On the Metro run to Crystal City, it was all she could do to keep her body from visibly shaking. She had not picked up the Write-on package from the Law Review office with its self-contained research materials and its limitation of a strict nine-day deadline. No matter how important it was to make Law Review, she could not compete again. She could not will her body to cooperate further.

That night, Judy did not rush away from dinner. For the first time since September, she stayed and enjoyed her son's company.

Shane's growing impatience with her habits had been blunted by phrases such as "Just a little longer," or "We're in the critical lap," employing a swimming analogy familiar to him.

"Sure, Mom," were the words he used to respond to these entreaties. But Judy would hear her son mumble under his breath. His disbelief in the veracity of her pleadings was becoming more blatant with each week.

That night as Shane rose to clear away the chocolate pudding, Judy said, "What do you want to do this summer?"

"I thought I had to work," he said listlessly.

"You're not going to. And neither am I," she said, shifting her priorities. Happiness entered her son's face. "Pick something you would like to do. Something fun we can do together."

"Do you mean it?"

"Try me. . . . What's it to be, Mr. Kruger?" Her body needed healing, their relationship mending.

"Camping," came back his answer decisively. "I've really missed the outdoors since we left Hollin Hills."

"Camping it is then."

"But you've never done that before."

"Then it's vastly overdue."

Judy researched their plans with the thoroughness that she brought to a legal research and writing assignment. She filled the kitchenette with pamphlets from the Virginia Tourist Association and from the United States Department of the Interior, Fish and Wildlife Service.

At the end of June, Judy presented Shane with the alternatives. "Here are the places I've found so far. . . . Option One: the Back Bay National Wildlife Refuge. It's something like Dyke Marsh Wildlife Habitat near our old home. But it's much better. The good news is it's right next to False Cape State Park which has nature trails and beachcombing. The bad is . . . Are you ready? Tons of mosquitoes and"—she paused dramatically—"water moccasin snakes up to two feet long. And poisonous."

"No problem, Mom," Shane's face lit up at the length of the snakes. "Let's go for it."

"Wait a sec, you haven't heard option two yet. Hiking and fishing in George Washington National Forest. Redeye, rainbow trout and perch." Watching delight spread across her son's face as he considered his holiday possibilities, Judy felt relaxed for the first time since last August.

Finally unable to restrain his excitement further, he implored, "Can we do both, Mom? Please?"

"I hoped you'd suggest that. That was my thought too."

Judy rented sleeping bags, a pup tent, backpacks and a Coleman stove from Army Surplus. They packed it all into the Volvo, as well as the requisite clothing for both trips.

The weekend after Shane finished school, they set off for the National Forest District. By early afternoon, they reached the village of Mountain Grove, their jumping-off spot for Lake Moomaw. At the Hitching Post they bought their provisions—powdered eggs, dried vegetables, peanut butter, jelly, tinned stew, macaroni and charcoal—rented tackle and made arrangements for a small boat. Then they drove the remaining mile to the lake. Shane chose a campsite close to the water and set up their tent.

Most nights they slept outside; the stars shone brilliant in the clear sky. The one night it did rain, they huddled closely together in the tent awake all night, bonded in discomfort. Droplets trickled down the inside skin of the canvas and splattered with precision onto their arms and chin.

Every moment was crammed with activities. Guided by suggestions from the forest rangers, they followed the hiking paths marked for beginners and explored the environs. Judy packed peanut butter and jelly sandwiches. They would pick a vista resplendent with lush pine and have their lunch; watch the waves of color, as cloud swept across the pine forest, rotating it from lime into emerald shades of greenery and back again.

On other days, they fished. Shane rowed the boat to rocky shoals, proud of his oarsmanship. Their bounty—perch with an occasional trout or redeye—was grilled for that evening's meal. And always there was a late-afternoon swim. The water felt like the smooth texture of velvet. Slowly, Judy felt her energy return.

Three weeks later, they broke camp at 6:30 a.m., repacked the car and headed for their second destination. Shane sat in the back, an Oriole cap squared on his head and a road map spread out beside him. He directed his mother meticulously through the complex of mountain roads.

"What a team," Judy said when State Road 39 actually intersected with Federal 81. "You're quite a guide." Her son looked up from his maps long enough to acknowledge her praise.

"I think we're pretty good too, Mom," he returned. A smile pleased his lips.

Five and a half hours after leaving Washington National Forest they neared the Back Bay National Wildlife Refuge. Shane had planned their arrival for midday, allowing enough time to transport their provisions, two gallons of drinking water and gear the five-mile distance over the narrow paths to a campsite in False Cape State Park.

"I want to see everything," Shane proclaimed as he clambered out of the car. Judy sat limply behind the wheel, recovering from the marathon. He continued through the slat of her rolled-down window. "Especially the snakes, the poisonous ones, two feet long." Judy wished his memory was not that precise. "Do you think we'll see any today?"

"I'm not sure."

"That's awful."

"It's all a matter of perspective," she chided, disengaging herself from the car.

"How much do you think we can get to see in three hours?"

She recognized the vocabulary of time pressure—the residue of how she had forced them to live during this past year. "We have no time limit anymore," she said in an effort to break the cycle and reestablish the pace of normalcy. "We can spend as many days as you want here."

From their campsite at False Cape, they often reentered the Wildlife Refuge. They would squat behind an embankment to await the birds. They saw the spindly-legged herons wade through the murky water, and the snowy egrets rest in the shallows, their bellies dampening with each ruffle of water. Frequently, they walked the one-mile seaside trail to the ocean to study the feeding habits of the larger birds. Shane was enthralled as the double-crested cormorant dropped beneath the water, to return with a fish dangling from its bayonet bill. He watched, fascinated, as the pelican left the marsh to plummet into the cool depths and reappear, its gullet swollen with prey.

They would climb the twenty-foot dunes. Judy led the way, while Shane tried to insert his steps into her sneaker tracks. Other times, Shane rolled down the mound, his body fully extended, and raced up again, pitting his strength against that of the sand. Near day's end, they would stop on a ridge and stretch out wide in the rejuvenating warmth of the sun.

Always, they would talk. The half-sentence fragments that began at Lake Moomaw and which, when she tried to encourage them, had been covered with "It's not important," began to recur. Gently, she persisted. He responded to her attention with renewed trust. In the quiet of nature, his hurts surfaced, as if drawn from some deep recess.

Last winter he had only made second string in basketball and was not permitted to dress for a game in the team's blue-and-gold uniform.

"But you made the swim team," Judy said.

"Everyone makes the swim team. At Jefferson, it doesn't mean anything. They're lucky if they can find enough guys."

They discussed his drop in grades in all his subjects: "How do you expect me to do well? The school sucks."

"Shane," she began the obligatory censoring of his vocabulary, then thought better of it. She wanted to hear everything that was bothering him.

"Well, it does. Ask anybody. It's an open school plan. Bet you don't know what that is. A bunch of different classes going on all at the same time in one big room. My math teacher bought some filing cabinets to block the noise. Told us she couldn't hear herself think. Boy, did she get it from the principal. But she kept them anyway. . . . I really can't hear what's going on in most of my classes. There's so much noise."

Of the students with whom he went to school: "Jefferson's sure different from my old school."

"Of course, a new school always seems strange at first."

"Not that." He dismissed her pacification. "A lot of gangs," he said conspiratorially.

"Gangs?"

"Sure. Blacks, Hispanics, Asians. And fights in the hall. We have really long halls."

"What does the school do?"

"Nothing. Why?"

"What do you do?"

"I have my friends too," he said, closing off that issue.

Shane had never been exposed to anything like this when he went to school in Hollin Hills. She shouldn't have sent him to the local public school without going there first and seeing it for herself.

Once he volunteered, "Do you know the only thing I like about Jefferson? They got a cool rec center. And there's pool tables and tons of video games. I win a lot of free games."

"Video games?"

"Sure. It's part of the after-school program. I go there until the late bus leaves. First bus leaves at two-forty and there's no point for me to take it—you're never home by then anyway."

Another time, she tried to delve deeper into how he felt coming home to an empty apartment. Shane blurted, "What am I supposed to do at home anyway? There's no other kids my age. Just old people and divorced people. . . . Sorry, Mom." He softened his last sentence.

"But there are almost five hundred units. There must be boys your age."

"Check for yourself . . . only one apartment has kids and no one would want to hang around with him. . . . Don't even think it."

Toward the end of their camping holiday, Shane startled her with how uprooted he felt.

"I can't go back there again."

"The apartment?"

"No, the whole place."

"The whole place? Crystal City?"

"Cement City. That's what it should be called. Towers of cement. Parks of cement. Artificial water. No trees, no grass, no birds . . . no crickets."

"There are trees, Shane." Honesty made her modify this absolute statement. "Some."

"No, there aren't. No real trees. They're stuck into cement. The wind can't even move them."

"And there are birds," she inserted.

"Who can hear them over the screech of planes? I can't. Those planes at National Airport never stop."

Through these snatches of conversation, Judy glimpsed the world that had become her son's in the past year; she heard his problems and disappointments, the ones for which since last August she had not had the patience. And his anger, which had been denied release.

On the final day of their vacation, she drove Shane the half-hour distance into Virginia Beach. They visited the Life-Saving Museum with its nautical artifacts, scrimshaw and ship models. As the day began to wane, they chose a seaside restaurant with an early-bird special. From their table overlooking the Atlantic, they watched sailboats making their way homeward, their yellow and orange spinnakers ballooning behind them.

"Mom," Shane said to her, his voice husky. "We should do this more often. . . . Have fun together," he clarified.

The following day, they backpacked their equipment and remaining supplies out of False Cape State Park. Judy's classes were to resume the last Thursday in August. Weary from the miles of hiking, Shane sprawled sleepily across the back of the car. Judy looked through the rearview mirror at her son. The road maps were still tightly held in his hands. Her thoughts flowed undisturbed, immune to the rock station to which Shane had set the radio. Nothing, she vowed, must ever come between her and her son. He had difficult pressures on him. Different from, but equal to, hers. She would never lose touch with what was going on in his life again. But each mile that brought her toward Washington also brought her closer to Georgetown Law Center, and with it a rush of anxiety. A certain fear that all resolutions, no matter how sincerely made, can be compromised.

*F*ive blue-gray envelopes were among the hodgepodge assortment that scattered across the mailroom floor when, after a six-week absence, Judy unlocked her mailbox. Shane scrambled to pick all the letters up. He shuffled and sorted them by envelope size, presenting to her the matched grouping on top. She opened the first of these.

Dear Ms. Kruger,
On behalf of *The Georgetown Law Journal*, it is my pleasure to invite you to join our staff. Your distinguished performance during your first year in law school has prepared you for membership on one of the nation's finest scholarly legal publications.

The experience you gain from *Journal* membership will be noted throughout your career by employers, judges and colleagues. . . .

She left the rest of the lengthy letter unread and tore open another. Her eye jumped to the critical passage: an invitation from Law and Policy in *International Business Review*. Two others, from *The American Criminal Law Review* and *The Tax Lawyer*, contained similarly worded offers and completed the complement of law journals at Georgetown.

But how was this possible? There had to be some mistake. She had not entered the Write-on competition. She considered the fifth envelope; its return address read Georgetown University Law Center, Registrar's Office. This time she inserted her nail respectfully under the glued portion—she did not want to disturb its contents.

"Official Transcript—Student No. 58703," read the computerized form. Her eye raced down the column of marks unmindful to which subject each applied. "A, B+, A, A–, B+, A, A." "Quality Point Index: 11," then an asterisk explaining: "This is based on a 12-point scale," and the words: "Dean's List: Top 7% of the class."

She reread her grades, slowly, in an effort to convince herself of their veracity. She felt Shane watching her. Softly she said, more to herself than to Shane, "I . . . we really did well."

"I knew you would, Mom." He raced up the steps leading to the elevators and called back, "So when are we gonna be moving back to Hollin Hills?"

∞

"Rule of thumb." Judy found herself joined by Jennifer, with whom she was now enrolled in the electives of Corporations and Security Regulation. "Nine out of ten who get summer jobs are offered permanent positions," the seer of statistics announced as they clambered down the L-shaped steps into the basement. "That's why the large law firms send their best recruiting teams here. This is it. The big push. Impress and be impressed." At the bottom of the stairs, Jennifer slowed down at the student lounge. Judy did not slacken pace. She continued toward the Placement Office, eager to extract herself from her classmate's company. "Judy," she heard Jennifer call, her voice loud enough to carry over the lunch-hour rush of students, "Even with Law Review, don't get your hopes too high. What major firm would possibly hire a divorcée, with a kid, most likely with emotional baggage—when they can have the pick of the litter? As if being older wasn't enough of a liability in itself. How can they possibly ask you to put in sixteen hours, seven days a week, which they expect from summer students and associates. They can't, therefore they won't. See you at Corporations."

In the aftermath of her most recent encounter with the Cassandra of the Law Center, Judy's confidence wavered. She indiscriminately put her résumé in the drop box left by every Washington firm or national with any branch office located in the District. She withstood the seduction of the Los Angeles, San Francisco and Chicago firms with their enticements of prepaid plane tickets and expenses for those who merited the call back to their head office. Her sight was limited to the Washington area; she did not wish to dislocate Shane again.

Judy added her Law Journal acceptance to her CV, and attached to it, as everyone did, the official transcript which gave her standing. If somehow a midnight team tiring through the piles of résumés collected from all the major law schools across the country were mistaken in their interpretation of the aforementioned honor, it was guaranteed one sentence would not be misunderstood: "This student's marks were in the top seven percent of the class at law school."

Neither would they misconstrue Judy's answer under the heading "Life Experience": divorced; custody of a child, male, age fourteen; former spouse Robert Kruger, now of Philadelphia.

Judy deliberately completed her résumé without subterfuge. She had accepted the realities of her life; it was now for others to do the same.

The first list of students each firm had selected to interview and the hour assigned appeared on the bulletin board outside the Placement Office the second week of September.

Judy hurried down the stairs to check the list before her Monday 9 a.m. Corporations lecture. Her name was on all Washington firms posted to date, including that of the most prestigious, Taft, Adams & Rogers.

Apparently she was not the only person who had searched for Judy's name before class that morning.

"You've still got a long way to go," begrudged her nemesis, plopping into the bolted metal chair beside Judy. "Only one in five of those interviewed will get a callback, and of those one out of three will be hired—last year's Placement Office Statistics. Plus, we're in a recession year and the big firms are cutting back their hiring. That translates into less than a one-in-ten chance you will get a job offer from Taft, Adams & Rogers. 'Many are called but few are chosen.'" Jennifer then swiveled her chair away from Judy to talk to the girl on her right.

Most of Judy's off-campus interviews were conducted in various rooms of the Hyatt Regency. All took the form of a verbal Rorschach test and were as varied as the style of the firms themselves. The only concrete and consistent question being one she had anticipated, some version of "Why are you interested in our firm?" Judy had left nothing to chance. She had researched the firms with whom she was to meet. She provided each with a compelling answer.

Five days after the initial interview, a callback letter arrived from Taft, Adams & Rogers inviting her to attend at their Connecticut Avenue offices at noon the following Wednesday.

On the scheduled day, Judy approached the narrow-angled building shaped like a luxury liner which fronted on Farragut Square and claimed an entire block of prime Washington real estate. Its upper floors bulged with encased square portholes.

She walked to its Connecticut Avenue entrance and took an elevator to the fourth floor, the lowest of the five occupied by the firm. Within seconds, its door opened onto a salon-style hallway with stained hardwood flooring. Shrubs set into ceramic antiques sat between each bank of elevators. Judy could not mistake the law firm's entrance. A long carved wooden valance spanned the full width of the corridor and was balanced by matched thick wooden Ionic columns. Set across its portico, the chiseled gold-embossed block lettering "Taft, Adams & Rogers" announced trust, stability and success. Solid doors opened and disappeared inward, ensuring the visitor an unobstructed view of both the elegantly attired room and the receptionist. A bouquet of partially opened roses was set to the left of her, arranged like a study for a Cézanne painting.

"I'm Judy Kruger. I have a twelve o'clock appointment," she said to the woman.

The click of her heels on the peg floorboarding was muffled as she crossed onto the Oriental rug that delineated the sitting area. She sat on a soft blue sofa facing two other candidates, both male, both younger. And all three of them a fungible product.

"Ms. Kruger, Garth Burns. A pleasure to meet you again." Judy rose to meet one of the lawyers whom she remembered from the Hyatt Regency. He extended a firm handshake. "Follow me, please. You will be meeting some of my colleagues in our corporations department, the area you said you wanted to practice in," he explained as he took her along the thickly broadloomed corridor to a small conference room. "One of my associates will be with you shortly. Please help yourself to the buffet prepared by our catering staff."

After he left, she lifted the lid of the silver chafing dish, revealing a garnished whole salmon, undisturbed by any previous diner. Beside this, two selections of salads, each abundantly heaped in a crystal bowl. A dry bar held beer, white and red wine and Perrier. Lime wedges in a small silver dish accompanied the latter.

Judy bypassed the delicacies. Instead, she chose a wing chair and, with her back to the window, faced the door: she did not want to risk being caught with a mouthful.

Her day took on a choreographed routine. During the course of the afternoon, she was routed out of and into this holding room for three meetings, a hiatus of at least a quarter hour between them. On each occasion, she was squired by a different junior, who, upon arrival, gave name, area of specialty and a handshake similar in both pressure and duration to his colleagues'. The names changed with each session: Don McGiven, Richard Bond, Glen Andrews, Ian Matheson, Gord Stephenson and Dave Costello.

The same information seemed to be sought by each interviewer, but was elicited in each consecutive meeting in an increasingly oblique fashion. Each of these lawyers, in apparel and mannerism, was a progressively older edition of his predecessor.

By four o'clock, Judy found herself back in the conference room. She worried whether she had handled herself properly? Had she revealed strengths or weaknesses? Where were their nebulous questions leading? How many other candidates were in rooms similar to this one, waiting?

A little after five, she was escorted up an inner stairwell and delivered into a double-windowed corner office.

"Brian McDug, partner," he said, extending the customary handshake. He neglected to give his specialty. He indicated she was to join him around a circular conference table at the back of his room, on which, she noticed, her résumé was placed. He took the chair across from her. Surrounding him were bookcases—the volumes aligned there were unusual in their uniformity. Trial practice reports, sequentially arranged by years, read their gold-embossed spines, in both plain and annotated editions. The arsenal of a litigator. Judy was forewarned.

"Who have you met today?" he asked pleasantly.

She mentioned the last person who had interviewed her.

"No, I know that." His smile disappeared as he repeated the question. "Which of my colleagues have you met today?"

This then was the reason each lawyer had pressed upon her his name. She must have been introduced to two floors of names. Disassociated, unrelated words. Her ability to recall them must be the firm's ultimate test of her memory, which she now clearly understood translated into a job offer.

She began to recite the collection. She was short one name: the man who returned her to the conference room after her second interview. "Don McGiven showed me his swim medal. What an honor being state champion," she enthused. Her mind, functioning on an alternate level, groped for the elusive name. "Ian Matheson and I discussed it on the way back from my interview with Don." Her digression undetectable, even to the attentive, as anything more than the respect due the achievement of a member of their firm.

"You must have met quite a number of us today," Judy said, her casual manner covering her near faux pas. She had forgiven him the trick. And relieved she had survived it, she began to relax.

"Actually, you're my first . . . of 'us' that I've met today," the litigator said. She had been placed back on alert. He picked up her résumé, and without glancing at it let its pages roll between his fingers. "I admire what you have accomplished. My mother took up a career later in life too. She's done exceptionally well. She's a nursing coordinator now at Providence Hospital." The intensity of his eyes belied the familiarity of his conversation and the casualness of his tone. It did not allow her the luxury of a lapse in concentration.

"She loves her work—she's working harder and putting in more hours than she did at nursing college. And you know the amount of time you have to put in at a professional school."

"I haven't found the workday disproportionately long in law," she said, skirting his probe. She had avoided the second trap. His reference and obvious pride in his mother had almost thrown her off guard.

"She really was wonderful. No matter how late she came home, she still did the cooking and laundry for me and my dad."

Was he sincere? Or was this another feint? His statements were couched in friendliness. She dared not risk his intentions.

"I'm fortunate. My son does those things." She mitigated the severity of her response, in case his admiration for his mother was sincere. "I feel mothers have an extra responsibility in raising sons these days. Today's generation of women require more help around the house from a man. I'm sure someday a woman will thank me for the training I'm giving my son," she said, smiling. "Don't you think so?"

He did not pursue this line of inquiry. He moved instead toward a greater level of confidence sharing. "I'm the youngest in a family of five. I was eleven when my mother started to work full-time. I remember I used to brag about her to my friends at school. But I missed having her home. I guess all teenagers feel that way."

This was the hardest statement to deflect. He had identified her jugular and gone directly for it. The pretense was over. The litigator must have been pressed into service to pursue the remaining issue which made the firm uneasy. Which would she place first: her career or her son? The determination of which translated into a ledger entry: the number of billable hours the hiring team could guarantee the partners she would produce for the firm.

She felt his eyes upon her, assessing her for weakness. A break in eye contact, a betrayal of body language and she was eliminated. There was no mistaking the admission he was seeking from her. Silence was deemed an admission. A litigator's tactic she had seen deployed against her at a larger conference table by an equally prestigious firm five years ago in Philadelphia. And just as innocuously. She could not waver.

"I can't relate to that. My son doesn't feel that way. He says I'm giving him a chance to control his own life. A growing space. And I think that's just as important as being home all the time. I agree with what the psychologists say, that it's quality of time, not quantity, that's important."

He did not wait for the tap signifying the end of the interview. He pushed his chair back, a sound rendered inaudible by the thickness of the cream rug. "Thank you, Judy."

Outside the door, she was reclaimed again and whisked back to her room. The salmon was discolored and crusted, a pungent odor rose from its carcass.

After more than half an hour, she could not confine herself to the high-backed chair. She paced. These intermissions made her uneasy and this one even more so. She was certain they were conferring about her. Should they interview her further? Should they drop her? Time was money to a law firm, never to be squandered. And partners' hours the most valued. Had she succeeded in convincing Mr. McDug of something of which she was uncertain? Would she really be able to balance the unyielding demands of being an attorney as well as providing Shane with the emotional security he needed?

Around seven o'clock, she was led from this place and zigzagged across three more floors connected by irregularly placed internal stairwells to the top floor. Her escort stopped before an open door of a large corner office.

"Mr. Hughes, may I introduce Judy Kruger? Judy, Mr. Hughes is our managing partner." A well-built man in his mid-sixties stood behind an inlaid wooden desk. Intelligent eyes were framed by a strong forehead, its domination reinforced by the absence of frontal hair. Short, bristly gray fringed his temples.

The decor of the room was acutely male. Glossy black-and-white photos of men in uniform dominated the walls. A ship's model, displayed on the front of his desk, replaced the customary pen set. A trio of shiny black elephants in attack stance with flared trunks sat benignly on a side table. The sobriety of black carpet and tufted upholstery was broken by the colors of the Stars and Stripes which was placed beside his credenza and formed the room's focal point.

Mr. Hughes waved her into the black leather sofa and took its matched companion armchair. He swiveled around to face Judy. Behind him, windows overlooked the top floor of a neighboring building and garnered the last orange streaks of sunset.

"You attended Swarthmore College on a scholarship. Graduated summa cum laude. Taught one year for the Alexandria County School Board in Virginia. Married Robert Kruger. Divorced from same ten years later. One child, male, now fourteen."

Unlike the others who had interviewed her, he had no résumé on the table beside him. Nor did his hands hold a clutch of notes. He rhymed off her CV as if he himself had prepared it. Then, without pause, disclosures she had not made.

"Out-of-court divorce settlement. Fixed dollar sum. Not indexed to inflation. Attorneys with carriage of the matter, Higgins, Stuart and Ross of Philadelphia, on retainer from Kruger Enterprises, Inc., the holding company of Kruger Clothing Industries. Listed on the American Stock Exchange. Robert Kruger remarried. Two sons, ages three and six months by present wife, the former Suzanne Walker. After the divorce and prior to Georgetown Law, Judy Kruger registered for and took employment as a substitute teacher with six school boards in Virginia and the District of Columbia. During this period, credit bureau reports indicate that house mortgage applications were declined by several leading Virginia banks due to J. Kruger of Hollin Hills being designated an unsatisfactory credit risk. Currently, and since divorce, sole support for her son and herself. . . . Would you say that is a correct reading of the relevant facts?"

"Yes, Mr. Hughes." Judy did not flinch. Impressive, she thought, as one professional evaluating another. And as dispassionately as if she were not the subject. They had done their research well. Even more thoroughly than she had.

"Are there any other relevant facts which we should be aware of?"

"No, Mr. Hughes."

"I thought not . . . I'm sure you realize by now you're not the usual profile for a firm like ours." His gaze still upon her, he assessed her as though she were not present. "We know how she will perform . . . top seven percent of her class at Georgetown, graded onto Law Review. And we do not need a corroborating opinion as to how she will motivate. . . . Like the very devil himself," he reflected thoughtfully, as if overruling his partners' consensus.

He swiveled his chair back toward his desk and rose. With a gallery of army men behind him, one a picture of two soldiers, arms tossed over each other's shoulders, another a more posed rendering of a military group, he said, "Profiles need amending periodically, like good laws. . . . I know you will do just fine. I look forward to having you on my team, Ms. Kruger. You will make a very welcome addition."

Rising from the sofa, Judy accepted his extended hand, "Thank you, Mr. Hughes." She turned to leave.

He held her back. "Judy, you have one advantage I'm sure you don't even suspect. Once you walk out of Georgetown and into this firm, your age is an asset. It gives you instant credibility with the clients. I should know. It was for me when I entered the profession at thirty. I completed Columbia Law School on the GI Bill after I served in Korea."

He accompanied her to the elevator and waited politely until it arrived. The receptionist had gone. The cleaning staff carts clogged the firm's foyer. Garth Burns and Ian Matheson walked by briskly—jackets off, ties askew, sleeves rolled up. Two who earlier had been fastidiously clad. For juniors and associates, it was still the working day. Each addressed the senior partner with a courtly "Good evening, Mr. Hughes," and to her, offered not a nod of recognition.

After that day, the academic year sped by for Judy, its passage barely noticed. The certain knowledge that financial security was within her grasp siphoned off the psychological component from her studies. Law school became nothing more than work and she could handle that easily. Ms. Brown, Mr. Hughes's secretary, phoned her during exam week as to her starting date. She relayed the managing partner's request that, due to a holiday of a second-year associate, it would be more convenient for the firm for her to start on May 19, the day following the completion of her last exam rather than a week later, as previously arranged.

"Of course," Judy agreed cavalierly, covering the disappointment she felt at having to forgo the camping week she and Shane had planned. First impressions, she knew, were always important.

The office Judy was assigned the day she reported for work at Taft, Adams & Rogers was one with a window. The eight-by-ten-foot room held a grained veneer desk and a credenza of matched finish, above which a nondescript watercolor had been placed. Her chair backed onto her only window, affording the client, for whom two high-backed chairs had been provided, the preferred view.

But Judy never met clients. She rarely was even in her office. From 8 a.m. until her day's completion, she was in the library on the sixth floor.

"Rumor has it a summer associate came in here at five o'clock one Friday night and was never seen again," a voice said through a slat in the stacks near the end of her second week. "Personally, I believe it."

In her concentration to locate a case, she had not realized she had backed into a carrel which abutted the row of stacks she was using. Its occupant bore an amused look.

"Terry Gibbs. Litigation associate. Medical malpractice. And I'm a whiz at finding anything. . . . You seem lost."

Her brief stint at the firm was apparently not sufficient to give her a facade of sophistication with the library.

"Let's see the blue memo sheet, the one from the assignment coordinator," he said, rising to a good six feet. Of medium build, with short-cropped hair and angular features, his hazel eyes arrested her attention. She passed the paper to him from beneath the weight of the three massive citators she was balancing in her arms.

"Uh-huh," he said as he scanned the sheet. "For Jim Bowers, Securities. I'd start with *Am. Jur. Secundum*. Never hurts. They're on this shelf. Then after the *Supreme Court Reports*, move to the *North-Western Reporter*. The librarian hides them over here." He steered her three rows over and pointed to a shelf reachable only by steps. "Next you'll need the *Virginia Reports*. Wonder why she left them at eye level—must be a form of state loyalty. . . . Anyway, they're here. And, of course, to update whatever you've found, you'll need *Sheppard's Citations*." He pointed to a shelf that was less than a whisk broom above the carpet. "That's the snakes and ladders for this memo. Have fun. And if you get stuck again, let me know. I love a challenge."

The six-day workweek was only the start of the expectations that Taft, Adams & Rogers set for its summer associates. Social activities with her colleagues occupied a minimum of two evenings a week: a cruise on a steamship out of Old Town in Alexandria, a revival at the Kennedy Center, a dinner at the Metropolitan Club for students and their mentors, a Baltimore Orioles game at Memorial Stadium. In addition to these special events, there was the six o'clock Tuesday night Law League baseball game at the Ellipse, played as a round robin competition against the other large Washington area firms. Around this was organized, and de facto enforced, a get-together for students, either burgers and draft beer at the Old Ebbit Grill, or black beans, Mexican chicken and sangria at Omega's in Adams-Morgan.

Judy could not extricate herself from these functions. Nor was she successful in injecting Shane into them. A pitch to the sports coordinator to include her fifteen-year-old son in a baseball game timed after this individual's predictable weekly lament of sagging partner participation was to no avail.

"Paralegals, yes, secretaries, maybe—if they're really good. But no kids —no matter how old they look!" Similarly rejected was her request to the social convener when at the last moment an Orioles ticket was going unused.

This compelled togetherness, Judy came to realize, was more than an attempt by Taft, Adams & Rogers to integrate newcomers into the firm. Their purpose was to speed the ultimate bonding: the recognition that all one's needs—for friendship, entertainment, as well as financial security —could best be fulfilled by the firm itself. A surrogate family, more capable than the one born into for meeting those needs, and in the best tradition of all families, expected from its members loyalty and unquestioning sacrifice.

Once this awareness was inculcated, it escalated the efforts a recruit would gratuitously put out for the firm—efforts, bankable in client development and additional billable hours. As such, these evenings were compulsory. Absences were not tolerated but treated as a breach in responsibility, and duly noted.

Judy could not afford to challenge the system. She required an unblemished record. She needed the hire-back and could not do anything which might jeopardize it.

How could she keep her word to Shane given at the time of the aborted camping week: "Once I get into the routine, I'm sure I can organize my work to be with you more. I'll spend as many of my evenings with you as you want." That promise had influenced her son's decision to get a summer job as a stock boy at Safeway, the grocery mart located in the Underground, the narrow, dimly lit subterranean mall which wound as a labyrinth of corridors beneath the residential towers of Crystal City. It was barely a ten-minute walk from their basement access to the store and, working the 7 a.m. to 3 p.m. shift, would allow him to spend the remainder of his day, until her return, at their outdoor elevated sundeck and pool complex. Set in a quadrangle, this was a facility which Crystal Plaza shared with three other sister apartments. With its Olympic-length lap pool, Judy felt confident it would draw other boys of Shane's age and interests. But despite her well-conceived plans for them to have their evenings together, Judy was rarely home by its sunset closing.

∽

Judy always seemed to be meeting up with Terry—due exclusively to his custom of usurping the carrel beside the *Virginia Reports,* the series of cases most consistently required for her research.

"How did the memo go?" he asked one July noon hour. Heat from the ninety-five degree day outside was filtering through the windows, making the climate-controlled library warm.

"Which memo?"

"That bad?"

"No, not really. Just a regular stream of powder-blue sheets to let you know you're wanted."

"How went the battle with the Bowers memo?"

"I've no idea. I haven't heard a thing."

"As long as you're not pulled into a partner's office again to explain, you're in great shape. Enjoy, enjoy . . . What are you working on now?"

"Updating a case. Due in at three o'clock."

"Good. Plenty of time. . . . Let's grab lunch." He swung his jacket from the back of his chair and onto his shoulders. As he walked toward the glass door leading from the library, he pulled up his tie. Judy had not moved. He walked halfway toward her. "What are you waiting for? You've only got forty-five minutes and it's beautiful outside. It's probably the only chance you'll get to see daylight today. By the time you leave this place it will probably be dark again. And I'm famished. . . . Come on, Lady J, we're wasting time."

Judy walked through the glass door Terry held ajar. They took the elevator to the main floor and purchased sandwiches from the Lunch Box, the concession off the lobby. Each carrying a white package with a bright green logo, they exited into the sun on the north side of I Street. Terry steered her diagonally across the road and into the block-long manicured greenery of Farragut Square. He chose the remaining bench in the shade, one under a large cedar. Sitting on its bleached slats, they faced the Metrobus stop and the fresh lime shutters on the side entrance of the Army and Navy Building. The twitter of birds pierced the screech from hastily applied brakes as vehicles sped around the square.

"I'm from New York. How about you?" he asked, lifting a tuna melt out from the box.

"I've always lived around here," she said evasively. She knew better than to volunteer anything. "What brought you to Washington?"

"Law school. And I decided to stay on. When you're twenty-eight and just out of Georgetown, Washington is a mighty seductive city."

"And when you're twenty-nine?" Judy teased.

"It still is," he laughed engagingly. Pigeons listened on the concrete walkways. "I'm going to give myself a few years here and then evaluate it. Medical malpractice is a growing field and I intend to grow along with it." His directness disarmed her. He had the flamboyance of the litigator and the brashness of youth. "So . . . what brings you to the law, Lady J, at this stage in your life?"

"I'm a late bloomer," Judy said.

"Good. They're always the hardiest of the species." He tore the soft center from his sandwich and tossed it into a cluster of pigeons. He asked nothing further of her.

Often, through the remainder of July and August, she and Terry shared their lunch break. They never strayed far from their home base—the intersection of Connecticut and I. Terry liked to eat outdoors, declaring it his duty to protect her from summer associate pallor. He embraced his passion for the law. He spoke of each pivotal precedent he had uncovered, talked of the tactics he intended to employ for a case, practiced on her and the pigeons who paced the cement paths of Farragut his deposition questions for the next day's witness.

Other times, he reminisced about law school. He regaled her with his fondest Georgetown recollection. Leaving his third floor Maryland Avenue walk-up at 8:55 a.m., cycling at full speed the two-minute distance, grabbing his bike at the foot of the stairs, and with it, spanning the two hundred steps leading to the Law Center's main entrance in under thirty seconds, locking it to the grill fence and always arriving at his nine o'clock lecture before the professor.

Judy was, in Terry's words, "a good listener"—by necessity. That was the surest way to reveal nothing.

Around five o'clock on the August Friday of her last working week at the law office, Terry insisted she take a break and join him for a drink across the road at the Barrister.

"Lady J, we have to mark this day with something."

They sat on the tall barstools, their drinks perspiring on the butterscotch leatherette counter. He gave advice on the third-year electives, and sought her opinion on a major malpractice matter he was working on with Frank Stephens.

A brief quarter hour later, Terry gave a nod to the bartender. "Got to go. I've a girl on the corner of Connecticut and K waiting for me. Can you imagine meeting every night at the same street corner in Washington? A little idiosyncratic, I tell her. She always does this to me to make sure I'm out of the office at a respectable hour. She's pegged me as being guilt-driven. Fallacy with her reasoning, I tell her—it can only be effective as long as we live in Washington.

"Now don't do those final assignments in detail the coordinator gave you, or you'll be here when Georgetown starts on Thursday." He leaned forward on the barstool and kissed her swiftly. "Lady J, I'm sure going to miss having you around." Then he went out the door. Hot, humid air seeped inside and hung heavily in the room. It caught the ice in the Perrier that had been abandoned by Judy at the opening of Terry's monologue and dissolved the cubes into the clear, chilled liquid.

Judy received a letter two weeks into her final year offering her permanent employment in the corporate department of Taft, Adams & Rogers. Its receipt immediately initiated two penned by her. One in writing officially accepting the position, the second, addressed to the assistant manager of the First Virginia Financial Corporation requesting a schedule of repayment for her loans to commence on the first of June and confirmation that upon final payment the lender would release all her security.

"That's it. We've made it through. We've done it," Judy said to Shane with relief, as both correspondences slid simultaneously into the mailbox in the lobby of their Crystal Plaza apartment. No mortgage burning, Judy thought, had ever generated the enthusiasm that accompanied that mailing.

For Judy, the remainder of the year completing the credits necessary to graduate was little more than housekeeping. Rather like sweeping up remnants after a New Year's party.

One Friday during the tedium of March, Judy descended the main hall's runway of terrazzo steps to see a figure set apart from the other foyer loiterers. He was slung against a cream pillar near the entrance doors, the relaxed posture of his body in contradiction to the intensity of his eyes, which were rigidly fixed on the glass partition of the library she had recently left and the twin stairwells leading from it.

"How is the soon to be Georgetown's newest oldest grad?" His salutation arrested her steps.

"Terry, what brings you here?" She came toward him, her hands weighted with casebooks.

"I live around here. Forget?"

"So where's the infamous bike? Do you have it on the concourse?"

"Nope. I've given up my bicycle. Too undignified for a second-year lawyer." He had not budged. He remained stalled against the column. "As undignified as meeting a girl on the corner of Connecticut and K. I gave that up too, officially three months ago. Most disconcerting to be regularly taken for a mugger whenever you go out socially. Don't you think so? Especially for someone who, an hour ago, in Federal Appellate Court made precedent in *James Torris* v. *Dr. Alfred Murdock.* Now, let's get a drink," he said, transferring her books under his right arm, "and I'll tell you the details of *Torris* v. *Murdock.*"

From then until term's completion in mid-May, Judy was not surprised to find Terry, usually at the end of the workweek, lodged somewhere in the central foyer unobtrusively waiting for her. On such occasions, they would stop at the Dubliner for a drink and, against a backdrop of piped-in Irish ballads, catch up on each other's lives. Terry would then walk her to the Union Station and the Metro run to Crystal City.

"Why so late again?" Shane asked Judy matter-of-factly at seven o'clock on one such Friday in May. He had uncharacteristically started to eat without her. A charred burger, empty Campbell's tin and a melting ice-cream container decorated the kitchenette's counter.

"I saw a friend of mine as I was leaving the school. We went for coffee."

"What's it to me?"

"I'm sorry, Shane. I would have told you in advance, but I wasn't expecting to see him. I never know when he's going to drop by like that. He's an associate at the firm where I'll be working."

"Spare me the details, Mom. I've heard it all before. I'm going out."

Chapter 6

B y the third week in May, Judy was back in her office on the third floor of Taft, Adams & Rogers. Her intended permanence after successfully taking her bar exams in July was asserted by her law degree hung conspicuously on the patch of wall in lieu of the standard print, and a photo of her and Shane in front of the sand dunes at False Cape State Park placed prominently on her desk.

The nature of her work changed, but not its hours. She rarely left her office. She was rendered invisible under a myriad of paperwork. From 8:30 a.m., her day was filled with minutiae—the paper shuffling government regulations generated. She examined for accuracy the minute books of the firm's corporate clients, verifying the recent home and business addresses of their officers and making the necessary corrections on the appropriate forms. She prepared their yearly filings within the requisite period and sent out the notice of annual meeting as prescribed by the Regulations to the Act. She often drafted minutes for these meetings as per the particulars on powder-blue memo; her attendance at same never requested. On rare occasions, she did the incorporation of a company, drafting its articles and bylaws and mocking up banking resolutions for approval. Upon direction from Fred Hughes, she inserted her name as a nominee director. The latter formality was a temporary measure often required by a client pending choice by them of a suitable candidate for that position and as a practice traditionally rectified at the first meeting of the board of directors. The one activity never permitted Judy was to meet with a client. The chairs in her office provided for that purpose remained unwrinkled with use.

"Remember Value Leasing, the subsidiary of our multinational client Mid-Atlantic Bancorp you were instructed to incorporate in June?" Judy was standing in front of Fred Hughes's desk. He flexed back his tufted leather swivel chair and stared joylessly into the midst of his marching ebony elephants. His voice looped over his back. "The one whose three choices for a name were rejected by the computer, thereby making it incumbent on me to seek direction for alternate names six separate times from senior management." The irritation of his tone made it clear that this memory still brought him aggravation.

"Yes, I do, Fred."

"Well, we all do. Unnecessary little episode." Fred Hughes left his elephants and turned to face her. He released his chair and let it snap to its upright position. "Alan Lewis, chairman of Mid-Atlantic Bancorp, phoned me five minutes ago. He is very anxious to activate the company. Says he cannot satisfy himself as to who the fifth director should be. He's still looking for a strong outside person. But at the same time, he does not want to delay the organizational meeting any longer. He intends to make his newest sub operational before his three-week biennial tour of his European and Asian holdings. He gave me the date of October 29 for the first directors' meeting. That's Tuesday of the week after next. Am I correct that you are listed with the state of Delaware as one of the five incorporating directors?"

"That's right."

"Then I expect you to attend on the twenty-ninth. Note it in your diary. Meeting to be held in Boardroom A at nine a.m. Send out the notice of meeting to all present directors, including yourself. . . . You may as well take minutes. You would have been writing them up anyway. And, Judy"—his words arrested her departure—"you are expected to say nothing."

∽

The six doors into the main boardroom were closed by 9:05. Judy was delayed due to a last-minute request from the chief financial officer to make available the firm's precedents for the company's proposed bylaws. She peered through the thin ridge of clear glass that rimmed the frosted beveled panels as a prelude to entering. Four men congregated near the coffee urn set out on the antique highboy.

The tallest of these formed the nucleus around which the others clustered. Well over six feet, of inestimable vintage, with a midsection that expensive tailoring could not conceal, Mr. Alan Lewis cut an imposing figure. Instantly recognizable by Judy from the photo inside the annual report of Mid-Atlantic Bancorp which she had read in preparation for today's meeting, his appearance was as impressive as the network of subsidiaries in Europe, Asia and North America spawned by this Washington-based conglomerate that he, as its largest shareholder at 11.2 percent holdings, personally controlled.

A man of erect carriage, slightly shorter, his lean frame attired in a similar but perceptibly less costly fabric, was compatible in years with Mr. Lewis. He had intense, deep-set eyes. Another was a curly-haired, plump younger man with a ruddy complexion. The remaining participant had angular features and a mustache.

Judy turned the wooden handle and, with the requisite documents under her arm, entered the cavernous room.

Mr. Lewis acknowledged her arrival by moving toward the double-pedestal mahogany board table around which forty-eight side chairs were set. He assumed the spacious, thick leather armchair at its head, the one in front of the life-size bronze bust of the founder of Taft, Adams & Rogers, a visage he easily eclipsed. The other three men sprinkled themselves on either side. Judy remained a deferential three-chair distance from the quartet.

The preliminaries complete and the coffee cups dispatched, the chairman brought his hands together on the spiral inlay of the table. Judy recorded 9:07 a.m.

"We all know why we are here. To hammer out the guidelines for our leasing company." The thick gray carpets and fabric walls in the nearly empty room were unable to absorb the magnitude of his gravelly voice. "I believe the climate has never been better to enter the leasing business. The economy is finally righting itself and we are well placed to capitalize on it. And Mid-Atlantic Bancorp, as Brian can attest as of year end, has come out of the recession with sufficient surplus funds to bankroll a leasing operation until it can secure its own credit line. We've an unparalleled opportunity to get into the leasing game, virtually on the ground floor. Management has decided on small-ticket leasing. That means nothing over twenty-five thousand dollars, gentlemen. With proper guidelines, that should place us at minimum risk. . . . Ted here knows the practical side of the leasing business. I stole him from our only potential competitor, but only after he was well trained," he said with measured levity. "And Roger, coming from a strong banking background, knows the credit end. Brian, as chief financial officer of Value Leasing, as with all my other companies," he said, acknowledging his senior executive, "will implement the controls we decide on today. Judy Kruger, as the incorporating attorney, is accommodating us by temporarily acting as our fifth director." He pushed his chair back from the table, his role in the meeting temporarily relinquished. "I invite your discussion." He waited.

"If I may suggest, Mr. Lewis, it might be useful to consider as the starting point the practice we followed at Econo-Lease," Ted said.

Mr. Lewis gave no encouragement. Brian drew lines aimlessly against the sticky adhesive of his legal pad but his eyes never left the speaker.

"The bulk of the leases were small-ticket items," he continued. "We lent on a signature and a solid credit check. Econo's security was the lease itself, together with the promissory note from the customer. That's what everyone in the low-ticket end of the market does. Wouldn't you agree, Roger?"

"I hear the same things from my contacts too. That's the norm in the industry. I endorse Mr. Bell's position." Roger's maroon leatherette writing pad sat unopened in front of him.

"Does everyone agree this is the appropriate security level for Value Leasing?"

"What Mr. Lewis means is whether we should adopt the practice in the industry. . . . Most definitely." Ted punctuated his opinion with an emphatic tap of his yellow ballpoint on the walnut table. It echoed in a quieted room.

"Mr. Lewis knows what Mr. Lewis meant. His question doesn't require interpretation," Brian said flatly, his hand now margining some geometric figure. "Alan?" he said, deferring to the man who commanded the head of the table.

The mechanical rhythms in the room became audible. Judy heard the whoosh of the air-conditioning system, the rush of air through the floor vents, the low-level hum of the fluorescents concealed above the grating, the bubbling of liquid percolating in the silver coffee urn on the highboy, and seconds later a remark addressed to her.

"Judy, as an experienced corporate lawyer, what do you advise?" Mr. Lewis demanded, placing his arms on the table and leaning forward.

Brian started to shade in his oblong design. Roger turned pleasantly toward her. Ted slung his elbow on the back of his chair. With his free hand he began a light persistent tap of his pen on the table's rounded edge.

"I'm sorry, but I can't agree with what's been said. As a director and your attorney, the minimum documentation which I'm comfortable with is Uniform Commercial Code registration. When a corporation with the financial reputation of Mid-Atlantic Bancorp by policy restricts itself to a twenty-five-thousand-dollar maximum, it clearly signals management's concern to minimize potential losses and to secure repayment. Without UCC registration, the corporation would have no legal right to repossess the property. Once a customer stops making payments, Value Leasing could lose its total investment in the asset. With no recourse . . ."

The tap from Ted's pen became heavier and more annoying. "With respect, Ms. Kruger, you're missing the point. Small-ticket lending is not asset lending. Once that fax machine or telephone system is installed, it's only worth twenty cents on the dollar—probably less."

"Ms. Kruger, I'm afraid I have to agree with Ted," Roger McPherson, the credit expert, said, continuing to play Guildenstern to Ted Bell's Rosencrantz. "Small-ticket lending is really a credit decision, not an asset security question. After all, we're not talking of leasing airplanes or tractor-trailers here, are we?" He chuckled, appreciative of his own humor.

"Not being able to repossess the equipment is an insignificant loss," Ted resumed, his credibility reinstated. "The greater loss is having an operating company and no business walking in the door." He let this image gestate before continuing. "This may be a new game for us, but there sure are loads of companies in it already. Not companies with our economic clout, I concede, but they don't have Ms. Kruger's addiction to forms. . . . Now I know salesmen. I've dealt with them for fifteen years. No office equipment salesman is going to take the time to fill out paperwork. He'll walk across the street. Somewhere where they wouldn't put him through the red tape Ms. Kruger is suggesting."

"I appreciate what you are saying, Mr. Bell," Judy said. "But the norm in the industry does not justify imprudent practice." Roger flinched. "Without registration, no one has notice that Value Leasing owns the equipment. The individual can borrow against the property or even sell it. Mid-Atlantic Bancorp, I believe, is looking for a new profit center, not a tax write-off."

"You're just trying to create legal work for your firm," Ted interrupted tersely.

Judy did not respond to the accusation. She held her calm as she continued. "Even though the economic climate is improving, no company can afford lax standards. And the documentation you put in place today may also have to see you through another economic downturn. And I wouldn't underestimate the deterrent factor of UCC registration. It's routinely computer-searched by banks, suppliers and credit bureaus to evaluate the creditworthiness of a potential customer. An individual will think twice before letting himself officially become known as a bad risk. It's a hard stigma to overcome." The financial information Mr. Hughes had amassed on Judy flashed through her mind, and with it, her humiliation. She worried she might have prolonged this issue unnecessarily and forced herself on to her next point. "The small-ticket items that Value Leasing intends to lease are the equipment essential to run a small business. If you take the photocopier, telephone system, fax machine and personal computer away from the small businessman, he can't function. The very fear of repossession of these items may be sufficient incentive to make him keep up the payments."

Ted was sweating profusely. His face reddened. He pulled the three-point handkerchief out of his breast pocket and, with it, dabbed at his upper lip and forehead. "Your registration idea is overkill," the salesman said, groping for a retort. "Even without it, you can sue them personally for the debt. Take them to court." His sentences had broken into staccato.

"Mr. Bell," she responded, "it doesn't pay to litigate for a few thousand dollars. A good attorney knows when to stay out of court."

Roger's lips were pursed. This time, he did not echo support for his colleague.

"Gentlemen, I could see your concern if I were advocating that you get a landlord's waiver for every lease. . . . If Value Leasing is to succeed long-term in the leasing business, the minimum documentation we should accept is registering the security."

Bancorp's prestigiously glossy annual report she had reread that morning—and its public relations thrust—came to mind. She returned to her core argument but with a different emphasis. "Public perception should be considered in determining this issue. Certainly a marginal profit in a new subsidiary looks better to the shareholders and the analysts in management's disclosure than would a loss."

The chief financial officer of Mid-Atlantic Bancorp put down his fountain pen, whatever irregular figure he had been doodling abandoned. "May I move, Mr. Chairman, that all the corporation's leases are to be properly registered in accordance with the Uniform Commercial Code."

Judy transcribed the motion.

"So moved. A seconder, please." Mr. Lewis looked into the abyss of the room, avoiding Ted's anxious gaze. "Judy, would you do us the courtesy of seconding this motion?"

"Certainly Mr. Lewis."

"In favor?" Brian Dell nodded assent, Judy put up her hand. "Opposed?" The hands of Ted Bell and Roger McPherson were raised. "Two for. Two against. . . . Approved," said Mr. Lewis, according to himself the prerogative of the chairman in a deadlock.

Mr. Lewis rolled his chair back, thereby silently terminating the meeting, and headed immediately toward the telephone in the nook of the room. Brian and Roger moved toward the coffee on the highboy. Ted remained at the table straightening his papers. He continued to obsessively align the edges of his pages, knocking each against the surface in front of him, a side at a time. Judy was still in her chair.

"Ms. Kruger." Judy had not heard Ted approach. She was preoccupied with filling in the details of the minutes. He rolled his handkerchief into a ball and wiped one damp palm against it, then the other. "I hope you're pleased with yourself. You've just made sure this business will never get off the ground."

Judy gathered her materials and left the boardroom, anxious to avoid further unpleasantness. The elevators refused to cooperate. She stared impatiently at the closed aluminum doors, considering whether it would be faster to take the stairs.

She heard an approaching heavy tread on the carpet.

"May I see you a moment, Judy?" requested Mr. Lewis. He steered her into an inside conference area and closed the door, thereby appropriating privacy for his conversation. He seemed more at liberty in their offices than she. He had ignored that this room with its oval cherry-wood table laden with documents was set up for another meeting, one due to commence at 9:30, according to the sign taped on the door.

Mr. Lewis remained standing. "I appreciate what you did for us today, Judy. Don't think I didn't see what was happening in there. With your permission, I'd like you to remain as a director, at least until we're over the formative stage. . . . Fred Hughes has acted for me and my companies for twenty-two years. All the work we bring in here comes under his direction. I'm on my way down to Fred's office now and I'm going to ask him to leave all of Value Leasing's legal work with you until my own people have these registration matters in place. And watch out that Ted and Roger don't try an end run on you."

⌘

"If that's what you say when someone specifically tells you not to talk, I'd better think twice before asking you to speak," Terry said, hearing verbatim the detailed thrust and tumble of Judy's morning meeting, the highlights of which she had told him earlier over lunch and which had led him to insist on this evening as a celebration and its update—the arrival by courier in late afternoon of Value Leasing's files along with a memo from Mr. Lewis instructing her to report exclusively to Brian Dell.

They sat at a balcony cocktail table on the roof veranda of the Washington Hotel. Before them, miles into the distance, blinked the brilliant color of the city night—the green of intersection traffic lights; the white beams from the Washington Monument topped by two flashing crimson eyes; the red blip from the undercarriage of planes on the flight path into National Airport. A cheese plate sat on the small glass oval between them, its wedged selections already dry. A filament of red was barely visible at the base of the carafe; the accompanying wineglasses were similarly drained.

Terry's teasing rolled over Judy gently. She was too happy. The happiest she could recall in recent memory. A tense meeting had broken in her favor and now she was here with Terry.

He leaned into the deep pocket of his turquoise wicker chair and looked at her appreciatively. "You're a gutsy lady. . . . A very impressive," he paused, "and a very beautiful woman."

Judy felt herself redden. She had never thought of herself as beautiful, not even in her early days with Bob: intelligent yes, sophisticated maybe, beautiful never. And since Bob, she never thought about such things at all.

Terry signaled the waiter and, pulling the table toward him, helped her out of the closely packed seating. Metallic legs scraped on the patio stone.

"I'm going to see you home to Crystal City," he said as they moved from the balcony into the corridor of the hotel's sixth floor. "But before that, I'd like to stop at Maryland. I have to argue before Judge Geissel after lunch recess tomorrow. Over the weekend, I took home photocopies of the relevant cases to have a further look at them and I'd appreciate your opinion on which ones you think would best support my motion. Okay by you?"

On M Street, walking toward the Metro station, Judy noticed the business traffic had thinned. The night people had come out. They were covered in layers of disheveled clothing, its weight bearing no relationship to the season through which they moved. Each wore a stack of hats: wools and thin cottons; gloves, their fingers torn through; a myriad of sweaters and vests; and some form of ankle-length protective covering—the preferred garment, a tattered heavy army coat. Gender was barely discernible—women sometimes identifiable only by skirts whose hems of varying length hung shapelessly about them. Men had on oversized trousers, belted at the waist by knotted string; their pant legs dragged through the filth of the pavement. The remainder of their possessions, limited to whatever they could carry, could be seen through clear plastic bundles, rolled severely into balls and clutched between reddened fists.

The destitute walked as in a trance, looking neither to the left nor to the right—moving to keep warm—unanimated, eyes vacant, unseeing and unseen by those who passed. Suddenly she realized that dating from the time she had been reduced to the degradation of welfare, she had been avoiding these faces. Thank God it never came to this, she thought to herself, and with that identified the fear that had driven her during her struggle to survive. A shudder involuntarily spasmed her shoulders.

"Let's take a cab. It's gotten quite chilly," Terry suggested, misinterpreting the origin of her discomfort.

"It's all right. We can take the Metro."

"Nonsense," he said with exaggerated gallantry, flagging down a cab. "I'll charge this to my client as a disbursement incurred 're: after-hours consultation with eminent counsel'—after today, Lady J, that's you."

The taxi stopped in the 600 block of Maryland and C Street.

"That's it," Terry said, pointing to a narrow house distinguished from the others in the row of slender walk-ups by the lime-green paint on its brick. "I promised myself I would upgrade after I graduated, but I got attached to the place. I have a habit of getting attached to things. . . . After you, Judy." He paid the driver, got a receipt and stepped from the car.

How charming this area was, each town house just a bit different from the others with oddly shaped fronts, jutting bay windows and well-tended miniature lawns. She followed Terry up the half dozen or so wrought-iron steps and then two flights to the third floor. He put his key in the latch and switched on the lights.

The door opened into a cozy room, a lovely turn-of-the-century Washington parlor. Across one side was a wrought-iron fireplace, the swirls on its grille reminiscent of that which was worked into the steps leading up to the house. Beside it was a metal basket filled with wood. Its mantel held a comfortable clutter of pewter drinking mugs and books. A beige rug remnant overlay most of the aged plank flooring.

"Make yourself at home." He indicated the butterscotch sofa across from the grate, over which a long-necked chrome lamp was arched. Sections of the Sunday *Washington Post* were piled on the almond acrylic coffee table. A chocolate velvet tub chair and ottoman were angled into the corner on the right.

"Be back in a moment," he said, disappearing through a swinging door. His steps echoed on the hardwood's bare surface.

Judy caught the faint slap of the opening of a drawer, followed seconds later by another. "Not doing too well," came his words from the distance, confirming her interpretation of the noise, revised with "Found it," and the clatter of a series of closing drawers.

He flopped down beside her on the three-seater and handed her the stapled bundle. His arms lazed across the back of the sofa, forming a sloped "T." "Do you like real fireplaces?"

"Uh-huh. I love the smell of burning wood." She looked up from the papers.

"Good. Let's inaugurate the first fire of the season in Washington."

Terry left her side, took the classified section of the *Post* and crumpled it. He crouched in front of the grate, arranged the paper, set slivers of wood on it and leaned three logs over this in a tent shape. He edged back to the coffee table and with a hand groped behind him for more of the Sunday sections. He rolled these lengthwise like a trumpet and ignited their far edge, then reached toward the structure he had prepared and tossed this firebrand into it.

Judy watched mesmerized as the kindling ignited, then the logs. Burnt particles floated from the grate. The sweetness of its wood filled the room.

"How did I do?" he asked, obviously pleased with his efforts.

"Extraordinary." Judy had long given up on her reading. She was comfortably curled into an arm of the sofa and followed this ritual and the boyhood enthusiasm he brought to it.

He flicked off the artificial lighting. Orange and red leapt from the iron grate. It caught them in its radius of light and drew about them a cocoon of warmth. A minute universe of two.

"Judy?" she heard him say, her name spoken as a question. The bravado was stripped from his voice, as surely as the uncertainty she had seen in his eyes when he had waited for her that first afternoon at the Law Center. "Judy?" he repeated, his voice husky and insecure.

She felt his closeness. He lifted her face to him and studied it lovingly. He kissed her neck, her eyes, her lips. Each in turn. Slowly, deeply. And she responded with an intensity new to her. Her arms welcomed his body to her, its press lithe upon her, his warmth a release from her solitude.

A log split and flared. Its sparkles shot high. It had been too long. A lifetime too long.

C h a p t e r *7*

*T*erry had changed the rhythm in Judy's life. The weight of her
responsibility to work and Shane eased as she felt the quickening excitement of being desired again. A Saturday evening in the intimacy of the
Japan Inn, dinner unrushed as sukiyaki bubbled lazily in its steaming
broth. Or crammed into the green enamel tables of Tout Va Bien, beneath
hanging plants and posters of Picasso; the dramatic rush of overworked
waiters. Late work nights and Fridays at Clyde's: pressed beside Terry on
a red leather bench as the colored liquid of the antique jukebox flashed
through lime, lavender and yellow. She tried to avert her eyes from the
slender oak bar and the equally thin young women who stood there three
deep and from whom came the flirtation of laughter, a sound Judy selec-
tively blocked. It worried her, being older than he. What was age? A
chronological gathering of memories—and she had collected far too few.

The explanations she offered Shane for her late evenings with Terry
had some credence. Saturdays were dismissed as "dinner with a friend
from the firm"; weeknight homecomings were justified as "an exceptionally heavy workload at the office." Both rationales went unchallenged by
Shane.

By the commencement of the third fiscal quarter, Mr. Lewis' business
acumen had proved out: a revitalized and buoyant economy was fertile
for lease financing. Leasing became the hottest growth industry and Bancorp's subsidiary was in place to capture the lion's share of the small-
ticket market of Maryland, Virginia and the District. Mr. Lewis' initial
mandate to Judy to implement documentation controls was extended by
Brian to have her oversee all UCC registrations and their prerequisite
searches. Value Leasing required her constant vigilance and in itself could
easily have consumed her entire day.

As Value Leasing grew, so did Judy's reputation and the business she attracted. True to the adage success breeds success, she drew to the firm other and equally lucrative financial institution clients.

In the ensuing four months, she felt pressured by the urgency of deadlines and the volume of new leases. Shane's infrequent calls to her office were dispatched with some variation of "Can't talk now. You'll have to call back," or intercepted by her secretary and left on yellow message slips.

Once again, her time was rationed, with little remaining for the mechanics of her household. Chores like small-appliance repairs, reorganizing the closets, oil and lubing the Volvo were postponed; some indefinitely, others ignored for months. With salary sufficient to keep current with her bills as well as make a respectable monthly payment on her personal loan, reconciling her bank statement with her checkbook somehow slipped into the latter category.

There were three bank machine withdrawals shown between January and March which, when she finally got around to this task, she did not recall making. For forty dollars, sixty dollars and eighty dollars. All were in the range she would take out when she had to buy last-minute groceries. Losing control of her expenses was troubling. Probably caused by having too much on her mind. When she had very little money, she knew how each penny had been spent; now with surplus dollars, she hadn't any idea where it had gone. Whether she was busy or not, she should never have let her bank statements go so long. It was too easy to lose track of money.

Laundry, done by her every second night, was one routine too entrenched ever to have its tempo altered; its frequency a carryover from her years of subterfuge. While Shane slept, Judy would remove the scattering of his shirts, pants and underclothes and return them, all washed and ironed, to his bedside for morning. She began this as a habit of pride. For her son in those latter Hollin Hills days, with but one change of clothes for school, there had to be fresh garments daily, and for herself, a credible cover story for the regularity of his attire. "Once boys this age find something they like, they certainly wear it over and over again" was her ready comment when queried by mothers of Shane's classmates. Although the rationale for her behavior was no longer relevant, she continued this practice. She would gather Shane's clothes every other night and take them to the coin machines on the basement level of their Crystal City apartment.

At the bottom of the hamper on one such occasion in January, Judy discovered a one-by-two-inch packet of papers, the thin transparencies used to wrap cigarettes.

Shane was doing his homework when she went into his bedroom to ask him about this. "I was picking up your clothes from the basket and I found something which I think belongs to you." She handed him the item.

"Oh, that? Thanks, Mom," he said, pushing aside the mop of hair that had fallen onto his forehead as he worked. He had been letting his shag cut grow out the past month. "You didn't have to bother yourself with that. It's nothing important." He flicked it onto his desk.

Judy made no motion to leave.

"Lookit, Mom. I intended to tell you I started smoking but I didn't know how you'd take it. The health bit and the cost of cigarettes . . ."

She pulled a chair up to his desk and warned him about the hazards of smoking, at the conclusion of which he said, "At least you should be happy I'm economical. I roll my own cigarettes."

∽

"This is Mrs. Fleet, executive secretary to Mr. Lewis," the caller said to Judy at 8:45 a.m., the morning following the third board meeting of Value Leasing. "Mr. Lewis would like to know if you would join him for lunch next Thursday at twelve-fifteen at the Prime Rib."

"What files does he wish to discuss?"

"I have received no instructions in that regard. . . . May I inform Mr. Lewis that you will be joining him?"

Punctually at 12:15 on the prescribed day, Judy entered the specified restaurant. She paused in its entrance, as her eyes made the adjustment from Washington's March noon-hour brilliance to the blackness imposed by the interior decor of ebony walls and dimly lit wall sconces.

"Ms. Kruger? . . . Mr. Lewis is expecting you," said the tall, tuxedo-clad maître d'. "This way, please." He led her past the center room and the crowd milling around the bar and through a low portico into an even more intimate dining area.

Mr. Lewis sat at an oval oversized table for four. With his back squared to the mirrored wall, he faced the aperture to the room and her approach.

"Thank you, Judy, for accepting my invitation," he said graciously, rising when she reached the table, surely as cognizant as she that a refusal had never been a possibility.

"Have you had lunch here before?"

"No, Mr. Lewis."

He opened the menu's heavy leather cover. "I've been coming here for years. Let me take you through the specialties. . . . You can always rely on their oysters. And if you like lobster bisque, they've got the finest in the capital. For entrées, I can recommend the roast beef or imperial crab. Whatever you choose"—he chuckled—"your doggy bag will do you for three dinners. . . . Carl, I'll have oysters, hearts of palm, New York strip, medium," he instructed the waiter, then directed him to take his guest's order.

She selected chicken divan, the least expensive main course she could find on the menu. No appetizer, no salad. She was not at ease with Mr. Lewis or this place.

"At the board meeting last week, that idea of yours for deferred commission—I like it. It's a concept I've never really put my mind to before. None of our other financial intermediaries depend so heavily on a commissioned sales force. . . . You know, when I was at Wharton nearly twenty-five years ago, there was no such animal as leasing. At least, not the type we do, the equipment-leasing business." His oysters arrived, presented on a bed of crushed ice with two condiments, one a vinaigrette, the other a red sauce. They looked meatier than any she had seen on the fish market counters in Old Town. "Tell me, Judy, have you given any thought to how we would structure such a deferral?"

"Yes, Mr. Lewis, I have some preliminary ideas, but, of course, they would require refinement and discussion with Brian." As he enjoyed his appetizer, salad and entrée, Judy groped to flesh out the alternatives for developing the commission holdback. Her chicken remained untouched; its Mornay sauce jelled into yellow thickness.

The waiter cleared away their plates, then with a monogrammed sweeper eliminated minute crumbs from the linen cloth.

"Judy, I have a real concern that with all of Brian's other responsibilities in our organization he can't keep on top of the boys at the leasing company. Not the daily overseeing that is obviously required. Ted is an excellent salesman but he has no loyalty to anyone but his own ambition. He and his crew need constant monitoring, as does Roger in credit. I need someone on my team whose loyalty is to the corporation and not to his personal agenda. I've decided that person is you, Judy. . . . I would like to propose a position as a senior executive with Value Leasing. You would be reporting, as you presently do, to Brian. We'd be starting you at double what second-year associates at Taft, Adams are getting.

"I think you should realize there are a lot of advantages to joining our organization. Not the least being, if I may say so myself, the financial benefits." He laughed congenially. "Bancorp has yielded over twenty percent return on equity in each of the last five years," he reeled off, his joviality vanishing with this statement of corporate achievement, "and is now trading at fifteen times earnings on the New York Stock Exchange. People who have been loyal to me, people like Brian, have already made themselves a tidy sum on their stock options. You could never possibly equal this in a lifetime of practicing law."

What he had said was right. She could barely believe her luck. Only a year out of Georgetown and she was being offered a chance like this.

Mr. Lewis sat back and regarded her, as if to assess her initial reaction, in this, his first breathing space since the entrée. She tried to conceal her exuberance.

"Of course," he continued when she had not replied, "you'll have the ability to hire your own support staff. With the volume we're writing now, you'll probably need at least two paralegals. You know, Judy, the position I'm offering you brings you into the Bancorp family at a very senior level. As *The Wall Street Journal* said last month, Bancorp is a dynamic growth company that's just beginning to tap its international potential. . . . And don't concern yourself with Hughes. I'll take care of Fred. The most that happens is I may have to lose a few golf games to him." Mr. Lewis clasped his hands assertively on the spotless cloth as one accustomed to conducting business in this setting. Then he pushed his chair back and waited.

She knew she was expected to be decisive. Too much time must have elapsed, for he said, "Opportunity knocks but once, Judy," and demonstrating his conviction, rapped the knuckles of his right hand firmly on the table's hard surface.

Judy did not respond to this subtle intimidation any more than she had to the fabulous salary offer. She disregarded it as she had Ted Bell's attack on her integrity six months earlier.

"Mr. Lewis, thank you for considering me. It would be a great honor to work for you. Would it be possible for me to have a few days to think about it?"

Carl poured the coffee from a silver service. An aroma richer and more satisfying than Judy had ever encountered tantalized her senses.

∽

"Judy, that's an offer a lawyer can wait a whole lifetime to hear and still never have it happen." It was an unseasonably warm March day and she was sitting next to Terry on the cement ridge that surrounded the fountain in Lafayette Park. The spray from its spout fanned into the light wind and cooled her back. She was facing one of the park's wide, red-brick walkways. The chess players were already busy at the collection of stationary stone tables near her. They moved their home-fashioned figures across the fading red-and-black checker squares set into the heritage granite's grimy surface. At one table, a ponytailed, raggedy-bearded man, with a soiled green velvet jacket and purple beret, played against a man with tattooed muscular arms. Beside them, two elderly men squared off. The thin vinyl chess mat which they had placed over the stone surface kept curling, despite the full complement of plastic knights.

Judy had lain sleepless in her Crystal Plaza apartment most of that night, weighing Mr. Lewis' proposal. The salary he offered, even without the stock benefits, was exceptional. But there was, after all, some risk. If she took his job, she would become merely an employee—she would lose her protected status as a lawyer acting for a major client within the relative security of a law firm. The very nature of the position he defined yesterday would force her to become caught up in upper-echelon politics with Ted and Roger. Mr. Lewis operated Bancorp as a one-man company. He could remove his protection at any time. And she could be fired at whim. An arbitrary, precarious situation in which she could lose everything; a scenario unlikely to happen to a lawyer, especially in a conservative, old-line firm like the one where she was fortunate to be employed. If she stayed with Taft, Adams & Rogers and continued doing Value Leasing's work, the worst that could happen if Mr. Lewis removed his patronage would be the loss of Value Leasing's account: a billing vacuum which, with her growing prominence in the leasing field and her present client base, could easily be filled.

It had been a herculean struggle to attain her present economic and professional status and she was hesitant to jeopardize it. For her, economic solvency came first; salary above this amount, a flattering nicety.

She finished her sandwich and tossed the Lunch Box's container into the red-brick receptacle, her trash tucked inside. "What do you think I should do?" she asked Terry, to whom, over this extended lunch hour, she had confided her analysis. She had picked this spot to do so, someplace away from the office. And someplace his arms could not distract her.

"Grab it. Lightning doesn't strike twice."

"Is that what you would do if you were in my position?"

"It's what anyone would do if they were lucky enough to be in your position. Think no more about it, Lady J. Take it."

Judy kicked off her flats and stretched her legs into the sun. Judy noticed he was appraising her motions.

"That new job of yours, Madam Senior Vice President, means but one thing: from now on, I'm going to have to make it my business to wrap up my morning ten minutes earlier in order to have lunch with you."

She would take the risk. Even though she would be giving up job security, this meant more money and faster advancement.

On her return to the office, Judy phoned Mrs. Fleet and requested a telephone appointment with the chairman and CEO of Bancorp.

"What matter should I tell Mr. Lewis you wish to discuss?" the executive secretary asked.

"The answer to Mr. Lewis' proposal," Judy replied without hesitation.

During the second week of March, Judy assumed her position as senior vice president of Value Leasing. The subsidiary occupied an entire floor of International Square East; its parent had the three stories directly above it in keeping with Bancorp's policy of consolidating its operations within a geographic region.

Flags of every nation proclaimed the international motif of the building. Their bright colors jutted festively from the marble facade over the height of the central concourse and its design of tiers of trees and a cascade pool with bubbling water. A glass side interior wall on the entrance level, set a generous corridor width across from the red-brick geometric external wall, ringed the expansive open courtyard and gave access to each of the four wings of the complex. The K Street East pod, with its twin sets of glass doors, prominent security counter and quad of swift elevators was the route by which Judy reached the company's ninth-floor premises.

Her office, situated opposite the open workspace shared by salesmen, collections, accounting, as well as her newly hired paralegals, had been decorated for Judy in her preferred colors, and with plants, rich fabrics, luxurious furnishings to soften the standard business accessories, collectively restored to her intense, stress-layered location a feeling of calm. A loose-cushioned, terra-cotta two-seater sofa was centered in front of her interior window and kitty-corner to this, separated by an apricot planter filled by a shrub with fanlike shoots, a set of pull-up side chairs in similar fabric. Her contoured high-backed chair of woven cream fabric rolled easily beneath a bleached-birch work surface and the return that extended perpendicularly from it.

From her desk, she looked through her expanse of prime window space into the center of the atrium. Patterns of cloud and light moved with regularity across the glass-and-steel roof. Ferns dangled from the balconies opposite and in the cavity in between, suspended by some invisible force, was an orb—a spinning, golden globe whose delicately lit spokes flashed color. When she would glance away from her files in her ninth-floor office and out at the play of blinking lights below her, she felt, from the events that had recently transpired, somehow above the universe.

"I can't spare the time to meet you for lunch today. I'm up to my neck with the appeal and everything. . . . You know how it is. . . . I'll phone you at the end of the day, whenever that happens to be, and we'll set up something for tonight. Okay?" Terry hung up without the warning of goodbye.

She had only been at Value Leasing for three weeks, but already things were falling into place. Sue and Donna, the paralegals she had hired, were working out well. They saved her from much of the tedium. In addition to ordering and picking up the Uniform Commercial Code printouts, they highlighted the relevant data for her to analyze. And with only one client to satisfy, Judy found her day less harried than it had been at Taft, Adams & Rogers. To date, Ted and Roger had not disputed her authority at the company.

But there was one disquieting concern which arose at work. Money was being taken from her purse with increasing frequency. Five dollars one day, twelve dollars another. Random amounts which, over the period since she had noticed this occurrence, totaled a hundred and twenty-three dollars. She could not discuss these missing amounts with anyone at the office. It would make her division appear mismanaged, and herself, so fresh at the job, foolish. And certainly, she could not accuse anyone unless she had solid evidence. With one hundred and twelve employees in a common area directly across from her, each with potential access, how could she possibly be certain who was responsible? She was constantly going in and out of her room—overseeing work, gathering reports, attending meetings. If she locked her door whenever she went out, she could stop the hemorrhage of her cash. But she needed to be accessible; such an act would send out the wrong message. As well, none of the other executives locked their doors during the day. It simply wasn't done. All she could do, she had previously decided, was to minimize her losses by limiting the amount of cash she carried to that needed for Metro fare, lunch and contingencies.

She hoped that today she had brought enough with her for an idea that had been gestating since Terry's call. As Sue and Donna had recently signed out for the District Court Office and would be gone for at least another hour, there was little she could do for now on her registrations and she had already attended to organizational matters earlier that morning. There was no need for her to remain at her desk during lunch today. And she didn't relish eating in the downstairs food court—it was too lovely a day.

She would surprise Terry. She would slip over to Connecticut, grab some sandwiches and sodas at the Lunch Box and phone him from his lobby. By now he would probably welcome a break.

Within moments of her decision, she left the office, took an elevator to the main floor, and as she did so, checked her purse to ensure her money was still intact, nodded to the security guard stationed at the pod's entrance, pushed open the glass door into the atrium, turned left onto the sloped pebbled walkway leading to the street and, to give her maximum time with Terry, grabbed a waiting cab.

That last action she instantly regretted—pedestrians were moving faster than the noon-hour traffic. Judy tensed forward. She kept a steady look out of her side window, comparing the pace of the walkers with the progress made by her vehicle, as if her impatience would in some way hasten the driver.

Near the intersection of Connecticut and K she saw Terry come out of his building. Accompanying him was a smartly attired young woman. The two crossed the street and headed into Hardee's.

"Here we are, ma'am. The closest I can get you."

"Keep going. And faster. Please!"

"Where to?"

"Away from here. Anywhere. Just keep going."

He brought her back to the cloistered safety of International Square in a return trip that seemed abruptly terminated within seconds. She remained in his cab, stunned. The driver extended his bulky frame over the ridge of the front seat and flung open a rear door.

"This is it. Where we started from."

She got out and began to walk despondently up the pebbled incline toward the impersonal structure.

"What about my fare?" came an irritated voice from the curb behind her in a volume loud enough to attract the attention of the constant stream of tower workers.

She retraced her steps and indiscriminately took some bills from her wallet, handed them through the cab window to the driver, then anonymously fell into step behind the others entering International Square. She walked through the set of doors left ajar by the previous user, passed the security desk without acknowledging its occupant, and did not engage in the pleasantries of the regulars with whom she rode the elevator. Avoiding her colleagues on her floor, she went directly to her office, shut the door and left her phone on call forwarding.

How foolish she had been. Naive and foolish. She had been deluding herself all this time. Living a fantasy. An illogical fantasy.

She was seven years older than Terry. Seven years. He never mentioned the difference in their ages but it must surely have been on his mind, as it always was on hers. It stood between them, a visible, unalterable truth.

How long did she think she could have held him—an attractive, witty, unattached, upwardly mobile lawyer? She saw how women looked at him in Clyde's, and everywhere else they went. Another month? Three months? A year at most? Maybe in another city. But Washington was not just another city. It was the nation's capital. And full of beautiful, bright, young and very available women. Women with no complications.

Shane may be the anchor in Judy's life, but to Terry her son must be nothing more than a nuisance. Terry never said that directly, but he had to feel that way. All the restrictions she imposed on their relationship for Shane's protection. After they had been together, she would never stay the entire night with him, but always left his place sometime around midnight. And she would never have him over to her apartment, not even for a meal. Nothing that might upset her son.

Was he at this very moment speaking to the girl he took to lunch, and casually dismissing Judy, as he had her predecessor, with an easy quip? "Oh, her? She's still at Farragut Square. But, as of last week, waiting for some other guy." Or "It's undignified for an associate of Taft, Adams & Rogers to be considered involved with a divorcée who has a seventeen-year-old son."

And Terry had never spoken of love. He never promised her permanence. He made love to her with the abandon of the uncommitted.

It had been nothing but an affair from the start. A beautiful passionate affair, but an affair nonetheless. She had never used this word, not even to herself, to describe her relationship. As if by denying it this label she could somehow alter the intensity of their intimacy and its inevitable end.

There was no purpose confronting Terry. He would just lie. Like her ex-husband had. Or worse, force her to end it. Today. Before she felt strong enough to handle it. Before she was prepared.

Judy remained at her desk waiting for Terry's call. Through a relentless, unproductive afternoon. He phoned at 6:50.

"I'm done. Barely. The Appeal Book just got served." His voice sounded worn.

Judy caught a snag of hesitation. "How are you?" was her reserved, cool inquiry.

"Awful. I got myself a case of heartburn. All for the sake of *Rose v. Dr. Schaeffer.*"

"How did you manage that?" she asked flatly.

"Had the great idea of taking Yvonne to lunch. You know, Yvonne, my new secretary. Figured if I ate with her, I could get her through lunch faster. . . . I got us in and out in under twenty minutes. Record time. But I'd rather not discuss the aftereffects." His lighthearted words could not disguise his obvious discomfort. "How was your lunch?" Terry tagged in afterthought.

"I picked up heartburn, too," she replied.

"We're sympatico, like I've always said," he responded with a return of his customary enthusiasm.

Despite Terry's explanation, Judy's sleep that night was troubled. More troubled than it had been for years. The thought of Terry and a younger woman refused to go away. Even if his secretary was not the one, it was going to happen someday. He would eventually drop her for a younger woman. Terry's words had not altered the inevitability, just the timing. Reality was pressing in on Judy's consciousness and clung there, stubbornly.

∽

"Mrs. Kruger, this is Detective Billings from Juvenile Division of the Arlington police. We have been trying to contact you since last night," echoed a voice from the cavern of her speaker phone.

Judy thumbed through the stack of pink slips that had already accumulated at the message center and had just been brought to her desk for her 8:45 arrival. There it was. "8 a.m., Detective Billings, URGENT, re:

son, 358-4330." Another one at 8:15 and 8:30. Judy snapped off the hands-free device and held the receiver to her ear.

"Is Shane Kruger your son?"

"Yes," her voice tensed, "has anything happened to him?"

"Your son was apprehended at 7:50 last evening at the Metro stop outside the Marriott in Crystal City for stealing a woman's purse."

"What?" The caller was unresponsive to her incredulity.

"Calls were made to the home and business numbers we had been given by your son." There was a pause, as if to consult notes, "at 8:15, 8:45, 9:05 and 9:30 last night. No reply was received. With no parent or guardian available to accept custody and on the authorization of a presiding court officer, your son was taken to the Juvenile Detention Center in Fairfax. He is presently being held there."

She had come back from Terry's around midnight. Shane's door was closed and his light off. Why hadn't she gone in and checked on him anyway, as she usually did? Then, this morning, she had slept in. It had only been for ten minutes, but when she got up he wasn't there. The county school bus reached his pickup point at 7:55. She was sure she had missed his departure by moments. She hadn't realized her son had never come home last night. How could she not have known this?

"But it was just a purse snatching," she defended her son and herself.

"Mrs. Kruger, in this state, there is no such charge as purse snatching; it's called a crime against the person. In Virginia, to steal an amount more than five dollars is a felony. The felony of robbery. It's punished accordingly."

"Where did you say he was? Please, may I come and see him?" Her mind was still trying to comprehend the situation.

"He's at Fairfax County Juvenile Detention Center—10650 Page Drive in the city of Fairfax." He reeled off the address, and then directions to get her there so rapidly that she was barely able to write it down. He concluded with "That's a good forty-five-minute drive from downtown Washington."

"Thank you, Detective Billings. Thank you for phoning. I'm leaving now."

She had not brought her car with her today and she had to get to Shane immediately. She spotted Sue signing out at the reception desk. Thankfully, she hadn't left for the Court Office yet.

Judy hurried from her room and over to her paralegal. "I'll have to take the company Toyota." She tried to keep the urgency in her voice under control. "Can you handle the filings by Metro today?"

"Sure," Sue obliged, taking a set of keys from her shoulder bag and handing them to her.

"Thanks." Judy rushed to the elevator. As she was waiting there, she caught a scrap of conversation from the area she had just vacated.

"What's her problem?" the paralegal asked the receptionist.

"I dunno. Except there were three messages from some police detective. Something urgent about her son."

Judy forced herself to block everything from her mind but the mechanics of driving as she wound her way out of the capital and past National Airport. Red, green, another red. Red again. The lights seemed to conspire against her. Everything did. Road construction, traffic congestion, trucks and erratic drivers.

Once on Highway 495, her mind ran unchecked; it raced with the speed of the car. What could possibly have gotten into Shane to steal someone's purse? Her son couldn't have done it. There had to be some mistake. She was a lawyer, she would straighten it all out when she got there.

The route she took brought her to an obscure part of northern Virginia and, even with the precise directions she had been given, the detention center was difficult to locate. After stretches of twisting farmland, she turned off Little River Turnpike at Judicial Drive, then made a right at a sign saying Fairfax County Juvenile Detention Center and parked in its sparsely filled lot. At first she just sat there, needing time to adjust to what lay in front of her. Before her sprawled an inhospitable, flat, red-brick, low-slung structure. It had slats for windows and all of them blackened, as if wanting invisibility. The institution was isolated by acres of unproductive land and tucked away inconspicuously in a remote part of the county.

She forced herself to leave the Toyota and, with apprehension, followed the winding cement walkway leading toward the structure. Pulling wide the heavy door, she confronted a uniformed guard. He stood behind a solid, chest-high counter built not more than two strides from this access. His eyes riveted on the entrance and her.

"I'm Mrs. Kruger. Detective Billings phoned me that you have my son here."

"Yes, Shane. We were notified you would be coming, Mrs. Kruger. We can let you have an interview room to meet with him."

"Thank you. But I would prefer to see my son where he is being held."

"We feel it would be better if we brought your son to you."

"I'd prefer to see my son where he is now," Judy said with determination.

"Very well. This is not our usual procedure, you understand, but if you insist, it can be arranged. Take a seat over there in reception, please. I'll have to get Superintendent Dawes. He's the only one with keys to take you back. . . . I caution you, this will not be a very pleasant experience."

Judy turned toward the adjoining area he had indicated. Paint peeled from its orange cement-block walls. She remained standing, as if to deny herself a presence in the building.

"Mrs. Kruger, I'm Superintendent Dawes," said a tall, husky man as he came toward her some minutes later. "Follow me, please." A chain was strapped to a belt loop on his trousers. From the wad of keys secured there, he selected one. "This is the intake area. . . . The only way in and the only way out," he said matter-of-factly. He unlocked the door and, once they had gone through it, relocked it on its other side. This dual procedure was repeated twice more in the short distance down the narrow passageway, and each time with a different key. The third door brought them into an internal, glassed-in circulation corridor, whose long sides walled in a grassy quadrangle. "That's where the boys play volleyball and baseball," he said. It was midmorning, yet no one was in the yard. The grass in that area was impeccable, with no ruts; in similar unblemished condition was the painted surface of a basketball court. Thick barbed-wire fencing jutted and thrust upward from all sides of the enclosure, forming a ceiling over this opening; its purpose, undeniable. Judy's gaze fixated on this barrier.

"We are a state-of-the-art facility. No bars," he said, compelling her to avert her attention from this location. "We use auditory surveillance. Not electronics. Here on the left side are what we call the living units. One person per bedroom, eleven rooms and an observation space surrounding a social area. Gives the counselors you see in there better contact with the juveniles than the standard design." As if to forestall any inquiry concerning two thin turquoise mattresses lying on the floor in each observation area the superintendent added, "We're temporarily overcrowded."

Through the Plexiglas windows of the compartments they passed, Judy saw teenaged boys. They were doing nothing extraordinary. Some were completing the morning's cleanup, moving the heavy furniture and vac-uuming under it. Those not so involved sat on chairs or extended their lanky frames over couches. Some were black, some white, a few Hispanic. Some scrawny, others athletic with enormous hands. A cross section of life. A few kids stared blankly into space. Or laughed at nothing. One was a skinhead. But mostly they looked normal. So ordinary. As ordinary as her son.

"What type of boys are in here?" she asked, searching for a rationale for Shane's confinement in this place.

"We're a medium-security installation. Probation violators, armed rob-bers, sexual offenders, drug dealers. Sometimes murderers, but there are none in here today."

"All mixed in together? In the same living unit?"

"Yes. We don't separate by crime but by age and criminal experience."

Her son was locked in with these people. She had to get him out.

The superintendent stopped before a third unit. "We'll find Shane in here." From his chain, he chose the key which admitted them into the common area. His right hand put the collection back into his pant pocket. It remained there, a bulky fist under the material. Now that he stood among the boys, the superintendent never took his hand off those keys; Judy was shocked and saddened, coming to her son's disenfranchised status afresh. What had she done wrong?

"Hello, ma'am," one black youth addressed her politely. "Come lookin' for someone?"

Her body became rigid. Involuntarily, she moved closer to the super-intendent, seeking protection. There were too many boys compressed into too small an area. She sensed pent-up anger and frustration, emotions not discernible through the sterility of Plexiglas, and that by being here, she had somehow raised their volatility. They seemed to resent her, per-haps for coming for someone who wasn't them.

Something was about to erupt, despite the presence of three street-clothed guards who suddenly became apparent.

"Who are you looking for, Mrs.?"

"Let me help you, Mrs.," another said, simultaneously sliding beside her.

"I'm fine. Thank you," she said, responding to their feigned politeness, her pleasantries emanating from fear.

"Ma'am, whad ya say your boy's name was?" said the first. Juveniles moved in around her. The attendants wedged between them, inserting their bodies about her as a shield, and edged her forward.

"Okay, Joe. That's enough. I'm sure the lady knows who she's come to see."

Judy saw the superintendent's arm tense. The bulge in his pocket became more conspicuous. The formation advanced her toward a closed cubicle. In an abrupt motion a key appeared and was inserted into a lock—the release of the final barrier that kept her from her son.

Shane sat on a poured-concrete slab that served as a bed in a barren four-foot-wide cell with a disproportionately high ceiling; his back framed by a harsh yellow wall, his eyes gaped vacantly through her. Hair, which he still left unmaintained, hung at chin level, scraggly, untamed and greasy. He wore the pocketless denims and coarse, dark blue shirt that she had seen on all the others.

Judy moved into the cubicle, its narrowness forcing her beside the glistening aluminum urinal. She had not expected this. She did not know what she had expected, but it certainly was not this. Her son in detention center clothes. Incarcerated. Locked in with rapists, drug pushers and thieves as though he were one of them. Her whole system rebelled. Cold sweat permeated every pore and she felt a wave of intense nausea. A band of pain seized her head, throbbing into her temples. "Superintendent Dawes," she uttered.

He was chatting with some of the boys in the main room.

Her breath was labored and short. "Superintendent." She tried to control the breaking of her voice. "Please, would it be . . . would it be possible to use the interview room? The one the desk sergeant suggested?"

The superintendent left the youths. "Certainly, Mrs. Kruger. . . . Come along with us, Shane." Swiftly, he conducted them from the room. Her son was made to walk always ahead of the superintendent, each door instantly secured behind them as they retraced their steps through the glass-lined circulation walkway.

Tears stung Judy's cheeks. The pain across her forehead intensified with each step. She did not permit herself to look to the side. She avoided the windows of the living units that revealed the motions of normalcy and kept undetected and silenced the frustrations that dwelt within.

He unfastened the door to the intake passage and brought her to one of the interview rooms adjacent to it. "You can use this for fifteen minutes."

"Thank you," she said to the superintendent as he was shutting the door. From the outside, he released the paper accordion blind which hung over its windowed portion for privacy. The latter act was an unnecessary gesture: their movements were visible through a wide rectangular glass surface located on the wall adjoining the administration area.

The room offered no warmth. It only contained a desk, and on opposing sides of it, two hard chairs. Shane took one, she the other.

"I want to know what happened," she began.

"Nothing." He tossed his disheveled hair out of his eyes.

"Something happened. You're here."

"Nothing happened."

"Shane, Detective Billings told me you were caught taking a woman's purse."

"I didn't take anything. It's a mistake. The stupid cops grabbed the wrong guy." He slouched down in his chair.

"What do you take me for? A fool? Police don't charge in cases like this unless they're sure. Damn sure. . . . You're not being honest with me. . . . If I'm going to get you out of here, you'll have to tell me the truth. Now what happened last night?"

"It was dark. I was coming out of the Metro near the Marriott. Some guy must have taken a woman's purse and got away with it. The cops grabbed me. The rest is history." He stared defiantly at her. "Don't you believe your own son?"

Judy contained her rising anger. She chose her words carefully, using only those of conciliation. She had to get him out of here, to a place where they could talk as mother and son. Away from this sterile, hostile environment. No mistake had been made—she was certain of that now. But whatever her son may have done, he didn't belong here. He would never belong here. She needed to get Shane home. Before he began to identify with the other boys and became lost to her forever.

"Shane, I love you. I want to help you. And we're in trouble. I can't get you out of here unless you tell me the truth. Now, please . . . tell me what happened."

Shane slouched deeper into the rigid chair. Nervously, he picked at his pants, then clenched and unclenched his fists, as if torn with indecision.

"Okay, I did it. I took the purse. Are you happy now?" Tears formed in his eyes. Clung stubbornly there and refused to fall.

"But why, Shane?"

"Money. For video games. Pool. That's why," he blurted in staccato.

"But why would you want money for that? That's ridiculous," she said, regretting that pejorative phrase as soon as it had been spoken.

"You didn't think it was ridiculous when you had me enroll in the after-school program at Jefferson so you could stay as late as you wanted at your stupid law school. I told you when we were camping that all we ever did there was shoot pool and play video games. You didn't object then. Not when it suited your convenience. Now, suddenly you do."

"Look, if video games and pool were so important to you, you could have come to me. Don't steal anything again. Ever. For any reason. Understand?" Her admonishment concealed her relief that his reason for wanting the money was not more serious. "If something is that important to you, I want you to talk to me about it, even if you feel I won't agree. At least give me that chance. . . . Now let me see what I can do to get us out of here."

Judy rose to look for the superintendent. Unsummoned, he approached from the administrative side of the interview room. He must have been watching through the glass panel.

"Mrs. Kruger, is it your intention to take Shane with you today?"

"Yes, thank you."

"You'll have to sign a recognizance."

"Of course. Whatever is required."

"John, bring Shane Kruger's personal clothes to the holding area." He waited until this man had removed her son from the room and then unfastened "intake" for her. The door opened onto the antiseptic place where, in what seemed a lifetime ago, she had come into the facility.

The superintendent went behind the reception desk. "Your son has been apprehended for robbery 18.2-58. He has been brought into custody in this detention center." He spoke a stilted, rote text. "I am empowered by the state of Virginia to release him on your recognizance. It is your responsibility to see that your son appears before the judge at the Fairfax County Juvenile Court, 4400 Chain Bridge Road, at nine a.m. on the twelfth of April. Do you understand?" He paused, as if assessing her comprehension. "This first appearance is an advisory hearing where the official petition will be read and a court date set. Legal-aid counseling will be available to you on that day. Do you understand?"

"Yes. Yes I do."

"Then sign here, please." She wrote her name and address. She likewise signed the release for Shane's personal belongings, anxious to speed up the formalities.

Sun streamed through the lobby window opposite, its brightness a heartening sight. She was grateful to see natural light again. They would soon be far from this place.

From a side drawer, the superintendent withdrew a white envelope. He emptied its contents onto the counter for Judy's inspection. A watch, signet ring, keys, ballpoint pen, coins, a wallet. The stub of a cigarette dropped from the bill section. The superintendent picked up the hand-rolled cigarette and slit it with a fingernail. A shriveled greenish-brown substance with something resembling flakes of parsley through it fell in clumps onto the counter. A sweet, pungent odor permeated the air.

"Do you know what this is? Marijuana, wrapped in cigarette paper. Fortunately no PCP," this latter phrase uttered more to himself. His hands deftly searched the other crevices in the wallet.

He put down the billfold. She felt his eyes fasten on her and maintain their hold. "This was in your son's possession when he was apprehended. Marijuana is an illegal substance which is contrary to the Penal Code of Virginia." His voice had again taken on its formal character. "I have the discretion to charge the juvenile with the misdemeanor of possession. I'm seizing the substance. I'm required to make a note of this possession on your son's file and on the notes that go before the Juvenile judge for sentencing. . . ." His tone softened. "You are very lucky, Mrs. Kruger. In your son's case, I have decided to exercise my discretion and not add the misdemeanor of possession to the petition for robbery 58. But you better make sure he never has drugs in his possession again."

"Thank you, Superintendent Dawes. Thank you very much. I'll have Shane at the courthouse on April 12." She took her son's watch, ring and wallet from the counter and slid them into her briefcase.

∽

"We have to talk, Shane," Judy said as her son, once inside their apartment, pushed ahead of her toward his bedroom. It had been a silent drive home, with Judy preoccupied organizing her thoughts for the confrontation she knew couldn't be avoided.

"Can't you leave me alone? I've had enough for one day." But he responded to the firmness of her tone. He arrested his steps and flopped onto the charcoal sofa in the sitting area adjacent to the window. She took the chair directly facing him.

"Here are your things they gave me at the detention center. I signed for them." She threw each item individually onto the glass table in front of him. One of the coins spun on its edge and without warning dropped. "I would give you your marijuana, but it was seized." She studied his face. His eyes averted hers, looking instead into the closed venetian blinds.

"I don't know what you're talking about."

"Shane," she said, lowering her voice, "I was there when Superintendent Dawes found it in your wallet."

"It's not mine. I swear it. It's not mine. . . . The cops must have planted it. Anything to get a conviction. . . . That's it. The cops did it. They had plenty of time."

"It was rolled in the same type of paper I found in the hamper, Shane. The paper you told me three months ago you used to make your own cigarettes," she said, unable to control the stress in her voice.

"Okay. I use marijuana sometimes. So what? Everyone in high school does. What's it to you?"

"You're asking 'what's it to me'?"

Turning back to face her, he glared. "Yeah, you don't care about me. You never have. Why should you care if I smoke grass?"

"Shane, I do care. You know I care. Everything I do is for you."

"You're always saying that. But it's not true. It's never been true. Everything you do is for one person: yourself. You're selfish, self-centered. You don't love me. You don't love anyone but yourself."

"Shane, I care about you and our life together. Law school, my job, it's all been for us," she said desperately.

"Law school? Your job? You did that for me? . . . Do you expect me to buy that shit? You did it for yourself. You thrive on adversity. Now you can add me to that list. You don't think I know about your boyfriend. But I do. . . . You say you're always home late because you're working, but I know you're with him. You didn't even come home last night. That's how much you care about me. You were with him last night, weren't you? If you'd been here when they called, I wouldn't have gotten stuck in that hellhole."

"I do love you, you're my son." She spoke this sentence with emphasis as if, in its simplicity, it absolved all misdemeanors of her neglect.

"You think you're so smart. Tell me, where do you think I got the money from for the marijuana? I took your bank card. Getting your pass number was no sweat. You're not very original. You picked my birthday. It only took me two tries to figure that out. And the cash you thought someone at the office took? That was me too." His confessions slid like a stiletto, deep into her.

She disguised her shock. To help him, she had to know everything. "Shane, are you taking anything other than marijuana?" Now he was talking freely, she had to hear it all. Every awful detail. She would not let his hostility keep her from probing. "Shane, is marijuana the only drug you're taking?" she rephrased.

He did not reply. His tirade had ended as abruptly as it had begun. He ran his hands through his hair. When it fell over his face, he looped the offending strands behind his ears and stared, as he had earlier, uncommunicatively into the sealed shutters.

"How often do you take marijuana?" she asked, trying to get him to disclose more. "Do you take it on your own or only with your friends?"

"So, you've finally come around to my friends, have you? Suddenly, you're interested. You've never been before. You'd never let me bring them home. They'd make too much noise and disturb your precious studying. Now, suddenly, you've decided you're interested in who I hang out with?"

"Look, Shane, we're on the same side." She was weary. The detention center and his anger had taken their toll, more than she would permit herself to show. And she couldn't take much more. She tried to narrow their discussion to the immediate and now. "We have a serious problem. This isn't a kindergarten charge you're facing. It's robbery. Fortunately, Superintendent Dawes has said he won't charge you for possession of marijuana. But that information will still go into your file and into the notes that the judge will have before him when he sentences you. . . . Shane, are you listening to me?" she said, becoming frustrated with his apparent indifference to his predicament. "First, we need a lawyer. I'm going to get Alvin Middleton. He specializes in representing teenagers in criminal cases. . . . Is that all right with you?"

"Do what you want to do. I don't care," he broke silence belligerently and sauntered out of the room, his steps exaggerated.

Pain knotted the pit of her stomach and lodged there. Deep and unforgiving.

What if Shane's accusations were true? Perhaps she was too committed to her career. She should have been with him more. Since she had been involved with Terry, she had been spending even less time with her son. She should have told him about Terry from the start. Why hadn't she been more sensitive to Shane? Why hadn't she made it her business to meet the new friends he had made since their move to Crystal City? Why didn't she spot the signs that Shane was on drugs? They were all there. They screamed out to be noticed: unexplained bank withdrawals, stolen money, the cigarette paper. He must have wanted her to discover them and help him. But she ignored them and him. She was too busy. Too busy and too self-absorbed.

What type of parent was she to have let this happen? The superintendent had been kind to her, even overly solicitous. He acted as if it were common for teenagers from good homes to be there. How could she have prevented this?

Her mind thrashed with these disturbing thoughts, through the assorted meetings with Alvin, the interval leading up to the advisory hearing to set the court date, and as the days inched toward the trial. Doubts and anxiety interfered with her work, unseating her concentration. When she would gaze distractedly away from her desk into the heart of the atrium and its core, the golden globe, she felt its unrelenting speed had hurled her reproachfully out of its orbit. She blamed herself with the same kind of questions with which her son had accused her. There was only one question she never thought to ask: Did she love Shane. For that was the one thing throughout this terrible nightmare of which she was certain.

Judy walked out of International Square at 11:45 in anticipation of lunch at the Prime Rib with the chairman and CEO of Bancorp, the first invitation of its kind since Judy had accepted Mr. Lewis' offer to become an executive with the organization. Mrs. Fleet, when notifying Judy yesterday of this appointment, had not indicated what matters he wanted to discuss. En route to her meeting, she considered the issues he might raise with her. Despite her concern over Shane, she felt she had a good grasp on Value Leasing's operations and would be able to handle whatever questions he might put to her.

In the twenty-three days since learning of Shane's arrest, she had been dividing her time strictly between her son and the office, confining her contact with Terry to the lunch hour. He had proven understanding, more understanding than she had expected, when told that for the next few weeks Judy would be spending her evenings with her son. She offered no fuller explanation for this other than she felt she had recently been neglecting Shane. Judy was unable to take Terry into her confidence. She felt too ashamed.

Judy's vision adjusted immediately upon entering the Prime Rib. An overcast sky had made the dark decor of the restaurant an extension of the outdoor environment. From the distance of the waiting area, she spotted Alan Lewis. He was in the small interior dining room, seated at the same table as he had been on the other occasion he had summoned her here. Alan appeared tense, an uncharacteristic departure from his usual phlegmatic manner. He was tearing chunks off the French loaf and discarding them impatiently onto his side plate. A waiter approached to replenish his breads. Alan waved the man away; his gesture denoted annoyance.

"You're Mrs. Kruger. Mr. Lewis is expecting you. . . . May I take that from you?" the maître d' said, slipping her light raincoat off her shoulders and escorting her to the Lewis table.

Her chairman rose for her arrival, his visage restored to the placidity normally featured there. "Judy, how nice to see you. What would you like to drink?"

"Perrier, thank you."

"Make mine the regular, would you, Carl."

Passing the slip of paper containing their beverage order to an assistant, Carl inquired, "Would you care to order now or later, Mr. Lewis?"

"Now will be fine."

Carl placed an open menu into her hands.

"Judy?" Mr. Lewis prompted forthwith.

She ordered roast beef. Medium rare.

"Make that two, Carl. With oysters, and hearts of palm salad." Their drinks arrived. "You know, Judy, I've been hearing good things about you from everyone. I can already see that hiring you was exactly what they needed down there at Value Leasing. You've been productive from day one. Instituting that system of yours, the one of deferred commission for salesmen, has already saved us money. And you implemented it without ruffling any feathers. Which I'm sure was no mean feat, knowing those boys. . . . Here's to you, Judy. And to your future with Bancorp." He lifted his martini in the affectation of a toast, took a swallow from it and rolled his castored black tuxedo armchair nearer to her. "You must really be pleased with how things are going."

"Yes, Mr. Lewis, I am." She now began to sip her mineral water. Previous to this remark, despite the affability of his conversation, she felt his gaze too intent upon her to do so prudently.

"Well, you should feel good about it. You've already more than justified my confidence in you. . . . Judy, I don't need to hand you any taffy, I've already hired you, but I want you to know I'm delighted with the job you're doing. You know, I don't see things like the other CEOs and chairmen of my generation see them. I fully believe that women senior executives are the way to go. An untapped resource. . . . You've a great future ahead of you with the Bancorp group of companies, Judy, in whatever avenue you find most challenging—whether at Value Leasing or any other of our subsidiaries."

Carl set down a tray of oysters in front of Mr. Lewis. He swiftly consumed them with none of the gusto she had noticed at their previous meal together. Rather, more as a nuisance that had temporarily derailed his agenda. The emptied shells were removed instantly and replaced by twin platters of prime rib; the conversation switched as abruptly as the courses.

"Hope today's weather doesn't cancel out the Orioles game. You know, we have a block of season tickets. Right behind home plate. Great seats —I arranged for them myself. Had them for years. Can't get tickets like these anymore for love nor money. . . . Does your son like the Orioles?"

"Yes," she said tenuously, uncertain where he was leading.

"Of course he does. Everyone does. Well, anytime you'd like to take that boy of yours to a game, just let Mrs. Fleet know." He took three large swallows, gave one grand wipe to his mouth, crunched his napkin and set his cutlery down. He pushed his entrée unceremoniously to the side, swept immaculate the crisp cloth where the plate had been, folded his hands into the center of its imprinted starched circle and leaned toward her in a confidential manner.

Judy abandoned her meal.

"You know, for many years now I've had my eye on a little factoring company in England. It's got a ninety-year history and a consistent earnings record. You never could reproduce a company like this today. . . . There are two key factors that make this an attractive acquisition for us. Firstly, no major shareholder." He unlocked his hands, traced his thumb and index finger across the cloth as if committing this point in writing upon its linen surface. He ceased this motion.

As he continued to speak, she felt him scrutinize the impact his words were having upon her. "Presently, the company is controlled by a consortium of French, German and English interests. No one investor has a big enough stake to call the shots. With Bancorp's management style, even with conservative projections, we could increase earnings by twenty percent in the first year. Then there's the European Common Market." He scrawled another imaginary notation on the cloth. "The directors don't see the potential of restructuring this London-based company as a full-service financial institution capable of serving the entire EC. Each of them operates a substantial business of their own within their own borders and are so myopic in their vision that they haven't even considered the international possibilities for the company they jointly control.

"For the last twelve years now, whenever I've been in England, I've visited with Lord Duffield. He's the chairman of one of the big clearing banks over there. I've been trying to get him to recommend my offer. Ten days ago, he phones out of the blue and asks me whether I'm still serious, and says he's now in a position to recommend to his investors a price of three hundred and fifty pence a share for the company. That's about eighteen million dollars U.S. Our British solicitors are presently working up the deal. I've learned it's always better in dealing with the Brits to have things done at their end. Makes them feel more comfortable when dealing with one of us Yankees. . . . Well, that's the origin of the paper that probably crossed your desk this morning. I told Mrs. Fleet to put you on the fax distribution list."

He settled back into the leathery thickness of his chair, the intimate part of the luncheon concluded. "Judy, we've got a problem. Brian has worked closely with me on all my acquisitions for over twenty years. But Brian is tied up on the Consolidated Regal merger. He's run into serious regulatory problems with it. I can't pull him off that without jeopardizing the deal. . . . In any event, it's time I started to groom his successor. I'm sending you over in his place to negotiate the closing and sign it up. The only way we're going to take this deal down is to put you on British Airways tomorrow with a banker's draft to buy them out fast. Real fast.

"My concerns are, first and foremost, a competing bid may come out of the woodwork. From my experience, when one person sees the potential in a deal, it doesn't take long until others come sniffing. I'm not going to give Duffield the chance to put the deal in play. No old-school buddy of his from Eton is going to bid three hundred and seventy pence and take this deal down." With the details of the pursuit he was becoming more animated, his language less refined. Muscles along the ridge of his forehead bulged prominently. "I'm counting on you to tie it up before the pack gets wind of it. That's why I've got to have one of my own people there. I must know immediately if another offer comes in so we can respond. No one's going to scoop this deal.

"Now, on the last-minute adjustments to the price. What the Brits called 'addenda.' " His voice, as he continued his briefing, had emptied its pretense of warmth. It flattened and became taut, its tone urgent. "I want you to know my numbers for buying this company are strictly based on the purchase price with no extras. So watch that we don't get nickel-and-dimed to death with severance pay, pension fund, cancellation of intercompany accounts." Three fingers spiked to attention as he enumerated these items. "When you add up all the gimmes they could put on the table, it could run us into the millions. Another ten percent over our purchase price, to be precise, and at that figure, the deal is marginal for us.

"And you better know this now—you'll have to negotiate this yourself. You'll get no help from our London solicitors. They're technically capable but they don't want to involve themselves in business details."

The waiter approached to clear away the dishes. Mr. Lewis gave him a stern stare to keep his distance. Judy dared not interrupt.

"And don't let Michaels and Michaels risk our deal by generating more paper. If any additional drafting is required, you do it. And keep it simple. I know the company. It's as clean as a whistle. And I know these people. I don't want to scare them off with complicated agreements and too many reps and warranties.

"And you'll have my private line at the office and at home. Don't be afraid to use it, Brian always does. I want to be kept in the picture.

"Judy, you'll know you've got yourself a deal when you see the big boys fly in from France and Germany. Once they've come to London, they're only there to sign and settle the menu for the closing luncheon." The intensity that had been steadily building throughout his remarks subsided with the delivery of that last sentence. Repeatedly, he rubbed his fingers across the section of cloth where earlier he had invisibly scripted his business analysis. He erased its indentations, as if by so doing it guaranteed protection for his strategy from potential competitors. Then he looked directly at her and added with determination, "It's essential to the corporation, Judy, that you drop everything and represent us in London. Knowing how capable you are, you should be able to wrap things up in a week."

This was the interval appropriate for her to express her gratitude. He was offering her an immediate increase in authority and in the long term the enticement of promotion: the possibility of becoming Brian's successor.

Judy's hands were iced in perspiration. "Mr. Lewis, I understand what this transaction requires and appreciate the confidence you have in me. But there are circumstances which make it difficult for me to leave tomorrow."

"You're going to have to overcome those circumstances."

"I have a situation I must take care of."

"Judy, I have situations. We all have situations." His voice clamped into tightness. "Our ability to detach ourselves from them, subordinate our personal interests for the good of the company is what's expected in the business world. With the power and title goes the responsibility. You must have known success has its price as well as its rewards." Eyes locked into hers. "I'm asking you to do what is required for the best interests of the corporation. . . . This deal requires mothering, Judy."

She gauged the steel of Alan Lewis' gaze, the bite of his words, the hard edge in his tone and then his ultimatum.

"Judy, I needn't remind you that what I'm requesting is expected and, I hasten to add, willingly given by every senior executive in my organization. I expect it. My directors expect it. And, Judy, I'm afraid I can't take no for an answer."

She felt cornered. She had already smelled the scent of blood and it was hers. Her mind groped desperately. Mr. Lewis was right. Sacrifice was expected of any person who held the position of senior vice president. And of any person in a large corporation who intended to keep that title and the power that went with it.

She would speak to Ron, the counselor Judge Arkin had assigned to their case at the advisory hearing. From the way Shane spoke after his sessions, it sounded like they had already established a good working relationship. And from her conversations with Ron, he impressed her as being genuinely interested in helping Shane. Sympathetic and competent. She would ask him to check on Shane in the evenings.

And spring break was over. Shane was safely back in school. That meant she'd be able to enlist the help of the Arlington policewoman who was routinely at his high school. That would provide additional coverage.

As soon as she knew where she would be staying in London, she would leave the hotel phone number with these people and instruct them to call her anytime, collect, at the first sign of a problem. Day or night.

One week, Alan Lewis said, was all that was required to wrap things up. She would be back in Washington long before May 29, the day set for trial. Alvin was confident that Shane, being a first-time offender, would receive a suspended sentence.

A week was really such a short time. With the professionals alerted, her son would be well supervised. What could possibly go wrong in one week?

"I would like to consider this matter resolved," her chairman said.

"Yes, Mr. Lewis, the matter's resolved," she responded. "I'll be on that plane tomorrow." Outwardly, she manifested a profound calm; it masked a pervasive inner uneasiness.

∞

"Ladies and gentlemen, we shall be landing shortly at Linate," announced a flight attendant. "Please fasten your seat belt, return your seat to the upright position and stow your tray table. On behalf of Captain Andrews and the crew, we thank you for choosing British Airways today and look forward to serving you again soon."

A stewardess, preparing the cabin for arrival, collected Judy's unused headset. Judy swallowed hard as the plane dropped in altitude after passing over a mountain range. Transparencies of cloud suspended below the aircraft, repeating their irregular shapes on the hilly, lush terrain over which they moved.

What was she doing landing in Milan when she should have been on her way back to Washington to be with her son? As soon as the deal closed, she should have gone directly home, just as she had originally intended to do. She had driven herself to finish the share purchase ahead of schedule so she could get back to her son sooner. She never should have let Alan change her plans.

Why hadn't Shane answered the phone at 7:30 in the morning? Where could he have been? Ron told her he had met with Shane the previous day and he was fine. If anything had been wrong, Ron would have called her back. Shane probably had slept in or gone to school already. She must stop worrying about her son. She had been making too much out of this. Maybe it was a good thing Alan had insisted she take a few days off.

There was a hard thud of wheels. They had landed.

DEDE

*T*he taxi, the only one Judy found available for hire at the Como station, lurched to a standstill before a three-story peach-colored villa. Magnolia trees, their leaves in the noon sun as shiny as if each had been hand-polished, stood in a perfect row in front of it. Through the glass revolving door and the oval windows beside it Judy glimpsed its interior. It was a narrow structure, and a companion door opposite of similar design permitted her to see what lay on its other side: the deep blue of a lake and, rising above it, the green of thick, sloped hills. A spun-crystal tulip chandelier hung beneath a scalloped ceiling and between a pair of snowy marble columns. Intrigued by these surroundings, Judy left the Fiat and passed through the door's rotation.

The concierge was occupied with the arrival of another guest.

"Anything not facing directly on the lake is not acceptable. Absolutely not acceptable. If my husband had accompanied me, I'm certain you would never have given me such a room. I demand to see the manager." The speaker had a rotund body, black hair, plain features and an unmodulated voice. She was extravagantly attired in a red crepe dress, expensive and in the latest style. A thick gold necklace yoked her neck. Her rising irritation was communicated by the gesturing of her right hand and emphasized by the resounding clang of her gold bracelet on the marble reception desk. Lined up behind her, a vanity and three enormous matching suitcases awaited the outcome. The embossed gold-leaf lettering on the owner's luggage outshone the gilt keys pinned onto each lapel of the uniformed man opposite. An assortment of Louis Vuitton hand luggage and a glossy Valentino parcel, its handles held together by ribbon, sprawled obtrusively across his counter. Elongated red nails clicked on the polished surface.

"I'm sorry, madam, the hotel manager is not available." He was the epitome of restraint; only a flush betrayed his momentary fluster. Confirming himself to be a veteran of such encounters, he continued, "I do have a room map of the spa, if Signora wishes to choose another suite."

"Good."

He swept a large card from behind him. With no remaining counter space, he extended it over her designer accessories. The woman examined the map with the intensity of one contemplating the invasion of a country.

"I wish to be shown this room here, and this, this and this." She punctuated each "this" with a demonstrative tap of her long nails on the plasticized plan. "I presume these are the best rooms you have?"

"Yes, madam." He acceded to her demands. Fistfuls of keys now dangled from the concierge's hands. He motioned to the porter who had been waiting at the foot of one of the twin marble staircases. "Please show Signora Talbot suites 203, 205, 207 and 208. Signora Talbot's luggage can wait here until she decides. . . . Sergio will show you the rooms."

He need not have bothered with the introduction. She had already headed to the lift before the clerk had completed his remarks, leaving him, in lieu of her appreciation, the debris of her hand luggage.

"*Alora*, Signora Kruger. Welcome to Itaro," the concierge said in the wake of the retreating guest. "I hope you had a pleasant journey." His greeting was effusive and without apology, as if she had only now arrived at reception. "We prepare for you a junior suite, at request. Room 112."

Judy had made a mental note of the rooms the woman was considering, 203 to 208. She was glad there was not the least chance of proximity.

∽

Dede wanted suite 205 the instant the porter unlocked the door. The antechamber would provide an additional noise buffer to the standard double doors. The curved ceiling moldings were more delicately carved than any George and she had commissioned for their house. Anyhow, there was hardly a comparison, the previous rooms he showed her didn't have ceiling moldings at all. Definitely a finer furniture collection than in the other rooms. The orange velvet Empire settee, high-backed chair, miniature writing desk and bed with gold-leaf headboard were obviously from the same suite.

All these pieces were positioned properly, set with a view of the lake. The teal-blue walls worked well with the antiques. And the treatment used to divide the bedroom from the sitting area—velvet drapes linked to a brass rod? A trifle heavy but effective. It gave an ambience of intimacy. The arched makeup table skirted with ruffles of organdy, though from a different period, was most compatible. Sensible too, angled as it was in the nook beside the window to catch the natural lighting.

Lots of closet space—something they never understand at home. They even had the good sense to provide a lock and key for them. Satin sweater hangers. Perfect. A full-length mirror, an added bonus.

She ran her hand under the bedspread, something she had neglected to do on the other inspections. Just as expected, good Irish linen.

"Bring my bags up immediately." The porter had been waiting unobtrusively by the door.

She felt the nostalgia of a homecoming. There was a feel to Europe. A texture of luxury. From the moldings in the hotel room to the manicured lushness of the greenery. Even the starched, crisp linen sheets she could not buy at home at any price. These things belonged to her. They were what she had been trained to recognize, taught to understand and appreciate.

Maybe it was because she was so young when she came to Europe the first time. Was she only seventeen, or was it sixteen? She traveled with her parents, staying a month in one grand hotel, then a second month in another. Marble bathroom, vaulted high ceiling and a vase, daily, of prime cut flowers. Silky white foot mat placed beside her bed. Meals on pure bone china imprinted with the hotel's crest, served always by waiters with the appropriate humility and a hint of an accent. The changed venue was identifiable only by the phrasing subtleties of the staff's English.

July was usually France. In Paris her father regularly chose the Bristol, taking an exclusive courtyard suite to avoid the city noise. They shopped avenue George-V, stopping only at the salons of Givenchy, Balenciaga and Dior, and on avenue Montaigne, Nina Ricci and Chanel. On the Riviera, it was Cannes, a waterfront suite at the Carlton overlooking the Croisette.

In Florence it was always the Villa Medici with the three concierges and the suite overlooking the quiet of a convent garden. With her mother, she had toured the gold shops that hung for generations from the Ponte Vecchio, learning to distinguish filigree finish from Florentine, handmade workmanship from a well-crafted copy. From the window of the proprietor's private office, she watched the brightly clad scullers practice on the Arno while her mother finished a purchase. Other days, they visited the Via Tornabuoni, which housed the best of the couturier collection from Milan.

Sometimes it was Venice, the Gritti Palace, a suite of course, overlooking the Grand Canal. She remembered their pilgrimages to the island of Murano, tirelessly journeying from factory to factory, searching for only the most intricate of crystal—a search which always ended, a month later, in the extravagant showrooms of Salvatini or Pauly and Company. They only used water taxis. The ferries were too crowded and, her parents warned, smells from the canal clung to your clothes if you were careless enough to take a gondola. Her mother always declared a month was not sufficient to include the galleries the guidebooks talked about. So they always sent her, without them, on an American Express half-day tour.

Dede returned to the sitting room and looked out at the lake. Then, turning the brass handle releasing the catch, she pulled one panel toward her, went onto the balcony and sat on a chair. Her body relaxed against the pliable straps. Involuntarily, she shuddered with exhaustion. Exhaustion for physical or emotional causes? It really did not matter why. All that mattered was she was here now. She was back, at last. After too long an absence.

The pool, which protruded into the lake, seemed a popular spot. That must be the floating dock she had been told about. Its deck cots sprawled with activity. A ball drifted unattended on the water's surface. She had registered for the spa program, but that could wait until tomorrow. Or the day after. Time was a commodity that no longer interested her.

Across the lake an ancient wooden boat slid through the water; the stillness of the day magnified its low, chugging vibration. Above it, coral-roofed villas nuzzled into the mountain's base. Gingerbread homes, she used to call them. The orange of their roof tiles, the painted stucco walls, a color splash against the emerald foliage. Cars wound up the steep cliffs. Periodically their steel surface caught the sun, transmitting a progression of moving bright flashes. Dede tracked their appearance as they curled up the escarpment, then disappeared into the thick undercarriage of greenery and the misted covering of the warming day. She continued to watch these metallic flashes until her eyes became fatigued and were distracted by the red-and-orange sheaths of hang gliders. She was intrigued by the fliers' daring as they hovered above the promontory behind the pool, then caught the wind to float out over the water, bringing them ever closer to her.

Their soaring, unhurried movement was mesmerizing. One hang glider came close enough to the balcony that, for a brief moment, she could make out his features. A strong face, chiseled with deep-set lines.

Mediterranean good looks. Large hands that gripped the wind stays. Muscular arms. Lean body. A physique and appearance like Tony's.

She followed his descent, the motion hypnotic to her. And her mind, responding, drifted as randomly as his flight. Back to Boston. Back to Tony.

∽

No, she could not say with truth she went to Europe every summer. There was one summer: the summer when she was twenty-one. It hadn't been easy convincing her parents to let her sign up for Harvard Summer School. They never understood why she wanted to attend. None of her friends were going there, they said. And studying was ordinarily not her preferred activity. They had had enough trouble getting her to attend Branksome Hall and recently Ryerson in Toronto. Why did she insist on doing this? they asked. None of their friends' children were going there, and they could not guarantee she would meet the proper people. Of course, her father said, he had business contacts in Boston, as he did in Philadelphia, Atlanta, Dallas and Miami. Every city where his U.S. subsidiary was presently putting up shopping plazas. But they had no real friends in the Boston area who could be relied upon to introduce her to their type of people.

But this was precisely the reason Dede was determined to go. She wanted to be somewhere where no one knew her parents, or the monetary significance of her last name. She wanted to be on her own, to find out who Dede really was.

Also, all reports had it that Boston was a fun place to be for the summer. Only a two-hour drive to Cape Cod. She could cut classes whenever she wanted and head out there. She heard the sand was white, the beaches long and romantic.

She met her parents' concern for supervision with a promise to live in an on-campus residence, their requirement for prestige with the status of the university's name. She heard her father brag to his business associates that his daughter "would be taking extension studies at Harvard," omitting the subtlety that it was only for the summer program.

Her parents insisted on accompanying her to Harvard and doing so two days before her residence officially opened. On a Thursday of the last week in June, they flew from Malton Airport to Boston. The timing of her arrival was the result of two unrelated factors: her parents' desire not to delay their departure, but to sail, as always, on the June crossing of the *Michelangelo*; and the application of her father's adage, honed in the shopping center business, that "the first one to stake the territory, always gets the best site."

Dede wanted her arrival on campus to be inconspicuous. Despite her protestations to the contrary, her father could not overcome the habit of a lifetime. He insisted that they be met at Logan Airport, as they were on all of their other outings, by a stretch Lincoln, and when they reached campus that the driver and the car remain at all times in front of Thayer Hall, Dede's assigned residence.

Rather than wait for assistance, her father, always impatient, insisted that the elderly driver carry Dede's three steamer trunks, two large cases and a picnic hamper up the steep flight to the third-floor landing. Dede told the man to make one further trip for her stereo, she wanted it carried separately for safety. She felt the driver should not mind. Her father always tipped generously.

Dede pushed open the door of room 301. The space was spartan. A square sitting area had only the basics in furniture: two Harvard spindle chairs, battered and black. The institutional white walls were soiled and ink-stained. A false fireplace, inset beneath a cement mantel, held neither electric logs nor charm. This area opened into a pair of smaller rectangles, divided from each other by a partition. A thin mattress, on top of metal bed coils, designated these as the bedrooms. A wood desk in each matched the chairs in the outer area in generation and decay—the type her mother usually referred to as "*Mayflower* originals without pedigree." A compartment held a counter-height, dented refrigerator.

Her parents pressed by her into its interior.

Initial silence was broken by her mother's words: "Dede, darling, there is nothing that says you have to stay in this place."

"Your mother wouldn't stay here, that's for sure. Not for an instant." Her father, rarely the second off the mark, had now caught up.

"I'm not my mother." Dede felt her comment was too hurtful. She tried to soften her initial response. "You must admit, Mother, if nothing else, the place has potential."

"Darling, you can still change your mind." Her mother was overlooking both of Dede's remarks. "Come with us to Europe. We'll just have the nice driver take your bags back down to the car. I'm sure when we arrive at the ship, Daddy can arrange an extra passage. Then all three of us will continue, as always, to Paris. Wouldn't that be fun? You know how much you like the Bristol."

"Dede's not going, Mother. Dede's staying right here." Dede never knew when she started to substitute her given name for the first person singular. Only that this affectation periodically popped into her vocabulary when thwarted. And why not speak this way? "I" was used so much in her family it seemed a good idea to unequivocally identify who was the speaker.

Her parents were unaccustomed to such determination. "Have it your way. It's your decision, God knows." She could tell her mother was becoming restless and was ready to move on.

Her father brought the discussion to an end. "I've a car and driver here that I'm paying by the hour to take us to the pier in New York. I want to board early to reserve your mother's favorite table for second sitting. If you're staying, Dede, let's get on with it." Her father gestured for the chauffeur to carry in the bags which had been placed on the landing and, as if he were on a construction site, began to pace off the dimensions of each partitioned space. He disappointingly proclaimed them to be exactly equal in size. Eight by ten feet. The difference between them was merely a view: one, a corner room, fronted on Harvard Yard; the other was interior, without a window at all. He seconded the former for her.

Next, he tested each bed as to firmness of springs and mattress. He chose the better component of each, and transferred it without compunction into her newly acquired quarters. The refrigerator was the only useful object that eluded his rearrangement. At first he tried to push it toward Dede's room. It did not yield. Then he planted his feet firmly and, gripping his plump hands on its upper surface, which came level to his chest, pulled on it. Abruptly, he stopped.

Guess he doesn't want to encourage my eating, Dede thought. She always felt self-conscious about the size fourteen skirt that hung shapelessly on her well-hidden waist.

Dede realized her father's concern rested elsewhere.

"This icebox is not worth getting a hernia over. Anyhow"—he swung open its door and looked inside for the first time—"it's filthy. Too dirty to use." To emphasize this statement, he smacked his palms together to rid himself of its unwelcome dust. "Well, that's over. So, baby, your mother and I had better be leaving."

With relief, Dede watched from her window as the limousine pulled away from the front of Thayer Hall. She was grateful the building was deserted. There were no witnesses to what constituted for her parents a normal arrival but what she considered to be a spectacle. She did not want them to ruin her plans for the summer. Being alone in an empty building for two nights was a small price to pay for avoiding the embarrassment created by her parents' ostentatious behavior. If anyone had observed their entrance, any subsequent attempt to blend with the others would be futile. She could not let them do anything to undermine the possibility of her acceptance, as previously they had done to her at home. That had been the reason she had to get away, in order to be herself. This might be the only chance she would have. She was safe now, they had left. Her only remaining concern was her roommate. She hoped, whoever she might be, that she would not compare the contents of their rooms too closely.

Dede settled into the business of unpacking. She only took out the things she felt essential for the night. She had no intention of using the rough university bedding. She had brought her own, which was of a similar color to the white presently there, but in a softer-textured Egyptian cotton. She tossed the coordinated peach lightweight duvet across the top of the bed. She hooked up the portable stereo unit in her bedroom, positioning it for her exclusive use. Dede kept her 45s and albums locked in a case. Her parents had taught her you could never be too careful. Never trust anyone.

She searched throughout the dormitory for the location of the telephone. There was none in the corridor outside or in her room; however, there was a jack beside the mantel. First thing tomorrow she would order a phone for herself, just as she had at home. The only comfort she was prepared to surrender for the summer was her red Corvette convertible. She had decided against bringing it with her to Boston. It did not fit the image she was determined to cultivate.

It was the dinner hour by the time she completed what she considered the basics. Not wanting to concern herself with where to eat the first night, she had asked their housekeeper to prepare something for her. Having been with her family from Dede's earliest recollections, Vera knew all her preferences. She did not have to tell her what to make.

Dede brought the hamper into her bedroom. She took out a pink place mat and spread it over the dusty, scratched wooden desk. She placed the companion napkin beside it. She withdrew a thermos, unfastened its taut cap and transferred its contents of chilled gazpacho into a china bowl. Then she ate liver pâté and cold breast of chicken amandine. The scrape of her silver utensils as they moved across the china plate were the only sounds she heard in Thayer Hall that night.

Dede slept fitfully in the stuffy, cavernous, empty dormitory. But it was worth it. Her identity was secure, her secret maintained.

At noon on the day the dormitory officially opened, an unfamiliar figure straddled the threshold of room 301. Lanky, with long blond hair falling into her eyes, and holding two suitcases, with a knapsack strapped to her back, she left no doubt as to her place in Dede's summer.

"Hi. I'm Susan McGoovin from Indianapolis. Your roommate."

"I'm Dede Ein from Toronto."

There was no name recognition. There had been no follow-up question. The curiosity Dede cringed from—"Are you one of *the* Eins of Toronto? You know the ones I mean, the shopping plaza people?"—did not occur. There had been no reaction to her last name. The moment of possible exposure had come and gone. She was secure, safe from possible recognition, free to be whoever she wanted to be. Her surname was not a threat to her here.

Dede watched Susan head straight for the other bedroom, place her bags on the vacant bed, reenter the sitting area and flop her tall frame onto the hard wooden chair.

"What do you think of this room?" Dede ventured.

"Awful. . . . Why?"

"We can fix it up. Let's go to Charles Street and pick up some interesting things."

"Are you kidding? You sure don't know anything about Boston. You can't afford to shop in that area." Hearing that comment Dede knew her instincts had been right. She had made the correct decision to come here. Susan rambled on, "Anyhow, what do you know about decorating?"

"Just what I like."

"Okay. What do you think would help? Suggest," Susan commanded.

"The place needs color. Atmosphere . . . a theme. Possibly Russian, with a touch of Spanish. A flashing bullfighter. Anything."

"If you're really serious about this, I think I know where we should look. A friend who was here last summer filled me in. Let's check out the stores in Downtown Crossing. Secondhand but select for the discriminating but impoverished buyer. . . . When do you want to go?"

"Today."

"Can't. Got too much to do. Have to be ready to register tomorrow. So do you."

Dede was apprehensive as Susan entered the quarters her father had co-opted for her and from its window looked out over Harvard Yard. Susan glanced at Dede's neatly stacked clothes, the readied bed and the suitcases stashed possessively under it.

"You must have been on the doorstep of old Thayer at nine a.m. today," she said without censure. "No wonder you want to get out. . . . Why not? I guess I can unpack later."

Dede left her Sportsac in the drawer. She grabbed an unidentifiable canvas tote, the one her mother had asked her never, under any circumstances, to wear with her. She tossed it over her shoulder and with Susan exited their room.

By the third store, Susan became fully committed to the project and supplied their theme. "What I'd like," her roommate said, poking through a box of discontinued fabrics, "is something that would put me in the mood for Revolution and Society in Comparative Perspective," her "must" course for the summer. "When I walk through that door, I'd like to feel I'm really in that period. You know what I mean—really live that time. Sound crazy?"

"Makes perfect sense to me," Dede replied.

Accordingly, their room officially went Russian, early twentieth century with, of course, reasonable modifications. That categorization actually was too specific. By the time they had picked from what was available, any Eastern terminology might equally have applied. Susan affectionately dubbed it "Czarist decadence" and, as such, the ideal atmosphere in which to pursue her subject.

Two hours later, they climbed up the stairs of Thayer, their arms heavy with purchases. Dede carried three enormous, nondescript brown bags. A tassel shade protruded from one. Crimson pillows from another. Fat candles with an unusual smell from the third. Posters popped in uneven heights from her roommate's package.

Dede dropped her bags inside the doorway and set to work. She moved a chair into position in the center of the sitting area. Without removing her sneakers she stood on it, herself adding to the history of that battered piece of furniture. Then she placed a ruby tassel lampshade around the exposed light bulb that hung from the ceiling.

Susan sat on the floor, watching the transformation. "What a subtle color. Provided of course"—Dede saw the beginning of a smile—"you consider red subtle."

Dede unrolled the burgundy cotton rug remnant she had found under Seconds and scattered upon it five oversized pillows in varying shades of violet, fuchsia, cranberry, orange and hot pink. She had suggested that an accent from another country be included. This was provided by a bull-fighter in full toreador regalia taunting a fierce El Toro. She positioned this poster, which had been featured in every store they had entered, above their mantel. His vivid costume matched their pinks; the price, the lowest on the street, their remaining dollar. The lady proprietor had been so grateful to finally be relieved of the dapper bullfighter that she had tossed in gratis a lithograph advertisement from a gallery opening. "For such good customers," she said in a thick accent. This they placed behind the door. They arranged the incense candles, found in an East Indian arcade, sporadically around the sitting area.

Dede helped her roommate unpack until the latter's compartment was as organized and tidy as her own. At ten that evening, the two sprawled on their thin carpet; candles flickered softly around them, their burning wicks releasing a peculiar pungent scent.

Dede was thoughtful. "What are you thinking?" Susan asked lazily from her half of the mat.

"Nothing. Nothing at all." And everything. Susan had no knowledge of the prestige of her parents' money. Their friendship did not depend on her family name. Perhaps her parents had been wrong. Money was not needed to ease relationships. Dede felt the stir of self-confidence, a feeling with which previously she had not been familiar.

Forty-eight hours later, summer school was in full swing. Dede and her roommate registered at Memorial Hall on Sunday, got their ID cards at the Science Center and were, at least in theory, attending classes by Monday. After studying the Harvard calendar with greater initiative than she had shown for any academic pursuit to date, she found her course: Introduction to Psychology. It had no prerequisites. Other students joyfully referred to it as a gut course. Its only drawback was its time: 10 to 11 a.m., five days a week. Not Dede's finest hour under the best of circumstances. But that would be no problem. Due to enormous enrollment, Introduction to Psychology had been assigned to an auditorium: no one would notice if she wasn't there. She wouldn't tell the others in

Thayer her class days, so she would be able to skip with impunity. Susan's lecture was in the afternoon, 1 to 3:30, and only twice a week. Dede wanted to have time to spend with her. Wasn't it summer? And summer was for fun. With Susan, she now had someone with whom to have fun.

She decided that since she was at Harvard anyhow, she might as well audit Renaissance Art and Archaeology. The passion in Michelangelo's *David*, the genius of Leonardo da Vinci and the other Renaissance painters in the Uffizi had intrigued her when she saw them in Florence. It wouldn't matter that she didn't have any formal background in art history. By auditing she wouldn't be embarrassed in front of the other students for her lack of knowledge. The class met Tuesdays and Thursdays from 6 to 8 p.m. Most of that was the staggered dinner hour anyhow. And the social scene in front of Widener Library didn't pick up until about 8:30.

She had never been a passionate student. She graduated Branksome Hall on a discretionary basis. At commencement, a special acknowledgment was given to her father for his endowment of equipment for the science lab.

It wasn't that high school had been difficult, it had just been boring, both the subjects taught and the girls she had to live with when her parents placed her in boarding.

Her parents told her of their decision the night they let her choose her favorite restaurant, and it was not even her birthday. They were getting older and wanted to be away for the entire winter.

"But it won't be so bad, darling," her mother said, interrupting her father's rationalization. "We'll make it up to you. In summer we will all be together. We'll still be going to Europe like we always do. Wouldn't you like that?"

The alternative they had considered and already rejected was leaving her in their Forest Hill home with Vera, who they felt was incapable of handling her. The older housekeeper didn't have the strength or desire to discipline her to their satisfaction. "Can't have a teenager running wild in the streets of Toronto. City's not what it used to be. Getting more like New York every year—violence, rape, bathhouses," her father sermonized. No, there was no choice—she had to go into residence whether she liked it or not. If she loved them, as her mother said they knew she did, she would want them to be away from the harsh, cold weather. She always had been a good daughter, her father interjected. "Well, baby," her father concluded with the plate of Lichee special chow mein and pineapple chicken congealing in front of him, "what do you think of this?"

"Whatever you think is best for Dede," she said stoically. "I'll do whatever you like." What could she say? Tell them not to go, not to leave her? That Dede hated to be alone? If they loved her, they would not do this to her, but would find some other solution. Like all her other friends' parents did: they were also rich and older. But none of them put their kids in boarding. They flew back every few weeks to be with their children. Her parents didn't have to stay away for a full five months without ever coming home. Not if they really didn't want to.

Anything was better than the stories she heard about boarding. She'd rather be with Vera, who cared for her, than in residence with girls who had been rejected like herself. But after her one sentence, she sat mute. She did not speak her pain. They didn't know that her stomach constricted, that her gut wrenched and she felt like vomiting. How could she tell her parents she ached inside because she felt they did not love her? Weren't parents the only people in your life you could depend on for love—real, unselfish love? She said none of this. Not wishing to let them see how deeply she was hurt, she dealt with the mechanics of the situation. She fought them on its implementation since they had already destroyed her with its theory. She became obstinate about the choice of school. "I wouldn't go to Pinehurst Academy. Only losers go there. Everyone knows that." . . . "No, not the Toronto French. How can I start there when everyone else had nine years of the language already?" . . . "I don't want to go to Trafalgar. It's in the middle of nowhere. I won't be able to see my friends."

When a compromise of Branksome Hall was reached, a girls' school in the exclusive area of Rosedale, her father was relieved. "Now that you've finally made your mind up, let's forget about it and enjoy ourselves."

Her father summoned Norman, the waiter he insisted serve him regardless of where this man's assigned station might be. Norman, according to her father, was the only one who knew how to take care of him properly. Her father reordered the chow mein and pineapple chicken—dishes that by now had formed a solid mass in the serving plate, instructing him to bring them "piping hot, like my little girl likes them." Her father also added some selections not ordered earlier, usually reserved by him for special events—Peking duck, all five courses, and phoenix chicken in a basket—thereby gastronomically identifying this evening as a festive occasion.

This was the first time Dede could remember she ate everything her father heaped onto her plate, and much more besides. Her appetite that night was insatiable.

But that was in the past. Her life was now for the first time under her control. She had a great roommate and the summer brimmed with possibilities.

C h a p t e r **I I**

*I*t was 8:45 on Tuesday of the second week of classes. Dede had just completed her third Renaissance Art and Archaeology class and was making her way back to Thayer, via the library. The July night was a particularly oppressive one, the type that proclaims summer has arrived in a city. More students than usual were congregating on Widener's steps. The dorms must be depopulated, Dede thought, as she surveyed the throng in front of the library.

Few with scholarly aspirations stood in front of Widener. Those types were already inside, their thoughts focused either on the past or on the future. Those who remained at the threshold or sat on the trimmed grass between the walkways in front of it were involved in the immediate and now—getting a date—a more pragmatic pursuit. Watching the nightly ritual of flirtation from across the Yard, she was ambivalent about whether she wanted to participate tonight. The patter was becoming tedious. "What's your name?" . . . "Where are you from?" . . . "What are you taking?"

This evening's Art and Archaeology lecture had wilted her. The session had followed the routine she had come to expect: two and a half hours of slides in a dimly lit, closely confined room with Dr. Grolin droning in his usual monotone. In order to ensure a dozing student did not miss the purpose of each slide, he would punctuate his monologue with a wooden three-foot pointer, the likes of which Dede had happily not seen since alphabet drill in grade one. And tonight's heat had not been foreseen. The air conditioning in the building had shut down. With the door closed to prevent corridor lighting from obliterating the clarity of the presentation, the small low-ceilinged room had become insufferable. Dede felt debilitated by the heat and unexpectedly antisocial.

As she was considering whether to venture through the crowds to join

Susan or to continue directly to the dorm, a male voice inquired, "Can you please tell me—to get to the Coop from here, do you go down this walk?" A long arm gestured to the left. "Or that way?"

"To make a long story boring," an expression she picked up since coming to Harvard, "I'm not too sure. I'm still learning my way around here myself. . . . I've got a map. I'll check." Dede unraveled the map from the back of her registration calendar and balanced it on the surface of her notebook. The outstretched sheet trailed down the front of the binder. She squinted at the paper. The markings were minuscule and, after the hours of slide watching, her eyes were having trouble focusing on it in the twilight. She brought the paper closer to her. "Can't find it. . . . Here, you look for it. Maybe you can see better." With those words she passed her calendar into larger hands.

He studied the map, providing her in the half-light an opportunity to look at him. He had a sculptured nose, square jaw, olive complexion and leathery outdoor skin. Short-cropped, curly black hair. Broad shoulders, muscular frame, an athletic-looking body, like a football player's. A person someone would notice. He's interesting . . . decidedly interesting, she concluded.

Dede's appraisal was interrupted by "Can't see it either. I appreciate your trying to help me. I'll find it when I'm here next time."

"You don't live on campus?"

He smiled broadly. "Nope. Not me. Wish I could, though . . . maybe someday." She realized then what set him apart from the others she had met in Harvard Yard. He was much older, probably around thirty. "How about you?"

"Sure do. Over in Thayer." She indicated the building in the distance.

"Lucky girl. . . . What are you taking?"

"Fun 101." She offered a flip reply, as she would have to any guy.

"I have a feeling it's more than that." He saw through her irreverence.

"Actually, yes. I'm registered in psychology. Since arriving, I've added Renaissance Art and Archaeology as an audit. I really like it, except tonight it must have been 105 degrees Fahrenheit in the lecture."

"Great subject."

"Are you in there too?"

He seemed amused by the question. "Nope. I'm here for Advanced Academic Speaking and Writing. I'm a part-time student."

"But I think you speak perfectly," she volunteered.

"Thank you, but my English should be better. I was born in Portugal. My family came to Boston when I was fourteen. There are similar courses I could take elsewhere, but I wanted to come to Harvard. I like the feeling of the university. These magnificent buildings—" He broke off, allowing the surrounding structures to speak for him. "Not what I will design some-day, but magnificent. That's why I've been taking the courses. Next year I'm going to college full-time. But"—his voice lilted, indicating a smile —"before I do that, I guess I had better learn where the bookstore is. Thanks for your help." He walked into the night.

That was how they met. But she didn't know his name. And he did not know hers. She only realized this when she was recounting their meeting in detail to Susan later that night: he had not even asked her name. It was the only time she viewed that oversight as cause for alarm.

That thought need never have troubled her. They happened into each other the next Thursday after her class in an aisle in the Coop. Her hands held Harvard-crested T-shirts; his were filled with textbooks.

"I see you found the place," she said.

"Yes, thank you. Got here just in time. They seem ready to close. How's Art and Archaeology going?" In the light of the store, she could see his eyes were brown.

"Great. Interesting course."

"Must be fascinating. . . . Would you like to go for coffee?"

"Sure." Who would refuse? He was by far the best-looking specimen she had met so far.

They cashed out and went to an off-campus diner. He said he came to Harvard directly from work tonight, without going home to eat. He or-dered the special for himself and asked her what she would like.

An invitation to coffee for Dede usually translated into a cheeseburger, fries, some luscious dessert and a cherry Coke. Now living on institutional food, she felt such indulgences a necessity.

She noted his plain slacks, his open-neck shirt, his workmen's shoes, his simple watch with its plastic band. She ordered coffee, with double cream and sugar.

He did not mention his work. He preferred to talk instead about ar-chitecture, the course he was studying, and the books he was reading. She asked him about his earliest recollection of Portugal. Her psychology pro-fessor was now into the memory component of the course.

"The sea."

"The sea?"

"The sea was always central in my life. We lived in the Azores, on the island of São Miguel. Wherever I would go as a boy, the sea was around me. I could not escape it. It was the main source of food and"—his voice turned solemn—"the barrier that kept us from the rest of the world. São Miguel is stuck out there, somewhere in the middle of the Atlantic." He dabbed his forefinger into his water glass and with the droplets drew a crude map upon the booth's Arborite countertop. "There's Spain, mainland Portugal, and there . . . way out in the middle of the ocean is my home, São Miguel." As if custodian of his secret, the psychological and physical distance traveled from birthplace to Boston, the moisture dried quickly on the glossy surface, taking with it his island. His past again became invisible.

"That is why my strongest memory is of the sea. And also," he added, "why I like to sail. I have my own boat."

Dede thought she must have miscued on his clothes. She could have the cheeseburger after all. The whole shebang. Maybe it was not too late to order now.

"I call her *Sereia do Mar*"—he smiled—"the *Mermaid*. She's a little boat. I'm her fifth owner. I had to do lots of repairs. I'm still not happy with the radar set. But she sails beautifully now."

She had paid no attention to these qualifying remarks. In her friends' parlance, there were no yachts, just "little boats." Everyone highlighted former owners and repairs, it was the appropriate complaint.

"Do you like to sail?" he asked.

She pictured the yacht basin in Cannes and replied, "Yes, I love to sail."

"I usually don't talk about myself like this. You know, you're very easy to talk to. I'd like to see you again. . . . I usually take the *Sereia do Mar* out about five. Lots of good light until eight-thirty. How would it be, if next calm evening after work, I come and get you?" He added uncertainly, "That is, if you don't have Art and Archaeology?"

This question, she sensed, was not about her schedule, but was whether she wanted to go out with him again.

She did not let him wait for a response. "I'm available. Any night," she was quick to add.

He walked her to Thayer. "May I kiss you?"

She turned to him and with practiced provocativeness said, "No. Not if you have to ask." With that she entered the dorm.

∽

"Feel like sailing?" Dede heard the following afternoon as she was coming back to her residence. Tony was waiting for her beneath a giant oak outside of Thayer. He was wearing a cutoff top, jeans and sneakers. His sunglasses were taped at the temple.

Dismissing his attire as the understated look, she hurried to the third floor and put on her nauticals—white slacks, oversized blouse to conceal what she felt to be an unidentifiable waist and immaculate Top-Siders.

Upon her return he asked, "Are you sure you'll be comfortable?"

"To make a long story boring, sure. This is always what I wear sailing."

She was not prepared for the stripped-down Pontiac, the one he told her he had purchased at the Boston Police Department's sale, nor when they reached the mooring for the *Sereia do Mar*. The boat was neither fashionable nor a yacht. It seemed to Dede the smallest-size vessel that could remain afloat on an ocean, surely smaller than anything in Cannes. But it was also the most cared-for sailboat she had seen. It looked freshly painted, its fore and aft decks spotless. It had a tiny cabin, with everything meticulously stowed, its neatness disturbed only by some scattered paperbacks.

Within minutes, Tony had raised the jib, started an auxiliary motor to propel them from the dock. When he reached midpoint in the bay, Tony told her this was where he preferred to sail. It was safer than the Atlantic and had sufficient wind. With those words, he handed her the tiller. Patiently he taught her how to control the wind, to tack and to bring the boat about.

"Do you know what I really like?" he said as he manned the mainsail. "This, the freshness of the ocean air. After work, I go home and change and, if it's not one of my school nights, come directly out here. With something to eat, of course. That reminds me." He went below. "I made this for you in case you couldn't last. Pressed chicken." He tossed a cellophane wrapped bundle in her direction.

She really felt no need of food, a welcome change. But he had prepared this for her and she would not disappoint him. She ate the sandwich. It tasted better than anything Vera purchased from Paul's French Food Restaurant.

He disappeared again into the galley. He returned with a book, its spine split with overuse and water damage.

"I like to read. Especially out here. This is my favorite. *The Fountainhead*," he said, handling its frayed cover lovingly. "It's about a man, Howard Roark, who wanted to be an architect. He would not take on work he did not believe in, no matter how bad things got for him. He did not accept a job he couldn't control. He did not let himself be compromised by any man or any woman. He lived his principles. That's how a man must live."

He opened the volume to an earmarked page and articulated it with passion. He read the words of the protagonist, but through them she heard the voice of Tony. She admired Tony's integrity and his desire to captain his own future.

She had learned much from him that evening. And related it to herself. Why couldn't she, like him, take charge of her own life, be responsible for it. She felt embarrassed by her pretentious behavior. She had to free herself from her background, from its language and affectations. Let it drift away with the other impurities salted and drawn out by the sea.

The next weeks proceeded at high speed. Dede attended lectures, sailed most evenings with Tony and talked into the morning with Susan—mainly about the conversation she had earlier with Tony. She even made her 10 a.m. psychology session. She hoped some lecture might illuminate her knowledge of Tony. But inwardly she knew neither Susan nor Introduction to Psychology could do that. Only Tony himself could. She attended that class and Renaissance Art and Archaeology because, she eventually acknowledged to herself, she enjoyed them. If learning was so vital to Tony, it should also be so for her.

Those weeks coincided with the emergence of her waistline. How much was owing to an absence of a compulsion to gorge and how much was credited to the inability to consume anything stored in the Danby was hard to delineate.

In mid-July, she had grabbed her usual midnight yogurt from the refrigerator to find its taste disagreeable. Cottage cheese, chosen in substitution, tasted remarkably similar to it, as did the deli chicken and peach she sampled in rapid succession. She removed the remaining contents of the shelf. A round glass bottle remained at the back, its liquid looking ominously indigestible.

"Susan, there's something unusual in our fridge. It's making everything taste peculiar."

"Oh," said Susan without looking, "that must be my Shalimar. I put it in there so the perfume won't evaporate. I never use much of it at a time. This way, it will last forever. . . . Dede, you don't mind, do you?"

How could Dede object? The refrigerator was the only useful item her father had not removed from Susan's room. Her roommate continued with the exuberance of one who has found the perfect solution.

"And don't worry about the food. I promise you, you won't be able to notice the difference soon. The scent will go away eventually."

But it didn't. Shalimar permeated everything Dede put into the refrigerator. Dede considered the likelihood of a permanently scented stomach. She removed the doughnuts, fruit, deli, cottage cheese and yogurt; replaced them with cans of Tab, guaranteed to be odor-resistant. Snacking lost its appeal for her. And why waste time eating, she thought, when there were now more interesting things to do? She abandoned the refrigerator, filled her thoughts instead with Tony. Her weight stabilized at 118 pounds. She was now a size eight, a size she had not seen since she was seventeen.

∽

"What a glorious day for sailing," Dede told Susan the following Saturday near the end of July. By late afternoon the temperature in Harvard Yard had become intolerable; the humidity, the radio kept repeating, had reached a record high. The air was close and heavy. Perspiration grew on her skin and remained, tiny bubbles that, when wiped away, reappeared. A futile cycle.

Dede hoped there would be a breeze on the bay. There usually was. Today she had put on khaki shorts and a T-shirt.

Tony began the motor to take the boat into the bay. The air in the harbor was still. There was some breeze, but not enough with which to stay cool. When they reached the opening that joined bay to open water, she declared, "It's stifling. We're frying here. It's hotter than on land."

"It can't be."

"Well, it feels that way to me. Can't we just take the *Sereia do Mar* out further so we can cool off? How rough can it get out there today?" She knew Tony would resist the idea. He did not like going out into the open ocean. "There'll be some wind there, but not too much for her to handle." Despite her comments, Tony did not alter course.

She persisted. In a mildly flirtatious manner, she said, "Let's go where there are no other people. No other boaters. Away from everything."

Tony capitulated. He took the boat through the strait and ran it for about fifteen minutes parallel to the shoreline. She sat on the inside bench beside him. "Dede, see that black building over there? The half-completed one, with the enormous crane? That's mine. I'm the construction foreman."

"It sure is large, even from here."

"It's going to be a trade center when it's finished." His face was resolute. He volunteered nothing more but brought the *Sereia do Mar* about and turned its bow toward the ocean.

She saw the Boston skyline become smaller, less significant. She thought she heard Tony's voice. Words seemed to form, then were lost. Perhaps a trick of the wind. She studied his features. His facial muscles appeared tense as if he were warring within himself, trying to make a decision. "What is it, Tony?" she encouraged.

She heard him force the words. "I told you I was fourteen when I came to this country. My father was a master craftsman in the Azores. He could make beautiful things with his hands. Miniature dollhouses, exquisite headboards, carved dining chairs. Everyone admired him. They said there was no one as wonderful as Senhor Picanco. Then we came here. No one wanted those skills. Everything was mass production. The only work he could get was in a factory. His mind was too old. He could not learn English. The woodworking plant had bad ventilation, and he got sick. He died when I was in the last year of high school. That's when I started in construction. My mother didn't want me to quit school. 'You mustn't, Antônio. Your father wouldn't want it. He came to America for you.' . . . My mother is a wonderful person. How could I watch her, a woman who could create such beautiful clothes, go into a basement workroom of a department store to machine-stitch alterations all night?"

With control he continued. "I left high school. From helping my father as a boy, I knew how to build. It was easy. . . . I've spent nine years with Moore Construction. The boss even sent me to trade school at night. 'Tony, you're the only one who can handle these men.' I didn't want the trade skills. But I did learn about mechanicals and reading drawings. One of my instructors lent me his books to study the theories of steel construction and reinforced concrete. That's when I knew what I wanted to be. What my father had prepared me for years ago when he had me sit in his shop overlooking the ocean and let me help him work."

She said nothing through this. She did not want to stop the words that would help her draw him to her.

"Dede"—his voice held strong against the current of the wind—"I'm going to be an architect. The Dean of Architecture at MIT has told me after I complete my English course this summer, I am eligible for admission.

"I am going to enter architecture next year or, at the latest, the year after. I will finally get to design the buildings I construct. Make beautiful places for people to live that fit in with the environment. Not cubicles, like I showed you, that obstruct the sky with steel. I don't like to be told what to build. In the meantime, I put on my hard hat and work. I study English and I read."

She appreciated his initial hesitation. The anxiety of opening a hurtful past—the fear of sharing the dragons and the dreams, the uncertainty of revealing too much of yourself to someone whose experiences were so different from your own that they could never understand: she could relate to all of it. The risk to himself had been enormous—a deepened relationship or rejection. He did not allow her to speak.

"How about more of Howard Roark?" With that he motioned for her to take the steering.

She did not place her hand on the tiller, but over his. She let it remain long enough for him to have the answer to the question she sensed he was too unsure of himself to ask.

He read her a passage, his voice resonant and once more relaxed. When he concluded, he stored the volume below.

The ocean had become flat. It was an endless, hushed surface. Gulls sat on its perimeter, miles off in the distance. The *Sereia do Mar* seemed as secure as if she were moored. There were no other boaters around. Everything was still. The boat drifted into irons.

Tony took back the tiller and started the motor. The buildings now seemed too far in the distance. "We had better start back. Anything can happen out here. We're in open water." As if cued by these words, a lone cat's-paw appeared and twisted into a squall. Swells rose from an unseen source. The six o'clock sky went black. His warning, "Coming about," coincided with a forty-five degree pitch to the boat. Dede slid unceremoniously against the gunwale.

"Do you think you can make fast the jib?"

"Sure."

"Good. Shift up slowly, Dede. No sudden moves."

She complied. She felt no concern: he was calm and in charge.

"Here's the mainsail. Can you handle it?"

"Yes."

Dede heard a distant rumble, saw a zigzag of light: the portents of a storm. They were stuck out in the ocean, all because she had insisted on it.

He must have sensed her fear. "Don't worry, Dede. There's still some time before the storm. All we need is a half hour. This is the type of weather I was taught to sail in. A real São Miguel storm. After this, you'll be an expert sailor." He had her put on a life vest, told her to sit on the floorboards. He sat on the side, braced his feet, hiked his body out over the waves, keeping both hands firmly on the tiller.

The wind tore at the mainsail. She was afraid its rope would break out of her hands and they would lose the speed necessary to take them to safety. Worse, sudden loss of the sail might cause the boat to capsize. Right here in the middle of the Atlantic. Where no one could find them.

She craved the sight of other vessels. She never should have made him take her out into the ocean. She clutched tighter at the mainsheet. Another gust of wind grabbed at the rope. Some of the line spun through her hands; her palms began to bleed.

Tony saw her wince. Took the rope from her. Held it in his hand and secured it with his foot. More thunder. Closer this time. Pellets of cold water hit her. They had passed unwarmed through the torrid air. Higher swells. Salt water stung her eyes, her arms. "Go below, Dede."

"No." She saw the control he had of the boat. The rain and surf lashing at his face.

He shouted, "Dede. Please . . . go below. Everything's okay. It's just like the Azores, on a bad day."

She shouted, "I'm staying here with you."

She saw the harbor opening appear ahead. She turned toward him to tell him they had made it.

A deep swell built off the stern. A wall of water moving in their direction. Twenty feet high and just as broad. Dede watched it hypnotically. It was subsuming the lesser waves. It took strength from the force over which it rolled, consuming and magnifying its destructive power, increasing in momentum. Its crest hung perversely over the stern, as if choosing the exact moment in which to drop its pent-up fury into their tiny hull, crush them as they struggled insignificantly against its massive strength. They were going to drown.

Dede screamed. Tony looked behind him and reacted. With both hands he brought the boat about. He swerved the bow into the brunt of the wave. Met it head-on, rendering it harmless. Its wash poured over the bow, spilled into the hull. He resumed his tack to safety.

They made the harbor. The water instantly became smooth. Bay and ocean, two worlds, each unsuspecting of the other. They were safe. Tony steered the *Sereia do Mar* to its berth.

But the wind was becoming fiercer. And the temperature seemed to have plunged twenty degrees from the combination of the storm and the night.

Her clothes were soaked. She began to shiver. "I'm freezing. Absolutely freezing," she called to Tony, who was cleating the boat.

"I have three large towels in the galley. Use them," he shouted. The *Sereia do Mar* was rocking at her mooring.

This time she did as she was told. She went into the galley looking for the towels. Her shorts and T-shirt were matted to her body. She peeled them off, squeezed them into a ball, hurled them into the sink and wrapped a threadbare rust towel around herself. The cabin was quite snug. She had not previously been down here for more than a few minutes. She looked through the porthole, but it was awash with ocean and rain. Then she thought of Tony still outside in the cold securing the ropes.

"All clear down there?" she heard.

The open cabin door allowed in a draft of cold air and rain when he slid down the stairs. Dede's body began to tremble uncontrollably, worse than before. Now that the crisis had passed, she was feeling its full aftermath.

Tony reached for a second towel and carefully wrapped her with it. The trembling subsided.

"I'm okay. Dry yourself off," she said.

He shook the water off his arms, his face, then looked at her with concern. "Are you sure you're okay?"

"Fine. Perfectly fine."

He found a third towel and ran it over his head.

"Let me do that for you. I'm sure I can do better with that. Sit down," she said with mock firmness.

Tony sat his six-foot frame on the bunk, bringing them both to the same height. She rubbed his thick black hair. Wet sprang from it, sprayed around the tiny cabin and landed on her body. He methodically licked the droplets off her, one by one. His arms moved around her waist, and pulled her closer to him. Dede did not know what to do. She had been a flirt, nothing more. She pretended nothing was happening and continued to rub his hair. His hands began to unwrap the towels, slowly, as one would a once-in-a-lifetime present. The towels fell around her feet. She made no attempt to pick them up.

She liked the warmth of his hands as they explored her body. As they moved from her waist, to her shoulders, then down the small of her back. In danger she had not felt fear, just the desire to remain with him. Now she wanted to be closer to him. To know the texture of his skin as intricately as she did his thoughts.

He brought her toward him. His wet clothes were an extra skin that could not keep him from her. He entered her with the gentleness of caring and with the passion of too long denial. She heard the rain pelt the deck. Felt a sudden surge of the boat, then a swell too powerful to resist. Now she belonged to him, as she would never belong to anyone again in her life.

When she thought of that afternoon, she did not know when understanding ended and love began. Only that it happened to her that day, that summer, and never again.

∽

From then on, they were together every moment Tony was not working. The boat became their home, their shelter, where nothing mattered except each other.

"Your arms are my favorite place in the world," she would say when they lay together, "the only world I need."

Susan never asked Dede about the night she did not return to Thayer —the night of the storm—or of all the similar nights thereafter.

Tony rarely asked about her background or her family, and when he did, she easily diverted his inquiries.

"What was it like growing up in your family?" he said on a quiet sail, the sea dimpled with wind.

"Quite uneventful," she said, "compared to yours."

"How is it you never talk about your parents?" he asked on another such occasion.

"There's not much to say. They're not that interesting."

He never forced himself through her reticence. He stood a respectful distance away, waiting for her, she believed, to volunteer what he had willingly shared with her. Or was this distance more than that, a premonition that her world was a place in which he might never belong?

Tony brought her to meet his mother. She had prepared for Dede as for the homecoming of a long-awaited relative. The table was laid with an embroidered lace tablecloth, a bridal gift, she said, from her own mother. The São Miguel dishes of *caldo verde*, shrimp croquette and caramel custard were placed in hand-painted porcelain dishes. This food, she explained, Tony had selected for her.

"You make my Antônio happy, you make me happy, too. . . . Now you must eat. It's not healthy not to eat."

Dede enjoyed her evenings there, especially the stories this lady proudly recounted about her son. Tony's first visit with them to Lisbon; Tony's design of a playhouse for São Miguel's grade school; how Mr. Moore had come to her apartment and told her that Tony had a wonderful future with him in construction.

Dede sensed the bond of respect between mother and son and the genuine caring. A loving interaction. Treating her as their own, they included her within its circle. She felt unconditional acceptance. For her, it was an irresistible draw. She returned eagerly and frequently to that immaculate two-bedroom, third-floor walk-up above the restaurant. She felt stirring within her a feeling of family, something she hadn't realized before had been absent in her own home.

They became engaged in August after a dinner in his mother's home. She must have known what her son intended, for the table that night held her best lace cloth, silver goblets, the anniversary gift her husband had brought her from Lisbon, and the prism decanter that had been her grandmother's. Reminders of family members loved and past, treasures of memory: they had all been taken out for that meal. They were present as if to be witnesses to Tony's joy, to see the Picanco past joined with its future.

Tony presented her with the filigree ring his grandmother had given him, her last gift before their departure from São Miguel to America.

His mother pressed Dede's smooth hands between her rough ones. "Antônio, he's a good boy. He will make you a good husband. Like his father, my Eduardo." Then she cradled Dede's face between her hands, her eyes searched Dede's for the answer to her plea. "And you be good to Antônio, no? You make him happy. Please. He's a good boy."

She wore the ring on a long chain. To be closer to her heart, she told

Tony. It hung unseen in classes under her shirt. Until she could tell her parents.

∽

They were strolling back to Thayer after their Tuesday night lectures. Tony was talking about the downtown project. That too much pressure was being put on him and his crew to complete by September 15. Mr. Moore, his boss, had preleased the building and was insisting it be ready for tenants by the first of the month. He had to have them in order to get the rest of the financing from the bank.

Mr. Moore told him to make sure it was finished by then. To cut corners, if necessary. Limit the quality checks on the mechanicals. Push the subtrades to exceed their daily production quotas. Take risks on safety—anything to make the deadline. Tony told her that Mr. Moore seemed desperate.

"No matter how I feel about Mr. Moore, I can't follow these orders. Doing it his way can weaken the building. Make it not structurally sound. . . . I know if he loses his bank money, I'm out of a job."

"You don't have to worry about that, Tony."

"What did you say?"

"You don't have to take Moore's orders anymore. You've no need to."

"I wish that were true."

"Listen, Tony"—she stopped walking and indicated that they sit on the grass—"you weren't really happy with the work you were doing even before this happened. Remember when we were sailing and you pointed out to me what you were building? I could tell you weren't happy then. But that can all be changed. You don't have to do that anymore."

"I don't understand you. You're talking in riddles." Dede sensed Tony was becoming exasperated.

"Tony, my father builds shopping plazas. In Canada and the U.S. All over. I know he's doing something in Hartford. And here in Boston. I can't remember what area he said it's in, but he mentioned it to me before I came this summer. It's around here somewhere. You must know it. It's going to be the newest shopping mall in the city. . . . You'll work for him. Run his U.S. projects."

"This is crazy."

"It's not, Tony. It's not. He's always complaining he has no one down here he can trust. He needs someone to run the U.S. operation, who knows the construction business and wouldn't cheat him. Someone loyal to him. . . . You want to be your own man. Run your own operation. My father's always saying construction demands on-site inspection and instant decisions. How can my father possibly run it from out of the country?" She did not give him time to think that one through. She had already done that for both of them. "He can't. You'd make the decisions. You wouldn't have problems like you're having with Moore. There would be no interference, Tony. You'd be in charge of the project from day one. I'm sure he'd give you input on the design even before you became an architect." She concluded with "It's a natural, don't you think so?"

Dede was surprised by his reaction. "I can't work for your father, Dede. I just can't. It's not right. I can support you, as I have all my family. But my way. And not with your parents' help."

"I didn't mean it like that, Tony. I only told you this because I can't stand to see you so worried. . . . I know what my father will say after he meets you. When he gets to know you, the type of person you are." She reached out her hand to touch his face, momentarily forgetting the purpose of her conversation. "How wonderful you are. Your integrity, basic decency, honesty. So many things about you. . . . When he finds out you're in construction and the level of your ability, I know what he will say. You're his type of man, Tony. I know you are and I know he will ask you to handle his U.S. operation for him. . . . Tony, my father is in his late fifties. He spends all his time running between Vancouver, Winnipeg and Toronto and now through the U.S. checking his projects. That is, when he's not on holidays in Florida." No matter how restrained she tried to be, whenever she mentioned her parents' extended absences she could not control the inevitable dig—the bitterness born in her Branksome Hall years slipped, unattractively, into her conversation. "He's always telling me that the best-run businesses are family firms. 'Blood,' he calls it. That he often wishes he had a son so he could set him up in the United States and not ever have to worry about his American company again. Well, you're going to be family. You're going to be my husband and he's going to get his son. A little late in his life"—she smiled—"but he'll get him anyhow. You're 'blood,' Tony."

"Dede, you're rushing things. He may not feel that way."

"No, I'm not." She could no longer contain her pride in him. "Tony, you know the construction business cold. No one knows it better than you. You've even admitted that yourself. No, Tony, you're wrong. I'm not rushing anything. My father needs you."

"Dede, this is crazy. Your father hasn't even met me. He certainly doesn't need me. And I told you, I don't intend to work for your family. I have a good job now, and can get another if I have to."

"Let's not discuss this anymore. Just please, Tony, all I want you to do is keep an open mind. You said my parents would eventually want to meet you. Well, they'll be coming by in a couple of weeks, expecting to pick me up. So now seemed as good a time as any to discuss this. . . . I know they'll love you like I do. And I'm sure my father will offer you the job."

Tony did not reply. In silence, they continued their walk to the dorm.

She had warned him, but not of the proper things. The things he really had to know. She repressed these, held them prisoner within her, refusing, with words, to acknowledge them. Feeling if she did not breathe life into her fears, they would rest invisible, unable to harm her.

The nights she lay contentedly in his arms in the anonymity of the dark, she had opportunity to tell him. Where he could listen to her, and yet not see her pain. But she did not tell him of the way her parents controlled and dominated her life and how powerless she always felt against them. She chose not to speak: of her parents' values, which she did not share; of their pretensions, which had driven away the possibility of real friendships; of the humiliation she felt being befriended because of her surname; of the loneliness during her parents' extended absences. She valued Susan as her first real friend and since the day of the storm, Tony had become her harbor, her place of refuge. The only happiness she had ever known had been with him.

She knew why she had not confided these things. Telling him held the greatest fear: he would be incapable of understanding her world, and feeling it irreconcilable with his own, would leave her. If she could remain silent, she convinced herself, the summer could last forever.

∽

"Dede, we're docked. What took you so long to answer the phone? Surely you must have remembered we were coming home today. Your father and I wrote you a nice postcard from Nice. Didn't you get it? It said we were landing on the seventeenth. Hold on, your father wants to talk."

"Dede, can you hear me? I'm calling from the pier. There's a huge lineup. Only one phone. Raced off the boat and beat everyone. Got to it first. Fortunately, I remembered from last time. Your mother and I are real tired, so I'll speak fast. We're coming to see you tonight. Make a reservation at Anthony's Pier 4. We'll be taking you home tomorrow. Driving. So start packing up."

"But, Daddy, there's something I need to tell you. I've met someone special. I'd like you to meet him."

"Sure. Make it a table for four."

"I also think you should meet his mother. May I ask her to join us?"

"How serious is this anyway?"

"Very."

"Why didn't you write us? We left you our itinerary."

"You know we've never been a family of writers."

"Well, where did you meet this fellow?"

"On campus."

"What's he planning to be?"

"An architect."

"Well, you better bring him along. And his mother."

"Daddy, he's very important to me. They're very important to me. Please be especially nice to them."

"Of course I will. . . . I've got to go. They've brought the bags off. Your mother's getting impatient. You won't believe the lineup for this phone. Make sure you reserve a view of the harbor. We'll meet you at Anthony's at seven, baby."

Dede's hand felt wonderful in Tony's as he accompanied her through the restaurant toward her parents. And how elegant Tony's mother looked in the silk brocade she had made herself.

Her parents were already seated at a table, their chairs overlooking the bay, a drink on the pewter serving plate before them. Dede saw her mother was impatient, she was already twisting her nine-point pearls. Her father got up as they approached.

"How's my little girl?" Dede kissed him and proceeded around the table to kiss her mother. "And this is your young man. . . . And his lovely mother," her father continued charmingly.

Dede introduced everyone in a manner that would have made the principal at Branksome Hall finishing school proud. "Mrs. Picanco, may I introduce my parents, Mr. and Mrs. Ein."

"Call us Stanley and Helen."

"Thank you, Mr. Ein. Please, I'm Maria."

They all sat in the seats assigned by her father, with a view of the lobster tank and their back to the bay.

"We're one drink ahead of you already. What will you have?" The remaining cocktails were selected. "Waiter," her father said as this man was about to leave. "Before you go, we want to order dinner. We have to make it an early night. Got a twelve-hour drive up into Canada in the morning. . . . Maria, don't mean to rush you, but we really need to make an early start tomorrow, eh, Dede? I'll have oysters, a one-and-a-half-pound lobster. Stuffed. Stuffed, Helen, I hear is the best, and an Idaho and put some of your delicious Boston cream pie away for me for dessert, will you? My wife here, she'll have the same. The rest will give you their own orders."

Once this man was out of hearing range, Dede did not delay. She had only this evening to settle things. Her parents thought she was leaving with them tomorrow and her father had just said he was making it a short night. She placed her hand on Tony's arm for reassurance. She began the words she had been practicing since her parents' noontime call.

"Tony and I plan to be married." Tony was looking confidently at her.

"Dede, this is quite a surprise. You didn't mention it was that serious," her father said.

"I wanted to tell you when I was with Tony."

"Have you two set a date?" her mother asked matter-of-factly.

"Not yet. I've been waiting for you to get back. And Tony thought you'd want to meet him."

"That was very considerate of him," her father said stiffly.

"Well, I suggest a long engagement," said her mother. "You two need time to get to know each other and I need time to organize things."

"Please be happy for me," Dede implored.

"We must have Taittinger. This calls for a celebration," her father said in his most affable voice. "We'll drink to our daughter's engagement and our safe return from Europe." The waiter was summoned, the champagne brought. Bubbles slid down the sides of their tulip glasses.

"Well, there's so much I have to do. Arrange things," her mother said in a festive mood. "I don't know what to do first. Where to start. Fortunately, your father and I brought you a little something from Rome. This will be your first engagement present." She reached into her alligator bag. She brought out a suede pouch stamped "Bulgari's" and placed it in front of Dede. "Dede has so much gold, we thought we'd give her something different this time." Dede made no motion to open it. "You know how much you like everything Bulgari makes. We got you something you can really use. Open it now. I'm sure Tony and Maria can't wait to see what we got you." She did not touch the pouch. "Well, you can open it later, if you like," her mother continued. "It's a diamond pin. We were lucky to find the exact match to the two-carat earrings we picked up for you last year. Remember them?" To explain her choice of jewelry, she added, "Dede loves diamonds. Well, I guess that's not so unusual. Most women do."

"Dede usually travels with us to Europe," said her father. "This is the first year she hasn't joined us in . . . let's see. In five years. I think she was seventeen when we first started taking her. I sure missed my little girl this time, but it looks like I'd better get used to it. Some other lucky man will be taking her to Europe now, eh, Tony?"

"We also got you the cashmere dress you asked us for. Found it at Harrods."

"We'd give it to you now, but your mother couldn't stuff that in her purse." Her father chuckled, always appreciative of his own humor. "Well. . . . Let's see the Rock. That's what's important to the ladies, eh, Tony, my boy?"

Dede unclipped the chain from around her neck and passed it to her mother. "This was given to Tony by his grandmother."

Her mother appraised it. "Filigree. The Portuguese do such interesting work, don't they? . . . How sweet."

"Well, Tony, wise idea. Mustn't rush a big purchase. Stake the territory, clean up the details later, that's what I always say. Helen, I'm sure Tony has someone looking for the perfect diamond for our Dede right this minute."

Dede saw Tony's teeth clench; his face grow sullen.

Oysters had been placed before her parents, tomato juice before the others. Her mother had used the occasion of her husband's comment to gently savage the oysters on her plate. In six swift scoops they had disappeared. She continued into the next item of her hastily drawn-up list. "We'll have to put a trousseau together. I'm sure Steven can help me. The Cutlers. They've become our dearest friends. On the ship, we were seated at the same table. They prefer second sitting too, like us. The husband manufactures designer suede goods. He insisted, Dede, that you and I come down and pick anything we want from his showroom in Manhattan. He's introducing his spring line already. Anyhow, you can discuss everything with him next week. He and his wife are such darling people. They'll be joining us in Chesterton for the weekend."

"Chesterton? Is that a subdivision of Toronto? Dede told me you live in Toronto." Tony tried to enter the conversation.

"I'm sorry. Didn't Dede tell you? Chesterton's not a subdivision. It's the name of our estate. Actually, there's Chesterton North," she said, emphasizing the "north," "because we have another place in Florida. Chesterton South." This time her mother drew out the word "south."

Tony did not question her further.

Her mother did not let this aside divert her from her topic. She took a sip of champagne and, undaunted, continued. "When Steven's up, you can discuss next season's style. Maybe he can have one of his designers make you a stunning suede going-away outfit. I'm sure he'd love to do it for you. Probably insist on doing it free, as a wedding gift." As if suddenly remembering the woman across from her, her mother swept Mrs. Picanco into the conversation, "Maria? Is Tony your only child?"

"Yes, Antônio, he is." She sounded grateful to be allowed to talk about her son.

"Then your family's all grown. How do you fill your time? . . . What charities do you belong to?"

Her mother must have valuated the gold-and-orange brocade fabric with its Bill Blass design and assumed it corresponded with an equally fashionable bank account.

"Charities? I do not accept charity. I make enough money to buy the food." Flustered, her English had become unsure, her words unstructured. "I make dresses."

Dede interjected quickly to cover Tony's mother's increasing embarrassment. "Mother, Mrs. Picanco makes magnificent clothes. In São Miguel, she was a dressmaker. The dress she's wearing tonight, she designed herself. Isn't it exquisite?"

Mrs. Ein regained interest in the conversation. "Dress designer? . . . I brought some exquisite silk fabric back from Como. I'm sure you know, they make the finest silk in the world there. With the exception of China, of course, but Stanley thinks that's too far to go for some fabric. You do beautiful work. Can you make the suit for me? As you're almost family, I really should give you the business, shouldn't I? I must insist you let me pay you. I can come to your place before we leave tomorrow."

His mother did not speak. She placed her utensils down; hid her swollen hands in her lap.

The entrées appeared. Sole amandine for Mrs. Picanco and Tony, swordfish for Dede and lobster for the Eins. The stuffed crustacean, split on its side, lay easily exposed. Her father swiftly dissected his. He removed the meat and tore off the claws. Ignoring the finger bowl, he wiped his hands on his white cloth bib and signaled for the waiter to remove the carcass.

Her father seemed to have heard enough. As she had seen her father often do in other situations when displeased, he took control. He abruptly changed the topic and his tone. He switched to his business voice, any pretended warmth stripped from its surface. He addressed himself only to Tony, who faced him, back rigid, hands uncomfortably clasped on the tabletop.

"How do you intend to support my daughter?"

"I love Dede. I will take good care of her, Mr. Ein."

"How do you intend to support my daughter?" said her father, not accepting this as an answer.

"I will support her well."

"How?"

"I work in construction. I've been with one firm, Moore Construction, for seven years. I make good money."

"How did you get into construction anyway?"

"I came from Portugal at fourteen. From the island of São Miguel in the Azores. When my father died, I went directly into construction."

"That means you taught yourself the trade. Or maybe took some night courses. But you are primarily self-taught, aren't you?"

"Yes, Mr. Ein. You could say that."

Her father's voice hardened. "Like most of the Portuguese boys I employ."

Dede had to interrupt. Make him understand how special Tony was, forthright, honest, respected. She would not let her father put Tony down. "No, not like that. The owner thought so highly of Tony he paid him to go to night school. Tony's work is wonderful. He's a foreman."

Her father siphoned what he required from her information, then continued the interrogation as if his daughter were not present.

"I'm surprised you even reached foreman. I wouldn't put anyone with that weak background in charge. Even if the whole crew was nothing but Portuguese. But you said you work for Moore Construction. That explains it. Simon Moore runs a cut-rate organization. Everyone in the business knows he'll do anything for the bottom line. He'll hire anyone off the boat. Anything to avoid union scale. Pays the lowest salaries in the Northeast, installs second-rate materials, builds to a price. That's his style. Standards barely good enough to pass the Massachusetts Building Code. Simon's even been charged twice with safety violations. . . . Owning one of the most successful construction organizations on the eastern seaboard, I'd say I'm somewhat familiar with the construction business. As a supervisor for Moore Construction I know the salary you must make. What you get now, what you can expect to make. . . . In Boston, knowing the market as I do, I'd say that only rents you a one-room walk-up. My daughter won't put up with that for more than three months, no matter what she's telling you now, any more than her mother could. Can you see Dede carrying groceries up two flights of stairs? Or even doing her own shopping at all?"

"This is only temporary. I hope to be an architect."

"Hope is not good enough. Everyone hopes."

"Mr. Ein, I will be entering architecture at MIT next year."

"That's commendable, especially at your age. How old are you?"

"Twenty-nine."

"Twenty-nine? And only now you decided what you want to be? Wouldn't you say it's a little late to suddenly decide on architecture? That's five years of full-time schooling with not even a foreman's salary coming in. That means for five years there'll be no money. You couldn't possibly be expecting Dede to work. Who do you think is going to support you? . . . Me?"

"No, Mr. Ein. I've been working toward this. I've saved up."

Her mother had appraised Dede's ring and found it wanting; her father had appraised the man and labeled him flawed.

Her father would permit no explanation, accept nothing but the quality in a son-in-law he felt he deserved. He seemed determined to break Tony, to expose him as an upstart. He worked methodically, with the precision honed against more formidable opponents. "When did you get this sudden urge to become an architect? After you met my daughter?" Tony did not answer. "Did a Dun & Bradstreet on her? On me? On Ein Construction? On my net worth?" Her father's questions built, accusation on inference, to a crescendo.

"That's not true, Daddy. You're wrong about Tony."

"A naive girl with a rich father must have been an easy mark for an experienced, slick fellow like yourself, eh, Tony?" He silenced her viciously, ensuring she would give him no further interference.

Dede heard the scrape of a chair moving against the planked flooring in the area where Tony was seated. She did not permit her eyes to leave her plate, she was mortified. She heard Tony's voice. Strained and controlled.

"We're leaving, Mother. . . . Now!"

Dede heard another chair move against the floorboards. The click of heels. Of footsteps withdrawing. She allowed herself to look up; her eyes followed their departure. Tony's shoulders were slumped; his mother, disoriented, stumbled uncertainly behind.

The waiter brought the Boston cream pie and placed it before her father. He cut contentedly into his favorite part, its soft center. Her father's work that night had been deft and accurate. He had maligned Tony's integrity and humiliated his mother.

Dede felt so devastated by her father's words that she had been temporarily desensitized to the effect they must have had on Tony. But now she reacted instinctively, running after Tony to the valet area.

A car pulled violently from the curb, its wheels squealing. She waved a cab from the restaurant taxi stand and felt into her bag for money. Only credit cards. She had no cash to give the driver. But how could she be expected to? Rich people, after all, aren't expected to carry money.

Her head spun from the words she heard, words that played upon her insecurity and tormented her through the long stretch of her last night at Thayer, during the twelve-hour turnpike journey home and throughout the sleeplessness that plagued months of her nights.

How could her father think that Tony had been interested in her only for money? He had never pressed her for information about her family, where they holidayed or where she went to school.

Or had her father's words all been true? From the beginning, he must have known she came from a wealthy family. It had been naive to assume that her rich mannerisms, body language and facile comments had not instantly tipped him off, affectations so flagrant they were impossible to conceal, like a physical deformity everyone can see and does not have to be reminded of. All she ever had going for her was their money. Was her need for acceptance so pitifully obvious he could not fail to notice it?

But Tony was not the type of person her father had described. He was not afraid of working hard. And he was proud that everything he had achieved since coming to America had been the result of his own efforts. He had never given her any reason to doubt that he loved her for herself.

If only she had found the courage to stand up for Tony that evening.

How could she have sat passively by, allowing her father to insult Tony and humiliate her. Why couldn't they leave her alone and let her be happy. They were always interfering in her life, telling her what to do, how to think, who her friends should be.

She should have defied her parents, remained in Boston and talked it all out with Tony. That was her only chance to be sure how he felt about her and her hope to salvage the happiness she had found with him.

Dede never heard from Tony again. He never reappeared in her life, either to slay her dragons or to return her dreams.

Chapter 12

Autumn began Dede's final year at Ryerson and the season's social schedule. Dede's attendance at lectures was inversely proportionate to her similar record for parties. She was committed not to miss any worthwhile after-hours activity: a University of Toronto football team dance at Varsity Stadium or its all-night continuation at some frat house with whomever she might have met there; the Friday night gathering at University College's Lit and Athletic Society's bar and, when the Junior Common Room closed at midnight, at the less exclusive Horseshoe Tavern at Bathurst and Queen; any recent acquaintance's un-birthday bash; the weekly wine-imbibing ritual at Phi Lam or Delta Epsilon; or, on the slow nights, with no makeup and black clothes, frequenting the downstairs coffeehouses of Yorkville. She never turned down a drive-in movie with a blind date, or an evening Corvette ride to Niagara Falls to watch the sun rise.

These things provided a diversion, something to occupy an unhappy mind. With those she met she never discussed last summer. She dismissed Harvard with the innocuous superlatives reserved for all summers.

It was not that she no longer cared about Tony; she no longer cared about herself.

After one such evening in April, she returned too drunk with her latest acquaintance to his St. George Street fraternity house. She followed him up the battered stairwell with its shaky banister. "For a nightcap," he had said. The room was unexpectedly empty.

She remembered him pushing her onto the cot, the weight of his body on hers, his roughness, the squeak of the worn springs, the shrill ring of the phone he paused to answer. The phone that jarred her back to reality.

The soft female voice that, pinned beneath him, she could not help but overhear.

"Hi. It's me. What are you doing now?"

"Nothing. Nothing at all," he replied.

"I hope I'm not disturbing you, calling so late like this."

"No, don't be foolish. Of course not," he answered. Lovemaking had become an emotionless act. It meant nothing to her anymore. And she certainly meant nothing to the man who was with her. What was she doing here?

She straightened her red dress, and fled down the stairwell and into the night toward the shelter of her car. She entered her Corvette, bolted its doors, rested her head against the steering wheel and, for the first time since that August night Tony walked from her life, she wept. She cried for herself, for what she had become, and even more so, for what she might have had with Tony.

By the time July had returned Dede was keen to escape from her life to Europe. They were to be abroad just four weeks. Her father felt it prudent to return home for the opening of his 650,000-square-foot enclosed shopping mall to greet the senior politicians from all levels of government who had facilitated this project. He had booked his prized fifth-floor suite at the Carlton, whose sitting room offered, through its center balcony door, a clear view of the Mediterranean and the yachts which presided there.

Entering the resort in Cannes after the absence of a summer, Dede observed it afresh. The public areas looked more excessively opulent than she had remembered. A crimson carpet in reception overlay chocolate-and-cream marble. From a vaulted ceiling, crystal chandeliers hung between a row of gilt-capitaled columns. Demi-oval mirrors set into the back wall below the deeply carved frieze rebounded the spectrum of glitter across the width of the room. Behind a sweep of mahogany counter, four concierges busied themselves.

Her father, as he ushered his family toward the open grilled lifts and the white-gloved operator stationed at the rear of the lobby, proudly declared, "Without question, this place is still the most exclusive address in Cannes."

Dede's day was spent on the Carlton's private beach. It was located directly across the boulevard from the hotel and was delineated subtly from other beachfront property by yellow-and-white candy-striped chairs that were coordinated with the awnings of the hotel and separated more authoritatively through the use of similar-colored wooden partitions. The purpose of these barriers was to prohibit the public from having access to the hotel's facilities.

Her parents habitually left the sea for their respective activities about three o'clock—her father for a late afternoon nap in the suite, her mother for an interlude of shopping in the exclusive couturier salons that proliferated beside and behind the Croisette. Dede's practice was to remain in front of the family's cabana until the sun's disappearance reminded her to return to the hotel.

On each of the afternoons that she had been there, she had noticed a man in his mid-twenties appear around the time the staff began to disassemble the beach—collapsing cabana partitions, stacking chairs and mats, removing parasols. From her chair, Dede watched his approach from as far away as five hotel lengths. Lanky and long-limbed, always in the same pink jersey, he was easy to distinguish from the others who wandered the public beach. He walked along the shoreline, sandals, towel and lightweight knapsack in hand, his powerful strides quickly bringing him closer. He would cut in at the Carlton's deeply recessed beach and pause. After a swift glance to ensure the cabana supervisor had abdicated his surveillance, he would authoritatively settle on a reserved cot which a hotel guest had conveniently vacated within the past half hour. He seemed to have a system as to which of these he selected. He deposited his towel upon it and sauntered to the Carlton's festive, wood-planked, open-air restaurant, arriving punctually just before its closing. He returned carrying the square cup reserved for espresso, and removed a newspaper from his pack. After reading every page in detail, he would spend the remainder of the afternoon alternating between sunning and sleeping. Sometimes though, when Dede had her eyes closed to the sun, she could feel him watching her.

On the fifth day of this routine, he usurped her father's canvas deck chair—the one immediately next to hers. She instinctively defended with the territorial imperative.

"You aren't a guest of the hotel, are you?"

"Nope, I'm a cot poacher," he said disarmingly.

"And a choosy one at that," she quipped.

"You mean how I picked my cot? I never take the fourth of anything. It's unlucky."

"To each his own," she replied.

"You don't mind if I sit here, do you?"

She had been bored these past few days and was enjoying the distraction. "Feel free." Her words were unnecessary. He had already stretched his legs, which dangled ungainly over the wood-frame canvas chair, more possessively into the sand. "Why don't you use the beach at your own hotel?"

"Can't. They don't have one. I'm staying at a pension up the hill there." A long arm indicated the direction of Vence. "Anyhow, this is friendlier turf, don't you agree? Well, usually friendlier."

His directness charmed Dede and short-circuited any further hostility. She had watched him for the past four days and not given him away. Now her questions became those of a fellow conspirator. He intrigued her. "Why this hotel?"

"Easy. Most comfortable cots, best-kept beach, a chef who excels at espresso and, lastly, but of paramount importance, the least attentive after-hours beach staff."

"What do you do when you are not poaching hotel guests' property?" She liked his turn of phrase and reused it.

"Wandering through Europe presently. Got it down to a science. Sixteen days a country. Finished England. Now doing France—eight days Paris, one day Marseilles, seven days Côte d'Azur—Cannes, Nice, Monaco. Then on to Switzerland. Germany. Home."

"Do you do this every summer?"

"Nope. This is my present to myself. For withstanding three years of graduate school. Before I start a real job and become a useful member of society."

"Who are you traveling with?"

"Myself. He travels fastest who travels alone. Talbot."

"Who's Talbot?"

"I am. George Talbot. Canada."

"Dede Ein. Same."

He leaned forward and offered her a sandy hand. "Have I answered all your questions satisfactorily?"

Dede still had not assuaged her curiosity. "Most. One more, the newspaper. You seem addicted to it."

"You mean this?" He lifted the section he had tossed to the side when they had begun to talk. "The international edition of the *Herald Tribune*. Yes, I always read it. It's my major budget expense for the day. I'll limit my breads to two rolls, count them when the waiters pass them cavalierly, but I'll never skimp on the paper."

"Why?" Dede was fascinated by a preference that chose information over food.

"There are some things you can't afford not to know. I have to stay on top of what's going on at home," he stated, adjusting his tortoiseshell glasses.

At first Dede could not pinpoint what made this man so compelling. He had well-defined features, an angular face and firm chin. A shock of sandy, wavy, thick hair, which, when he became animated, fell onto his forehead and was nonchalantly pushed back. A tall frame void of unnecessary fat which he agilely controlled. These features blended together in a pleasing unity, but were not individually exceptional. Rather, what elevated him to distinction was his confident manner and the intelligence and the wit this sparked.

"Are you staying here?" he asked.

"Yes." Her days of pretense were gone. Anyhow, how could he help but know? He had observed her here for the last four days. Unless, of course, he thought she was like him, an interloper.

"With your folks?"

"Yes."

"How long?"

"For the month."

"Well, now we've done the formalities, let's not waste the afternoon. Like motorcycles? I've rented one. Best way to see the Riviera. Like to go?"

"Sure, but not now. Not dressed for it." She had only her swimming gear with her. "And can't grab my things from the room. My father hates motorcycles and the people who ride them. Calls them hoodlums and bums. I'll have to get my things when he's not there."

"No problem. We'll do it another time. Like to go out on the pier?" he asked, bringing his hands against the chair's wooden arms and lifting himself up.

They walked the length of the water-skiing dock, then sat on its smooth planks, their feet resting on its ledged overhang. How wonderful the offshore breeze felt tossing her hair and the fresh scent of salt air. Between the slats, schools of striped fish could be easily spotted in the clear turquoise. Sun played upon the shallow transparent liquid, and with the sandy bottom, cast upon it golden, undulating geometric patterns.

Sitting on the wharf they talked of trivia, the inconsequential things designed to acquaint and amuse, but reveal little of importance. They lingered until the sun plunged radiant and splendid into the sea. Then he strolled with her across the Croisette to her hotel.

How it happened, Dede could not recall. Somewhere during that conversation, he had invited himself to join her and her parents the following morning at their cabana.

"What are you planning to be, George?" her father began where he had left off last summer with Tony. Never one for small talk, he opened with the only thing that interested him in a man. George had presented himself at the Eins' cabana, the reserved row closest to the sea, with the scrubbed look of someone who just emerged from a shower. He had arrived, not via the beach, but as would a hotel guest, down the steps of the rope-matted gangplank. He now sat upon the family's third and remaining chair, the one next to her father, balancing the Vittel the older man had ordered for him. Helen Ein, beneath a parasol, was perusing *Paris-Match*. Dede lay on her back, arms hung over the sides of the yellow mat on the sand, a collapsible wooden head rack propped behind her. She listened to the lull of the Mediterranean against the pebbled beach and the conversation of the two men, her eyes shut against the sun's strong eleven o'clock rays.

"Serve in government, sir," came back the answer, direct and immediate.

"I like that answer. Spoken like a man who knows what he wants. But what makes you so sure you'll be given the chance to?"

"I've already been vice president of the Young Liberals of Canada. Held that position before I went to Stanford. I was asked by the campaign committee before the last leadership convention to come back to run the Youth Delegates for Lester Pearson. Delivered them all, to a man. Did debating right through seven years of university. Been prime minister of model parliament and, in my last year of honors political science, I was president of the student body. That sort of thing. Nothing is for certain in politics, but I think I'm pretty well positioned."

"So you're going after power. Good for you."

"No, not power. The real power in a country is in the press and the TV journalists. The people who subliminally interpret the news for you. Tell you indirectly what to think, who to vote for. . . . It's not power that attracts me to government, it's the opportunity to do something useful. To contribute what I can to society. . . . At Stanford, my doctoral thesis was 'Forms of Government for Emerging African Countries.' I presented models for how their government should be run."

"An idealist too. That can be dangerous."

"I'm what you call a safe idealist. A pragmatic idealist, if you need a label. I know my limitations. I also know what I am capable of doing and, with luck, I'll get a chance to prove myself. Work for my country."

"When do you plan to come home?"

"This is my last trip away for a while. It was great receiving a Woodrow Wilson Fellowship and taking it at Stanford. Couldn't beat the professors . . . or the weather, for that matter," he added, smiling engagingly. He delivered his next remarks directly to her father, as he had all the preceding ones during this interview. "But I want to get back to Canada. Get started. I'm an expatriate from Ottawa, returning home." George reached up and placed his drink on the knee-high wood veneer stand that lay between the two men; a minuscule ridge prevented the bottle from tumbling off its surface and into the sand.

"A fellow countryman. Returning to his roots. I like that."

George accepted her father's invitation and joined them for lunch at the seaside open-air restaurant.

"What will you have, George?" The younger man had left his menu unopened.

"Whatever you order is fine with me, sir."

"Good. We'll have pâté de foie gras and sea bass. For four. Make that two fish, not one large one. . . . Tastier that way, George. . . . My regular wine, of course. Evian and Badoit. And raspberries."

"No dessert for me, Stanley, thank you. Just my regular café au lait."

"No raspberries for Mrs. Ein," he said, amending his instructions. "Just café au lait. And bring that at the end of the meal." Leaning toward George, he added, "Dede's mother here, she's a chameleon. She acquires the eating habits of whatever country she happens to be in. Isn't that right, Helen dear?" He thumped her shoulder affectionately. "Anyone else want something different?"

George did not deviate from her father's suggested menu. Neither during this meal, Dede noticed, did he count his rolls.

At three o'clock her parents rose to leave. Her father turned to George. "What do you two have planned for later?"

"I don't know, sir. I was going to ask Dede if she would like to go for a cycle ride."

"Of course she would, George. Why wouldn't she? Only way to see Cannes" was her father's unexpected reply.

It was the perfect Mediterranean night. The air remained warm, despite the nine o'clock hour. They sped along the Croisette, the boulevard's lush greenery of royal palms and sycamore on one side, the sea, dark and luxurious, on the other. The evening, to Dede, seemed a profusion of sparkling jewels. Stars, brilliant gems, lit up the deep beaches by which they rode. Lights flickered randomly from the salons of the hotels tucked around the nape of the bay and from the yachts moored in the harbor. A string of lanterns hanging funnel to bow outlined a cruise boat anchored for the night in the deep water of New Port, which, visible everywhere they traveled, acted as their silent guide. From a cliff overlooking the city came the illumination of the tenth-century watchtower, Canois Castrum.

The salt air rushing onto Dede's skin made her feel an unexpected vitality.

George pointed out sights not found in a guidebook. She had never experienced Cannes like this before. He showed her mounds of raw fish piled crate-high—oysters, crabs, shrimp—displayed outside the seaside restaurants, and their proprietors, white aprons snugged around rotund midriffs, who darted around the corner to ogle the quality of the competitors' products. He spun through the labyrinth of lanes and passageways behind the main boulevard. He took her to the fish market, which at this hour gaped emptied and spotless, but from where, George explained, the morning's catch would be bargained from portable wooden stalls. They bumped down cobblestones to an alley alive with all-night cafés. Street performers—a pantomime magician, a violinist and a trio of guitarists—entertained in front of them.

He stopped the cycle before a pastry shop and ordered them a Napoleon *crème* and a mammoth sugared *palmier*. The shopkeeper selected these with care and passed a small white box over the counter with the hesitancy of someone delivering gems. With this purchase, they circled back to the main thoroughfare and, locking the machine, strolled the wide sea walk in the vicinity of the hotel. George located a pair of turquoise metal chairs on the isthmus of grass beside the road and lifted these over to the broad yellow ledge overlooking the Mediterranean. He offered her one, then sat in the other, placing his loafers against the slanted protective buttress before them. The sky held its translucence.

"*Voilà. Pour vous, mademoiselle.*" He urged a pastry upon her.

She selected the more innocent piece, leaving for him the creamy, chocolate Napoleon. The fine sugar ridges collapsed sweetly in her mouth. Haltingly, she responded in kind. "*Le petit gâteau est très délicieux.* . . . How's my French?"

"All it needs is a crash course in confidence," he replied.

It was easy to relax to his repartee shared above the rhythm of the sea and the light, consistent hum of traffic behind him: the hilarity of his adventures with another student who had flown standby with him to England; the elderly couple whose hospitality of bed and breakfast he enjoyed and who on parting refused to accept money from him; the unique system he used to rate the places he had been. His nonchalant manner disarmed her.

She responded forthrightly to his interest in her travels, the hotels she and her parents stayed in, the restaurants in which they dined. Why shouldn't she tell him? she thought as she watched a breeze toss a lock of wavy hair into his eyes. Last summer had shown her the futility of subterfuge. Perhaps if she had told Tony, hidden nothing, let him assimilate the information of her affluence as their relationship evolved, he could have withstood her parents' behavior that night. Concealment had ensured the shock; it had intensified the gulf of money and background that existed between Tony and her. It made these differences too difficult to overcome at such a critical juncture. Or maybe nothing she could have said beforehand could have held him for her. Whatever the reason, she would not handle things the same way this time. She no longer had the fortitude for pretense; the aftermath had been too brutal, her devastation too complete.

She would not conceal from George the details that described her lifestyle and wealth. She would not extract herself from her background. She could no more easily remove herself from her family's womb than a newborn could emotionally be severed from his mother by a slash of the umbilical cord.

This time she would answer all questions, would let him see the total entity, her and her parents. Neither would she atone for or renounce their values and pretensions. He would have to evaluate for himself what he would see, separate what she was from what she might be perceived to be—just as she would have to assess for herself his character.

It was well after midnight when George pulled his cycle into the front parking lot of the Carlton. A concierge in white jacket and trousers hurried down the steps.

"No, no!" This man's index finger articulated from side to side to dispel any confusion that might be caused by the phrasing of a translated language. His head shook with passionate disapproval as if the cycle's presence there were a personal affront. "If you are a big movie star"—Dede saw George's eyes quicken with possibilities for a positive resolution but the concierge did not pause—"still not possible. May I have the doorman take that from you, monsieur, and place it at the rear of the hotel?"

The man to whom he referred had been present since the initiation of this discourse. His wincing visage, gesticulating shoulders throughout, made him an equal participant in the conversation.

Amicably, George relinquished the keys of the offending vehicle to the doorman and, unperturbed, accompanied Dede up the trio of marble steps, between the atrium's pillars, through the spinning door and into the humid lobby. Clad in his short-sleeved pink jersey and chinos, George was not intimidated by the disdain from the layers of staff—concierges, receptionists, night managers, porters and pages—by whose stations he passed en route from curbside into the lift. He strode easily, with the facile manner of those who habitually summered there.

He escorted her right to her room, whose entrance along the air-conditioned corridor was separate from that which opened into the family's center suite. Before parting in front of her pink-ribboned double doors he brashly inquired, "Same time tomorrow at the cabana?" Dede did not try to dissuade him then or on any other occasion from joining her. Nor did she discourage her father, before he would leave her and George at the beach in the late afternoon, from assuming George's automatic inclusion in their evenings—dining with them at La Réserve de Beaulieu and the other gourmet bastions they frequented—and later playing, at her father's expense, at the gaming tables of Cannes's casinos.

George's easy charm had become a part of the pleasures of Cannes none of the Eins had any intention of forgoing.

George did not leave Cannes after seven days, as he had originally told Dede he planned to do; instead he remained the entire duration of her stay. He remarked to Dede and her parents at the cabana, on what would have been his last morning with them, that there were too many things still to see on the Côte d'Azur, places he had subsequently read about in his Michelin which he wanted to show Dede.

That same day Dede heard him discuss his career choices. He did not direct his thoughts to her, but courted instead her father's advice. George presented his alternatives succinctly, judicially weighing each for her father's consideration. "I've been offered the job of running the constituency office for Joe Bradley. You've probably heard of him. He has the best winning record in parliament. Been elected four consecutive times."

"Of course I have. Put in good money myself to make sure he kept his seat. I've one plaza in his riding and plans pending for a second. I like to know where I stand with a man, if you know what I mean. You can count on Bradley to show you the ropes."

"That's my opinion exactly. He spoke for my nomination the first time I ran as a Youth Delegate to the convention. Those delegate seats were hotly contested. I've always remembered what he did for me. He's really been my unofficial mentor. . . . That's the reason I was tempted to accept when he personally phoned me at Stanford and asked me to give him a hand."

"He's always been straight with me. He's a good man. I don't understand why you don't grab the job."

"If I accept his offer, sir, I'd have to move to Toronto. It will remove me for two to three years from the mainstream, Ottawa, where all the decisions are made. Also my folks live in the capital. I really had wanted to be closer to them now that they're getting a bit older."

"What else you got?"

"Just before I left for Europe, I was asked to be executive assistant to the Minister for Small Business. It's a junior ministry in the outer cabinet, but it is an EA position. It would put me in the center of things. They say it's a rare opportunity. Gives me access to everyone important. Also, the best possible grounding to run for parliament."

"Solid thinking. I like a man who knows how the system works." Her father seemed equally intrigued with the younger man's opportunities and flattered by being taken into his confidence for what he always said was the most critical decision of a man's life. "Hard decision, George. No one can make it for you. Have to look yourself in the mirror and decide. But you're on track either way. Definitely on track."

To his wife and Dede in the privacy of their suite, he later confided his definitive conclusion. "That's a man who thinks right; who appreciates who butters his bread. That boy is going places."

A few days later, George asked and received permission to take Dede for the evening to the neighboring principality of Monaco. Both dressed as fashionably as an hour's motorcycle ride would allow in order not to be excluded from its world-famous casino.

They took the paved roadway parallel to the sea until a marker pointed the route to the narrow cliff pass that would take them to Monaco. As the cycle climbed higher, each spiral twist revealed to Dede a more splendid postcard setting. From the cliffs, the fishing villages that nestled along the sea became a winding ribbon of fairyland lights, like a fiery Victoria Day wand that, as a child, she used to hold in her hand with fascination as it leapt with brilliant silver sparkles. Then down toward the principality in swift hairpin turns. George handled the cycle confidently on the stretch of twisting cobblestone, adroitly navigating between the jutting cliffs and the precipice that sheered into oblivion a few meters beside it. Small, stacked stones piled as a low curb along the ledge provided the pretense of a barrier. Dede fastened her arms tighter around George's waist and did not relax her grip until the narrow road widened again beneath the terraced hills of Monaco.

At the city square near the casino, George locked the cycle, clipped onto his collar the tuxedo bow tie he had brought with him for this purpose, then escorted her into the glittering salons of the Monte Carlo Casino. The decor of the main gaming room was plush, with mirrored walls, thick dark floral carpeting, lush wooden high-backed chairs. Ceiling-painted seductive cherubs watched amorously behind wide elaborate crystal chandeliers. The casino's clientele, George said, came from the list of society notables and the less well-connected who, for a few hours, aspired to their ranks. Diamonds, pearls and emeralds decorated the evening attire of those who gambled there. The mood was of a private party where all the invitations had been hand-delivered.

After the casino, they motored through the principality. George pointed out the Prince's palace, magical in its evening lighting.

At the cabana later that morning, her father acknowledged her 4 a.m. return with no more concern than "You two have a good time? . . . Good."

During the next two weeks, they spent most evenings exploring by motorcycle the areas around Cannes together.

Two nights before Dede and her parents were scheduled to go home George remarked, "You can't leave the Côte d'Azur without seeing St.-Paul-de-Vence. That's my neck of the woods. Literally. That's where I stayed when I first got here. All the great artists worked in that region at one time or another. Renoir, Braque, Matisse, Miró. The air up there is fragrant from the giant pines. The cones are so huge, they fill your entire hand. . . . You know, we really should make a day of it."

It was a steamy Mediterranean afternoon. The air rushed refreshingly cool over Dede's back as the cycle sped along the A8 Autoroute for over an hour, wound up a two-lane road at Cagnes-sur-Mer and, upon approaching the town of St.-Paul, took a steep left toward the Maeght Foundation.

"Like to sit out here before going through the gallery?" George asked as they entered the art museum's gardens.

"Sure," she replied, walking over to a reflecting pool, whose lilies, she noticed, were awakening into gentle flower.

Resting on its ledge, they shared thoughts on the selection of sculptures scattered beneath the pines. Dede's favorite was a fluid, graceful bronze by Henry Moore, displayed on a rough stone bench; George admired the mobiles by Alexander Calder, which, he pointed out, responded to their contact with air, light and wind.

They toured the exposition halls illuminated by creative quarter-cylinder roofs—"light catchers" was what the plaque at the entrance called them—designed to provide each room with the lighting most compatible with the works on display. Then they strolled through the charming patios and courtyards which adjoined these galleries, discussing as they went the paintings, mosaics, drawings and sculptures before them, works of such masters as Chagall, Matisse, Bonnard, Giacometti and Miró.

"And now to St.-Paul. It will be hotter than here, but it's a must-see," he said as they retraced their steps downhill to get their vehicle. Wild red poppies grew randomly through the field beside them.

The cycle angled down the jut of mountain, edged around a deep valley and spiraled up a rocky spur toward a walled town. Strung together in tight geometric shapes, from the distance the peach stone structures resembled a miniature toy ceramic village.

The half mile quickly traveled, they were soon strolling hand in hand beneath ramparts on a narrow street en route into the medieval community. Moss protruded through its feudal stone. The muzzle of a cannon stationed in the wall faced them as they continued toward the only entrance. "That's the Lacan Cannon. Taken in the battle of Céresole in 1544. A beauty, isn't it? . . . Don't worry, it's not manned," he said good-humoredly as he steered her directly in front of it and then up the tunnel's arched incline into the belly of the town.

From a nearby shop, they purchased a pouch of goat cheese and from another, shiny cherries and grapes selected from its wicker basket's outdoor display. They sampled these as they climbed the cobblestone passages, perusing the art galleries and ateliers of artisans and painters.

The afternoon wore hot and muggy. A shaggy pup leapt his forepaws into a centuries-old horse trough and greedily slurped its runoff. "I think he's trying to tell us something," George quipped. "Ready for an aperitif?"

He guided her out of the fortified town and diagonally across a powdered, clay square, a presently unengaged, informal *pétanque* court, then into the elongated, low-slung structure parallel to it. His rubber soles left wide crimson marks on the highly polished ceramic tile.

"*Réservation pour Monsieur Talbot, s'il vous plaît. . . . Cinzano, garçon. Pour deux,*" he said as they were shown to a cliffside table on the outdoor terrace. Below lay an expanse of valley resplendent with its dress of greenery: spirals of tall, untamed cyprus, thickets of orange groves and olive trees, vegetation so lush it grew as the chronological companion to the ancient town. Villas were embedded into the hills on the opposite side of the valley, their orange ceramic roofs, a distinctive *tuiles romaines*, a tranquil accent.

George continued to order for both of them. His gaze rested throughout the meal, not on the landscape, but exclusively on her. The sun began its descent; the temperature slipped to balmy.

"Before the light goes, I want to show you a little more of the area. The pine forests I told you about. Cool, scented and unspoiled."

It had been an exuberantly carefree afternoon. Galleries and this romantic city.

"Shall we?" he asked.

She rose in direct answer to his question.

They skirted along the perimeter of the dusty, earthen patch toward his cycle, past a game of *pétanque* now in progress. The elderly players were stooped, their concentration locked on the roll of the balls.

"Ready?" he asked engagingly as he kicked the dry crimson powder off his loafers before placing them on the running boards of his machine. They sped down the hill, veered around a bend and, after the respite of a brief plateau, swerved right, simultaneously spiking the cycle up a perpendicular. The engine pulsed beneath Dede as it struggled for altitude; its vibration stirred within her a surge of excitement. She locked her arms tighter around George's waist, snuggled deeper into his back. He called out not to be afraid, he knew this road well.

Just when Dede was grateful that the route had leveled off, George cornered left. The road narrowed. George geared down. She ventured a look. Gracious villas were concealed by fences of laurel or split bamboo. Iron gates reinforced that seclusion. A coach lamp fixed on top of an entrance pillar prematurely lit the large block lettering *"Le Mas d'Artigny"* and an equally imposing *"Propriété Privée."* This warning and a length of stone wall deterred those without reservations from accessing this exclusive resort compound. After these gates, the road became a slender, deserted pathway. The homes on either side of it seemed abandoned and in need of repair. Untended wild shrubs bred around them. Neglected cyprus and olive trees abounded. George cut his speed further. He yanked off his helmet and looped it through his arm. A stone Roman-tiled *mas*, a cat snoozing in an alcove window, was deserted. Clumps of yellow miniature blooms, dark-throated blue iris and stabs of vibrant orange poppies continued their blaze of color in the dissolving light.

George pulled off into an untouched enclave of greenery. Ivy wound rampant up a slender oak, dressing it in intricate emerald. George balanced his cycle against its side, placing his helmet on top of the handlebars. He reached for her hand and guided her beneath the arc of trees. Fat cones scrunched soft and luxuriant beneath her feet.

Deep in this wooded area, George beckoned her to sit beside him beneath an ancient pine, its roots bedded in moss. She leaned against its crusted bark into the pliable covering. The sky shimmered with the last rays of the summer day. The wild foliage and play of light on the sloped, rugged trunks and entwined boughs enthralled her.

Dusk deepened into night. The branches thickened about them. Only threads of moonlight seeped through their tangled arms. A rush of air carried on it the sweetness of Scotch broom and the intoxication of the fragrant myrtle. Crickets pulsed in the anonymity of the dark.

In this sultry Mediterranean night scented with wildflowers, she yielded to the softness of the moss, the vacuity of her haphazard existence. And to George.

They spun down from the hills into Cannes as the fishermen were bringing their catch into Old Port under the cloak of predawn. The pine, as George had promised, had been sweet.

In the waning hour before the Eins had to leave their sunning to ready themselves for their transatlantic flight, George, in a voice audible to all in attendance at the family's cabana, remarked to Dede's father, "Sir, thought you might like to know what job I've decided to take when I get home. I was thinking over what you said. Feel I really owe it to Joe Bradley to give him a hand. I realize it will probably set my career back by two years. But I can make it up. Just means later on I'll work a little harder."

"I admire your decision. That's the type of loyalty I always look for in a man."

A sandy lock tumbled over George's forehead. He brushed it away with his hand before he casually added, "So I guess I'll see you folks in Toronto then. When I see you off at the plane, I won't have to say goodbye after all."

When they returned to the hotel, her father had the concierge make the necessary arrangements to ensure George would be brought from the airport in their stretch Mercedes directly back to the Carlton's beach.

Dede kissed George goodbye at the first-class flight lounge with his promise they would be together in five weeks in Toronto.

Two hours after the Eins left for North America, George, as he had told Dede, resumed the schedule he had postponed for twenty-seven days. He headed by prepaid Eurailpass, second-class coach to Switzerland.

∞

From the day George arrived in Toronto she dated him exclusively. The executive marketing job which she accepted at Ein Construction after her graduation from Ryerson filled her daylight hours.

George drew her into the hemisphere of politics, a part of the world previously unknown to her. Responding to his encouragement, she threw herself into the life within the extended family of a political constituency. She accompanied him to all the area association meetings and the gatherings he had to attend. She even, upon George's urging, threw a corn roast at Chesterton North for all the residents of Joe Bradley's riding. This was the first major function George had organized since his professional commitment to politics. She was pleased when Joe Bradley thanked George for arranging the affair and said, "In all my twenty years of politics, this was the best turnout for any constituency event I've attended. You sure were right, George," the veteran politician concluded, "big draw having it at this fabulous home."

Regardless of the pressure from Bradley to take him everywhere on the weekends he came to the riding, George never let this interfere with the family dinners the Eins asked him to attend.

George asked her to marry him on her twenty-third birthday. Wasn't he everything a girl would have wanted? He was intelligent, confident, worldly and the personification of charm; the indicia of a man who, her father never ceased telling her, "had a future." He had been good for her.

He made her feel desired again. She shone in his reflection. Others considered her more important now, sought out her advice and her company. Attracting a man with wit and charismatic good looks had given her a status she had never before enjoyed. George seemed devoted to her; he refused to leave her even for a weekend to visit his parents in Ottawa.

But she was unsure he loved her. Dede forced the doubt away. That feeling was no more than the residue of her insecurity after Tony.

She would make George a good wife. The wife an aspiring statesman required. After these four months, she knew exactly what was needed. She would be the perfect hostess, and with her polished private school manners court with him the power brokers. She would use her parents' connections to accelerate and smooth his career, use the cover of her restricted clubs and family money as a deceptive counterfoil for his ambition. She would even encourage her father to bankroll that critical first campaign for parliament, the one in which an unknown candidate like George would find it difficult to raise the cash without which, her father had often told her, a potentially attractive candidate's future was doomed. Her life was inextricably entwined with his. Somehow, her marriage seemed destined, as if it had been predetermined since that first afternoon on the Carlton's beach.

Eagerly, she accepted the unspoken terms and his proposal.

George gave her a one-and-a-half-carat pear-shaped diamond during a family dinner at the Rosedale Golf Club. The suggestion as to the stone's cut and size had come from Helen and Stanley Ein; the money for its purchase, George later told Dede, from the Talbot family's only pledgable asset, the cash surrender value of Mr. Talbot, Sr.'s life insurance policy. The ring was presented with no more spontaneity than could be expected from a carefully paced transaction, one which only required the transfer of an asset to bind its execution.

The engagement announcement received quite a different response from the one that had taken place over a similar dinner in Boston a little more than a year ago. Dede noticed that her father looked exceptionally pleased. She did not know if he was pleased for her or for himself. This was the type of son-in-law she knew he would welcome—a man who had a future and who needed his guidance.

"George is someone," he told Dede many times since the younger man had come to work for Bradley in Toronto, "who can be relied upon to feel gratitude." That meant a person who would appreciate her father's help and return his favors in kind. "George is a man," he had told Dede on many occasions, "who will listen to reason. A man who can be counted upon to come through for you." That translated into a man he could control.

It was an extravagant wedding, even by Ein standards. Held in March with that month's erratic weather, it was decided, for the convenience of the guests, to hold both the ceremony and the reception at the same location. The Confederation Ballroom of the Royal York Hotel was chosen, a place with both the luxury and the capacity necessary to accommodate eight hundred of the Eins' most intimate acquaintances and a representative sampling of the Talbot family.

Her mother brought an interior decorator up from New York to redesign the ballroom for the occasion. Not satisfied with the room's dark paneling and artificial lighting, she instructed him to make everything "airy." He lapped layers of cream French voile over the mahogany walls and replaced the standard brass sconces with gilded equivalents so ornately fashioned that they looked as if they might have been on loan from Versailles. The hotel's crested heavy china was set aside for the elegance of translucent Limoges.

The requisite mood was completed with greenery. The outdoors was transplanted inside: trees in pastel pots, plantings of spring flowers and branches of orchids. The designer ordered such an abundance of these that her father mused guests at nearby tables might never see each other.

Dede's wedding dress was a bonded model from France, delivered via the salon at Creeds—yards of tulle over French satin, embroidered sleeves and a short, oval train. Her father urged Dede to walk down the aisle slowly: "At the price that dress cost me, it's a thousand dollars a step."

The society orchestra, swelled to triple size to accommodate her mother's desire for continuous music, broke into a waltz after dessert was presented.

To the applause from politicians, developers, a sprinkling of relatives and the muffled clap of one hundred and fifty white-gloved hotel staff, Mr. and Mrs. George Talbot came to the floor for their first dance. They were joined by her parents and the Talbot, Srs., whom George had arranged to arrive one hour prior to the nuptials and to retire shortly after dinner.

C h a p t e r **13**

"*B*aby's dropped. It can be anytime now. Phone my service when you feel the first contraction," warned Dr. Sutton on her January 3 appointment. "Now remember, phone immediately. If we get that storm they've been predicting, we'll both need all the time we can to get to the hospital."

Dede had long ago given up driving, her figure too swollen to fit behind the wheel of a car. She had come by taxi, not wanting to bother George. She felt herself lucky to get a cab immediately, the wind and thickening gray sky the prelude to a winter storm.

About 3 a.m. she woke with pain. Then awareness of high wind and something pelting against the bedroom pane. Ice or freezing snow, she thought. She was not going out in that. She'd wait until morning.

The next spasm ended that resolve. She roused George. While she called the doctor's service and managed to dress between the increased bouts of pain, she heard George turn on the shower.

She went to the vestibule of their apartment. Without a chair and unable to bend, she balanced precariously against the wall and pulled on her leather boots, one by one. She stood there and waited for George. She heard the sounds of him still dressing in the other room. Then saw him cross to the study and meticulously reorganize his briefcase.

"Can't you leave that for now?" she pleaded.

"I want to have these files if Joe calls me from Ottawa."

George finally joined her at the door. He looked dressed to escort Joe Bradley to a formal dinner, not his wife to the delivery room of a hospital. She walked from the lobby of their Rosedale apartment into the brunt of the season's first storm. It was as if all the hostility of the winter had been saved and hurled without remorse in one brutal onslaught. Snow covered the walk, concealed the outline of the steps, converting them into a seventy degree hazardous slope. Sleet stung Dede's face, the exposed skin of her hands, and settled into her hair. Wind gusts pushed against her body as Dede inched forward hesitantly, trying to keep her footing. George supported her with one hand, his briefcase with the other. It took nearly fifteen minutes for her to reach the car.

Wind had swept snow high into the undercarriage of the Corvette. George scraped enough ice off the front window to allow a porthole of vision until the defrost could take over. He turned the starter. The engine clicked in, tires spun ominously and finally gained traction.

George moved the car into the deserted street. One unplowed street slid into another as they wove among the labyrinth of Rosedale's corridors. Snow swirled into the windshield, swiftly as a kaleidoscope, with them imprisoned at its vortex. It blanketed the glass too swiftly to be removed by the wipers. She was grateful when the maze wound downhill, emptied into the main thoroughfare of Avenue Road.

She finished her expedition to the hospital behind a University Avenue snowplow. Her involvement in reaching the hospital had temporarily anesthetized the pain. Now it was intense, as if taunting her for her earlier neglect.

The emergency room nurse clocked contractions at two-minute intervals. She wheeled Dede directly into the labor room.

The pain seemed too severe to handle. Everything was happening too rapidly. She could not bring herself under control. A woman's voice said, "You're hyperventilating. Breathe into this. Draw long breaths." A brown bag was placed over her mouth. "Good," Dede heard. The emotionless voice continued. "Dede, we're going to help you get yourself into the breathing routine you studied. Do it exactly as we taught you in the Lamaze classes. Go into stage five, the final stage."

"Final stage?" Dede asked when her present contraction subsided.

"Yes. You've cut it close. You've missed the earlier stages. You'll just have to wait until the next child to try those."

Dede was unable to appreciate the humor: she was in too much pain.

The woman took her hand. "Here we go now, Dede. Breathe . . . blow out . . . breathe . . . blow out. Rest between the contractions. . . . Your husband is going to take over now."

Dede felt the reassurance of George stroking her hand. Heard the click as he placed his stainless-steel watchband on the metallic tabletop. His soothing voice replaced that of the woman. Dede focused, as taught, on her breathing. She felt calmer.

The voice cut her concentration. "Dr. Sutton will be here shortly."

"He's not here yet?" she heard George ask.

"He'll be here shortly, Mr. Talbot," the nurse repeated curtly.

"Why isn't he here?"

The nurse hesitated, unable to avoid this issue a second time. "Dr. Sutton called in just before you got here. His car won't start and he's taking a cab. I'm sure he'll make it on time. He's never missed a delivery yet. In any case, we have a competent obstetrical resident on this floor. We're a teaching hospital, you know."

Dede lost her count. The next pain caught her off guard. Threw her again into hyperventilation. A brown bag clamped over her mouth, a clinical hand substituted for her husband's.

"Dede, we can't afford to have that happen again. If that occurs, we'll have to give you something."

"No. Nothing. No painkillers for my baby."

"All right, Dede. You can do it. I'll help you. Breathe one, two . . . blow out. Relax. You're doing well, Dede."

"Dr. Sutton just arrived," announced someone.

"Move her into the delivery room. Immediately."

"Which room?"

"Room four."

"Room four? You can't use that room," came back George's voice. "Any other room number, but not that one."

She heard whispering. It must be about the delivery, something pertaining to her condition. Dede strained to hear. The contractions were now stronger and coming one after the other. No rest time seemed possible at all.

"There's no other room. That's the only one that's been set up."

"That's impossible. There must be another delivery room ready."

"No, we're short-staffed tonight."

"She can't use that room."

"Why?" interjected some male voice. "Is this her request?" demanded the same person when her husband did not reply.

George would not respond to the challenge of the intern who had confronted him. He was not going to admit his superstition about the number four.

"We're wasting time we haven't got, Mr. Talbot. You have a choice. If you insist, we can prepare another room. To set it up will take at least twenty minutes. The baby's been ready for some time now. We'd have to further delay the birth. We've already held the baby back so Dr. Sutton could get here for the delivery. To wait any longer will certainly be more painful for the mother. It could put more stress on the fetus. What's it to be, Mr. Talbot?"

No one thought to consult Dede. They were talking all around her. She was merely the centerpiece.

"Another room," came back her husband's answer without hesitation.

"Mr. Talbot, are you sure this is what your wife wants? This is her first delivery."

"I'm quite aware of that. She must have a different room number," he said flatly.

Dede's bed was wheeled through a door into the middle of a room with glaring lights and metal surfaces. She was screaming uncontrollably, her breathing rhythm forgotten. Footsteps and voices filled the room. She involuntarily tore at the straps which held her onto the narrow aluminum table, rolled from side to side with the swift, sharp stabs.

The nurse's voice she had heard earlier in the night returned. Cool and detached, it continued as if no interval had lapsed between sentences. Dede grabbed at her words, the only stability in this endless, ghastly night. "Now breathe . . . blow out . . . breathe . . . blow out . . . breathe . . . blow out."

Another pain. Automatically, Dede seized the waist of this woman who stood beside her.

"That's all right, Dede. Squeeze me when the pain comes. Keep up the breathing . . . blow out. Breathe . . . blow out. . . . That's good, Dede."

"Is this full natural childbirth, like the peasants in the fields, or is it just my imagination?"

"Full natural childbirth," came Dr. Sutton's calm answer.

A sharper pain. Further down. Involuntarily, Dede started to push.

Dr. Sutton's voice commanded, "Don't push yet, Dede. We want to give you something for the delivery."

"A local. I know. Go ahead. . . . Quickly."

"No, an epidural. There doesn't seem to be a local here."

"I won't take it. It's not good for the baby." She had to pause to allow a contraction to subside. "We agreed no drugs. You promised. I took those breathing classes to avoid that." Pain ripped beneath her belly. The baby had no intention of waiting for them to debate the point.

"Dede, I'll have to make a small incision in the skin to allow the baby through. You've a big baby here. I've got to do an episiotomy. If not, this baby will rip you apart like an onion skin. To do the procedure, I need some form of anesthetic. I ordered a local, but I don't see it here. Seems to have gotten misplaced in the shuffle. You've done well with natural childbirth so far, but we've got to give you an epidural. There's no alternative now."

"It will affect the baby."

"No, the baby won't be affected. Dede, the anesthetist is on his way. I've already called him."

"I won't let you give me anything."

"Tell you what, Dede. If you're concerned about the epidural, I only have to wait five minutes from the time the freezing goes in before I make the small cut. That's the minimum time we need to get some benefit of the epidural. You're still going to have some pain, but this way there shouldn't be any drug effect on the baby. Now, roll onto your side, curl up into a fetal position as best you can. Don't move." A sharp jolt soon followed that phrase. "Now watch the clock."

She turned onto her back again. Her lower body grew numb. She watched each tick of the second hand until it drew into the one-minute mark and rotated four more times.

"I'm cutting now and I bet you can't feel a thing. . . . Okay, Dede. Now it's your turn. Push. Give me a big push. . . . Good. Now another one, just like that."

A moment after, she heard a baby's cry.

"You have a son." The doctor placed the small form on her stomach. "A strong, healthy, big boy. Congratulations. You did very well."

The room emptied. They left her on the table, holding a pink squirming newborn. A fragile, tiny life that she had already been unable to protect from the assault and precarious whims of the world. A nurse appeared and took the baby away from her. Two nurses transferred her to a stretcher.

"You had a lot of pain during your labor," one said to her. "Natural childbirth and then an epidural at the end. You did beautifully." As the nurses were leaving the room, through her exhausted, dazed state, she thought she overheard one say, "Can you imagine giving an epidural so late?"

She was wheeled upstairs to a private room on the maternity floor. George was waiting there.

"Thank you for my son, Dede."

"Did you see him?"

"Yes. Worn out from his big day, though. He's sleeping now. Something his mother should do too." George sat on her bed, kissed her forehead, then headed for the door. "I should let you sleep."

"Maybe just for a few minutes. I am tired. But if I do sleep, George, do you promise not to leave? I don't want to be alone."

"I won't leave."

"Promise? Sure?"

"Yes, I'll be right here in this chair. Go to sleep now, darling. You don't mind if I use the phone here, make some calls?" He brought his briefcase and chair closer to the telephone as he was completing the sentence.

"No, go ahead. Make sure you call my parents in Palm Beach."

"I already have."

"Call everyone else, then. I want everyone to know."

She heard him dial his office. Ask for his messages. Then Dede drifted into drugged semiconsciousness. She heard, as if from a distance, the vernacular of politics—talk of the constituency schedule, riding meetings, Bradley's agenda and the words "I'll be in shortly."

Dede woke with a start a half hour later to find the room empty. Both George and his briefcase were gone. A note in her husband's familiar handwriting was pinned to a nosegay of flowers on her nightstand.

Bradley's speaking to a House Committee. He needs me
immediately. Had no choice. Knew you would want me to go.
I'll phone from Ottawa.

> *All my love,*
> *George*

P.S. I saw our son. He is beautiful.

Dede's hand felt along the rim of the counter for the telephone that she recalled seeing there. She could not feel its outline. George, she now remembered, had been using it. Her arm groped further; other limbs did not follow. She fell, a dead weight, onto the damp linoleum floor. She could not get up: her legs were numb and without strength. Using her elbows and forearms to wedge herself toward the bed, she arched her upper body and grabbed, with both hands, for the plastic cord of the call buzzer. Its ribbed orange tubing ran futilely through her palms. Pinned to the middle of the bedsheet, the buzzer was still beyond her reach.

The door to her private room was closed. She did not have enough strength to make herself heard through it, only to release the tears that involuntarily streamed down her face, tears she had no will to wipe away. Fumes of freshly mopped disinfectant rose to nauseate her as she remained lying in its sticky wash.

On the shift change, two nurses found her there, chilled and despondent, hair wet with iced perspiration, matted as if the delivery had occurred only moments before. "You poor dear," one said to her as in unison they lifted her back onto the bed. "I told the young man that was here when we brought you up that it was dangerous to leave you alone until the anesthetic wore off. Lucky you didn't break anything, falling like that."

The flowers began to arrive a few hours later. Each additional presentation outdid its predecessor in creativity. Cut flowers in a ceramic holder with "It's a Boy" scripted in glazed blue lettering. A large planting set into a boat-shaped container. A chocolate wicker basket with a profusion of blue irises tumbling from each side. A cutting from an orchid branch. An enormous white mum, designed with pipe-cleaner eyes, nose and big blue bow to resemble a bunny's face.

The cards the nurses handed her bore the names of her parents' friends, the obligatory tokens in acknowledgment of the first Ein grandchild.

By nightfall, the room was pungent with floral scent. The dresser held two tiers of flowers, as did the recessed window siding. Nursing staff brought in spare tray tables to hold the overflow.

George did not telephone.

Around eight o'clock, Dede rang the call buzzer. She asked the nurse to remove all the flowers and to hand them out to anyone on the maternity floor with none of her own. "Give this away first," she said, reaching for George's nosegay at her bedside and, tearing his note off the crystal vase, pitched the message into a large green hospital pail. "Give this one to the mother who looks the loneliest."

Alice, the expensive professional baby nurse Dede had hired for two weeks to allow her to regain her strength after the delivery, stayed on indefinitely. This woman seemed the only one who could quiet Adam when he screamed with spasms of colic that erupted like clockwork precisely at eleven-thirty and lasted until dawn, the hours in which her husband required his sleep.

By the time this ailment had disappeared, Dede had come to rely on this woman for everything. She was best at ridding Adam of the large gas bubbles that plagued his gastric system long after Dede had nursed him. Alice knew how to make baby food from scratch—something Dede was not confident enough to do. She prepared daily his peas, beans, carrots and meat, refusing to use "those store-bought jars," condemning them as being "chock-full of unnecessary additives." Adam seemed more willing to accept foods introduced by her rather than by his mother. Dede noted Adam was generally more placid when left in Alice's care.

Why shouldn't she keep Alice? Thanks to her father's financial benevolence, his "baby gift" as he referred to it, money for this was not a problem. It was important for Adam to have unadulterated food. It would make him healthier, help him to grow better, probably enable him to gain that weight the pediatrician was forever asking her about. How could it possibly be detrimental to Adam's development to have someone look after his physical needs—prepare and give him solids, change and bathe him, soothe him the instant he woke. Someone who was more qualified to handle him than she considered herself to be in these areas. This external care, so vital to her son at this stage in his life, was only one aspect of his world. Dede would still provide the nurturing. She would continue to nurse Adam and never be away from home during his waking hours. She would be the one to play with him, wind the mobile that hung above his crib as he gurgled and reached to grab its elusive forms. And when Adam became a little older, she would take him everywhere with her. She would never inflict upon him the loneliness she had experienced in her childhood. With someone so small, whose function was to eat and sleep, it didn't matter if she temporarily handed over his bodily care into more competent hands.

Ten months after this decision, Dede entered the nursery at 2 a.m. to discover Alice putting unprescribed drops into her baby's mouth. Horrified, she realized that this woman's success with her son had been achieved by giving him regular nighttime doses of a strong liquid sedative.

After dismissing the nurse in the middle of the night, she took full control of Adam. She vowed never to entrust her son to anyone else's care again.

∽

George was collapsing the recently vacated metal chairs which had been brought into the church basement for the constituency's March meeting.

Dede and Joe Bradley were sitting side by side on two of the uncollected ones.

"George, come on over here, I want to talk to you. Bring yourself one of those legendary chocolate doughnuts they always send in for my speeches. Get yourself some coffee and sit down here." George pulled over one of the remaining freestanding chairs. "How do you think I did tonight?"

"Good, sir. You know that."

"No. I'm not so sure anymore. When you do this political bit for as long as I have, you get stale. Begin to repeat yourself."

"You didn't give this speech before. I checked specifically for that."

"I didn't mean the exact same speech. Not the same words. But the same content. . . . A person has to get stale."

"Everyone recycles ideas, Joe. That's not unusual."

"For a while now, I haven't thought my speeches were having the same punch as they used to."

"You're being too hard on yourself."

"You know, George, in Ottawa they say I'm getting a little long in the tooth."

"Not you, sir."

"I'm not getting any younger, George. It's not easy putting in the type of week I do in Ottawa, waiting in those Friday night crowds at the airport for a flight, working the riding on the weekends, then flying back to Ottawa Sunday night. Doing this week after week.

"You know, I've always told you, no matter how secure a politician thinks he is in a riding, he's still vulnerable. He can't afford to skip one constituent's function. That voter will never forgive you. So you have to go to them all. Every single damn one of them. Remember that rule, George, a politician is always vulnerable, no matter how popular he thinks he's become. . . . Besides, all this running begins to wear on you after a while. Even on me."

"I understand."

"I've done it sixteen years now. It's pension time, George. Time to pack it all in."

"You can't be serious, sir."

"Why so surprised, George? I told you that the first time you phoned from California and asked me for a job. Before I agreed to hire you, I told you this would probably be my last term. I'm sure you must have realized even an old warhorse like me couldn't go on forever."

"But you have so much yet to do. Things to accomplish."

"Even if I did, I'd never be able to get it through. I've been around politics too long not to realize if they don't make you a cabinet minister after two terms, they never will. At this stage, I'm nothing but an effective ward heeler. It's time for me to move on, George."

"I don't agree with you."

"I appreciate your loyalty, but my mind's made up. What I want from you now is to prepare a list of possible successors. I want the riding to pass into strong hands. For example, Mario Fellini, the alderman who represented this district for twelve years. The boundaries for his municipal ward are fairly close to our federal ones. He's a good possibility. Pulled the votes for four elections there with bigger wins each time. Strong ethnic ties, second-generation Italian. More Italians moving into the riding all the time, George. That influx was something that was beginning to worry me for my reelection even with my track record. Sound him out. See if he's interested in running as a Liberal.

"Then there's Peter Luellier, president of Imperial Oil. Hear he runs a tight ship over there. If he runs Imperial Oil, I'd say this man is already in politics, and probably survived the worst of it. Right, George? He'd be a strong candidate. He'd have no problem raising a healthy war chest. Big name in the city. On the boards of the Heart and Stroke Foundation, United Way, Hospital for Sick Children. Seems to get himself involved in all the high-profile charities. And gets good press for doing it. Has high name recognition. Know he's been a lifelong Grit. There's no trouble there. But speak to others in the riding, see how they feel about him. Maybe he's too establishment. May have too privileged an image for the ethnics.

"Then there's Joan Landon. Been on the airwaves for fifteen years now in that same rolling-home-time slot. A media phenomenon unto herself. Survived the fickleness of audiences. I hear from my advertising friends she even keeps increasing her audience-share ratio. Her pull straddles the whole community, ethnics and blue bloods. They feel it's her compassionate subject matter, the variety of people she profiles, the big names she manages to bring into that studio of hers, her warm voice, that everyone's-best-friend image. . . . No matter for us. All we need to know is if we get her, we'd overcome the ethnic factor and at the same time solidify our traditional base. She'd give us broad-spectrum appeal. She's got high visibility and credibility. But she'll be a tough cookie, George.

She prides herself on being apolitical. Don't know if we can rely on her to toe the party line once she hits Ottawa. Also, may be a hard sell to convince her if she's hung up on job security. Those media czars make it hard for journalists to return once they've been tainted with a party label. They don't like any appearance of biased reporting. You'll have to test the water, George. Maybe do it in stages. May take a fair bit of time, but she'd be worth it. That lady would be a hell of a vote getter.

"Can you think of anyone else? I can't."

Dede saw George's usually enigmatic face go scarlet. He looked stunned.

"Anyhow, if you do, feel free to add in anyone else's name you think I should consider. And, George, please try to make it as concise as possible. I don't expect another Ph.D. thesis like 'Emerging African States' or whatever it was you sent me to read from Stanford when you applied to run my constituency office. But do a thorough job, will you? I'm counting on you."

Joe Bradley, never known to be an astute judge of people, misread the emotion on her husband's face. "And, George, you don't need to worry, I'll give a good reference on you to whoever it is that succeeds me."

Joe Bradley left them and walked across the basement to pour himself another coffee. Dede saw the veins bulge on George's temple and neck. This was the first crack in his immutable mask that she had seen in the three years they had been married.

Bradley turned and faced George from a widened distance. "One more thing. Make me a list of what you think are my future career opportunities. For someone who is an unqualified expert in everything and knows everyone. And directorships, George, don't forget those, the ones with the healthy per diems."

Dede did not have to wait long to hear her husband's response. No sooner had they entered the privacy of their Rosedale apartment, and before she could make her nightly inspection of the nursery, than he said tersely, "It's time for me to make my move, Dede." He seemed unusually controlled for what had just taken place. "I've let this go on long enough. I've decided to bring this up with your father after Sunday dinner. I may need you to back me up. Will you do that for me, Dede?"

Dede understood the significance of what she had overheard that night. George had not told them the truth in Cannes. It was not Bradley who had sought out George; it was George who had persuaded Bradley to give him the influential constituency job, knowing full well how soon the sitting member would be retiring. "Positioning himself," as George would call it. Gaining Bradley's confidence, doing his bidding, encouraging the older man to become dependent on him, making it natural for Bradley to consider him as his successor. But Bradley had passed over him, treated him as being of no consequence. Not even given him the courtesy of rejecting his candidature. Humiliated him.

She would not let anyone humiliate her husband. Not the way she had allowed her father to do to Tony in Boston that summer. She would not let Bradley do that to George. Hadn't she worked as hard as George for Bradley? Hadn't she always worked alongside of George, helping him all the way? Of course she would support her husband.

George had not waited for her answer. By the time she thought to reply, George had already gone into the master bedroom, removed his sport jacket and shoes. The question for him had been purely rhetorical.

∽

It began as a typical dinner at her family's Forest Hill home: George chatting at one end of the table with her father while she, seated beside her mother with Adam between them in a high chair, alternately fed herself and a less than willing son. This meal she felt she looked more in need of a bib than did her one-year-old. She was splattered with squashed peas, carrots and bits of sticky, mashed chicken which had been tossed with slingshot accuracy by a cranky Adam. His gums were now pressed firmly together against the intrusion of the long silver spoon. He was resolute in his refusal.

When the adults at the table had completed the Cornish hen and soufflé, she considered this the opportune time to keep her promise to George. "Vera," she said to the Eins' long-standing housekeeper, "could you finish feeding Adam for Dede?" and asked her mother if she would supervise. She adjourned with George and her father to the library, exiting with the sentence that peaked mothers traditionally invoked to excuse such behavior in their offspring: "He's really no trouble. Adam's just a fussy eater."

Her father settled possessively behind his desk of smuggled contraband luxury confiscated from his bourgeois counterparts, the disenfranchised rich of Castro's Cuba. Enormous and ornate, with inlaid wood and bronze gargoyles, this piece of furniture dominated the study. George sat on the short cushioned sofa opposite. Dede slid the thick walnut-paneled doors shut and joined her husband on the sofa.

"Thought you'd like to know, sir, Joe Bradley spoke to me about retiring."

"About time too," her father said sarcastically.

Her husband did not become sidetracked. "He's asked me to draw up a list of potential successors. He's told me to put on people like Mario Fellini, the alderman, Peter Luellier, Imperial Oil's CEO, and Joan Landon, the broadcaster."

"What did he say about you, George?"

"I wasn't on the list."

"Not on the list?" her father repeated incredulously.

"He also asked me to make up a list of what I consider to be astute job or career opportunities for him. He's anxious for directorships. I believe the exact phrase that he used with us, didn't he, Dede, was anything with 'healthy per diems.' Guess he's not retiring so much as redefining his priorities."

"What do you expect me to do, George?"

"Nothing. I just thought you'd want to be kept informed. I remember you said in Cannes you had one plaza in his riding and another nearing completion. I thought this was information you'd like to have. I know how you try to keep on top of things where you have business interests."

"Quite astute, George. You show good judgment in bringing this to my attention."

George rose to leave. Her father remained, a contented look spread across his face.

"George, do you think you could win the riding? Assuming, of course, you got the nomination?"

"One hundred percent, sir." He addressed her father as he had in Cannes. "I know the riding cold. The polls, bus-stop locations, factories, all the community leaders. Single-handedly, I've organized every rally and every successful function Bradley's had over the past three years. I've increased the party's membership. I'm well known in the riding. I can win it. What I can't do, sir, is deal with a man like Bradley."

"I know Bradley's type. He's a tough son of a bitch, but easy to handle when you have the key. You're in my neck of the woods now. Leave it to me. . . . Dede, how would you like having your husband in parliament?"

George's gaze clamped down on her. Wasn't whatever was best for her husband best also for her, Adam and their marriage? Without a moment's hesitation, she answered, "That's our life, Daddy." Her father rose, the matter settled. "I'm not promising anything, but I wouldn't concern myself with Joe Bradley's successor list if I were you, George. I hate to see a smart man wasting his time when he has more important things to do. There is only one person Joe Bradley is going to find worth considering."

Dede heard her father hum happily to himself as he put his arm solicitously around his son-in-law and the two of them left the room. She noticed her father had the look, reminiscent of a picture in a pop-up storybook that she had shown Adam, of a wolf let loose to frolic in an opened chicken coop.

A major Toronto newspaper covered the nomination convention of Spadina Riding, the earliest selection process of its kind to be held in that city for the yet unannounced election. The press were eager for information on when the Prime Minister would bring his minority government back to the electorate and equally keen to learn what type of candidate the ruling Liberals would put forward in the next election at a time when their leader's popularity was sagging. A dearth of more controversial information elevated what should have been a local news story to the editorial page. It appeared under the caption:

THE CHANGING OF THE GUARD—OR IS IT?

Last night the Grits came out in full force. 1,200 of the party faithful trooped into Harbord Collegiate to pay homage to an old veteran and pick a new warrior in Spadina Riding, a bastion of Liberal support since the affable Joe Bradley captured it 16 years ago.

His baton passed last night surprisingly uncontested, despite the pundits' predictions that this riding would produce a hotly contested fight. The party leadership under Joe Bradley's firm stewardship put in nomination only one name. An anonymous source from the Association's hierarchy said the young candidate, George Talbot, was Joe Bradley's choice, foisted on a less than enthusiastic executive.

In an unusual, but not unprecedented move for an outgoing member, Joe Bradley, victor of four elections, gave the nomination speech himself. Mr. Bradley referred to Mr. Talbot as "brilliant and forward-thinking." He called Mr. Talbot's candidature "a sign of the new breed of Liberals—young, committed and with the vitality to move the party into the eighties."

Spadina Riding conducted a coronation last night, not an election. It was the proverbial "laying on of hands" for a handsome, debonair, unruffled and totally inexperienced heir.

This pundit predicts the Conservatives and NDP will nominate strong candidates in an effort to break the Liberals' 20-year domination of this key riding. We doubt that Joe Bradley can pass his seat so easily to his chosen heir.

On page three of that day's business section a less obtrusive item appeared. It announced the appointment of Joe Bradley as a special government public relations consultant for Ein Construction. It enumerated his directorships to date, three in number. All of them were wholly owned downstream subsidiaries of Ein Construction, the corporate names of which had been carefully selected not to reveal to an unsophisticated public any affiliation with the Ein Group of companies.

The well-attended nomination meeting failed to attract an avalanche of supporters. The handful who did offer help were mostly the elderly and the riding executive. These workers were looked upon by George warily as being "party loyal" not "candidate committed" and as such, he told her father, not a reliable source to form the nucleus of a winning organization.

Two weeks later, the volunteers from the local Liberal youth wing, the ones George had once led and had predicted would join his campaign, had still not come forward. The absence of these, he explained to his father-in-law, was due to the unflattering press coverage.

George countered with high-priced political mercenaries. He joined those who journeyed downtown for the spring sport season; he went to see those who played hardball. He gained the commitment of John Ambros, a top election mechanic, with a personal visit and a handshake containing a check from Ein Enterprises.

John in turn got Rudolph Consultants to agree to accept George into their fold. This top Grit political advertising firm was credited with the successful marketing of major Liberal candidates. Together these professionals devised the strategy to convince the electorate to choose Talbot to represent them in parliament. They created the image, literature, physical appearance, sell line; they selected and staged the events George would attend.

The only staff position integral to every election which George did not have to fill was that of finance chairman. Dede's father and his business associates made this usually critical position unnecessary.

The location of the committee room was chosen by Ambros for its broad window exposure and high traffic count. Its size was spacious enough to satisfy the paid staff who had to be hired to augment their traditional volunteer counterparts. From his glassed-in command post and adjacent conference room, Ambros kept an eye on every aspect of his tightly knit organization.

Dede worked from 8 a.m. until 6 p.m. in the common area at the front of the campaign office where the volunteers gathered. It was expected, George said, for the candidate's wife always to be visible, encouraging those workers to put in longer hours, lauding their efforts, making them feel welcome and appreciated, listening compassionately to their polling experiences, the praise and the complaints they siphoned back. This function, George told Dede, could not be delegated.

Dede complained she had to spend the full day away from Adam doing little more than gratuitous hand-holding. George responded by assigning to her the title Cordiality Hostess and reiterated that her role could not be subsumed by a professional. Any of her slack time, he said, could be filled with handling requests for lawn signs, registration complaints or looking up phone numbers for use by the poll captains on election day.

At six o'clock, Dede accompanied George on his nightly round of door knocking.

Dede refused to consider leaving Adam with a baby nurse or a self-described nanny. Her experience with Alice fueled a resolve to take Adam everywhere with her despite the inconvenience to herself or her son. Her conviction never to let him know the loneliness that she had experienced in her childhood remained unshaken. If the campaign necessitated her full-time attendance, it also required the same of Adam. She moved into the committee room laden with the entourage that accompanies a toddler—playpen, high chair, stroller, portable crib, jolly jumper, assorted baby-food jars, warming dish—and set up a play area for him near her desk.

"What do you think we're running here, a nursery?" she heard John Ambros say to her husband a few days later. "My people will never put up with this." George asked her to move Adam to a less conspicuous spot. Adam and his things were relocated behind the supply partition at the rear of the room, away from the comings and goings of campaign workers, curious constituents and her attentive vigilance. Dede found herself dependent on the kindness of one of the back-room staff to inform her when her son required to be changed or had woken up, eyes mischievous and bright, eager to play.

Having Adam there presented difficulties. It was not easy to keep her son's utensils and plates separate from the coffee mugs and cutlery discarded near the sink by the staff. The self-contained room had no facility to warm up, wash or prepare his food. Dede overcame the latter inadequacy by opening fresh jars of baby food for each feeding. Despite endless pleading and ultimately, in frustration, a stenciled sign posted on her son's playpen, she would find Adam gagging on what suspiciously looked like bits of stale doughnuts or dried pizza crusts—treats from well-meaning workers—the residue of fast food that abounded in constituency workrooms.

Dede would seclude herself behind the partition to feed Adam, but often was interrupted by an impatient constituent who demanded immediate gratification and would only be satisfied receiving it from the candidate's wife. At such times, Dede would shift Adam into her arms and carry him with her while she dispatched the intruder as quickly as possible.

Before Dede left to go with George on the evening's canvass, she had Vera come to pick up Adam, take him home and put him to bed.

Dede was satisfied she had achieved her most important goal, to have her son with her as much as possible. To let him know he was loved.

The editorial writer's prediction proved correct. Neither the Tories nor the New Democrats were prepared to forfeit the riding. Both opposition parties analyzed it was possible with a hitherto unknown Liberal candidate to wrestle Spadina Riding from the Grits' control.

Wedged between these contenders, Rudolph Consultants carefully drew George's political image. To counter Kingsley's strength of thirty years of political experience compared with George's lack of elected office, they presented their man as not just a politician but someone with a track record for idealism and statesmanlike thinking. They drew upon Talbot's doctoral thesis, "Forms of Government for Emerging African Countries," as evidence of his commitment to aid underdeveloped areas and his understanding of his country's role in a larger community of nations. George's Ph.D. from Stanford was juxtaposed against Kingsley's high school diploma and Simon MacGrugen's well-meaning but unsubstantiated sincerity.

Kingsley's record for being a friend of underprivileged minorities and the disadvantaged, with his Head Start program, which had crowned his administration as mayor, was blunted through pamphlet photos showing Talbot among the faces of immigrants he had helped reunite with their Canadian relatives and through radio endorsements from some elderly constituents on whose behalf he had petitioned Ottawa to secure their disability pensions. All of these activities had been initiated and concluded under Joe Bradley's aegis but were now unequivocally claimed as George's personal accomplishments.

Sensing the start of the youth-worship decade, they attacked Kingsley's age vulnerability with the phrase "yesterday's man." In contrast they played up Talbot's energy, labeling the handsome, charismatic candidate as "tomorrow's man" with "the vitality and dynamism required to give this riding a significant voice in Ottawa."

Assessing his appearance as one of his most salable features, they renovated his physical image. George's tortoiseshell glasses were replaced by soft contact lenses. The sandy tuft that, when he spoke passionately, tumbled lazily over his forehead and was brushed carelessly away, was now to be professionally groomed and sprayed before any encounter with the public—an all-candidates meeting and even the daily door-knocking ritual. Starched white shirts, gray pinstripes and black oxfords were substituted for George's preferred pastel button-downs, sport jackets and loafers. When his rich debating voice was added to his redesigned appearance, he became the product the literature promised.

The candidate was delivered to the electorate in glossy pamphlets, leaflets that were sent by special householder mailings or that were thrust in pedestrians' hands at targeted locations, and through the speeches his writers had psychologically crafted.

The "spin" the consultants devised was of a dedicated, highly motivated, brilliant young man. A Canadian Kennedy. Preferably, unhandicapped by the stigma of wealth. To mask his in-laws' fortune, John Ambros stipulated that Stanley Ein was not to be given an opportunity to flaunt his connection with the candidate. He was not in any way to be visibly associated with the campaign: never allowed at any function or even permitted inside the committee room.

Three weeks before the nation voted, the same paper which had covered George's nomination profiled Spadina Riding. Their sample polling devastated the candidacy of George Talbot. They predicted an easy walkthrough for the Conservatives' Benson Kingsley, giving him an eight percent lead, their figures, of course, subject to the usual two percent margin of error.

Unfazed, the Talbot campaign implemented their plan, a strategy formulated months earlier by Rudolph Consultants in their St. Clair Avenue offices and timetabled for delivery during what Ambros called "the decisive twenty-one days." They attacked, using the full arsenal of an unlimited war chest.

Fresh mailers were hand-delivered by paid workers to every home in the riding three times a week. A cassette tape labeled "George Talbot Speaks on Your Future" had been scripted by Ambros himself and was performed with sincerity after media coaching of the candidate. It also contained well-edited passages from previous all-candidates meetings, each selected to show Talbot's command of the issues in contrast to the less than stellar performances excerpted from his rivals. This tape was distributed by a second team of paid workers under instructions to make sure it was placed directly into a voter's hands. The candidate also handed these out personally at subway stops and factory walk-throughs.

A well-publicized open bar became the norm, sponsored by the Friends of Talbot Committee, an unofficial organization funded by Ein Enterprises. This bought for George's speeches the widest possible media and public exposure during these critical days of the campaign. Pizza and beer in the committee room helped recruit and reward youth workers after the two exhausting blitzes of the riding that definitively identified the Talbot vote for Ambros' professional crew on election day.

On a tour of all the Toronto constituencies, Pierre Elliott Trudeau made a brief stop at Talbot headquarters to wish the candidate well. This photo opportunity was caught by the professional cameraman permanently assigned by Ambros to cover George's candid moments with the electorate. The final piece of literature of the Talbot campaign featured a picture of George and the prime minister above the caption: "I want this man in my government."

Every maneuver to this point had been in preparation for election day. Nearing this date, the Ambros machine locked into high gear to pull out the vote: to ensure that every confirmed Talbot voter and the undecided who were leaning toward George, as had been previously identified through door-to-door and telephone canvasses, cast their ballot. Professional telephone callers prodded those people at intervals throughout the polling hours to go to vote. Their numbers were augmented during the crucial five-to-eight time slot, the hours most people could be counted on to be at home. A steady line of taxis remained from 8 a.m. outside Talbot headquarters. These cabs, in addition to the service normally extended to the elderly and the solicited requests, provided a free ride to anyone targeted through these calls who might accept a lift to go to the polls. Nannies waited at the committee room and were driven to relieve homebound mothers in the brief interval it took to make the round trip to vote. This special group, Ambros' research revealed, were predisposed to support George, seeing in him, also a new parent, an identity of interest.

Outside poll captains were issued sweatshirts with "Talbot Campaign" blazoned in large red letters upon them, cleverly circumventing regulations which prohibited advertising near the polling stations on election day. Those who still had not voted by six o'clock were visited by a pair of veterans of previous Ambros-run campaigns and cajoled into leaving dinner and going immediately with this team to the polls.

For Pierre Elliott Trudeau, election night, July 8, was a reaffirmation. For George at ten-thirty at the Inn on the Park, where three other Liberal candidates were also holding their receptions, it was a precarious evening. As winners were declared elsewhere, election groupies and party loyalists gravitated to the Talbot party, which offered the only remaining undecided contest in the hotel—and was also rumored to have the best food. These people milled about ravaging extravagant platters of smoked salmon, roast beef and turkey, and consuming volumes of liquor. Tallies were being phoned in from the polls by on-site workers and transcribed onto an oversized blackboard elevated on a podium at the front of the room. With more than half the vote counted, Kingsley was leading her husband by six hundred votes.

At 11:15 p.m. the pivotal polls started to report in, the ones which Ambros had targeted for an additional Sunday door-to-door swing through the riding by the candidate's family—George and Dede and, in a stroller, baby Adam. Ambros rushed these returns to George. When George received them, he did not relay these, like the previous ones, to his assistant at the blackboard. Instead, he brought Dede and Adam with him onto the platform. He had personally selected Dede's outfit: a simple cotton suit with a corsage pinned to the lapel. George stepped back, giving his wife central position. He insisted she transcribe for those in attendance these key figures. Fifteen minutes later, when the largest of these polls reported in, Dede chalked the numbers that put her husband over the top.

George, with Adam in one arm, took Dede's hand and lifted it in victory. The signal had been given. Balloons tumbled from their netting; streamers zigzagged across the room; whistles went wild. Champagne gushed from oversized bottles. "Happy Days Are Here Again" spat from trumpets and horns in a ragtime rendition.

It didn't matter that George had reduced the vote in Spadina Riding to its lowest Liberal plurality in forty years in an election that conversely saw his party and its leader returned with an even greater percentage of the popular vote. Nor that a national paper in a column entitled "Campaign Postscript" reported that the Talbot campaign spent three times more than had previously been spent by any other candidate across the country. It cited these excesses as unabashed vote buying, an abuse which soon after this election was made illegal. But the public, in typical post-election lassitude, promptly forgot which candidate had most flagrantly violated the spirit of the incoming legislation.

∽

Dede wanted to be present to see George participate in the pageant of the Speech from the Throne, which was to be his first day sitting as a member of parliament. He told her he would leave for her, on the kitchen counter of his Bronson Avenue bachelor apartment, the one guest ticket which he had been allocated as an MP.

George had encouraged Dede not to break up their Rosedale apartment and move the family to Ottawa. As a new member of the House, he was sure he would be occupied every night, either working or meeting with his colleagues. She would find she had become a parliamentary widow. He felt she would be happier remaining in familiar surroundings and in the same city as her parents and friends. She and Adam would be able to visit him, he said, as often as they wished, courtesy of the airline pass the government issued to spouses of members.

For Dede, this was going to be the first of such visits. She was taking Adam with her, as she did everywhere. Grandma Talbot in Ottawa had told her she would gladly babysit her grandson during the ceremony. Dede prided herself that, since Alice's abrupt dismissal, she had never left him behind regardless of any inconvenience to herself.

That muggy September Tuesday, Dede packed two bags for her Ottawa overnight. A small case for herself, which contained the crimson suit, eyelet organdy blouse and floppy-brimmed matching hat, the ensemble which she planned to wear at the ceremony in the Senate chamber, a green cocktail dress for evening and her nightclothes. A larger one held Adam's necessities: two dressy outfits, five sleepers, diapers, crib sheets, extension bars for the rental crib she had ordered for the Bronson apartment, the Busy Box he played with to put himself to sleep, his chunky Fisher-Price family, mud-brown teddy bear and a two-day supply of baby food.

She jockeyed the luggage into the car, collapsed his stroller into the trunk, strapped Adam into his car seat and headed west on Highway 401. At the airport, she unloaded at curbside, placed the car in the terminal parking structure, snapped together the stroller, then rushed herself and Adam to the Rapid Air Counter at Terminal Two. She completed all this in time to make an earlier shuttle than the one on which she had been scheduled.

The short flight was a difficult one. The air conditioning on the plane malfunctioned. Within moments of being sealed in the aircraft perspiration appeared on Adam's forehead and his pudgy arms grew sticky. Dede removed his white boots, socks and the light jacket she had brought in anticipation of a normally chilly aircraft. She still could not make him comfortable. He was becoming increasingly irritable. At the Ottawa airport it took her three trips to transfer her bags from the conveyor belt to the Blue Line cab stand, each undertaken with a cranky Adam hoisted against her body. She had told George not to meet them, knowing he was involved all day in parliamentary matters.

She had the taxi stop at the apartment and remain, meter ticking, to ensure she could proceed without delay as soon as Adam was settled. The driver hauled the bags and stroller up the stairs; she followed behind carrying a drowsy son.

She phoned Grandma Talbot in Vanier to tell her they had arrived earlier than expected. Dede constructed the crib, set in its mattress and completed it with sheets, extension sides and toys. She put her son within its secured sides. She changed hurriedly into her red outfit—then went into the kitchen to get the ticket. It was not on the counter or anywhere else in the apartment. Dede phoned George's parliamentary office. He had not yet hired a permanent secretary. The temporary had no idea where George or the ticket were. She told Dede they were now distributing the remaining seats on a first come, first served basis at the Center Block of the House of Commons.

Dede took Adam's blue sailor suit from his suitcase, switched him into it while he lay there, unprotesting, weary from his travels. She could not delay any longer for Mrs. Talbot or else she might not be able to get a seat. Why come all this distance and miss everything? Anyhow, it would be nice for Adam someday to be able to say he had attended his father's first Throne Speech. And how pleased George will be when he finds out his son was there.

She scooped a sleepy Adam into her arms, hastened downstairs and into the cab.

All remaining seats had been distributed when she reached the parliament buildings. Dede gained access to the upstairs North Gallery behind a tardy journalist. She shifted Adam onto one hip and with him thus camouflaged walked up the back steps under the gaze of a less than diligent guard. She slid into a vacant seat in the fifth and last row of the gallery as the procession was commencing. As she settled, she readjusted her red suit and hat, colors acutely noticeable among the somber tones worn by the dignitaries. Television cameras tucked into the corners of the Senate on the side of the chamber opposite to her were tracking the proceedings.

She propped Adam up on her lap in order that he could see better. The Gentleman Usher of the Black Rod, in his formal black jacket dipping into calf length at the back, was followed by a sergeant at arms, the Speaker of the House, clerks attired in black official robes and finally the members of parliament, George among them.

The pageantry over, Governor-General Jules Léger began the Throne Speech. Its text contained the government's stated plans for the upcoming session of parliament. It was difficult for her to see Her Majesty's representative. She was sitting at the rear of the third balcony, directly above the place the governor-general was reading. She felt detached from what was transpiring on the floor below her. She overheard someone whisper that the speech was scheduled to run forty-five to fifty minutes. He had only begun, and already she was finding it difficult to concentrate. The monotony of his delivery, the rhythm of the repetitive phrasing, the drone of a prepared script, the stifling heat and the closeness of the air from the height of her last-row gallery seat conspired as a sedative after her frantic day. She shut her eyes, confident no one would see her.

Adam had already fallen asleep. He snuggled contentedly against her. The slow, even draw of his breath further relaxed her. Her body slid deeper into the chair; her hat drooped over her face. She, like her son in her arms, dozed in half-sleep.

The eleven o'clock network news that went coast to coast that night excerpted, as expected, highlights from the Throne Speech. It concluded its segment with a lingering shot of a sleeping woman in a red suit and floppy, wide-brimmed hat, holding across her lap a similarly reposed child. The voice-over of the Ottawa correspondent said, "Not everyone found the program proposed today by the Trudeau majority stimulating. Not even among those nearest to them. Even at this initial stage, it put one member of parliament's wife and child to sleep." The media, exhibiting uncharacteristic charitable restraint, did not identify which particular member's family.

Chapter **14**

Dede's life in the period after George's election splintered into two identifiable parts. Time-heavy weekdays without George bridged by late-night calls and then, when he returned to the riding on the weekend, tightly scheduled togetherness Joe Bradley style—a frenetic round of constituency parties, ribbon cuttings, bar mitzvahs, christenings, weddings, riding functions and the inviolate dinner with the Eins. Neither provided Dede with companionship or Adam with a father.

She gave birth to her second son on a Tuesday, a year into George's term in parliament. George had not returned from Ottawa to be with her, even though she had let his East Block office know before she left for the hospital. He had given his third speech in parliament that afternoon. "A blockbuster," he said when he telephoned after the delivery. His absence, he explained, had been unavoidable, but he would see both her and his new son on Friday night. He would be on the first plane for Toronto after the House rose for the weekend.

This time Dede kept all the flowers. Most were sent from constituents and political acquaintances. She felt she had earned them.

Two months after Michael's birth, she moved them out of their Rosedale apartment and into a house in the same neighborhood. Uncertain of George's help at any time now, she felt it better to move before winter, rather than delay until parliament broke for Christmas.

The place offered the features Dede had been looking for. The five-bedroom, three-story house was a center-hall plan with the master suite overlooking a ravine and it seemed designed for a family of boys: it had numerous nooks and crannies, funny-shaped geometric areas, secluded spots where they could go to play and never be found by an adult. It was apparent that every aspect of the house had been carefully considered. There even was a pull ladder tucked against the third-floor ceiling that allowed trapdoor access to the roof. A good example of the architectural thoroughness of the 1920s, Dede told Adam when they had explored the attic together.

Dede renovated and decorated the house with only minimal consultation with her husband. This was in accordance with George's wishes. His involvement in other family-related matters similarly was limited. His concentration, he told Dede, simply could not be distracted from his work.

Whether to personally show support for his leader's policy on multiculturalism or primarily due to the ethnic composition of his riding, her husband crammed his hours with language immersion. George took Italian lessons to make himself, in Ambros' words, "more palatable" in future elections to those voters who, as had been predicted, proved to be George's soft underbelly in the campaign. He worked on becoming similarly conversant in Portuguese, after noting the trend for recent immigrants from the Azores to settle in the city's core. Conversational French he studied with a government-provided tutor for an hour each morning in order to become bilingual. "To position myself," he said. This familiar phrase, Dede knew, signaled his next ambition—a cabinet portfolio—a goal lightly camouflaged by the caveat: "Just in case the prime minister should require me."

The next election promised to be an easier one for her husband. The Conservatives and the NDP seemed reconciled to have Spadina Riding remain Liberal: they both placed their stronger candidates and big money elsewhere. Ein Construction again bankrolled the Talbot campaign. This time, however, it was augmented by contributions from traditional Liberal corporate sources.

On the final weekend before the Tuesday election, a published Gallup poll revealed that the Liberals and Conservatives were deadlocked nationally in popular support—each party had 37.5 percent of the decided vote.

But George had worked hard in the past five years to solidify his base and reach out to new supporters. He spoke the language fluently of whatever constituent's home he entered—Italian, Portuguese or English. The electorate replied with appreciation and eliminated the unarticulated ethnic factor; they rewarded him with their votes.

"Clark scores minority victory," read the headlines in the *Winnipeg Free Press* the next morning as Joe Clark's Conservatives won 136 seats to fall short of a 142-seat majority and the Liberals dropped to 114 members. "With the class that has always marked his best performances, Prime Minister Trudeau turned over the reins of office to Conservative leader Joe Clark after conceding election defeat at 1 a.m. today."

George's win was impressive, especially viewed against the national trend. For him, it was a reversal of the previous election. He doubled his plurality in a scenario that saw his own party disappear into official opposition.

In the political reality of a minority government, every Grit seat and every member became important. It allowed George the window of recognition for which he had been preparing.

When George came home the first weekend after Parliament reconvened, Dede saw he could hardly contain his exhilaration. He hurried her upstairs to the bedroom and conspiratorially shut the door.

"They've noticed me." He paused. His right hand made tight demiarcs, a mannerism he had when, speaking without notes, he searched for the most effective way to introduce a topic. "Dede, I was invited for lunch by a highly placed senator. They call him 'the Rainmaker.' . . . Well, he took me to lunch by myself. I sat at his corner table at the Four Seasons. Do you know the hotel keeps a table permanently reserved for him?" As he spoke, he excitedly paced the length of the bedroom. "He told me they'd been keeping an eye on me. They saw how I built my vote. And he told me straight out—they wanted me to be one of the group to rebuild the party. . . . The senator knew a lot more about me than I figured. He was really impressed with how I turned around my riding. And he says I did exactly what he would have done to woo the ethnic votes. He says there are thirty to fifty other seats out there that can be had with a good multiculturalism policy. And I forgot to tell you the best part: I'm definitely going to be appointed to the shadow cabinet." He sat down beside her on the blue chintz love seat and took her hands. "Well, what do you think?" Dede saw George's animation. Heard excitement percolate through his voice. She enjoyed the intimacy of being his confidante. He gave her no time to applaud. "This is our chance, Dede. Clark can't last a full term. The NDP can bring them down at will. Trudeau needs every vote he's got. The people around him will be watching to gauge who the loyalists are, who's prepared to go the furthest to rekindle the party's support. The senator told me as much. . . . When Clark goes, Trudeau will reward those who have been the most faithful during his interregnum. Dede, I intend to be one of those people." He dropped her hands, stood up and, with his back to her, looked out the picture window and across the ravine. Without returning to face her, he completed his thoughts. "The senator made a big point, Dede, that I was a good family man with a capable wife. . . . Apparently, he'd heard a lot about you from the Ontario organizers and everything you did for the last two elections."

"What are you asking me to do, George?" She should have realized it was uncharacteristic of George to confide anything. Dede had begun to understand the workings of her husband's mind. He never gave out extraneous, personal information without a purpose.

"I want you to come to Ottawa more often."

"Why, George?"

"To be with me. We will be attending functions like we did in the Joe Bradley days. Work the room together. You should get to know the wives of the other members. And the press corps. Also, get involved at headquarters at the social end of the policy conferences we're going to be initiating. Network. Encourage more women to become involved in the party. . . . Well, how does this sound to you?"

Dede was speechless.

"I realize you don't like to leave the boys. Don't worry, we'll work something out." He returned to her side, put an arm around the back of the two-seat sofa which contained her and, facing her, said with urgency, "Dede, I need Trudeau to notice me. And the boys around him, they're going to be watching how I perform. . . . I need to be more visible." Self-consciously, his hand moved to push back the hair from his forehead. It was a superfluous act. His hair, sprayed in place, could not possibly have tumbled into his face. The election over, he still retained the lessons it had taught. He concluded with what was for her his most disarming appeal. "Dede, you're the only person who can help me."

She was flattered and delighted. For a long time now, she had felt excluded from George's life—isolated and unnecessary. She had missed being needed by him, missed him and the glamour that surrounded him. And regardless of the pretext he had given her, she knew he missed her.

She had no idea how she would manage, but she would go to Ottawa whenever he required. They would be a team, as they had been in Toronto, and work Ottawa as effectively as they had the Spadina constituency. She had not let him down before, she would not let him down now. He could rely on her as usual.

∽

When the House resumed after the summer recess, the schedule George set for Dede necessitated her attendance in the capital at least three days a week. With Adam entering grade two and Michael in junior kindergarten,

Dede felt it unwise to disrupt their routine. Overcoming her reluctance, she decided to hire a housekeeper.

George considered this an opportunity to demonstrate his support for the ethnic population he represented and urged her to employ a recently arrived immigrant. He told her if there was any difficulty in communicating it could quickly be resolved with a call to the multilingual member of George's constituency staff or, if not urgent, await his return.

Although she acceded to his wish and hired Maria, an Italian girl with a ready smile and a willing nature, Dede felt uncomfortable with the situation. Maria's sweet disposition and efficient management of the house could not overcome the artificial barrier of language. Dede did not know how to deal with the frustration that built in the articulate seven-year-old Adam and to a lesser extent in his younger, less verbal brother. Adam would chatter to this young woman only to receive no response. When his questions remained unanswered and his demands unfulfilled no matter how often they were repeated by him, Adam could not be appeased by Maria's hugs. He would scream and throw his toys. He became in stages angry and then, seeing the anger was to no avail, sullen and withdrawn.

Maria had been in their employ for almost a month before Dede realized how distressing this situation had become for her son. Late in October, she arrived home on an earlier than usual flight. Michael was sitting on the counter in the kitchen, singing happily to himself while Maria prepared the vegetables. Adam was nowhere to be seen.

When she asked Maria, *"Dove ne, Adam?"* the young woman led her to the third floor. Upon entering the room, Maria called out to Adam. There was no reply. Although it was four-thirty, the room held only the half-light of winter. Dede searched through the irregular-shaped compartments that comprised the attic.

She found her son with his face pressed to the wall behind a stack of packing crates. When he saw his mother, he abandoned his hiding place. He leapt into her arms, his spindle legs locked around her waist, and refused to release her. He buried his face into her shoulder, clinging to her ferociously.

It was in this manner she carried Adam down from the attic and conducted her conversation with the constituency office. Dede unraveled the explanation for Adam's behavior after a tedious translation process. She now fully comprehended the magnitude of the problem.

But it was already late October. The Ottawa social scene was in full operation. She did not have the luxury of time to remain at her Rosedale home and train help. And what guarantee was there that a new person would not present a different and perhaps more serious problem? The devil you know is better than the devil you don't know was a philosophy to which she subscribed. Dede let the arrangement stand.

She chose to handle her son's exasperation by explanation. Despite her constant reassurance that Maria's unresponsiveness to his conversation and requests was due to the housekeeper's lack of facility with the language and not of her own volition, her eldest remained unconvinced—especially when, in his father's presence, Maria seemed able to understand everything.

Dede's week was closely scheduled. She would wait for Maria to return from her time off and then, already dressed for a reception, take the dinner flight to Ottawa, stop at the Bronson Avenue apartment to drop off any additional suitcases she had brought, then meet George at the first in his series of functions.

Her daytime hours had now become as tightly clocked as her evenings. In mid-September, she had begun as an assistant on official caucus functions. As George had anticipated, her flair for creative entertaining did not go unnoticed. Members and their staff appreciated her passion for detail, the calligraphy invitations that became the signature of a Dede Talbot-organized function, the distinctively wrapped favor each guest took away as a memory of the event.

Trudeau's chief of staff acknowledged Dede's preeminence as their most capable party giver. He requested that she organize, with a select committee of members' wives, the December 13 Liberal Christmas party. This was, unquestionably for her, the most prestigious function that she had been assigned to date.

Dede deliberated every aspect of the evening, checking each thoroughly with the leader's office. Whether to retain the party's traditionally used orchestra or move to a more "with it" group. Would she offend the sensibilities of her older guests? Whether to serve the customary hors d'oeuvres passed by tuxedoed waiters with silver trays or have trolleys of sushi, and have these wheeled by their Japanese creators in kimonos. Would this be considered too flashy and unorthodox for the establishment? Whether, except for the head table, to allow open seating. Color of cloth, style of calligraphy, wall decorations and choice of favor mired her in a similar dilemma of detail that consumed her time.

On Wednesday, November 21, less than three weeks before her Christmas reception, Ottawa was jolted from its usual staid complacency with the news that Trudeau was quitting. "Pierre Elliott Trudeau, who towered over Canadian politics for more than a decade, stunned his own party and even some close advisers by announcing that he was stepping down as Liberal leader," ran *The Globe and Mail's* front-page story. "He will ask its national executive, meeting in Ottawa this weekend, to call a leadership convention for March."

An editorial in the same paper analyzed the Liberals' precarious position in the wake of Trudeau's resignation, concluding the Liberal party to be in a state of leadership "poverty."

> How can a party be healthy when it has been reduced to opposition after 16 unbroken years in government, when it has only 3 federal MPs west of Ontario, when it holds power in none of the 10 provinces and when it has no commanding figures ready to lead it?
>
> The abruptness of Mr. Trudeau's departure makes it almost impossible for an unknown to establish himself in time to make a real run for the leadership.

Conservative strategists viewed this lame-duck period as the opportune time to introduce their first budget in sixteen years: the Liberals, leaderless and in disarray, pending the choice of Trudeau's successor, would not possibly choose this moment to bring down the government. They would not force a general election before their leadership convention. On Tuesday, December 11, John Crosbie, the droll finance minister from Newfoundland, standing in the House of Commons in Labrador mukluks in keeping with the tradition of wearing new shoes when bringing in a budget, tabled what was considered to be a draconian, belt-tightening budget.

Working against her deadline, Dede was grateful she had fewer functions to distract her than was usual at this season. George was tied up in the House long hours, as were other opposition members, preparing for the debate spawned by the motion of nonconfidence which customarily followed every major government initiative.

Dede was determined that her Christmas party would be a success, both for herself and for George. She would be able to deliver to George the visibility he had asked her eight months ago to help him achieve. More importantly, she would provide him with access to the outgoing leader. As organizer of the event, she was given the honor of being placed with her spouse at the head table. When assigning the specific seating for that table, she put her husband next to Trudeau, guaranteeing this placement through the use of name cards.

George had always said that all he needed was five minutes to sell himself to anyone. He would have the time span of a five-course meal to ingratiate himself with Trudeau: to ensure the leader knew the work both he and his wife had undertaken while the party had been in opposition —and to reaffirm his continued personal allegiance to the man himself. As senior statesman of the party, Trudeau's advice was being actively sought by all the leadership contenders. Who better was there to recommend to his successor that George be considered for inclusion in any future Liberal cabinet? George would have a surfeit of opportunity.

For Dede, this was also going to be a pinnacle evening. Most members brought their wives to Ottawa to join them for this prestigious affair. Now these women and the social columnists, as well as the Hill's male-dominated community, would know who was the capital's most outstanding hostess. After December 13, she would be known for her own achievements, and would be sought after in her own right, and not only as George Talbot's wife.

Dede had purchased a spectacular cocktail dress to wear for the function that she had spent three months planning. It was a bias-cut yellow chiffon with a beaded bodice. Like the party she had organized, she hoped it would be appreciated for its style and elegance.

On the morning of the reception, Dede made a final check of the room at eleven. A morning telephone canvass she had instituted successfully contacted the personal secretary of every Liberal MP, senator and party luminary. All previous RSVPs were recanvassed and assured. At three, Dede relayed this information to Trudeau's chief of staff. He confirmed that all was on schedule for the leader's nine o'clock entrance. The vote on the motion of nonconfidence over Tuesday's budget was slated for five-thirty. The House would rise at six, as usual.

She just managed to finish these duties in time to make her after-school call to the boys.

"Grandpa's here," Adam told her excitedly. "Can I go back and play with him?"

"Sure, sweetheart." Her father regularly dropped by whenever he was in the city and the boys loved his visits.

"Grandpa says good luck tonight," Adam added.

At four-thirty, Dede took a taxi to the apartment. Over the driver's radio, she was pleased to hear a political commentator predict easy defeat for the nonconfidence motion, as only a handful of Liberals would be present: "Most of Her Majesty's Loyal Opposition will be elsewhere at five-thirty. They will be preparing to attend their elaborate annual Christmas merrymaking."

When George did not appear at their apartment as arranged at eight-fifteen, Dede proceeded by cab to the party. She was keen to oversee the final preparations. Sushi chefs were arranging their ingredients in the lounge, the orchestra was testing the amplification system. All was in readiness, waiting to be activated into full life by the arrival of the guests.

By nine-thirty, no one had appeared. Busboys, waiters and musicians looked impatiently at their watches. An intense maître d' asked Dede what she wished him to do. The turkey would be shriveled if they delayed much longer; his kitchen staff wanted to conclude and go home; his waiters, if she insisted they remain, would require overtime—at union scale, of course.

It was ten-thirty when Dede heard the news. The vote of nonconfidence did not take place at five-thirty. By unanimous consent of all parties, the hours of parliament were extended to ten as party whips scrambled to assemble their members for the late-night vote. After the bells had ceased ringing for division at nine-forty, the hastily orchestrated coalition of Liberals and NDP in a 139 to 133 vote—a mere six-person margin—had toppled Joe Clark's Conservative government.

A grim prime minister had risen to address parliament. He advised that he would be meeting the governor-general early next morning to tender his government's resignation. He would also request His Excellency to call a general election. His announcement at ten-twenty had launched the next federal campaign.

These events were recounted by *The Ottawa Citizen*'s parliamentary reporter, who had been sent to get comment from the first prominent Liberal who made an appearance. But none did. No Liberal members appeared, prominent or otherwise. There was no celebration in the ballroom that night, either for Christmas or for the brilliantly orchestrated coup d'état.

Senior Liberal organizers went directly into an all-night session to find a way to lure Trudeau back from his announced retirement and convince him to remain as leader through the now imminent election. Members of the shadow cabinet sequestered themselves behind closed doors to devise election strategy. Exhausted backbenchers waited in the caucus rooms for further developments and reveled in the tactics that had brought the demise of the short-lived Tory government. Lights burned long and low in the offices of the meeting rooms on the Hill that night. Most ad hoc gatherings broke only at dawn when the first flight of the day jetted members to their constituencies to begin again the elusive quest for power.

At 10:35 p.m. Dede stuffed herself with cold turkey and *gâteau saint-honoré*. She sat behind the regal calligraphy place card scripted "The Right Honorable Pierre Elliott Trudeau" in a ballroom holding the debris of the party that had never been.

∞

The February 18 election which swept in Pierre Elliott Trudeau's party with an absolute majority returned George for a third term. Trudeau made the official telephone call to George inviting him to become Secretary of State for International Development, a junior ministry with specific responsibility for generating closer ties with the Third World. Commentators credited his inclusion to his political savvy and his wife's activism.

Her father had contributed heavily to George's campaign despite the fact that the official agent told him his donation this time around would be superfluous, as the Talbot coffers were already filled. He was adamant in making what he now called his regular contribution.

George did not seem predisposed to jettison the Ein connection. He reciprocated the patronage. Her father continued to enjoy the benefits of the unspoken bargain that he had made with George in Dede's presence years before in the family's study. With federal officials, Ein's requests for meetings no longer required a three-week lead time, but were expedited usually within a twenty-four-hour period and always at an hour convenient to him. No one in Ottawa risked alienating a member of George Talbot's extended family, lest it impact adversely on their careers. Her husband, capable and eager, had been recognized by the astute as someone to keep on the good side of—a "comer."

George made sure his father-in-law was included in select, intimate power gatherings attended by businessmen and notables whose coups were featured regularly in *The Globe and Mail*'s Report on Business. Stanley

Ein's wealth equaled theirs, but their social position surpassed his, thus normally rendering them inaccessible. He now entered their inner circle and called them by their first names. He was no longer considered "just another rich developer" but had become something rarer: a possessor of the elusive title "well connected." George had paid him back in the currency her father most coveted—respectability and status—the intangibles that, despite all his fortune, he had never been able to acquire.

George's elevation to a cabinet post coincided with Dede's disengagement from her husband's political career. George had crossed the critical threshold to minister. His "political Rubicon" was how he referred to it, and he now abandoned her on the other side.

It was no longer necessary for Dede, he said, to come to Ottawa on his account and to sacrifice more time away from the boys. He knew how much they missed her and how torn she had been to be away from them. And he did not wish to put any further strain of travel on her. He could handle things from this point on. With his new position came a staff executive assistant who, he explained, could accompany him to social functions. "An official version of what I used to do for Joe Bradley," he smugly mused. It was no longer unusual for Dede to receive a Friday afternoon call from George, telling her some minister or senior official wished to have a late Friday conference with him which, unfortunately, would delay his return home until the next morning.

In addition to his Ottawa extended absences, George, as part of his portfolio, made extensive Third World tours. Most of these were to various countries in Africa.

"How would you like some company?" Dede ventured six weeks before a Kenya trip.

"Too rigorous a schedule for you," he responded. "Be switching cities every day."

"I'm up to it."

"All that packing and unpacking. Flying by night. Difficult climate. After a few days, you might begin to think of it as a nightmare."

"Nonsense."

"Then great, why don't you come? It would make the stint seem less like work. . . . You realize, of course, we wouldn't be staying in first-class hotels. External doesn't like that. And the department won't let us upgrade ourselves. They feel in countries like this it can hurt. Be bad for our image there."

"Don't worry about that. It's not a problem for me."

"Then it's settled. I'll tell my EA you'll be joining us. Kenya's fascinating. You shouldn't have any trouble keeping yourself busy."

"What do you mean?"

"I'm there on official business. All of my time is accounted for. I'm afraid I won't have much time to be with you."

"There must be some time we'd be together."

"Sure. On planes, during official receptions . . . things like that."

Dede never again raised this topic. Or suggested accompanying him in the future on similar travels, journeys which seemed to arise with greater frequency and less advance warning.

In the next three years, George's time home became even more abbreviated. Her husband—conscientious, loyal and aggressive—was rewarded by the prime minister with additional areas of responsibility. He was made the unofficial liaison between the cabinet and the Liberal party in Ontario. Recognized as an interesting speaker, proficient in four languages, adept at handling the press, he was increasingly in demand. George never turned down a request to speak at an annual meeting or fund-raiser. How could he pass up an opportunity for enhanced media exposure?

George's most recent flurry of activity meant but one thing: her husband was "positioning" himself again. "They're grooming me for one of the major cabinet posts. External Affairs, Communications, Manpower and Immigration," George confirmed for her. She watched anxiously as these commitments intruded deeper into their lives.

Dede discussed her mounting concern for her boys' welfare early in the school fall term on one of the infrequent occasions when she and George found themselves both together in their home. George was propped up in bed, two king-size pillows behind his head, a third under his writing arm. In the evening room, the tensor light on his Louis XIV night table arched across his half of the spread. The quilted chintz duvet cover was barely visible under the scatterings of official ministerial correspondence, as George rotely appended his name. Not the best environment to have this conversation, Dede evaluated, but an opportunity she dared not waste.

"George, that parent-teacher night I attended for the boys two weeks ago," she said, taking residence on the sofa across the room. "Remember, I phoned your Ottawa office and left a message with your secretary that I was going to be seeing the children's teachers, and asked her to see if you had any specific things you wanted to ask? Well, I went, and even without my asking her anything, the teacher told me she was concerned about Adam. Miss Rose said he avoids playing with the other boys. When she asked Adam the reason for this, all he would say was he didn't want to. I don't think that's it, do you?"

George did not make use of her pause. The rhythm of his signature remained unbroken.

"I just think he isn't good enough in sports and doesn't want to be embarrassed. You know boys this age, they have to be the best at something or they won't do it at all. What I really feel he needs is more exposure to sports. Get some confidence in himself. Then he'll join in. . . . George, how would you feel about bringing some young man to live in the house? A university student. I was thinking, someone enrolled in teachers college would be best. That should make sure he's interested in children. He could help the boys learn baseball, football. The male-type things I can't do for them. . . . And I know you're much too busy. But these things are still important, George. Adam's ten now. If he doesn't learn these skills soon, he never will. They say boys communicate through sports. If he continues to refuse to play, he may have a difficult time making friends. I'm worried he could become a loner," Dede said, hesitating to add that Miss Rose had voiced the same concern. "Having a person like that in the house, who's interested in sports and in the boys, could make a difference. What do you think?"

George's hands had not ceased from their task. His right hand signed the page, his left expedited it onto the completed pile. Both moved in tandem as if regulated by an invisible force.

"What do you think, George? How would you feel about a man living in the house? The boys need a male influence."

"Uh-huh."

"George, this is an important decision. I'd appreciate if you would put these papers down. You're not paying any attention to what I'm saying."

"Of course I am," he replied, looking at her over the frame of his horn-rimmed glasses. He always removed his contacts before bedtime.

"You can't read, sign and listen at the same time."

"I'm not reading. I never read these things. My senior civil servant answers my mail, writes the replies and delivers these to me." By way of illustration, he picked up the collection of papers which still remained to be signed and dropped them. Their collective weight flattened the duvet. "I just sign them as a formality. I've told you that before. . . . Donald wrote them before I came into this portfolio. Undoubtedly, he'll write them after I'm gone. . . . Hopefully," he mused, "to External Affairs."

A smile lifted the corners of his mouth with the pleasurable thought he had just placed in his mind. "I'm listening, I really am. I assure you, you have my undivided attention. Now go ahead, I'm beginning to get tired and I still have another full briefcase to get through tonight."

Much to Dede's chagrin, George did not cease his activity. He had not even done so to deliver those sentences; nevertheless, she pressed forward. "With someone else to share the driving, I could enroll them in hockey. They'd probably have to begin with skating lessons, as they need the basics. Also, I'd like to get the boys into swimming. You know what I mean, the sports that you can't just pick up on your own. With all the driving I normally do, these extra classes just seemed too much for me to handle. . . . Also, there's always something that needs to be done around the house. I could use someone to shovel the snow, do some small repairs, put out the garden furniture in the spring. Having a man around would take some of the responsibility off me. . . . We have the bedroom, so there's no problem with space. And the house is so big, probably you wouldn't even notice he's here. . . . George, do you think it's a good idea?"

His indifference had become annoying. "Well, George, is it yes or no?"

He still did not respond. Dede left the divan and walked nearer to the bed. George had fallen asleep in an upright position, his pen poised in inertia near the pile of unsigned letters.

Any attempt to discuss this matter with him at a later time would prove equally futile. She would have to make the decision herself.

On Monday, she phoned the College of Education and asked if the dean's secretary would be so kind as to post a notice on the student bulletin board. "Physical education major. Free accommodation, food, in exchange for family responsibilities. 781-5932."

Bill Carter was ensconced in the guest room by the end of the week or, as Dede now preferred to measure time, in preparation for the hockey season. She had interviewed the five applicants in her home so that Michael and Adam could be there with her, playing innocuously throughout each meeting. Her basis for hiring rested on how the individual responded to her questions and equally on who she felt related best to her boys.

Bill seemed to establish an immediate rapport with them and he offered, in addition to the specific sports skills she required, the attribute of being a proficient downhill skier. He was from British Columbia, with a sturdy, athletic build. He was lured East, he said, by the cold, crisp climate instead of the dampness that characterized the B.C. winters. He wanted to try this part of the country before deciding where he wished to permanently locate. As all his references were from out West, Dede felt it prudent to check further. She called the dean.

"Mrs. Talbot, we appreciate what you're doing, taking one of our out-of-towners into your home like this. But I can't offer you much information on Bill, or any of our other young men you're considering, for that matter. They're all from the one-year program, which has only been in session for two months. I did speak to Bill's instructors on your behalf and checked over the comments that came in from his practice-teaching placements to date. All were very positive. Bill's a keen student. I know this isn't the sort of information you wanted from me, but it's all I have at the moment. I hope it will be of some help."

It was not surprising that the dean had said he was a good student. Often aloof, he spent the bulk of his free time studying in his room. As had been agreed, he gave three hours each day to Adam and Michael. By the end of week one his athletic program, practiced on the snow-barren street in front of their home, had Adam and Michael adept at holding a hockey stick and passing a puck. Dede cued to Bill's words that signaled her boys' reentry into the house.

"That's it for today, guys. We'll pick it up from here tomorrow."

She delighted in her boys' raucous laughter and was grateful to see pink cheeks replace their pallid whiteness, when after their session in the crisp air they raced inside the house for hot chocolate. She enjoyed the feel of her boys' cold faces against her warmer one as she hugged them.

At month's end, they were already in beginners' hockey. By taking them skating to a nearby indoor ice rink daily after school over a three-week period, Bill had advanced them directly into a program with others of their own age.

Their enthusiasm captured for one sport, Bill carried their interest over into another. He prepared them for skiing. Starting with indoor exercises to further strengthen their muscles, he soon had them practicing balance on a small slope in their backyard.

Around the house, Bill fulfilled his responsibilities willingly. He relieved Maria of taking the garbage out to the street. In the predawn following a snowfall, from the warmth of her bed, Dede would hear the comforting scrape of a shovel. Having a man living in the house made her feel safer when night settled around her ravine home.

George, on one of his weekend visits, offhandedly remarked how well Bill seemed to be working out.

At the next parent-teacher night, Dede asked Miss Rose if she noticed any difference in how Adam was interacting with the other boys.

"Interesting you asked me that, Mrs. Talbot. Mrs. Inglis, Michael's teacher, asked me the same thing only recently. His proficiency is up in the sports he plays, but for some reason he still avoids participating," she went on as if mentally ticking off items from a list. "When I encourage him to join the other boys, he becomes belligerent. He has the skills now, but he doesn't seem to know how to use them in an appropriate manner."

"Why would Mrs. Inglis discuss this with you?"

"Because she's noticed the same behavior with Michael."

She was disturbed by this information, but felt her boys' attitude would change once they were more comfortable with their newfound physical prowess.

By Christmas, Bill had abbreviated the time he allotted to the boys. Any genuine interest in being with them or pretense of flexibility had disappeared. Michael and Adam apologetically entreated Dede with requests for lifts to hockey practices and games. She would hear Michael's or Adam's footsteps pad eagerly to Bill's room in early evening, to retreat immediately, the step labored and slow, accompanied by such mumbled disappointment as "Sorry, Bill. Didn't think you were still busy."

Bill also became more circumspect and guarded. Dede did not recall when she realized that instead of keeping his door open throughout the day, as he previously had done, he now kept it shut at all times other than during what he considered his official working hours and that this recent desire for privacy was reinforced by a small padlock.

With increasing frequency, Bill brought home a male friend or two from class. At first he asked Dede for permission to do so, then continued the practice at will. He ignored Michael and Adam, ensuring their exclusion by taking his friend immediately to his room. At these times, Dede often saw Michael sulking outside Bill's room. Adam was also upset by this. He would refuse to do his homework and retreat to the third floor. When Dede went to get him, she would usually find him playing by himself with the model railway his father had given him on his seventh birthday and had spent most of that parliamentary recess helping him construct.

Bill was entitled to have his own friends, Dede thought, but that didn't give him the right to treat her boys so rudely.

She balanced Bill's conduct. He did provide a male role model, had ability in teaching sports and was above reproach in the work he did around the house, his willingness an example for her sons to see. But he lacked any sensitivity to Michael and Adam.

She did not have to wait for the next parent-teacher meeting to hear a report on her boys. In January, around Friday midmorning, a guidance teacher phoned and inquired the reason for Adam's high absenteeism that month and, in the course of the conversation, mentioned he was not in school today. It appeared that although her eldest son, along with his brother, had been driven to school by Bill, he had not gone to class.

Dede panicked. She reached George at his Ottawa office and synopsized the information.

"Dede, it's nothing. All boys do it at one time or the other. It's spring fever."

"George, don't make light of this. And if you haven't noticed, it's the middle of winter. . . . This is serious. Have you ever given Adam permission to skip school? Today or any other time? . . . " Her tone begged for an affirmative answer.

"Of course not," came the cavalier response.

"Then we have a big problem. How should we deal with it? I didn't want to discipline Adam without consulting you."

"You're on the spot, you make the decision. Whatever you do is fine with me," came back the voice which held the lilt of an upturned smile.

"George, are we alone? Is there anyone else in the room with you?"

"Of course not."

"Is Joan there? Or that other EA of yours, Ted? Are they both there?"

"Sure. They're always here. Why?"

"Never mind, George. Never mind. . . . Sorry to bother you with something as unimportant as your son's welfare."

"Give my love to the boys," George replied, oblivious to her sarcasm.

How could she tell him whatever transpired within their home was meant to be private? As intimate as making love. Something only between husband and wife. Not to be shared or casually overheard by strangers. His lack of interest in anything going on with his family infuriated her. This was as hard to reconcile as the news from the school. She terminated the conversation, unwilling to endure more of his banalities.

She confronted Adam by herself. At first he denied his truancy, but

Dede persisted. "Adam, I'm not going to punish you if you tell me the truth. I just want to know the truth."

No answer.

"At least tell me where you went."

"Skiing."

"Skiing?" Dede repeated incredulously. "Why?"

"I wanted to. I like skiing."

"I didn't know you liked it that much."

"Well, I do" was his belligerent retort.

"Why didn't you ask me for permission?"

"Didn't think you'd let me skip school."

"You're right, I wouldn't have let you." She felt relieved by how benign this turned out to be, but wanted a fuller explanation. "How did you manage to get there?"

"Bus."

"From where?"

"Took the subway to Yorkdale. Got the bus from there."

"Where to?"

"Up north."

"Up north?"

"Snow Valley, Hidden Valley, Horseshoe Valley. Those places."

"But why wouldn't you go skiing on the weekend when there was no school to miss?"

"It's too crowded then. By the time I'd get a ride up from Toronto, it would've been afternoon. Best snow is finished for the day."

She wanted to believe Adam, wanted the loose ends disposed of and his story to be consistent and conclusive. She did not press this line of questioning further, but moved with practicality toward the future. She wished to end the scene that pitted her unwillingly against the son she loved. "Okay, I'll make you a deal. If you don't skip any more school for three weeks I'll ask Bill to drive you to the slopes. If you want, you can even go up north the night before and be the first one on the hills. What do you think of that?"

"Can Michael come with me? I don't want to go without Michael."

"Sure he can." Adam's insistence on having his younger brother join him gratified but puzzled Dede. The guidance teacher had told her Michael had been in school every day. He had never been a conspirator in Adam's unauthorized absences.

Dede kept her promise. Three weeks later, after confirming Adam's perfect attendance, the trio of Bill, Adam and Michael prepared to drive north of Barrie to Horseshoe Valley. They would be sleeping at the adjoining inn that night so Adam could get an early start. When the boys' skis and bags were all placed in the car, she gave her final instructions to Bill.

"Make sure you keep the room for Saturday. Michael will need to have a rest in the afternoon. Don't forget, he's still only nine. He shouldn't be skiing all day." Dede watched the family station wagon—her ultimate concession to child rearing—move out slowly through the thick snow.

She saw a small figure bob up and down. Michael was bouncing on the seat, his habit when excited. Although George was not home this weekend, she had dismissed the notion of joining them. Not able to ski, she did not want to hold them back. Besides, skiing was Bill's forte. Even if he was somewhat detached, he would give them a good time. Now, watching her boys' exuberance as the car pulled away, she wished she had gone with them.

∞

They returned Saturday near the hour of six. Darkness had already enveloped the house. The aroma of roast beef, a favorite of the boys, filled its corridors.

Dede did not meet her sons' entrance, it was executed so swiftly. She had been waiting for them in her bedroom. She was ready on Michael's arrival to give him a bath, to warm him after what must have been a cold day skiing.

"Where did everyone go?" she called from the top of the stairs. "Michael? Adam?" She turned on the bathwater, then went looking for her boys. She went downstairs and into the kitchen. Maria said they had not come in there. Dede passed through the dining room. The table was laid for dinner. Nothing had been disturbed. They were not in the family room either. Dede walked back upstairs. She returned to the bathroom to switch off the tap. She found Michael standing there, staring at the water gushing into the porcelain tub.

"Have a good time?"

"Nope," said the small boy. His eyes avoided hers. They were transfixed by the flood of liquid coming out of the pipe.

"I'm sorry, I thought you would enjoy today."

Michael offered no comment. Nor did his eyes move. He stood cold and shivering, his back to her.

Dede crouched to his level to hug him. He pulled away in advance of her touch. "What is it? Michael, what's wrong?"

"Nothing."

"What is it, Michael?"

"Leave me alone. I want to take my bath."

"Okay. I'll help you." From a squatting position, Dede started to undo the buttons of his plaid Vyella shirt. She tugged at one sleeve.

He jerked his arm from her. Flailed the words at her, "I said go away. I can take a bath myself." Suddenly, he turned around. A somber, drawn face stared at her with the look of the betrayed.

"Okay, Michael. I'll wait outside. Call me when you're through." Dede retreated from the room.

Twenty minutes elapsed. Michael did not call. Nor in the interval had Dede heard the slosh of emptying bathwater. She pushed open the door. Michael was sitting in the tub, scrubbing harshly at his skin. A thick film of soap clung to the surface of the water, the debris of too much lather.

"Okay, Michael. Enough is enough. . . . Out."

Obediently, he left the tub. She reached for a towel. "Brace yourself for the big rubdown. Here we go." These were words that signaled the game Michael so enjoyed. Her son would plant his feet firmly into the yellow pile mat and she would seesaw the thick towel from side to side, rapidly, in short strokes, drying her son's slender frame as he erupted in laughter. This time, there was no game, no laughter. He grabbed the oversized towel out of her hands. Placed it over his nakedness.

"No. I'll do it." In a low, determined voice he said, "No one ever touches Michael again."

Bewildered, Dede left the bathroom. She had to find Adam. He could tell her what had upset his brother. "Adam, where are you?" No response. She went to his room. His door was closed, the lights off. The brown duvet was tightly drawn around her son's familiar form. Was it her imagination, or did she hear muffled sobs? She stood over his bed, waiting. There was no motion. No further sounds. She bent down to hug the huddled form beneath the covers. He shifted position. She put her hand on the comforter. Her son rolled over and pushed it off, emphatic to rid himself of her touch. Whether he was sleeping or only pretending made little difference. It was apparent he intended to tell her nothing that night.

She went downstairs. Bill was at the table having dinner, unconcerned about the two untouched place settings beside him.

"Bill, do you know what's bothering Michael?"

"He's had a very active day. He's just overtired. It's nothing to worry about," he replied between mouthfuls.

"There's got to be more to it than that. And I'm very worried about him."

"I'm sure it's nothing. He'll be fine in the morning."

There could be no accusations, no recriminations. Her only certainty was Bill did not intend to explain everything that had taken place during the twenty-four hours her boys had been alone with him.

When George came home the following weekend she did not tell him she had fired Bill or her suspicions behind this decision. Her explanation for their employee's absence was "Bill needed more study time for his year-end exams," adding, "I don't think it's necessary to replace him." Bland words, chosen not to arouse George's curiosity. From her husband, she had learned to be self-protective.

Bill's name came up one more time. It occurred the following winter on a February night as George was speeding through his late-night signing of the correspondence prepared by Donald.

"Got a request for a character reference for that phys ed guy who once lived in our house. That boy from the West. Bill somebody." Dede saw George was groping for the surname.

She supplied the answer. "Bill Carter," she said coolly.

"That's right. Some boys' boarding school in northern B.C. is thinking about hiring him as a housemaster. I told Donald to prepare a good solid reference for him."

"May I see it?"

"I don't understand why you'd bother yourself. But it's here, if you want to look at it. . . . That's if I can find it again." It was already buried four letters deep. He exhumed it. George sent the pages across the bed toward her, as a boy would a darted paper plane. "That finishes me for the night. I'm done." He dropped his work on the carpet, turned off his bedside tensor light and placed his glasses on his night table.

Dede went to her side of the king-size bed. She reviewed the letter from the headmaster of Cavendish Academy for Boys. It was clipped, as was all of her husband's incoming mail, to his assistant's prepared reply on George's ministerial letterhead. She read Donald's exemplary reference on Bill.

Dede walked down the corridor. Outside Michael's door, she listened to the sobs that since last March periodically troubled his sleep. She entered Adam's bedroom and studied the enigmatic face of her eldest son. In the span of these eleven months, he had still told her nothing.

She had been unable to substantiate anything in the entire interval since Bill had left. Nor to dispel her fear that her sons had been molested.

Her responsibility was to the innocent and to herself. She ripped the letters: both the headmaster's request and George's signed reply. Shredded the correspondence into indistinguishable pieces. If only she could eradicate the anguish Bill had caused her boys as simply as she had this reminder of him.

Chapter *15*

Georon was a survivor of the September debacle, unlike 107 of his less fortunate colleagues. "The Conservative tide has swept through the Metropolitan Toronto region with unprecedented force, leaving only a handful of Liberal MPs clinging to the basis of the party's once solid bastion in Ontario. . . . The Liberal losses reduced the party from a political powerhouse in Canada's largest metropolitan area to an isolated pocket of six heavily ethnic-populated ridings in Toronto's west end," ran *The Globe and Mail* beneath the headline "Tory Landslide" as virtually two decades of Liberal rule came to an end. Pole-vaulted through the mechanism of a leadership convention into the position of prime minister on Trudeau's second and permanent retirement, John Turner had been unable to preserve for his party his promise of power. George Talbot returned to the shadow cabinet of a decimated party.

Her husband now was in Toronto only every third weekend. More of his hours, he said, were required in the capital since "we have fewer of *us* to watch more of *them*." The only operational change that distinguished this out-of-power period from the previous one was he did not suggest Dede join him in Ottawa and declined her offers to do so. His reasoning was based on the different political realities this time. "It's not necessary," he had said. "It's too soon to start reorganizing. There's no mileage in it. Mulroney's going to be around for a full four years. . . . Joan has consented to continue her escort function."

In addition to his reduced status, the election caused him further personal embarrassment. It had rendered obsolete his cards, embossed with its red ministerial insignia, on which was written "The Honorable George Talbot, Secretary of State for International Development," and with its loss left him with the inconvenience of personally readying himself for international travel. He attended almost as many out-of-country conferences as before, but in a diminished official capacity.

In preparation for another of these sojourns, Dede was assisting George with his packing. It was a warm June day and through the expanse of window in their bedroom, Dede saw that deepening shades of green were returning to the ravine. She felt lighthearted as she usually did at this time of year.

"Is this the suit you want to carry on the plane or should I pack it?" A veteran of too much lost luggage, George now took a garment bag onto the aircraft. She held the blue fleck suit up for his inspection, the one he routinely took on all his government-sponsored African trips. Classic, but not too ostentatious a cloth, it projected the middle-of-the-road image he sought: a look, he always said, that made the officials of the host country more receptive to his proposals. An early proponent of "dress for success," he carried the concept in the reverse direction.

"Neither. I'm not taking it."

"Why not? It's your uniform for your African trips." She was enjoying their banter.

"We may be talking about Third World problems, but we're doing it in European luxury."

"Where's it being held?"

"France."

"Which city?"

"The South of France."

"No kidding. Where?"

"Cannes."

"We haven't been there since the summer we met. It would be nice to go back."

"It's going to be five days of intensive sessions. You said after all the conferences you worked on you had no desire to attend another one in any capacity. Not even as a guest."

That was true. She had had enough of the segregated women's programs. And she abhorred the artificial conviviality that typified a convention—being propelled into friendship with people she had no desire to meet, these relationships being dictated and strategically choreographed under George's tutelage. But Cannes was unique. And worth making the exception. She would put stipulations on her presence. Confine her attendance to the opening reception and the black-tie gala.

"I'd really like to go this time."

"You wouldn't know anyone there. We're only going to send the policy person from our embassy in Paris and, of course, Jack, the assistant deputy minister in charge of African Affairs. You've never liked him."

"Good. Less people to have to be nice to."

"Dede, I don't think you understand my predicament. Even though I'm not from his party, Mulroney named me the official Canadian delegate. He's been experimenting in putting high-profile members of the other parties into positions of international responsibility. He's sent a confirmed NDPer to be Ambassador to the United Nations. I'm going to have two sides watching my performance at this conference. My own, of course, and the Conservatives, to gauge whether Mulroney's policy is shrewd politics or just promoting the careers of their rivals. If I distinguish myself here, I may make it easier for other backbenchers to be effective in this parliament. I really want you to come, but I can't afford to have any distraction."

"I promise not to be a distraction. At least, not more than a minor one," she said teasingly. Not giving him opportunity to reply, she continued. "Don't worry, I have lots of things I can do to keep myself busy. Dior, Balmain, Saint-Laurent." She counted them off on her fingers in playful exaggeration.

"Dede, that's what I'm afraid of," he mock-chastised. Then he switched moods and regarded her intently as if weighing the determination in her request. "Okay, let's do it. But try to stay out of the shops. Seriously. At least the ones on the Croisette."

"Who else from Canada will be joining us?" she asked as an afterthought.

"No one you know."

"There must be someone," she said, aware of the entourage that circles an official visit.

"Like I said, only the assistant deputy and a policy adviser from our embassy. That's our delegation."

She no longer concerned herself that she was plump. She was twenty-two again and carefree. And this was Cannes, the place where they had met. Her mind had returned there and was already planning their days and evenings.

Their lives, she felt, were becoming unglued with the relentless business of living. Its adhesion stretched thin by the exigencies of miles and responsibilities. It had been twelve years of separated weekday nights, with George in Ottawa or on solitary international journeys and herself in

Toronto, a de facto single parent, consumed with the anxieties of child rearing. In their snatches of life together, they could do no more than not disturb their deteriorating bond. She needed to get them back to a less complicated existence. If they went into the hills of Vence, where the pine was sweet and fragrant and everything had begun, they would be able to re-create what they first had.

"Do you know where I'd really like to stay?"

"No."

"Mas d'Artigny. That beautiful hotel we passed on our motorcycle that night."

"What night?"

Dede's memory had returned to France of more than a decade earlier; George's thoughts remained stuck in their Rosedale home.

"If that's what you really want. . . . But remember, it's at least a forty-five-minute car ride from there to the convention center. It's going to take me longer to get back and forth and be much harder on me than if we stayed in Cannes at the Majestic with the rest of the delegates. . . . But consider it done. If it means that much to you, we'll stay there."

Dede was pleased how easily George acceded to this request.

∽

Their private stucco cottage at Mas d'Artigny was opened up by a stout porter whose age seemed to match that of the hotel's. He gingerly placed the heavy wooden key in the latch, pushed wide the thick, wooden door and with a hand bid them enter. A lean assistant in his twenties brought their luggage. Dede followed immediately behind the younger man. Before releasing the duo, she made a room-by-room inspection of the suite. Often these sorts deposited the bags and fled, an event she could forestall by this method. Usually she required at least one room change before she was satisfied for the night, and their stay here was going to be almost a week.

Dede ignored the sitting room and proceeded directly into the bedroom. George's office must have been effective. This was the most perfect room. She committed every detail of it to memory. Fabric walls of pink and yellow florals with winding green stems matched the twin chairs, bedspread, drapery and valance box. A vase of pink roses, yellow lilies and wide green foliage stood on a dresser in front of one of these walls; it drew the silk print into three-dimensional life. Ceiling moldings and doorframes were trimmed in pink. A line drawing of a pair of birds hung opposite the bed. One flirtatious and alluring, her wings enticing in a dance; the male, superimposed upon her breast, remained passive, as if confident of his control. Near the bed, a narrow glass door opened onto a private garden and a miniature pool.

She reentered the sitting room she had so curtly bypassed. A finely carved wooden desk and chair with a floral cushion matched to the walls was placed before a large garden window. A full branch of lavender blooms, rich and luscious, an offshoot from the climbing vines outdoors, framed the left side of the window's portico. Curious whether this aperture was mere decor, she twisted its lock; it swung into the garden. Freed from its constraint, the branch of lavender bougainvillea spilled into the room. Dede had returned to the place where all things again seemed possible.

"This is perfect. We'll take it," she said.

A most fortunate decision, as the corpulent porter, unconcerned with her inspection, had long since withdrawn, taking his assistant with him. The latter had strewn their six bags in the center of the sitting room.

Dede flopped into a pink chair. She was exuberant. "Isn't this place wonderful? Just what we needed."

"Dede, why don't you take it easy tonight? With the change of planes in London, we've been traveling for ten hours. And there's a six-hour time difference. Why don't you skip the reception? I wish I could." George was already in the process of disengaging his gray pinstriped suit from the garment bag he had carried with him onto the planes. "I'm used to these long flights. This is a short hop compared to Kenya." Her husband made one of the two en suite bathrooms his own and was starting to shave.

She spoke above the rush of water. "I'm okay. Really I am. And I'm totally organized for tonight. My hair survived the time zones with no trouble," she said happily. She had her international travel hair routine down to a science: she had it blown, as always, three hours before departure; carried her clips with her onto the all-night transatlantic carrier, calculated when the other business-class passengers would be asleep or too absorbed in the in-flight movie to notice her, then set her hair into rollers. Afterward, she would sleep carefully in order not to disturb her work.

"Really, it would make it much easier on me if I went alone. Otherwise I'd feel under pressure all night to get you home. In addition to the reception, I've got to meet Jack and the person from Paris I told you about. To be briefed before we start tomorrow."

"I don't feel a bit tired, George."

"I don't know how long I'm going to have to be there tonight. I don't want to keep you up late unnecessarily. The secret of beating jet lag is to fall in with the local time. . . . I want you to have a good day tomorrow."

She did not protest further. She thought of the elegance of her en suite bathroom with its circular whirlpool tub and the seductive bottle of scented bubble bath beside it—and her fabulous bedroom.

She gave in to the pulsing sensation that now was beginning to affect her body. "All right, George."

"Be right back. I just have to jump into a fast shower." Through a partially open door, hot water steamed into the room. "Now about to-morrow," came a deepened voice resonating from the surrounding tile. "This is my schedule. . . . I'll be leaving early. About eight o'clock." His monologue ceased. She was not certain whether George's information was complete or had become temporarily overpowered by the water. His voice returned above the buildup of pressure. "With the rush-hour traffic, I'll need a full forty-five minutes. . . . We're having a keynote speaker during lunch. Sessions all afternoon. Delegate dinner. The typical opening day. I'll be back late. . . ." Dede heard the snap of the shower handle, the cessation of water. Steam began to dissipate into the sitting room. "Now, what are you going to do while I'm away?"

"I think I'll stay around the property tomorrow. Enjoy our garden and pool."

"Sounds good." She heard the hiss of aerosol. "You know, I've read that this place has a four-star restaurant. And I bet they'll deliver to our patio. Sorry I can't be here to enjoy it with you. . . . With that long drive back from Cannes, I'll be quite late, but I'll slip in quietly."

The conversation terminated with George's emersion from the dressing area fully attired, his wet hair sprayed into place. He was elegantly turned out. He retained no visible sign of the tedious day of travel.

The Mercedes limousine which had been waiting outside their cottage sped away the sole Talbot who was attending the reception. As she watched the taillights disappear, her body, suspended far too long in a pressurized environment, shuddered involuntarily; then with recurring fre-quency. She bathed in the luxury of her surroundings and fell asleep instantly. She slept soundly, oblivious, she realized on waking, to both George's return and his early-morning departure.

Not wanting to miss George for a second morning, she had set the bedside clock radio for seven-thirty. Two nights of going to bed early sandwiched between a day of rest on the property had eradicated her jet lag. She wished to have breakfast with her husband, even if to do so meant getting up at this unaccustomed hour.

George was already out of bed. She slipped a dressing gown around herself and, walking barefoot over to the glass door, looked for him in the garden. A basket of croissants, a square dish of berries and a thermos had been set upon their terrace table facing the pool. She pushed ajar the slender door and descended the narrow single step onto the cool, fresh grass of their secluded garden. The face of the purple bougainvillea had already lifted toward the sun. The sweet red fruit of the *arbousier*, which Dede had been told blooms best in the South of France, hung ripe and full. She walked beneath its branches and sat down. George joined her minutes later, wearing his most fashionably tailored suit. She passed her husband the breads, the plate of choice raspberries, and poured his coffee, then chose a chocolate croissant for herself.

Although confining her intake, Dede had never fully relinquished her passion for food. Rather, she compromised by taking small bites of all she loved best. With such practiced restraint, she began breakfast.

She methodically demolished a croissant, eating only the crusty sections. She unfurled the brown buttered top, then layered it with the assortment of jams the waiter had left. She removed the top strand that encrusted the soft middle, ladled thick marmalade upon it, then ripped off one of its nubby tips and plunked it into a pot of raspberry preserve. The fourth piece, she reserved for the kumquat. She savored the different taste sensations, chewing delicately as she listened to George.

"Since you're up already, let me fill you in on today's agenda. It's the key day of the conference. A symposium with four guest speakers. This panel is the whole reason Mulroney wanted me here. They've brought in Evans from the U.K., Grosky from Moscow, Bing from Australia and that Graham man from Washington. The topic is 'Famine and Plague Risks over the Next Five Years: Preventive Techniques.' Catchy title. Sounds somewhat reminiscent of my Ph.D. thesis, doesn't it? . . . Anyhow, I'll be tied up there all day. Symposiums always run late. Especially when they take questions from the floor. So don't worry. . . . Any idea what you'll be doing?"

"Not sure."

"Here's my Michelin for the French Riviera and some pamphlets. I picked them up for you at the front desk. . . . The Maeght Foundation we cycled to the summer we met is only a five-minute ride down that hill. And you remember where we were in St.-Paul? Well, it's only a few kilometers further along the same road. The Colombe d'Or is there. Worldwide reputation. Got fabulous food and their balcony has a terrific view of the medieval town. I know you'd enjoy having lunch there. . . . Together they would make for a great day. Wish there was some way I could do it with you. In a couple of days, my schedule lightens up." As he stood up, he took a gulp of coffee. "Too bad we opted for this place. If we'd stayed at the Majestic like everyone else, we'd have had more time together. Enjoyed having breakfast with you, but I've got to get going."

"Where will you be if your office needs you? There was a call yesterday, but I didn't know where to refer it."

"The convention schedule that has the location of our meetings is in there on the small table." He glanced in the vicinity of the sitting room. "But they'll never be able to get me if they phone the convention center anyhow. The place is enormous. It's a mammoth complex. Better just take a message and find out what time I can reach them tomorrow. Anyhow, it can't be anyone important. Turner said he wouldn't need to talk to me this week. I really must go, it's eight-thirty," George said as he hurried up the patio steps and into the chauffeured Mercedes. The driver handed George the *International Herald Tribune*. Her husband had begun to leaf through its pages before the car pulled away.

Facing the interior of the garden, Dede dallied over breakfast and with it savored the beauty of the ripening day. The sun fell on two large stones which dominated the space beyond the pool. Their raw power was caught in its refraction. The seven-foot black one jutted to the left, angular and uncompromising; its appearance unaltered by erosion. Accompanying it, softened with the backdrop of a crimson tree was an equally massive stone, its contour and color different. It was a round rust formation; its lines chiseled with weather. Its shape resembled a woman in prayer; its position was supplicant to its companion. She read nature's order in their form and placement: the male's strength; the female's vulnerability. But these were nothing more than debris disgorged by the centuries around which a garden had been sculpted.

A loud plop dislodged Dede's thoughts. A bullfrog was enjoying the exclusivity of her pool.

She did not bother with the Michelin. She was not enthusiastic about gallery hopping alone. Nor did she relish eating unaccompanied at any restaurant, world-class or otherwise. Anyhow, she had not come all this distance to sample the environs, but to be with her husband. She would save both of these delicacies to share with George. Maybe tomorrow they could visit the Maeght that George had said was nearby. He told her his sessions were lightening up.

She left the garden to locate his convention brochure. She found it in the place where he had indicated, its glossy pages damp from his shower. She looked at day three. Full. Her eyes moved back to day two. George must have misread the program. The symposium was listed, but only for the morning. Lunch in the afternoon read "at leisure." Hadn't George said only this morning that he regretted they hadn't spent more time together? It was only ten-thirty. If she left now, she would be able to catch him before the symposium broke. Perhaps have lunch, like they used to, at one of those fish restaurants that ringed the harbor. She probably should leave him a message that she was coming. She scanned the brochure again. There was no specific contact number listed.

She would surprise George. She rang the front desk. "*Un taxi, s'il vous plaît, immédiatement.*"

"Fifteen minutes, Madame Talbot," he replied in flawless English.

Having made the decision, she felt exhilarated: it was the Côte d'Azur and she was rushing, as she had so many summers earlier, to meet George. She dressed in her favorite suit, this season's Anne Klein—a hot-pink linen jacket with a wraparound black skirt. Everyone always complimented her on the jacket. She wanted to look her best for George. She tucked the convention schedule into her purse for reference.

She was waiting outside her villa when the Peugeot arrived. "*Palais de Congrès, s'il vous plaît.*" She did not need to add the encouragement of "*vitement.*" The driver did not slow for speed bumps and went around the traffic circle at La Colle-sur-Loup and past the town of Cagnes-sur-Mer at full throttle. The charm of the French countryside was obscured in an unidentifiable blur. He took the hairpin turns with the swiftness reserved for a highway; the autoroute of A8 as if it were a lap at the Grand Prix. He jolted to a sudden stop forty minutes later before a small white building on the outskirts of Cannes.

"*Palais de Congrès,*" he proclaimed. "*C'est là.*"

This did not look at all like the place George had described. In a crisis Dede could not rely on her French. Instead, she leaned over the driver's seat and pointed to the address printed on the pamphlet. He shrugged and pointed impatiently at the same structure.

"*Ici, Palais de Congrès vieux. . . . Nouveau, là.*"

She asked him to proceed to the correct location. He refused with a nonnegotiable, "*Non. Trop difficile avec un auto.*" She did not delay further. She extended her open palm, which held an assortment of francs from which he could take his fare, then slipped out of the taxi.

From the pristine sky sun flooded down upon her. It was warmer here than it had been in the hills of Vence. She felt buoyant and somewhat relieved to have regained control of her destiny as, undaunted, she began her six-block journey. She crossed the street to the side nearest the Mediterranean. Her heels forced her to slacken pace over the granite blocks that comprised the Croisette as she proceeded toward the imposing, geometric edifice which dominated the waterfront.

She enjoyed the activity and the sights she always associated with Cannes. A landscape of yachts stretched as far as the eye could see: smaller ones moored at the docks closer to shore; the larger, more exotic ones, rested in deeper waters. A potpourri of boats stood in dry dock; bare-chested men scraped at their barnacled hulls. Sightseeing launches full of tourists were coming back from the morning excursion. Snack vendors sold from makeshift kiosks, whose presence, when she came closer to the city's center, cluttered the sea walk. An unaccompanied child wove on a skateboard in front of her as, nearing her destination, she regarded the complex.

The conference center comprised more than a city block, and its multitude of glass doors and terracing made it difficult to decide which was her correct entrance. She went to the information gallery and inquired how to get to the *Salon de Presse*, the room listed for today's symposium. The shortest route, she was told, was to take the orange door in front of the merry-go-round and the lift to the third floor. It was now approaching twelve o'clock. She quickened her pace. She had to locate George before they broke for lunch.

For what seemed to be a further quarter hour, she followed the circumference of the building until she spotted her first marking.

The carousel, to which she had been directed, was uncanny in its realism. Stallions and mares frothed and leaped, their enamel prime colors bold in the steaming June sun; tigers and lions snarled, their painted, glistening bodies poised to spring from the gyrating platform. Mirrors exaggerated the animal shapes and glossy lacquer. Beside this spinning mechanism, fountains jetted water, its rhythmic splash unable to overcome the pounding tin cacophony from the calliope.

The blare and color disoriented Dede and she had to once more circle the building before coming upon the bright orange entrance. She took the lift to the third floor.

The elevator opened, then swiftly shut behind her. Its portal instantly became unrecognizable, its aluminum exterior blending with the gray fabric walls on either side.

Turning to her right, she faced an explosion of light and color. Raspberry suede walls and chartreuse carpeting assaulted her senses. Metal pipes jutted like projectiles from a drop ceiling. Tips of burgundy neon lit, like a runway, the labyrinth of corridors off of which were reception pods and clusters of meeting rooms. Each pod was identical in shape and size. She was alarmed. She had no idea which of these hosted the African conference. There was no wall directory and the entire floor was emptied of humanity: there was no possibility for assistance. She would have to go pod by pod, tediously checking the small placard which stood in front of each meeting room for the words *"Le Salon de Presse."*

After searching along three halls, she spotted the sign and next to it one which confirmed she had reached her destination: "World Conference on Aid to Emerging African Nations. Simultaneous Translation." There was no one outside the room. She came closer and listened at the door. There was muffled speaking, then brief applause. More speaking. She relaxed. She had made it before the session ended, despite an erratic cab ride, a bewildering complex—altogether a chaotic morning. She spanked the creases out of her linen skirt in preparation to meet George and the others to whom he was certain to introduce her.

Dede looked through the round, blackened one-way glass. The speaker's podium must be in front of her: the delegates faced in her direction. The all-male room sat in ties and fully exposed white shirts. The moderator must have suggested that they, gentlemen all, remove their jackets for comfort. A plastic Evian bottle and tumbler glass were set before each of them. A large card with black lettering spelled out each country represented. It sat neatly in front of each delegate.

Through the invisibility of her one-way window, Dede looked for "Canada." The countries were in alphabetical order, making each impossible to miss. George was not behind the placard. The chair was vacant;

the Evian bottle undisturbed, its accompanying tumbler unused. The space was clean even of paper scatterings. George was not there. It did not appear that George had ever been there.

Polite applause repeated itself. Then the scrape of metal chairs straining on wood. She must escape. When the doors opened and the audience spilled out, she would stand out, the only female among them. And in the vainness of her hot-pink jacket, she would be a beacon among the somber suits. Exposed and humiliated.

She had to escape. Embarrassment gave way to panic. She was unable to find her way through the maze of corridors. The intricate ceiling of brash, fluorescent tubing that had guided her entry became instead the grotesque lighting of a carnival, discharging patterns, jarring and raw. It was a repeat of the vibrant carousel she had just left outside, a glare of psychedelic light and mirrored trickery. The delegates' voices, audible behind her in a host of tongues, were a dizzying additional layer of confusion.

She could not find the elevator; its shiny, camouflaged exterior remained hidden to her. She fled down the steep cement blocks of the chill back stairs, the exit meant only for workmen or those escaping from fire, and reentered the harsh sun of midday. Glare, both from the unprotecting heavens and from the reflection of the sea, assaulted her vision. She ran along the Croisette's sea walk, continuing in the direction that an hour earlier had brought her here. In her flight, she was not concerned about the snag of her heels between the stones, the heat of the one-thirty hour or the scenery she hurried past. She rounded the neck of the bay toward the string of open-air seaside restaurants, the chic comfortable ones with pampered decor and a sidewalk screen of thin greenery which lined the motorway across from the most picturesque and discreet section of Old Port. Only then did she break stride. And when she did, it was involuntary.

George was sitting in the atrium of the restaurant: at a choice front location, his back flush against the fully extended glass partition; his hand rested over that of the woman beside him. He had no need for Evian—champagne and some other wine chilled in a brass cooler near them. Apricot roses in an earth-tone ceramic vase stood on a peach linen cloth next to the steaming bouillabaisse they shared.

Dede could not mistake this woman anywhere. The lady who George had said "consented" to continue as his escort in Ottawa when the party returned to opposition—Dede's stand-in—Joan, his former EA. The EA who had been with him for five years, but was no longer on his staff. And a name coincidentally omitted from the roster he gave of those she might know at the convention. Dede had no fear of being spotted. George's eyes never left Joan and his look was unmitigated, explicit and reciprocated.

Dede stood rooted to the sidewalk with the fascination and compulsion of the voyeur. She felt immune to discovery, an invisible spectator at her husband's infidelity. Her throat constricted. Noxious fumes spat from the unbridled exhausts of buses, cycles and lorries; they rose to nauseate her. Tears flowed down her face, tears of humiliation and anger.

She bolted. Briskly, she continued along the Quai St.-Pierre until at Sofitel Méditerranée she requested a taxi from the doorman. The kindness of this stranger wrought from her a spontaneous return of tears.

∽

She rose early, arranged for the menu and the location of breakfast to be a repeat of yesterday's and, as dawn opened into morning, waited outside for her husband. George, direct from his shower, entered the garden wearing the scrubbed look of the innocent. On his way to the patio, he brushed against the vines, knocking their fragile petals carelessly to the ground. As she had on the previous day, she poured George's coffee, offered him the croissants, the plate of jams and the fullest bowl of raspberries.

"Did the panelists have anything interesting to say?"

"Not really. Same old stuff, but reworked."

"Some of it must have been new."

"Grosky, you know the agronomist from Moscow? He reported on some innovative production methods."

"Anything else worthwhile?"

"The other speakers were pretty pedestrian. Lots of recycled ideas." He dug heartily into the raspberries.

"What was the rest of the day like?" she asked.

"Lunch. Then more of the same."

"That's too bad. Sorry your day was so disappointing."

"How did your day go?" George took a wash of coffee.

"Disappointing too."

"You never left here?"

"No, not that. I took your suggestion and went off the property. I decided to go down to Cannes. To the conference center." She kept her tone unrevealing, flat and controlled.

"Enormous complex. Have you ever seen anything like it? . . . Quite an architectural achievement. Where else did you go?"

She wouldn't let him sidetrack her. She kept her voice unemotional. "I went inside. To the *Salon de Presse*. To join you for lunch. Thought I'd surprise you. But the surprise was mine—you weren't there." Her voice cracked, betraying her tension.

"Most of us stepped out between speakers. Jack asked for a word with me around that time. . . . I really feel badly we missed each other. . . . It's quite a difficult building to find your way around if you've never been there before." Going off on this tangent, he had effortlessly sidestepped the issue.

Her voice took on a hard edge. "Then I walked along the seaside . . . toward Gaston et Gastounette." He did not interrupt her again. "You do remember that place, don't you? You should, we used to go there together. And our special table? The one Alain used to set up for us on warm days when they'd push back the glass partition. . . . You'll never guess who I saw there. Right in the front."

George did not respond. His croissant remained locked between his thumb and index finger.

"And do you have any idea who was with that person?"

Her husband remained impervious: a politician skilled in difficult questions and tight situations. An advocate of "the best defense is offense," he tried, as she had anticipated, a confronting assault.

"Dede, you think I'm having an affair. Then I confirmed your suspicion when I didn't explain the circumstances behind a business lunch, especially after you had so elaborately staged the opportunity for this." He lifted his hands, sweeping the cozy breakfast arrangement and the majesty of the landscape together into one passionate gesture of futility. "Well, I'm sorry to disappoint you, but I have nothing to confess. Nothing was happening there. I realize you're worked up. And I can understand how it happened. Coming all that distance down to join me and then not knowing why I wasn't there. . . . I guess you could say it was my fault. I should have kept you informed of the goings-on in my office. But I really didn't want to bother you with the nitty-gritty. . . . When we went into opposition, as you know, I lost my staff. Just this year, Joan was reassigned to our embassy in Paris. At the last minute, her new boss ordered her to accompany the policy adviser, who you will remember I had distinctly told you was going to be present at the conference. . . . The first I knew of her being here was when I saw her at the informal briefing session the night we landed. . . . I thought I should take her to lunch."

"Is Auld Lang Syne so important to you that you skipped the symposium which, you made a big point of saying, was the only reason you were sent here at all?" His offhand manner had become unbearable.

"If you must know, yes. I thought I owed it to her. She did the personal things I didn't have time to do for myself as a cabinet minister. And she accompanied me to parties in Ottawa so as not to inconvenience my wife. . . . Yes, I thought I did owe it to her."

"Did you owe it to her to hold her hand too?" She gave him no chance for rationalization. "How long has this been going on, George? For the entire five years she was your EA?" As she asked this, everything suddenly became crystal clear. "Is that why you didn't want me coming to Ottawa once you became minister? Not even when you went into opposition again?" Question provoked question, igniting her memory and further incensing her.

She had said it: the things she had sworn to herself she must never say. The words that revealed to him, unequivocally, the intensity of her pain.

"I'm not going to dignify that with an answer. But you're wrong, Dede. Dead wrong." She stared through him. . . . "Okay, Dede. It's obvious that unless I tell you everything, you'll never be satisfied. And I know I shouldn't be doing this. It's a confidential matter. . . . You realize you're forcing me to break a confidence," he added as if gauging the level of her anger.

Dede made no effort to stop him.

"Joan's been miserable since her transfer," he continued matter-of-factly. "The ambassador Joan works for is a hard-nosed politico. He sees everything in terms of party: our party, their party. Daily, he's making her life difficult for being associated with the Liberals for so long. He refuses to overlook it, as if it were some terrible transgression for which she can never atone. Joan wanted my advice. Whether to request a transfer, which would be viewed as a black mark, or hang in. I was trying to calm her down."

Dede pandered to his explanation. "And what did the seer advise?"

"After some bouillabaisse and champagne, which I'm sure you observed," he replied, mimicking her sarcasm, "I managed to convince her to stick and stay. I told her nothing is easy in government. There are always personal concessions to be made. You have to consider the big picture. When you're a career civil servant, you have to take the good with the bad . . . as with everything in life."

Dede refused to let herself become drawn further into the conversation. She had heard his self-justifying rhetoric before.

He must have sensed her mounting irritation. "Do you think I'm so stupid that I would have taken her to our restaurant and sat at our table in broad daylight if there was anything to hide?" He posed this as a rhetorical question and one which obviated any further rehashing of the event. "While I was there I made a reservation for us for tonight. Would you like to go there or would you prefer if I made it elsewhere?" he asked, confidently projecting their marriage into the future.

She refused to be so easily appeased. "Why didn't you tell me this when we were sitting here yesterday morning?"

"Would you have believed me?" he said with uncharacteristic simplicity. "Look at you now. The foolish way you've upset yourself. And this unnecessary scene you just choreographed for us." He spoke with the indignation of the victim. "My darling Dede," he said, his tone softening, "you've always been so insecure. I don't know whether it's the teenage weight problem you still imagine you have, the rarefied childhood your parents put you through that prevented normal relationships or simply not really having a college education which undermined your self-confidence. These are things which happened to you years before we met. Hurts for which I'm not responsible, but still have to live with the consequences. . . . I'm sorry, maybe I shouldn't have said that, but you know it's true. That's the only reason you don't seem to realize how much I love you."

George had accessed her vulnerable area. Her questions stopped. Embarrassed, she avoided his gaze, which, like his words, had become overlaid with sympathy.

"Do you know what I'm looking forward to, Dede?" he resumed. "When you've lived with me for as long as you've lived without me. That will be, let's see, in only nine more years. Then maybe you'll forget everything that happened to you before we got married. And you'll be happy with our life together. Like I am."

He had brought her full circle to her last question, leaving her no loose ends to consider. George picked up his chair, which had become embedded in the softness of the grass. As he moved it aside, he said, "Dede, I don't like to leave you when you're like this." Leaning down, he gently kissed her on the forehead, then proceeded to the limousine, cautiously stepping around the ruby fruit of the *arbousier*. Overnight, a branch from that tree had loosened, splattering its protected harvest.

The chauffeur held the door open. George called back, "Then tonight? At Gaston et Gastounette? The reservation's for seven." The door closed, the car sped away.

Dede remained at the patio table, her breakfast untouched. Wasps hovered above the neglected pots of jam. One, too eager, had plopped into the pot of honey. Its wings fluttered futilely, trapped in the sweet, thick nectar.

She considered the rock formations across from her. The juxtaposition of their stone life. The submissive female supplicant acquiescing to her uncompromising counterpart. Nature's order.

What choice did she have but to accept her husband's explanation? She had no desire to end up divorced. After all she had gone through with George and everything she had done to help his career, she did not want to find herself alone and have to start over.

∽

Returning from abroad, Dede began to reassert her credentials as Mrs. George Talbot.

George's sins of commission rimmed their lives but, she reasoned, equally did her omissions. For men in politics, power was a seductive lure and female parliamentary staff were reputed to be predatory. A cabinet minister, the position George had held for the bulk of his career, was one of the most sought-after of prey. If infidelity was inevitable, her behavior might have made it so. Since George had been elected to Ottawa, she had been torn between two cities and two generations of Talbot males, and might have overinvested her energies and emotions in her boys to the detriment of her husband.

She blamed his indiscretions on her neglect and resolved never again to give her husband cause to repeat them. She monitored George's incoming invitations with both his local secretary and her Ottawa counterpart to ensure her own availability for those functions George wished to attend. Without waiting to be asked, she appeared every second Wednesday in the capital, remaining to accompany George home on Friday.

Dede dealt constructively with the deficiencies of her own that George had mentioned. She took a more dedicated approach to weight reduction, hiring herself a personal trainer. She successfully shed inches and pounds, but refused to diet to excess. A slightly fuller face, the beauticians advised, pressed out wrinkles. So why ravage the one positive feature nature had allotted her? With a slightly plump face, reduced thighs, hips and waist, for the first time she felt confident in her appearance. She endeavored to make herself more intellectually appealing to her husband. She enrolled in extension studies at the University of Toronto, taking classes at the St. George campus every Tuesday night. Her choice of course was Africa in the Twentieth Century and this added an extra layer of communication to her life with George. It also gave her the ability to insert at the appropriate juncture of conversation the correct buzzword the occasion demanded when, with George, she socialized with others in his field. She knew she could not possibly span the educational gulf that lay between George and herself, but she could make herself comfortable speaking with him about his work. Their Mercedes station wagon now regularly transported, in addition to Adam and Michael, periodicals on African studies.

Her husband seemed appreciative of her efforts and similarly made concessions. He became more attentive and reliable. He returned every Friday on the six-fifteen. She no longer received phone calls from him canceling his weekly visit. She knew exactly when to expect George home and planned accordingly.

On Fridays she encouraged Michael and Adam to have a snack when they came home from school.

"We're dining tonight at eight o'clock. Gourmet food and a gourmet hour," Dede would say often to her boys when, nearing seven-thirty, they grew hungry.

Within a month their complaints had ceased as Adam and Michael learned they could depend on their father's appearance. The boys savored this reunion. They thrived on their father's attention and the structure he brought to their lives.

George seemed to be enjoying their companionship. On one such Friday in February he turned to Adam and asked, "What do you think of all of us going to visit Grandma and Grandpa in Palm Beach for school vacation? Not just you and Michael and Mom like it usually is. But all of us. As a family."

"Sure, Dad."

"Michael, would you like that?" Michael left his chair, encircled George's neck with his arms. "Then it's settled. I'll tell them at caucus I'll be away for March break. . . . I'm all yours."

Plans were made; the air tickets reserved well in advance to guarantee there would be no disappointment at this peak travel season. Adam went to the attic less frequently after this. During their weekday meals with Dede, the boys talked of little else but their upcoming holiday with their father.

Adam usually delayed his packing for similar trips to his grandparents, a tactic which resulted in the task being performed by default on the eve of the flight by Maria. But this March it was different. A month before they were to leave, his room had become a hazard course which only the wary could negotiate after lights out. He had laid his clothes in neat piles all over his floor, and took delight in explaining to his family, and to Maria whenever she threatened to remove them to vacuum the room, what he intended to wear for each activity with his father.

The week before their departure, Adam was flopped on his stomach beside Dede on the duvet watching TV, his long skinny legs kicking absently behind him, when George phoned.

"I'm swamped with all the work I've got to get done before I can go away. At this point, I don't know why I'm even going," he said. In order to guarantee the optimum coverage for his Ottawa office, he had moved up his secretary's vacation to two weeks before his own. "A mistake," George pronounced. "The temp's a disaster. She's capable of making the simplest task her life's work. She can't seem to get my correspondence out. Kim's only been gone five days and already everything is backed up. If I'm going to be able to get away, I'll have to stay in Ottawa this weekend. Do my reports and letters in longhand and hope she'll somehow find her way to type them. I have to get them out before I go."

"Can't you think of any other way to get them done without staying over? The boys are going to be so disappointed. You know how they look forward to these Friday nights."

"I can't see any other alternative. The caucus will be critical of me if I don't get these things finished."

Adam heard his mother's end of the conversation.

"I want to speak to Dad. Don't let him hang up." He raced out of her bedroom and down the stairs. "Dad, why can't you come home?" she heard him say with disappointment from the phone in the kitchen. Adam, in the midst of adolescence, was the one who craved his father's attention the most.

"Your mother will explain it all to you."

"I want you to tell me," her son persisted.

"Got to work all weekend. To get things cleaned up so we can go away." Adam did not reply. "I'm doing this for us, Adam. You and me. So we can have lots of time together. I want to make sure we're going to have two great weeks with no interruptions. My days will be completely yours. . . . Now, is it okay if I work the weekend?"

"Sure, Dad," he said reluctantly.

"I've got big plans for us in Florida. We'll fly up to Orlando on my Air Canada pass. Spend a few days at Disney World. And we'll drive over to the Blue Jays' spring training camp in Dunedin. Take in batting practice, check out the new players they've signed and get lots of autographs. . . . How would you like that?"

"That's great, Dad. See you next week." When he came back to her bedroom, he had his Blue Jay hat skewered firmly on his head. He did not return to lie beside her, but instead watched TV from the foot of the bed. At ritualistic intervals, he tugged at the peak of his cap.

Dede called George's direct night line at eight-thirty and again at ten. It rang nine times, finally to be answered by the House of Commons' main switchboard.

C h a p t e r **16**

*T*he intense storm predicted by weather watchers to be the last of the season struck the city in the morning two days before they were to leave for Florida. The temperature throughout the precipitation hovered barely below freezing, rendering the snowfall heavy and moist, the consistency which Adam and Michael called packing snow and joyfully patted tightly into snowballs. Following this assault a drizzle had begun in late afternoon and deposited upon that accumulation by dawn a thick ice glaze.

Through a shallow sleep, Dede heard the roof groan. It shifted, as it always did in the old Rosedale home, under the stress of the extreme changes in temperature. The sound was welcome company, stable and comforting.

Around midmorning the phone rang. She picked it up in the family room. School had already broken for spring recess. Both boys were there. Adam was helping his younger brother select a board game to take on the plane the next day.

"It's your father," she said to them as, dropping into the mocha couch, she glanced out the leaded windows. Whipped snow clung to the bark of the trees. Sun glistened off its glazed surface. The day was warming up. A chunk dropped off the roof. "Hi, George. You'll never guess what we're doing. . . . Packing the boys' flight bags."

"Dede, I just can't go. It's impossible. You'll have to take the boys without me. External Affairs made a special request to have me included in an emergency fact-finding mission to Ethiopia and some of the other countries that have been hard hit by the drought. It's considered important to see things firsthand. That's the only way to know for certain what's happening over there. It goes this Tuesday for four weeks. . . . You know how I feel about these assignments now that I'm just the opposition critic.

There's no way I can refuse. And there's something more important at stake here: the sincerity of my commitment to the Third World could be challenged if I don't accept and instead head off to Palm Beach. . . . Apologize to your parents for me. I know the boys aren't going to like this too much. Can you please explain to them what a spot I'm in?"

"Everyone here was counting on you," she said wearily.

"You're great with the boys, Dede. You can handle it. You usually take them to Palm Beach yourself during March anyhow. They probably won't even notice I'm not there. . . . When I return from Africa you can count on me being on the six-fifteen from Ottawa every Friday. . . . Just think of all the fantastic stories I'll have for the boys."

Adam had also been a participant in the conversation, the inconspicuous listener intently interpreting his mother's reactions. "What did Dad say this time?"

She sensed Adam's apprehension, the anxiety underlying those few words. He got up from the floor and stood in front of her, his thin arms held rigidly at his side. An eye twitched.

She tried to minimize the anticipated impact on her son. "It's just gonna be me and youse guys," she said mimicking the style of the Cagney videos of which Adam had recently become so fond. "It's just going to be us three. The famous triumvirate. The threesome that brought you Nassau and other great sun spots returns to bring you Palm Beach." When there was no response, she switched her approach. "Wait until Grandma and Grandpa see you. They won't believe how much you've grown." Her forced gaiety did not work.

"Dad's not coming," Adam said flatly.

"No, not this time." Dede dealt with her eldest son forthrightly now, met his bluntness with a corresponding directness. Adam continued to stare at her. His deep-set, penetrating eyes demanded more of an explanation. "The prime minister insists Daddy make a fact-finding trip to Ethiopia in these two weeks. Daddy had no choice." Dede's charitable revision of the facts was to soften Adam's disappointment, not insulate George. She concluded with "I know you're disappointed. . . . So am I."

Only Michael heard her last comment. Adam had escaped from the room before its completion, his heavy tread audible on the uncarpeted wooden steps leading from the second floor to the attic.

A little over an hour later, Dede readied herself to leave the house. The CBC announcer had said it would be five degrees Celsius. "Large meltdown expected today. Final storm of the season as March goes out like a lion."

Dede shed the mink-lined trench coat she had worn all winter. George permitted her to have a fur provided its contentious pelts were safely concealed inside and unable to offend the less affluent or the ecologically minded constituents. The same reasoning permitted their station wagon to be a Mercedes as long as in predelivery servicing the dealer removed its telltale hood ornament, thereby camouflaging its pedigree by turning the vehicle into a Chrysler look-alike.

She refused to dwell on the reason behind George's sudden change of plans. He could rationalize anything. She concentrated instead on the tasks that remained to be done. George had said he wanted to look after the tickets and traveler's checks himself. With his withdrawal, she now had a myriad of things to complete if she was going to take the boys away on her own tomorrow.

Around noon, after these last-minute items were done, she turned her Mercedes into their circular driveway. Its interlocking stone had already been scraped clean. Robins hopped on top of the plowed stacks. She moved her car as close to the front entrance as possible before she got out: a crisp ice crust covered the lawn's snowy surface. She scrunched over the remaining deposits toward the house. A heavy thud of snow smashed onto the walkway in front of her.

Instantly, she looked up to see what had happened. Someone was up there. Pain knifed her unprotected eyes, unaccustomed as they were to the combined clarity of the winter sky and the glare off the glistening surfaces. She squinted, pulled down her Vuarnets from on top of her head to cover her eyes. She focused again. It was Adam. Perched precariously on the ridge of the roof, legs pinched up beneath him, hands gripping the shingles. He sat in a dry pocket of sun. The morning's direct rays had melted that patch first, bored through its ice shield until it released its burden and sent it plummeting to the ground. As the sun approached its most intense hour, it was beginning to loosen the snow which had accumulated there. Clumps of thick, raised snow still adhered to the roof, fastened to the shingles by the ice rain. They projected out ominously from the gable above his head. At any moment they would dislodge and bring her son down in an avalanche, shattering his fragile body as surely as the snow that lay fragmented near her feet.

Icicles hung from a false window spire beneath the apex of the roof.

The cycle of warm weather and freeze had tapered their spears to dagger points. Now green prisms of death, they poised directly over her unsuspecting son.

The high repetitive screech of hawks broke the silence, a chorus incessant and irritating; their sleek black wings circled wide and terrible against the clarity of the sky.

Dede ignored the heavy pounding of her heart. She had to bring her fear under control. When she felt she could trust her voice not to betray her terror, she asked, "What are you doing up there?"

"Nothing." His answer fell quickly to her through an eerie stillness.

"Why are you up there?"

Silence.

"Adam, please come in now."

"Why?"

"I'd like you to come down so we can talk."

"There's nothing to talk about."

"When are you coming down?"

"Maybe never."

"I want you to come down so we can talk about what's bothering you."

"I don't want to talk to you. I want to talk to my father and I'm staying here until he comes home."

A slice of snow pitched from the roof and smashed. The same would happen to her son if she couldn't get him down quickly.

"If I phone your father and he agrees to come back from Ottawa to talk to you, will you come down off that roof now?"

No answer.

"Okay," he finally said.

Dede was afraid to leave Adam and use the phone in the house. She worried what might occur in the interim. She wasn't sure what was going on in his mind—how he might think or react. Nor could she risk upsetting him further. In advance she told him everything she intended to do, hoping his prior approval would somehow guarantee his safety.

"I'm going to call Daddy from my car. I'll find out exactly when he'll be home. Then I'm counting on you to come down. Is that all right with you? Do we have a deal?"

Adam did not reply.

She got into the station wagon and left the door ajar. She started the ignition, activated the cellular phone and punched in the digits of George's Ottawa office. Then her eyes returned to Adam.

One ring. Two.

"Mr. Talbot's office, *bonjour.*"

"This is Dede Talbot. Put me through to my husband immediately. It's urgent."

"Mr. Talbot's in a meeting. He left instructions not to be disturbed by anyone, Mrs. Talbot."

Dede snapped shut the car door. Pressed up all four power windows, soundproofing their conversation. "I'm not just anyone. And I must speak to him."

"Mr. Talbot's at caucus in the West Block. Do you wish me to transfer you?" the temp asked.

"No, I'll take the number." She didn't want to risk being disconnected.

Dede hung up without a pleasantry. Again, she entered the area code, then the number.

"National Liberal Caucus, *bonjour,* Caucus Nationale—"

"This is Mrs. George Talbot," she said, interrupting the bilingual salutation. "It's imperative I reach my husband. Please take this message in to him. 'Adam's life is in danger. I have to speak to you now—Dede.' . . . Hurry, I'll hold on."

Minutes later the efficient voice returned. "Mr. Talbot read the note. He wrote on it, 'Can't take call now. Will phone as soon as caucus over.' "

"You'll have to pull him out of that meeting. It's a matter of life and death. He can't phone back later."

"Mrs. Talbot, it's impossible for me to reenter the room. I'm sorry" was her unequivocal reply.

"Please. You must! You must help Dede. . . . Please," she pleaded for the first time in her life.

"I'll try, Mrs. Talbot."

"Thank you, Priscilla" were the words Dede heard from George. Professional and polite, words obviously addressed to the secretary. "I'll take it in the members' side room. . . . What's the problem, Dede? I'm really short on time," she heard a few seconds later.

"Adam's on the roof. Possibly going to jump. The snow is breaking up all around him. George, even if he doesn't jump, he could be killed. He won't come down unless you promise to come home."

"Dede, you pulled me out of an important caucus meeting. Surely this could have waited twenty minutes."

"George, when can I tell Adam you'll be home?"

"I'm not coming home until after the Ethiopia trip. Four weeks. You knew that before you phoned."

"Didn't you understand what I just told you? We have to get him down right now. Before something terrible happens."

"Dede, calm down. Nothing's going to happen to Adam," he said patiently. "Wait a sec." She heard a hand being placed over the receiver. "Okay, Mike, I'll be right in" were his muffled words. "Dede, I'm being called back," he said, sounding stressed.

"George, Adam knows I'm phoning you. What do you want me to tell him you said?"

"Tell him to come inside immediately. And that I love him. But Dede, you know what to say better than I do." Frustration dominated his voice. "I've got to go."

"George, don't do this to Adam. He's your son. He needs you. I need you. Don't do this to us."

"Dede, I'm sorry but I can't stay and talk to you. Foreign aid's up next and, as shadow minister, I'm expected to be there. If I don't get in right now, I'll be noticeably absent. I really must get back to the meeting. I'm sure you can handle it. If you have to speak to me again, you know where to find me."

"George, you have to—" A dial tone replaced her husband's voice. Through the windshield, Dede looked up at Adam. He looked so vulnerable and pitifully frail on the roof of the old house.

"Just spoke to Daddy," she said as she got out of the Mercedes. She trudged closer.

Adam was watching her, but did not ask what his father had said. As if he already knew the substance of the call and that he could expect nothing. "Daddy's coming home. He's taking the first flight out after the caucus meeting. He told me to tell you he loves you very much. Like I do. He said you are to come in immediately."

Adam did not budge. He seemed to know that she was lying.

Silence, broken only by the bounce of liquid onto a frozen surface. The erratic sound of dripping she had heard earlier had been replaced by a steady splatter. Its persistence had perforated the glazed snow at random intervals along the perimeter of the house, forming ruts of chill water. The icicles along the eaves were accelerating their melt. So too, she now noticed, was the heavy, jagged cluster which, suspended directly over her son, was dripping continuously onto his leather jacket.

A metronome measuring the remaining minutes she had left to save her son's life.

One piece along the ledge shifted and dropped. Its tip pierced into the ice crusting beneath it, and embedded there.

"Adam, I'm coming up to talk to you. Okay?" She did not wait for acquiescence. Dede covered the two flights to the third floor with a speed she did not know she possessed, and entered the place where her son spent endless solitary hours. Her eyes, readjusting after the brightness of the outdoors, groped through the dimness, desperately seeking the suspension ladder which would take her to the roof. But they were drawn, unwillingly, to the site where Adam had his miniature village and train collection—the project father and son had labored on over several holiday seasons. Together they had set down a network of track over embankments and sidings, through model villages, tunnels and stations with elevated platforms, even installing breaker switches that flexed cautionary flashing signals. The realism of its village had been complete to the detail of a farmer waving from a grassy field of grazing, polka-dotted enamel cows.

But now everything was destroyed. Two black diesel locomotives had been crashed headlong; their bodies locked together, tangled and prone. The miniature sign crossing was torn; cows, farmers and homes strewn across the room. Model cars, selected by Adam and presented by George at three successive birthdays, had been smashed. The Union Pacific passenger car, a perfect 1860s replica and George's most recent gift, the worst mangled of these. Its fine velvet seats and embossed gold doors had been methodically crushed. This was the debris and destruction of all which she knew had come to symbolize for Adam his father's love.

Dede's panic increased. Her eyes located the ladder and the opening to the crawl space. She maneuvered her body through its slender passage, wedging her hands against its rotting timbers. Her eyes remained fixed on the bright light ahead.

Reaching the porthole, she hoisted her lower body against its side, and stretched her hands toward her son. He remained an arm's length beyond her reach.

Her son watched her efforts impassively.

"Adam, I thought we had a deal. You said you would come in when you knew your father was coming home."

He didn't move.

"Adam, come in. Now."

Another clump of snow dislodged. Slid through the narrow corridor dividing Adam and herself. She heard it break on the cement. She glanced down. From this precipice, the three-story drop was more terrifying.

"I told you, Daddy will be coming home after his caucus meeting." In desperation, she added, "He said if he finds you on that roof when he gets home he'll spank you, regardless of your age."

That embellishment gave authenticity. Adam now seemed convinced of the veracity of her statement. He extended his hands toward her. She saw they were trembling.

Dede braced her feet under a joist, flung her length across the wet shingles, frantically straining to span the critical distance between them. Stretched until she grabbed her son's hands, cold and immobile, within hers. Constricted in the same position and wearing only the lightest of apparel, he was showing the effects of having been out in the cold too long. His body seemed wooden. She brought him toward her, his legs outstretched, a dead weight, dragged behind him.

A dense, ice-coated mass of snow broke from the section directly above Adam, threatening to knock him onto the pavement in an avalanche of snow. It struck his lower body, his legs pivoted from beneath him; they dangled over the ledge of the eaves trough. Dede clutched her fingers around his fists, her nails dug deeply into the flesh of his palms, the bones of his thin wrists. She pulled him back to her, toward the porthole and safety, through a source of unknown strength.

She knew she pulled him away from death that moment as surely as fifteen years ago she pushed him forth into life. Again she grasped him in her arms and held him even more possessively than she had at birth.

There was very little Dede had to say when George finally telephoned at nine-fifteen. In the aftermath of the rescue she relived the incident and along with this came other thoughts until, dominant, these obsessed her and drove out everything except their resolution.

George had never loved her. Love she now knew was too complicated an emotion to attribute to George Talbot. He only saw others in terms of what they could do for him. He may have married her for her parents' financial usefulness to his political career or possibly her social prominence. He probably remained married to her for an equally unflattering reason: for the illusion of unavailability that marriage provided for the career-driven, or because a divorce, no matter how adeptly presented, could derail the career or at minimum dim the political prospects of even the most entrenched politician. She knew Joe Bradley had schooled him well in the vulnerability of his chosen profession. One or an amalgam of these reasons bound him to her. But he compounded apathy with betrayal and deceit. Could he consider her so gullible, himself so glib, that she would believe he would expose himself to criticism by missing the most significant session of an international conference just to help a former EA chart her career moves? Hardly in character for a man who wouldn't step out of a routine meeting to take an emergency phone call concerning his son. Or as recently as two weeks ago, after all she had tried to do to eliminate his desire for other women, brazenly revert to his former style of last-minute cancellations with his signature excuse of having to stay in Ottawa and work the weekend, ostensibly to ensure he could join them for a family holiday, but probably to sleep with some other staffer. He was a credible liar, seduced by his own arrogance, a man for whom charm came too easily, to whom everything is given without effort being expended.

But she had known these things for a long time, and had forgiven him. Until today, his conduct had affected only herself. She would not allow him to extend this treatment to her children. Adam deserved better than this. And so did Michael. She would not permit him to do this to either one of them again.

How could he be so insensitive to his son's needs? Disappoint him, time after time, and turn his back on the situation his selfishness had precipitated? Even to care so little as to refuse her call about Adam's safety and then, with full knowledge of the imminent danger, deliberately ignore his son's desperate bid for his attention? George's rejection of Adam—cruel and heartless—could never be rationalized. She didn't want to think of what might have taken place if she didn't come back when she had.

What was she going to do about George's indifference and the harm it was causing? She couldn't change that, but she couldn't live with it either, not with what almost happened today because of it. And she wasn't sure how much longer she'd be able to tolerate George's steady stream of affairs, or his lies.

It was clear now she was the only one who could be responsible for her boys. But with all the problems she had with George, how could she possibly be expected to give them a normal family life? All she could do at this point was to go to Florida, spend as much time with her sons as possible and hope things would settle down. There was so much for her to consider.

When she spoke to George from the family room at nine-fifteen she revealed none of these thoughts. She provided him with only a terse, emotionless, abbreviated account of the day's events, to which George's response was "I told you there was nothing to be concerned about."

After five minutes she ended their conversation by telling him she still intended to take the children to Palm Beach in the morning as originally planned.

"Have a safe flight," George replied. "Sorry I can't be with everyone. I'll phone before I leave for Ethiopia. Tell Adam I'll talk to him then."

She placed the telephone back in its cradle, and, depleted emotionally, unable to force herself from the sofa, raised her head and looked out through the window's welded glass squares. She could not believe that everything had returned to normal. Tranquil and ordered. All that remained of the storm was a light dusting of snow.

∞

Dede returned on an early Thursday morning flight twenty-four days later after extending March break an extra week and a half. She felt she needed more time with her boys.

The following day she set into motion the plan she had outlined to Adam and Michael in Florida. She drove them to school and, once more, went over with them that she would be going away today because she had some personal things to sort out and needed to be alone to do it. She kissed them goodbye, promising them she'd only be gone for a short time. On her way home, she picked up Gertrude, the German nanny she had hired from the city's most prestigious registry to assist Maria. This woman's services were so much in demand among her Rosedale contemporaries to supervise their children that she usually could fill only repeat bookings. After explaining to each of them their duties, she took Maria into the family room and handed her a detailed list of instructions and a glossy brochure from the hotel where she would be staying containing any information the maid might need. Then she asked her to bring down an additional bag from the attic.

Dede removed her lightweight informal attire from her Palm Beach luggage, repacking these, and the third of their initialed set, with her designer collection of dinner clothes and better casual wear. Once this was completed, she snapped off the hanger her high-neck red crepe purchased nine months earlier in Cannes. She put it on, not slowing to examine herself in the mirror, and added her parents' most recent travel gift, a braided gold necklace. She stuffed a matching bracelet, along with a single strand of pearls, into her purse.

George was due back from Africa later in the week. She leaned a pink personal-size envelope against his bedside tensor light, its color and size selected to clearly differentiate it from the brown government variety already stationed there.

At four o'clock, she had the limousine driver carry her suitcases to the car.

At six o'clock, she answered the final boarding call for Alitalia to Milan.

BARBARA

Chapter **17**

Sitting on the balcony of her junior suite at Itaro, lost in recollection, Dede was slowly nudged into awareness by the persistent, heavy clang of bells. Her eyes adjusted to the brilliance of the late afternoon light. Her gingerbread homes were still across from her, safely locked into the depth of thick greenery. On the lake below her, a boat similar to the one she had been watching earlier traveled across Como's expanse at a pace equally slow as its predecessor. A float plane dipped between the hills. But there was no sign of the hang gliders or their festive sheaths. Her hang glider was gone like the fringe of a dream. But not the memories that had been stirred or the turmoil of emotions.

She looked at her Rolex. Eleven-thirty North American time. She quickly made the six-hour forward calculation. Five-thirty. Too early for dinner in Europe. Too late for anything else. Perfect for an aperitif. But not here in her room. She needed a distraction from the intrusion of these recollections. She would have a cocktail outside in that nice bar she spotted coming in, the area overlooking the pool. They probably offered an interesting drink, something blended with herbs and natural ingredients. She would unpack later. How wrinkled could her things have gotten anyway? She had placed everything between tissue paper. Memories had tired her, more than she would have thought possible.

She forced herself out of her chair and reentered her suite. Abruptly at the threshold of the first of the two doors that led to the corridor, she altered direction; headed instead toward the closet and observed herself from all angles in its full-length mirror. The straps of the elasticized balcony chair were imprinted onto the back of her red jersey. They compounded the creases acquired during that tiresome transatlantic flight and the subsequent hour drive up from Malpensa in the Mercedes the spa had sent for her. No, she certainly couldn't go downstairs like this. What suitable thing could she easily get her hands on? The black crepe. It was indestructible, even without pressing. She unzipped the largest of her cases, felt around inside it, located the fabric between the tissue and pulled it out. "Better. Much better," she concluded after a follow-up inspection. With that, she grabbed her wide-framed sunglasses, tossed them into her purse, picked up her key from the boudoir table where the bellman had placed it and left for the lift, jangling its heavy metal against the adjoining gold tag throughout her routing to the lobby. The concierge greeted her with refined cordiality and no hint of their earlier encounter.

"*Prego, signora,*" he said, acknowledging with these words both her and the key's return.

She took the first entrance leading outside, pushed the revolving door and headed across the pebbled walkway toward the terrace bar. She spotted a gazebo. Leaves emanating from branches of circling trees wound around its white slat sides and curved roof. Their lilac-like flowers fascinated her. Such a secluded and elegant location. She entered and sat beneath it in one of the patio's low-slung chairs.

Still too early, even for cocktails, she thought. The staff were preparing the area, shaking open white cloth squares over iron tables and placing on each a silver cup brimming with delectables. All was being executed with a relaxed chatter and a proficient ease. She was not disturbed by them; she was used to others working around her. The elevated platform of the gazebo provided her with a perfect view of the pool. The sun was in her eyes; she squinted. From her Chanel bag, she withdrew her sunglasses and slipped them on. The beach attendant had begun collecting the day's debris. He picked up the discarded turquoise towels and pitched them into a portable rack; the mats he hoisted onto his shoulders, circumventing the chaise longues still in use.

Two ladies on cots next to each other were enjoying the late afternoon sun in the uninhibited, topless European manner. Neither of them looked as if they required spa facilities. A teenager on her stomach, legs flexed in the air, hunched over a paperback. Much too skinny, Dede thought. And that woman near the end of the dock—the one lying on the huge orange beach towel? Her towel isn't at all like those the attendant is gathering. She must have brought her own. Very déclassé. Wonder where she's from.

She turned her attention to the waiter who was now poised attentively beside her.

"Signora?" he asked, presenting her with the aperitif selection card.

∽

I am finally relaxing, Barbara thought, succumbing to the gentle rocking motion of the suspension dock, and placed her face deeper into the tangerine towel which she had spread over the mattress of her cot. Time for her was measured in achievements. Now she was taking the usual pause with which she always rewarded herself for successfully concluding an exhausting task. On this occasion she had chosen a more glamorous locale, one appropriate for a woman at her new juncture in life.

Those wonderful chimes again. She felt enfolded in their layers of musicality. They must be coming from the cliffs behind me. She sat up, seeking to locate their source. No, not from there. The bells continued, allowing her to track their sound. It was coming from the lovely church tower down the lake.

From her altered position, she noticed a lanky, auburn-haired teenager on the opposite side of the dock. She was sitting by herself, the places on either side not taken. It's Jenny. Eagerly, Barbara started to get up, instinctively responding to this recognition. No, not Jenny. Of course, she knew it couldn't be her. It was only a similar-aged girl whose features and mannerisms uncannily resembled her daughter's. One of the quirks wrought by distance and desire, endowing the unfamiliar with what we wish to see. A contrivance of the mind that I must guard against, as, for the first time, I am alone.

I must be winding down already. I'm not even curious about what book that girl is reading, whether it's a collection of short stories or a novel. Already a sign of improved health.

She lay down again and assimilated her surroundings. The lake was calm, its surface dimpled like pores of skin. A sycamore stood rigid as plastic, its leaves motionless. The bow of a speedboat had been pulled onto shore, its motor angled above the water.

She looked into the still water. In reflection, these solid forms had changed: boat and tree had split into component parts. They had become slabs of overlapping layered strokes, unidentifiable shimmering globs of color. An Impressionist landscape, she mused, a profusion of individual marks, each unrevealing in itself; its images achieved by illusion.

I am anonymous here, a painting on a wall no one looks at, and I intend to remain that way. I must stop this metaphor and allow my mind to rest. I must relax. And as someone accustomed to being aware of her thoughts and able to control them, she tried to get her mind to cooperate. But this afternoon she was not successful. She was a forgotten painting on a wall. But who was with her in the painting?

"Imagine you are a painting on the wall. What type of painting would you be?" was the question with which the journalist had opened the four-hour session over lunch. A tape recorder had been placed before her in lieu of an entrée.

"Probably a portrait," she had replied.

"In this portrait, are you alone or are there others with you?" he asked, not allowing her a moment's reprieve.

She was unnerved. He wasn't using the question about the painting as simply an interesting way to open a traditional author interview. He was asking psychological questions, the kind devised to reveal her innermost thoughts. Even New York's best media training wouldn't be able to protect her from his questions.

"Are you a solitary figure on the canvas?" he persisted, rephrasing the query she had left unanswered. A shrewd newspaperman, he had sensed her vulnerable area and seemed determined to take advantage of it.

"Okay, let's try something else," he said in the face of her continued silence. "You don't seem to like this line of questioning—we'll begin with statistics. How tall are you?"

"Five foot one and three-quarters." The descendant of a tiny grandmother, the three-quarters had always been important to her.

"What color hair?"

"Depends on the time of month," she wanted to say, but thought better of it, answering, "Brown."

He avoided the obvious—age. The one fact with which she proudly had no hang-ups. The only things that age well are wine and writers.

"What is your best feature?"

"My eyes."

"Why?"

Avoiding an objective answer, she replied, "I have been told my eyes penetrate, invade." She omitted "make people uncomfortable."

"When were you first told this?"

"A long time ago."

"By whom?"

"A friend."

He let that answer pass.

"That wasn't so difficult, was it?" he said encouragingly. "Now here's an easy one. What do you look like?"

Despite the two weeks between that question and now, she still couldn't answer.

"I never look in the mirror," she said. Had she wanted to be more forthcoming, she would have told him why she did not look there—that skin, face and bone structure, the garb we wear through life, hide all that is essential: the pulse of the mind. But who would believe such a reply? Her colorist, whose payments on a new Audi correlated with the depletion of Barbara's bank account, especially before one of her TV appearances or press interviews such as this? However, she thought, that's merely insecurity camouflaged as vanity—a mask making it possible for me to reveal ideas, the only thing really worth talking about.

"I'd like to pursue my original line of questions. In the painting, are you alone or with others? . . . Are they proportionately large or diminutive? Proud or humbled? . . . How close does each stand to you? . . . Where is each placed on the canvas? . . . Does one figure dominate? . . . How do the others regard you?"

If only she could get her mind off this interview. But with the soothing sway of the dock, the lilting, seductive rhythm of a foreign language spoken in an unfamiliar locale, she found herself slipping deeper into memory. Her mind scanned as a computer program, searching back in time for the key to unlock the answers to those questions.

C h a p t e r **18**

The scorching July heat, the highway haze dissolving into a barren, desertlike landscape, the black sticky asphalt gumming the tires of the rented Pinto—those were the images she remembered of the desolate California roadway that had taken them still further into the interior of the state. Other drivers must have chosen not to travel on such a hot day. Traffic was relatively light.

Married such a short time, Paul was still at the stage of acquiescing to most of her suggestions. He had agreed to this detour to visit Sharon, a journey which was becoming with each passing mile more like a pilgrimage, and gave her a chance to tell Paul about the origin of this friendship.

"I spent three years at the National Music Camp in Interlochen, Michigan, a place for the study of the arts. To call it a camp is simplistic. It's much more than a traditional summer of trees and fresh air. It was founded on Dr. Maddy's conviction that art transcends the boundaries of language and nations—that it can break down the artificial barriers that divide people."

"Did you really believe that?" he interjected.

"Actually, yes. All of us who attended the camp in those early years did. We were committed to art and the understanding that could be transmitted through it. Art, commitment, understanding. We saw Interlochen as an ideal of what could be accomplished if all one's creative energy was channeled into art.

"Can you imagine how exciting it was to be thrown together with people of different religions, languages, races and countries, but all having one thing in common—art?" she asked rhetorically, too caught up in the concept to pause for a response. "This incredible mix of people was done deliberately. To provide a microcosm of the world community. And everywhere you went, there was always music. Day or night. I remember at twilight some evenings, a soprano with the sweetest voice I ever heard would wander between the cabins singing 'Summertime' from *Porgy and Bess.*"

"How did you come to go there?"

She maneuvered the answer away from the personal, a protective device she had employed since childhood. "You couldn't just enroll. You could only get in through a process of auditions and recommendations. I met people of extraordinary talent."

She had tactfully avoided telling him what had compelled her to seek such an environment: her love of books; her mother's mock indignation at constantly finding Barbara, long after she should have been asleep, reading by flashlight in bed; the librarian's statement that she had nothing further to recommend for someone her age. Then writing her first short story—the way words flowed effortlessly, surging from a source she could not identify. That exhilaration was a feeling she never forgot. She could not predict when the writing would start. When the words began, she felt part of something greater than herself, a creative force for which she was merely the conduit.

She remembered how embarrassed she had been in grade seven when, during a chemistry lab, the principal cut into the school day with a PA announcement congratulating her on having a story published in *The Ladies' Home Journal.* This was the first she had known about it; her grandmother had submitted her writing without telling her. Faces turned to stare at her sitting in her usual spot at the back of the class. Collectively, their look was one of disbelief which changed within seconds to ridicule. Exposed, she returned her classmates' stares with concern. A writer did not fit the stereotype of the carefree teenager, an image she had been ardently cultivating. She imagined herself evaporating from the chemistry room, a phenomenon which unfortunately did not transpire.

From that day onward, wanting nothing more than to be accepted, she told no one about her writing, nor did she permit any story to be sent in for consideration. But she continued to write: it gave substance to her life. She tucked the stories away as one does memories. At seventeen, how could she not have been attracted to a place where she might find others with the same values as herself?

"You know, we had all those political fears then . . . Khrushchev and the Cuban Missile Crisis. We all worried about the Bomb. Did you ever have a 'Ban the Bomb' button? I did." She really didn't think he would have. She looked skeptically at Paul, not sure he would approve of her next concept, but she went ahead anyhow, intent on sharing her anti-establishment thoughts. "I figured that if the world managed to blow itself up and Interlochen was a pocket of life that somehow survived, like the natives in *Lost Horizon*"—she loved the James Hilton novel and was always injecting it into conversation—"that the new civilization begun with these values would form the ideal society."

She got back to the point of her story. "Anyhow, that's where Sharon and I met. Sharon was a music instructor as well as a counselor. She had the most talent of anyone I knew. She would play for hours in those hot practice cabins. When I would be falling off to sleep . . . you know how you can just feel yourself drifting off?" She stated that as a question. Living together was still so new, she was checking to see if they shared the same responses. "I would hear her piano. The beauty of her music was always the last thing I heard before I fell asleep."

"Why was she so determined?"

"It wasn't that she was determined. It was rather"—she reached for the exact word to describe her friend—"a passion. You should have seen her play. The expression on her face. She was transported. I hope she'll play for us." She changed that to "I'm sure she'll play for us."

Darling Paul, he really doesn't know me yet, doesn't know what he's gotten himself into. Perhaps that's best, she mused. She could sense he was often uncomfortable with her friends. He had told her that he found them different from her and even different from each other. But that had made him even keener to meet them all, especially those most important to her. Perhaps he was wondering what type of person he had married. "Naively married," she thought briefly, remembering how they had met. Paul had been billed as having goals, ambition, honesty, brains—a checklist of virtues. A "catch" was what her aunt consistently called her neighbor's son whenever the topic of Barbara's age was coupled with her single status. "Straight," her college friends would have labeled these identical qualities, their synonym for boring, and with that assessment have ignored him. But Barbara enjoyed meeting new people, something not as easily accomplished now that she had been out of college for five years and in confining clerical jobs. Curiosity overcoming her reservations about him, she agreed to a blind date. She admired his focused energy and quiet determination, and sensed he was drawn to her intensity, so like his own.

"Now I wonder what brought you and Sharon together? We know it couldn't be music," Paul said, teasing her good-naturedly about her off-key singing of hit tunes during this mammoth drive.

"You're right. It's definitely not that," she joked back, then turned serious. It was something more basic than music. She hesitated, not wanting to alarm her new husband with a philosophy of which she was not sure he entirely approved, then continued. "It was what we were just talking about—the belief that the cultivation of art is the highest attainment one can work toward in the world."

With her last statement, he dropped this subject.

"You know she's about six years older than me, bright, and has an intense enthusiasm for life. I think you'll really like her."

"How long ago did you say Joe and Sharon were married?"

"About three years. Her wedding was the last time we saw each other. Sharon used to write twice a week, wonderfully detailed letters about her lessons, the ones she was taking and the ones she was giving. Anyhow, after she got married I guess she had less time, as there were fewer letters and I thought they were"—she paused, again searching for the correct word—"too mechanical."

"She must have been glad to hear you're coming."

"After all this driving I put you through, I certainly hope so." But his comment unsettled her. With each mile, Barbara was becoming increasingly apprehensive. When they landed at San Francisco Airport and she had phoned Sharon to tell her of her proposed visit, her friend's voice had seemed restrained. In Barbara's excitement, she had put it down to surprise and lack of advance warning. The recollection of that call and the hostile barrenness of the area they were traveling through combined to increase this uneasy feeling. It seemed such an unlikely spot for someone with Sharon's sensitivity to be living. Barbara believed the mind needed a fertile physical environment in which to expand and this place certainly did not qualify.

Just then a subdivision emerged, which, with their speed of travel, they had almost passed. Barbara was struck by the development's absence of personality, the castration of individuality. Each home was a replica of the other in size and design, Meccano pieces locked together in one seemingly endless rambling line. They wandered about the housing tract for an inordinate length of time searching for unit thirty-nine; the numbers were the only key to the identity of who lived inside.

She had expected an effusive welcome from her friend; instead, when she greeted her at the door, Sharon was reserved and ill at ease. She showed them into a room where drinks had already been set out. This area contained all the accessories for daily living: the television, rabbit ears pointing east and west, provided the focal point, its location Barbara always used as a bellwether of values. Knickknacks were precisely placed in the room and a gun collection was mounted on the wall. No flowers dangled from romantic angles. In fact, there were no flowers at all.

Sharon toured them through the two floors of the house as emotionless as a robot. Obviously a routine, Barbara thought, and felt loath to interrupt it. Their bed, tables and desk were all devoid of the clutter of living. The house seemed uncomfortably tidy, and too functional to belong to Sharon.

Once back on ground level, Sharon took the group to the garage where her husband was tinkering with a car. "This is our proudest possession," she said. Barbara knew she was supposed to respond with some superlative, but before she could think of one, Joe enthused, "Great Porsche. It's a beauty, isn't it? I race it!" Expensive tools hung on the walls and surplus car parts were everywhere.

The tour complete, Sharon took them back to the room with the guns. They sat on opposite sofas, placed boy/girl like at a formal dinner party.

"Easy drive, wasn't it? Great highway," Joe opened, avoiding any appreciation of their marathon trip. "Ever see a group of guns like that? I don't know anyone around here who has one as good as mine."

"I haven't seen anything like it." Paul's compliment was truthful. To the best of Barbara's knowledge, weaponry was not in her husband's repertoire of experience.

"What do you think of that sawed-off one there?"

"Nice."

The conversation stalled. A new vehicle was required.

"We loved San Francisco. We must have walked ten miles a day. We refused to miss anything. Everything is so different, charming. You must find it a very creative environment, Sharon. What are your favorite haunts?"

"I've never been up there, Barbara. It's a long drive away," said Sharon.

"Actually, with the highway . . . " Paul began. His eyes locked with Barbara's and he aborted the sentence.

"Joe and I like it here. There's no point to go traveling."

All Sharon needed was the right question to open her up, Barbara thought. Then everything will be like before. She just had to ask her something concerning her music. Barbara recalled a letter she had received two years ago from Sharon about a recital she had arranged for her students.

"Sharon, how many children are taking piano lessons from you now?"

"I don't teach anymore." Suddenly Barbara realized what was missing from Sharon's tour—her baby grand.

"Where's the instrument par excellence?" as Sharon used to refer to it.

"Sold for the Porsche," Sharon spoke stoically. "I have an upright now."

Barbara could hardly believe it. The car had replaced Sharon's music? But she said there was an upright in the house. "Please play for us," Barbara cajoled. She desperately needed to see Sharon's excitement reappear, hear her voice lilt with anticipation when she announced the piece. Barbara wanted her friend back as she remembered her.

"I'm sorry. It's in storage," Sharon replied woodenly.

"What do you think about that gun?" asked Joe. "I bet you'll never guess where I found it. But before I tell you that story I want to show you what we've done with the backyard. It was nothing but a mud heap when we bought this place. Come on, let's all go outside. Everyone, follow me."

Sharon remained seated. Her face grew taut. Lines of tension emerged. A high-speed lens shutter captured the withering aftermath of a life with brutal, devastating speed. What remained was a reduced form.

Joe continued his monologue, ignoring his wife's transformation. "We'll go out through the kitchen. That's the fastest route." Joe left with Paul in tow.

Then a voice emanated from the form Barbara barely recognized. "I need to go outside," Sharon said when they had gone. She rose rigidly.

In silence, Barbara followed her out the front entrance. Sharon took a footpath leading away from the complex. Her friend walked as if blind; sensing her route, she headed toward the open space, the area unrestricted by concrete. The land Barbara had earlier dismissed as barren was, she realized, Sharon's closest link with nature. They sat among the hard brush.

"Barbara, you must promise you'll do something for me and you must do it now. Before it gets too late. Before it becomes impossible." Her voice broke, then she regained her composure. Staring into the distance, she continued. "There are some things you have to do for yourself." Then Sharon turned to her. "What are you writing now?"

"Nothing. I've been . . ." Sensing Sharon's unhappiness, she did not want to upset her friend by saying this, but Sharon had always insisted on honesty. "Too happy. I don't want to take time away from Paul and myself. I can always get back to my stories."

"There are some things you must never put aside. Or you can never get them back." Sharon's voice had attained passion. "Don't lose your identity in your marriage, or you'll lose yourself. You must start now, when you're happy, when everything is fresh and exciting. . . . Write. Take the time to build your career. That way, when things settle down, you will always have your creative energy and the skill and confidence to know how to use it. Barbara, never take for granted the gift you have been given or question why words flow through you as music does through me. I mean, used to flow through me. If he loves you, he will accept this as part of you and grow to love it too. If not . . ." Her voice faltered. She had no need to finish this thought; her intended meaning was clear. "Barbara, your eyes, they're extraordinary. I hoped you wouldn't see what I have lost. But I realize by watching them that you have."

Barbara never forgot how ashamed she felt for the horror her eyes must have held for her friend and for the anguish of confession they had elicited. Nor had she forgotten Sharon's advice that from that day on gave focus to Barbara's life.

Chapter *19*

*B*arbara checked on Jenny to make sure her daughter was in bed before she resumed her final preparations in their New Rochelle apartment for their guests. Barbara deposited the centerpiece of sweet peas and baby's breath, as usual, between the silver candelabras. All had been set for the biweekly dinner party that Paul's law firm had come to expect. She had done these "evenings" so often, she had it down to a fine science. Drinks. Hot hors d'oeuvres of pigs in a blanket, sweet-and-sour meatballs, first all passed around, then left on a warming tray. Grapefruit freely laced with sherry for the meal's appetizer. She had discovered the more sherry she added, the more agreeable the evening became. Caesar salad was served as a course by itself. Roast beef followed, medium rare, cut very thin. No one noticed how thinly it was cut, just that it was beef. Although expensive, this was the entrée she always used when Mr. James, a founding partner who wavered between total health and the beginnings of an ulcer, attended. This was accompanied by eggplant parmesan, for those with more demanding palates, and green beans with roasted almonds. Dessert was always sherbet in scooped-out orange skins. This had the advantage of being made days in advance and frozen, one less thing with which she had to contend on the day of the dinner.

Tonight was the senior partners' turn. Two weeks ago she had a similar evening for the associates; Paul believed it prudent also to invite to his home the colleagues with whom he worked on a daily basis. Then, when they heard the partners had been entertained they would not be resentful of him, nor would they know for certain whether he was attempting to ingratiate himself with his superiors. His real motive would remain disguised: to move upward from associate to junior partner to full partner as swiftly as possible. Paul did not feel the firm's social occasions gave him enough opportunity to interact with the partners. The parties in his home gave him unqualified access and the chance to show his wife as an asset. Most corporate clients expected to be entertained. James, Benton & Collins placed great emphasis on spouses of their lawyers, feeling they could call on not just a lawyer but a couple to represent the firm.

Barbara was in the kitchen, where she spent virtually all her time during these occasions. They had reached the salad stage. She poured her Caesar dressing over the romaine lettuce and sprinkled on the parmesan. She served Margaret Benton first, then Karen Collins, Mr. James, Phillip Benton, Wayne Collins and lastly, Paul. She left her salad at her place setting, implying an imminent appearance at the table, which she knew she would never make. This way no one would feel uncomfortable as she served them, not that that had ever happened. No one in this elitist group had yet commented on her absence. She cleared away her full plate at the termination of each course. She was accustomed to their insensitivity to the point where it no longer bothered her. She couldn't relate to these people. No matter how often they came to her home, she knew they weren't her friends. They were insular and superficial. But Paul was intent upon impressing them and, since this was important to him, she did all she could to help him. Paul worked long hours—8 a.m. to 9 p.m. weekdays and most Saturdays and Sundays. But this was expected of him and of everyone at his level. Paul had explained this to her and insisted these parties were the surest way for him to make partner.

Barbara was beginning to understand her husband of three years. It was not primarily money that motivated Paul, although she knew they could certainly use it, just as this was not what had prompted him to choose law. Paul required respect and in selecting a future career had limited himself to the professions that he felt provided him with instant prestige. Law, the giving of advice, was a natural for him. Regardless of the rationale her husband gave for this ambition, Barbara sensed he was driven by an inordinate need for respect. It probably stemmed from his immigrant background. He often quipped that everyone in the country was at most two generations "off the boat." But Paul was only one generation removed. His father had been a rug peddler as a young boy; in later life, he became a five-and-dime store clerk and finally the manager of a small retail chain. He had brought the family economic security; his son strove to improve himself and take his father's immigrant dream one step further, to respect and social prominence. Barbara believed that associating himself with James, Benton & Collins, a midsize white-shoe firm, after graduating from Fordham was her husband's attempt to achieve this. Although she understood Paul and wanted him to realize his aspirations, the idea of respect as an end in itself troubled her. Barbara considered respect an intangible, elusive commodity, not an absolute. When would he feel he had attained it? Would he ever have enough?

The most animated conversation at these dinners always occurred midway through the entrée. Barbara attributed this to the effect of two glasses of wine and whatever protein had been ingested from the thin slices of beef.

"We'll take them. No question of that." Wayne Collins was the firm's sports organizer, a position in James, Benton & Collins which rivaled that of managing partner. He had played Davis Cup tennis through college and continued it during law school. To get it approved by the law school faculty who looked down on such time-demanding activities, he had pleaded poverty. But that wasn't his main reason: he loved the sport, pure and simple, and would have done anything to keep on playing as long as possible. On the court he was seeded in the top ten; in the classroom he was in the bottom third. He announced the summer he took the bar exam would be his last season. When he retired from tennis he was retained by many of the sport's highest-earning players to handle their contracts for them. These professional athletes trusted him: he knew their special needs, their fears and, to a lesser extent, the law. At fifty-five, his build was still muscular, his smile engaging. His athletic activity was now channeled by the firm into the society sport of competitive sailing. He worked out daily and routinely bicycled to work. "We'll take them. Don't worry," he reiterated.

"But we need a good passer for quarterback," added Benton. "I told you, Paul, before you offered that student the job, to feel him out about whether he was prepared to join our regular Tuesday night game. You said it wasn't a problem. So where was he last Tuesday evening?" Benton, although flabby and out of shape, never missed a game. Paul often described to her how this man would puff down the field to position himself to receive the ball. The other firms by now knew to watch Benton, for once he arrived upfield and readied himself, the ball invariably followed. No junior felt so secure within the firm that he would dare deny this senior partner his moment of glory. When he wasn't playing football, Benton's sport was lethal office politics.

"He was sent to the County Court building in East Orange. Had to close fifteen lots. He phoned in to say it was going down to the wire."

"Paul, I know you will never let this happen again," Benton said rigidly. Paul's face reddened. Barbara knew procuring athletes was not what her husband had envisioned when he joined the firm. He had to get above being on the receiving end of everyone's orders.

The silence at the table was blissfully broken by Mr. James. No one ever thought in terms of addressing him by his first name. He had a ramrod-straight back and a perpetually florid complexion. His body seemed to deny his age. The city's legal elders and those who worked closely with him knew this was a petrified appearance, the accumulation of years of brandy abuse. But he still commanded a devoted following, exclusively older clients, who came perhaps more due to social affinity than to any legal imperative. Most came to review old wills or have annual returns witnessed, then stayed to chat. To the chagrin of the junior partners, Mr. James would not bill these old friends for the nonlegal time they spent with him. Between these visits, he sat behind a mostly empty desk and compulsively pitched balls of crushed paper into the wooden garbage pail he had placed half a room length away. Paul had suggested to Barbara that the firm's sport obsession could have originated with him.

Mr. James returned to the only legal issue raised. "Did they close?" he demanded.

"Did what close?"

"Did the fifteen lots in East Orange close?"

"Yes, Mr. James."

"Well done, Paul," he said with exaggerated emphasis, a mannerism Mr. James used to thank all those who gave him satisfactory information.

"Who are we playing next Tuesday?" Benton was not going to let this conversation be put on the bench.

"Miller, Olsen & Treepot, sir."

"My good friend Tom Miller. We had a big case together a few years back," said Mr. James. "The Outland estate. Interpretation of a will. Miller phoned me and said his client might consider settling. He was always cagey, even in law school. I knew if he wanted to settle, I must have had a stronger case than I suspected. So I went to the library. I read through all those old cases and got him. Bar review editors called me later to discuss the ramifications of the case. Did you say Miller was playing touch football next Tuesday?"

"No, Mr. James, his firm is playing our firm. Not Mr. Miller himself."

Paul did not add that Mr. Miller had resigned from his firm due to their policy on compulsory retirement at sixty-five, even for a founding partner: something the juniors, when alone together at Barbara's dinners, suggested Mr. James should do. They attributed Mr. James's behavior to encroaching senility, opening him to charges of incompetence and exposing the firm to liability.

Obviously delighted that Mr. James had returned the conversation back to football, Benton resumed, "We can take Miller, Olsen & Treepot. We did it two years ago, we can do it again. Just make sure the student is there, Paul."

"If we take that game . . . when we take that game," Collins corrected himself, "we'll win the league. That's no longer an issue." Collins had the habit of inserting legal phrases into nonlegal subjects. "Do you want the victory banquet at the Marriott or at my club? What's your pleasure, gentlemen?"

Barbara was relieved her apartment was not in the running.

"Food wasn't so good at your club last month. Book the Marriott." Benton made the firm's decision.

The business of a celebratory dinner having been resolved, the men became chivalrous in what they permitted to be discussed. "Margaret's taking classes at the university." Benton proprietarily put his arm around his wife's chair.

"Tell us about it, Margaret," Mr. James requested. Margaret now held center stage, a position she enjoyed as the wife of the senior partner with the largest billings.

"I'm taking a creative writing course. I was chosen for it."

"Well done, Margaret." That was apparently enough information for Mr. James.

"You must find it very interesting. Please tell us more about it," said Karen Collins. A brunette and strikingly lovely, she was a physical complement to her athletic husband.

Barbara thought how difficult it must be for Karen, prominent in volunteer work, to sublimate her ego at these gatherings to Margaret's forceful personality.

"Jane and Della took this course before. It fits in nicely after our regular bridge game."

"When did you start?" Karen inquired. Barbara was surprised that Karen asked this since these two women, co-veterans of years of office social gatherings, always seemed to know exactly what was going on in each other's lives.

"Three months ago. I go once a week, after bridge, as I said."

"Do you think you're actually improving?" Barbara thought how uncharacteristic it was of Karen to let her hostility toward Margaret show—uncharacteristic and dangerous for her husband's career.

"Of course, why wouldn't I?"

"How do they teach creative writing?"

"We're given a theme and we have to write a story about it."

Barbara stopped removing the dinner dishes. She sat down behind her uncleared, totally cold plate of roast beef. She wanted to hear this conversation.

"What do you discuss in class?"

"The instructor usually reads his own work and we analyze it. He marks our writing and returns it the next week with his comments."

Barbara asked, "What writers are you studying?" The group, even Paul, stared at her. They were unaccustomed to her joining in the discussion. Until she spoke, they probably hadn't even noticed she was at the table.

"No one in particular."

"What are you reading yourself?" Barbara asked.

"Nothing."

"But you can't write unless you read."

"Where did you get that idea?" Margaret replied. "We are given assignments and we write. That's how real writers work. They write. They don't have time to read."

"But they have to read." Barbara noticed Paul flinch.

Karen was quick to join the attack. "I think Barbara's right. A writer should read. I myself read. Jackie Collins. Even some Hailey."

"Those are not quite the type of writers I was referring to. I meant the masters of literature. Do you like short stories? If you do, you'll love Somerset Maugham. His short stories are wonderful. Most of them are set in Malaysia. Or if you want something wittier, with a New York locale, try Dorothy Parker. I could lend you my favorites, if you like."

"Do you have many books?" Karen sounded intrigued.

"Yes. Actually, I find it best to read anthologies rather than too much by any one author. I find if you read any one person too much it can affect your own style." Barbara corrected herself: "I feel if one writes, as Margaret does, it could influence your style too much. It's better to be an original something than a copy of a Hemingway or a Katherine Mansfield. The aim of a writer is ultimately to develop a unique style, something no one has done before." By this time, Barbara realized she had spoken too much. She rose and went to the kitchen, taking the remaining plates with her. An embarrassed silence followed.

"I gather your wife likes to read," Collins remarked heavily.

"We both do," Paul covered. "Who wants coffee? Wayne, Phillip, I know you do. And Margaret and Karen take tea. Mr. James, what may I get you?"

"Coffee with a little brandy would be nice, Paul."

Her husband seemed relieved that he had smoothly put her controversial topic to rest. "How are you enjoying your new health club?" he asked Collins congenially.

"Glad you asked that, Paul. They've got the best equipment I've found yet in a club."

With that the conversation did not again stray from its conventional content, the women's allotted time deemed misused and over.

The partners left punctually at eleven. Paul always helped clear the dessert dishes. This time, when the apartment door closed, he sat down in his dinner chair overlooking the debris on the table. He looked distraught. "What happened there, Barbara?"

"I shouldn't drink wine," she replied, remaining standing.

"You never drink wine. Barely Perrier. What happened to you there?"

"Nothing. I just got too involved in their conversation."

"It was more than that. You were quiet the entire meal. But as soon as Margaret Benton mentioned her writing class you monopolized everything. You know how Margaret loves to brag. She lives to impress people. Benton gets a charge out of it too. Makes him feel important. You upset her and embarrassed me. What came over you?"

No answer.

"You must have had a reason. Why did you do this to me?"

"I didn't do it to you. I couldn't let her talk that way. She didn't know what she was talking about."

"My instant expert on literature!" he said. Sarcasm dripped from each word.

"Paul, she wasn't talking about your firm's games or where the banquet should be held. She was talking about something important and she happened to be wrong."

"How do you know she was wrong? Whether you have to read to write or some nonsense like that? And since when do you come to be giving advice to a senior partner's wife on what books she should be reading? Even if you did know . . ." He stopped himself, appearing for the first time to hear his own words. "Barbara, what do you know about writing?"

"I write," she said quietly.

"Everyone writes," he said sharply. "I write legal briefs. What are you writing? Letters?" The cruelty of his remarks silenced her. She began picking up the dirty plates.

"Look, I'm sorry, Barbara. But it's just getting to me. All this money I have to spend on these parties, the work you have to do by yourself. No one ever offers to lift a finger. Not even to help with the cleanup. Just 'See you at the office on Monday, Paul' and 'Another great party, Barbara.' It's important to me that these evenings go well. You know how much I want to move up in the firm so we can be done with these dinners once and for all. I'm sorry to have to keep putting you through this."

Still silence.

"Barbara, I'm sorry. Please talk to me."

"It's okay, Paul," she replied, continuing to clear off the table.

"Now tell me. What was happening at dinner?"

"I already told you, Paul. I write."

"Write what?" The same words, but this time softness reentered his voice.

"Short stories. I have for a long time."

"I've never seen you do it." He appeared to be trying to absorb this concept, as if wanting to make it more palatable and incorporate it into his life.

Leaving the cleanup, she sat down in the chair next to him.

"I do it during the day when Jenny naps. Or sometimes I write at night after you're asleep. When we were first married, if an idea occurred to me during the night I would make myself go back to sleep and hope I could remember it in the morning. I didn't want to disturb you. But often it wouldn't return. It would be lost forever. So now I get up, write the basics down and come back to it the next day. You know, you're really a very sound sleeper."

"Why haven't you told me this before?" This was more of an accusation than a question. The look he gave her was reminiscent of the one she got from her classmates years ago in that grade seven classroom and immediately she felt apprehensive he would change his attitude toward her the same way as they had done years earlier.

"I'm sorry, it was just too hard to share."

"With me?"

"With anyone," she replied, averting her eyes.

"Why?"

"I wasn't sure how you would feel about it." She forced herself to make the correction. "I wasn't sure how you would feel about me." It was out now. She continued, "I felt I would be too vulnerable. Too exposed. It seemed safer to keep it to myself." She did not let herself stop. No more fear of how he would react. Whatever the consequences, she would face them now.

After that they talked until the early morning hours. She told him what writing meant to her. She even told him what Sharon had said when they had been alone that sweltering afternoon in the California field. Words that were etched forever in her memory, words she had felt she could never confide to anyone. As Barbara repeated Sharon's phrases and re-called the passion with which she had spoken them, it reinforced her friend's message and its timeliness: "Barbara, there are some things you must never put aside. Or you can never get them back. Don't lose your identity in your marriage, or you'll lose yourself. . . . Write. Take the time to build your career. That way, when things settle down, you will always have your creative energy and the skill and confidence to know how to use it. Never take your gift for granted. If he loves you, he will accept this as part of you and grow to love it too. If not . . ." In her own mind, as she watched Paul listening to her story, she finished Sharon's unarticu-lated conclusion.

Barbara had gone through the worst. She had told Paul everything. She did not have to wait long for his response. He rose from the table and walked toward her. He kissed her slowly, deliberately. Then made love to her with all the gentleness of the first time.

*D*uring the next year, Barbara began to change aspects of her life to accommodate her writing. After much consideration she chose a place to work. Jenny's room had been a possibility. It was cozy and she liked the sweet baby smell that still permeated the room. But Jenny was now five and had become too sociable. Recently, whenever she entered Jenny's room, even if there had been no noise coming from there, her daughter would jump up and greet her. It was useless after that to try to settle her down again. Barbara's only real alternative for writing space was the bedroom.

Paul eventually accepted the idea. He moved their king-sized bed to the side of their small room. She found a compact brown antique desk with matching chair in a secondhand store. The desk had a worn leather top and fluted legs. The elderly shopkeeper, a lady with gray hair tied in a respectable bun, told her this piece had formerly belonged to an authoress. Which writer it was eluded her memory. Barbara did not know if the proprietor's chronology was genuine or prompted by Barbara's comment that she was a writer, but she bought it anyway, both the desk and the story. The desk had a history and that appealed to her. Perhaps she would fashion a story around the desk. She would provide the background of who previously had sat there, this woman's physical description and what her life was like.

Barbara positioned the desk in front of her eighth-floor bedroom window. From here she enjoyed an uninterrupted view. Below her to the right, about three hundred feet away, the construction site for another apartment building had been cordoned off by an orange mesh barrier. It still allowed her a full view of Travers Island and of the children who played there. She observed their spontaneity as they ran their kites or kicked their legs from the swing into the vastness of the sky. She watched the fall of the rain. She still could not adjust to the sensation of being part of the sky: of seeing the drops fall before her and yet not hear their accompanying splatter. Rain or snow, the apartment's altitude made them silently identical. But from her window she could see them and she imagined the rest.

Once Barbara had found her location, she needed to create a pocket of time in which to write. She restructured her day to do so. Her mind was freshest in the morning. As she slept, ideas percolated into her consciousness. Characters would invade her dreams, their purpose and personalities becoming clearer, permitting her to delve deeper into their stories. All she had to do was get up and jot down their words. These came easily, almost effortlessly. Had she truly her choice of time to write, it would have been immediately upon waking, the time closest to this awareness, when the handful of early morning commuters drove with their lights on and most of New Rochelle huddled deep in their beds.

But Jenny and Paul also laid claim to these early hours. Jenny had continued her habit of rising with the first light. Barbara would position herself outside Jenny's bedroom waiting for her to awaken. This had been her practice ever since Jenny was an infant. Paul thought it was a novelty and would pass. But it went deeper than that: it was born of an intense conviction that she wanted her child to know she was loved, and loved just for being herself. She believed love to be the only legacy of significance.

Once Jenny was up, Barbara would help her choose her clothes for the day. She was pleased that Jenny liked her room. Barbara had chosen a circus-tent motif and Paul had decorated the ceiling with it. The walls of Jenny's room were hung with her own art. Bold brushstrokes of primary colors and huge, smiling faces on stick figures abounded. Barbara interpreted this to be a healthy sign: it meant her daughter was happy and content. While Jenny worked at dressing herself, Barbara kept her company. Jenny would chatter nonstop of playmates, school and *Sesame Street*, everything that had caught the attention of her keen mind.

"All ready, Mommy," she would say when attired, pleased with this accomplishment, and raise her arms eagerly for her mother to lift her up. When Barbara held her, it felt as if her daughter had suspended her breath. She did not move but nestled her small face deeply into Barbara's shoulder, her slender arms wrapped snugly around her mother's neck. For that brief moment, the only motion Barbara could detect in her daughter was the beat of her heart. It was as if she did not want this hug to end, her tangible reassurance of her mother's love. Barbara could not describe the joy of these moments to anyone. The intensity of emotion she felt for Jenny was impossible for her to capture in words.

After they all had breakfast together, she waited downstairs with Jenny until the bus taking her to the Montessori school picked her up. The private time with her family had ended and her workday officially began. Barbara let the dishes sit on the table. She allowed the jam to lie spilled beside the napkin, the cereal to cake in the bowl. She left the beds unmade. She pushed away the normal clutter of living, the everyday matters that would have consumed her hours. To enable herself to write, she had to tolerate this unfinished business. She freed her mind to create. She pulled out the wooden chair, set her arms possessively on the antique desk and stared into the distance: a prelude to all her writing.

She worked until the hour to meet Jenny's bus. Then they would do the housework together. Barbara tried to make this enjoyable, a game in which Jenny participated. To make cleaning up Jenny's room fun for her, Barbara had found a wicker giraffe laundry hamper. All Jenny had to do was lift up the neck of the yellow animal to deposit her dirty clothes. Initially she had to stand on her toes to accomplish this. Now after a year she was as tall as the animal and no longer needed to stretch. She would race around her room picking up everything she had wearily shed the night before, lift the lanky neck and plop them in.

Saturdays were set aside for Jenny, something she would not intrude upon for any character or plot, no matter how critical its stage of development, time just for the two of them while Paul was away at the office.

Jenny enjoyed these shared activities with her mother; it was Paul who experienced difficulty accepting the changes in Barbara.

Barbara withdrew from her dinner entertaining, explaining to her husband that she just couldn't keep on with such a time-consuming activity. It took her a full two days to prepare for the event, which included specialized shopping, cooking and flower arranging, and another half-day to restore the apartment to normal, polish and put away the silver. She suggested to Paul that if one of the other women could help her she might be able to continue, but after all the years of doing these evenings by herself a spontaneous offer of assistance was unrealistic.

Her husband later mentioned to her that the associates had not been a problem. They were his peer group and dismissed it as a nonissue. A few had chided him with some comment about having a liberated wife.

But she never knew what explanation he had given to the partners. Karen Collins held executive positions in charity organizations, but that gave Collins admission to an additional social circle. Her work outside the home, Paul often informed Barbara, had helped expand Collins' client base. Margaret Benton's activities were encouraged, if not directly picked by her husband, in an effort to keep his wife busy. When not fully occupied, she would constantly phone Benton. A disgruntled secretary counted and surreptitiously circulated the information around the office that in one day alone she had phoned Benton twenty times. Margaret's creative writing class was nothing more than a flirtation, one in a long series of similar, short-lived affairs. Mr. James, a widower, never tired of telling how the firm could not have prospered without his wife. Whether this was the actual situation, or an idyllic recollection that evolved after her passing, was of no consequence.

No, none of these men would understand the reason his wife was no longer actively supportive of his career. How could he possibly have told them that she needed to fulfill herself? That she required time for her writing? No matter how he might have couched such information, they would conclude he could no longer control his wife. Then would come their corollary: a man who could not control what was happening in his own home could not be trusted to handle the firm's major clients. He might be upset, his judgment unreliable; an unncessarily risky situation for the firm. Barbara was familiar with their reasoning process. Her husband had often speculated with her that this was the basis on which a promising associate who had been to their apartment for dinner was denied advancement. Paul might be concerned his honesty would result in similar repercussions. Barbara did not learn until later that Paul had procrastinated in giving any explanation to the partners.

Barbara was writing regularly now. She did a story about the Great Depression through the eyes of a farmer's child. She tried this in the style of the 1930s period. Then she reworked it in a clipped, upscale manner. The message that came across was totally different. Something similar happened when she rewrote other pieces. Which was better? How should she write? After struggling by herself with concerns like these for close to two years, she felt input from other writers would help her and decided to join a workshop.

Barbara phoned Margaret Benton. Margaret seemed delighted to be back in the role of dispensing advice.

"There is only one group in the city to join. You really don't have a choice. None at all," she said dogmatically.

"Who would you recommend?" Barbara prompted when Margaret hesitated.

"Dr. David Stafford." A pause. Circumspect silence. "Of course you've heard of him?"

"Well, I . . . " Barbara was on the threshold of admitting ignorance.

"World-class," Margaret said. "Absolutely world-class," she reiterated, as if enjoying the use of the superlative. "Of course, the entrance requirements are rigid. Most of his students are published."

Barbara thought of her *Ladies' Home Journal* piece. Perhaps that might help. "How recently would someone have had to be published?"

"I'm not sure." Margaret had imparted her advice and seemed bored with the specifics. "He has evening classes at NYU. That's not too far for you." Location, Barbara knew, was always Margaret's prime consideration when selecting a course. "But as I said, it's difficult to get in." Then, unable to resist the attraction of a parting suggestion, she said, "Why don't you apply? It can't hurt." With that, Barbara heard a click. Margaret had terminated the call.

Barbara told Paul about her conversation. He was pleased she had contacted Margaret. Both knew Margaret would mention the call to Benton, who would be complimented that his wife had been consulted. Paul seemed concerned that Barbara might not follow up on Margaret's recommendation. Before he left for the office one morning, he dialed Dr. Stafford's home number, which he had extracted from the university, then called Barbara into the room and told her whom he had on the phone. He thrust the receiver into her hand.

"Yes? Yes?" Barbara heard a brusque voice demand. "Speak up."

She did not want to do so. She wanted to hang up. Then she could pretend this call had never happened and the embarrassment could be avoided.

"Hello? Anyone there? Yes? Yes?" he repeated curtly.

"I'm sorry to trouble you. I'd like to know if I might qualify for your workshop," she heard her voice respond.

"My class is pregnant."

How could everyone be pregnant in the class?

He must have detected her embarrassment. "Pregnant. You know, FULL!" he boomed in clarification.

Barbara's palms were wet with perspiration. The telephone slid in her hand.

"Okay," Dr. Stafford continued. "Send me a portfolio of your work. I'll look at it. But my class is full."

Without any warning the call was over. Barbara was left gripping the phone, trying to assimilate the brief conversation.

"You won't believe what he said. It's fantastic! Absolutely fantastic! He's actually agreed to read my work. He asked to see my portfolio. Paul, I appreciate you making the call, even though how you went about it was unnerving."

"I knew you could handle it once you got started. You just needed a little help."

Barbara returned the phone to its cradle. Paul came over and kissed her lightly. "Must go. I'd better get down to the office before they miss me. Why don't you phone Margaret and thank her? I'm sure Benton would appreciate that."

Barbara reviewed all her work in preparation for submission. What had seemed exciting and innovative at the time of writing now appeared ordinary. She was uneasy. How could she explain two stories written in different styles? She chose what she considered the best, and forced herself to send it in. If nothing else, at least she would get an opinion on her work from a well-respected writer.

Two weeks later, NYU sent her a registration form for the course. No notification from Dr. Stafford had preceded it.

To enable Barbara to make her session on time, they agreed that on the night of the course Paul would leave his midtown office punctually at five and she and Jenny would have dinner early so that as soon as he reached home she could drive the few minutes to Pelham station to catch the 7:08 train to Grand Central.

That first session, Barbara was the first to arrive. The walls were unfinished and pitted with pen marks. Chairs were scattered about the room haphazardly. The blackboard was cracked, dark stress lines showing through. The upper portion of the lectern had been decapitated, its top severed from its stand, and tossed in a corner. The place seemed cold, antiseptic and inhospitable. Not an environment conducive to a writing workshop. She went to the back of the large room, brought a chair toward a desk and sat down.

People straggled in one at a time. By the scheduled hour, eight others had assembled in the room and, like herself, had taken places at the back. Barbara smiled inwardly that writers' psyches at least have one thing in common.

Dr. Stafford's entrance did not permit her time to digest his appearance. He arrived in mid-sentence. Twenty minutes late, he felt no need to offer an explanation. He bashed a sentence on the board. The chalk snapped in two, splintering on the floor. "Is that a good line?" He read aloud what he had written: " 'I think that I shall never see / A poem lovely as a tree.' Well? Well?" Again, the abrupt manner she had heard over the telephone. "That's an often-quoted line. You all probably had to memorize it in school. Well, is it good?"

No one answered.

"Why would you have been made to memorize it if it wasn't good? Look at the unusual metaphor comparing a poem to a tree. Is it good or not? Well? Well?"

The person beside her answered, "Yes, of course."

"Are you sure?"

"Yes." The person seemed less convinced.

"Wrong. It's horrible. One of the worst lines inflicted on the English language." Dr. Stafford made more frantic scribblings on the board. "Is that a good line? Well? Well?" This round, everyone chose silence. Left to respond to his own question, Dr. Stafford declared, "This is a good line. Hear the music; the rhythm of the words. You must first learn what constitutes good writing. Just because you were told something was good does not necessarily make it so. You must not allow anyone to dictate taste to you again. Including me. You must become the sole arbiter of what is good. Just as you, I'm sure, by now know the difference between right and wrong. You have developed your own intrinsic value system. So it also must be with literature. You will feel your way, learn the texture of words, then ultimately be able to judge for yourself."

Barbara was mesmerized by his dynamism and his ideas.

"I will present to you excerpts from short stories. Some are chosen from the works of the great; others from those who deservedly have been relegated to obscurity. So as not to influence you, I have deliberately deleted the authors' names."

He began to circulate sets of mimeographed sheets. As he passed these around, Barbara tried to assess Dr. Stafford objectively. He was about forty-five and quite short. Limbs attached to a gaunt frame. His short-sleeved shirt showed dark rings of perspiration; his arms hung painfully thin. Hair, bristled and askew at the sides, disappeared into a shiny, bald pate. His nose was hawkish, his eyes deep-set and his face intense. Each physical characteristic, as itemized and noted, was singularly unattractive. But when Dr. Stafford spoke, a metamorphosis occurred, his eyes became vital, his body energized. The individual features merged with the passion in the man to produce the composite: a compelling, charismatic individual.

When Barbara returned to their apartment after eleven o'clock, only the lights in the hall were on. Paul must have gone to bed already. She was disappointed. Throughout the mechanics of her return—the thirty-one-minute train ride to Pelham station and picking up her Pinto there —she had been looking forward to sharing the events of the evening with him, reviewing and savoring it in its aftermath.

As was her habit before she went to bed, she checked on her daughter. She brushed away the wisps of fine hair that had fallen over Jenny's eyes and stroked her small face with its delicate skin. She found herself talking to the slumbering child about the creative excitement she had felt in the workshop. Lids, heavy with sleep, opened. Petite hands reached for Barbara, pulled her drowsily into their arc, then went limp again. Barbara leaned down and kissed Jenny's forehead. How she loved this little girl.

She went into their room, where Paul was deep in sleep. She was too stimulated to go to bed; instead, she decided to write. Used to going from bed to desk during the night, she knew her route as precisely as a sleepwalker in a trance. She reached there, ran her hands over its carved legs, its weathered leather inlay, and wondered about the woman who had worked at this desk in a previous generation. She gazed into the night with its thick complement of stars. Her mind, a bud almost killed by frost, began to open. It was alert and receptive. Phrases, characters and speech patterns flooded her thoughts. All she had to do was write them down. With her page lit only by lanterns that hung in the sky, she began the outline for her next story.

∞

Future classes followed the format established that first session. The nine would discuss an excerpted passage. Dr. Stafford would advance the same question: "Is that passage good? Yes? Yes?"

When a student thought the demands of the voice had been satiated, inevitably came the parry: "Explain." No one was exempt from this challenge. It was impossible to predict how Dr. Stafford would react to an answer: whether he would let it pass or press for a more insightful analysis. Barbara dreaded it when the voice was directed at her. Dr. Stafford merited the expression "he does not suffer fools gladly," and she never knew when she might inadvertently enter that category. She sensed he was employing this as a technique to force them to reveal more of themselves to him and to each other, and conceded this might be necessary if he wanted to mold these introspective, noncommunicative individualists into a cohesive, supportive group.

Although after the first week Barbara had shed her suit and heels for Levi's, sweater and sneakers, her clothes still set her apart: the canvas of her running shoes was too clean, the cut of her jeans too classical. And she was a few years older than most of the others. She also discovered that she was the only person in the workshop who valued a full-time committed relationship. In this subculture, Barbara felt she was the nonconformist, the interloper, the intruder. But as the weeks passed she was able to transcend the differences in clothes, age and lifestyle. The walls of individuality and protective silence that had initially characterized the group began to crumble. She no longer saw the others as unapproachable, but understood them as students who, like herself, were struggling to gain insight into themselves, to tame and direct the force that had compelled them to write.

Rita, a playwright with three productions to her credit, was a master with dialogue. She could dissect any speech, identifying why a phrase needed to be employed or should have been deleted. Barbara was mystified at first as to the reason a dramatist would be interested in a fiction workshop. But her attraction to the course became clearer as the sessions progressed. Rita continually chose the chair directly in front of Dr. Stafford and her eyes never left him. If Barbara had occasion to speak to him after class, Rita would also be there. She would remain behind perusing that night's material with as much concentration as if it were a piece of business in a play while another temporarily held center stage. Rita would wait Barbara out, ensuring her own exit would coincide with Dr. Stafford's. Stafford treated Rita with detachment, as if not unaccustomed to female adulation.

Beside Rita sat John, the Ph.D. candidate. He had had one story published in a minor magazine. His attendance in the group was due less to his literary interest than to the credits he needed to earn toward his degree. As no student in five years of Stafford's course had yet received a failing grade, John, with a minimum writing output and a careful reading of both the instructor and the syllabus, had found the one course where he could float.

John had bright eyes. Possibly that and his bony nose were the only things you could identify for certain. A full, well-tended beard which he stroked appreciatively throughout each two-hour session concealed the lower portion of his face. Whether this was for affectation or a counter-balance for a receding hairline was open to speculation. His stocky frame was invariably clad in charcoal slacks and a button-down blue shirt.

John preferred the role of academician to peer. A passive spectator, he would rouse himself only to offer literary witticisms and pedagogical foot-notes. This grated on the others, most of whom prided themselves on a conscious rejection of formal education. After three months, his pedantic extravagances only drew smiles from his classmates, no longer inciting the courtesy of a rebuttal.

It was with Lennie that Barbara felt the greatest kinship. He worked as a copywriter for a Madison Avenue advertising agency. He was a creative wordsmith with an agile mind. During office hours, he composed the words that seduced the public into buying Holiday Chicken, the agency's key account; in his free time, he crafted the motives and story line for the people who lived in his imagination. Not willing to risk his salaried job lest one of his characters offend a client, he published under a pseu-donym. Barbara overheard him say that he worked up to the minute he left for class and usually arrived without dinner. Despite these pressures, he was always easygoing and unhurried, as if he had an abundance of time. This appearance was enhanced by an old pipe that rested unlit in his hand during class. About six foot two, he carried his height awkwardly. He never quite knew how to position his body in the molded chair. He alternately scrunched his legs under the seat, or stretched them out in front of him. This latter position created a hazard for Dr. Stafford, who, when absorbed in a thought, paced with passion. Eyes, a feature Barbara usually noted, were hidden behind thick glasses, a result of years of close paperwork.

With his lean frame and curly black hair cut conservatively long, Lennie would have been considered handsome were it not for the deep pitted pores, a legacy, she assumed, from adolescent acne, which scarred his face and apparently his confidence. He preferred the company of one person at a time and was reticent about entering into the group's discussions. Barbara understood his sensitivity and was careful never to rebuff any overtures of conversation. That was why, when he invited her for coffee one evening after class, she felt unable to refuse even though she would not get home until well after midnight.

"I guess you're wondering how I stick it out in advertising," Lennie said, as the waitress set down his cheeseburger and her Coke, then left them in the privacy of their corner table.

She waited, not knowing how to respond.

"If you can write, you can write anything. Literature or copy. They both deal in words, the difference is how each makes me feel about myself. When I'm doing advertising, I feel I've sold out. I'm just service for hire."

His bluntness disarmed her.

"Lennie, don't you think you're being hard on yourself? Most people who write creatively have to work at something else to support themselves. At least you work where your ability lies—with words."

"That's how I used to think when I tried to rationalize spending ten hours a day doing copy. Maybe as I've gotten older I've become more honest with myself. . . . I'd like to be able to do serious writing. Work on something worthwhile for a change. . . . Something that I consider worthwhile," he clarified.

"I understand."

"You know, most people don't consider writing important. It's not a value shared by Middle America."

"No, it certainly isn't," she agreed.

"I want to do something meaningful with my life. Or at least try to," he said.

As Lennie spoke, he articulated and reinforced sentiments that had often gone through her mind. She felt less isolated artistically.

"Look, I've sold some stories," he said, "but it's really not enough to live on. It's barely enough to starve gracefully on. I need to sell more. You know the bind we're both in: the more you sell, the easier it is to sell."

"But you've already been published in some prestigious magazines."

"Not really that prestigious. And unfortunately not that frequently. I'm hoping Stafford's direction will give my work focus and make it more marketable. It's hard to explain to a layman, a nonwriter, why I'd give up my high-paying, socially respectable job for something as financially in-secure as literature. . . . People say I'm pretty good at what I do. But anyone with some skill with language can knock off copy. If I weren't at the agency, somebody else would be writing it. I'm just a component part. A sophisticated microchip. But utterly replaceable." He had been looking directly at Barbara up to this point. Now he turned away, em-barrassed.

"I see the people on my staff. We work together, supposedly as a team. But as I supervise them, I know they're all eyeing my job. Do you know why? Because each one of them knows what I do, that any of them could do it equally well." He leaned toward her and spoke more softly now. Behind his glasses, Barbara saw the intensity in his eyes. "But not everyone can write fiction as I do." Somehow coming from Lennie, this admission did not seem egotistical, but forthright and honest.

"You know, I believe being able to write creatively is a gift. A gift that should never be squandered."

As she rode home on the train, she considered Lennie's words. She no longer felt obliged to apologize for her writing, something she too was beginning to think of as a gift, a commitment which required relentless pursuit.

Chapter 21

It was nearing six o'clock on an already darkened November evening. Barbara and Jenny had just finished cleaning up from their early meal. The fare had been Barbara's abbreviated version of a Colonel Sanders chicken dinner, minus the fries, soup and salad. At least on these Thursdays she had not yet resorted to paper plates, the final stand of the time-conscious. Freshly cooked chocolate pudding waited in the refrigerator, the snack Paul was to give to Jenny at bedtime.

Jenny gave her mother a big hug and scooted to her bedroom. Barbara began collecting her books and papers, readying herself to leave for her class as soon as Paul reached the apartment.

"I can't stay home this evening," Paul said as he came through the door.

"What did you just say?"

"I have to go out later." He hung up his coat, sat on the sofa and reached for the newspaper on the Parsons table before him.

"Out later?" She repeated the phrase as one struck with unpalatable news and, with the papers she had put together for class in her hand, went over to where he was sitting.

"I told you how great we've been doing in interleague hockey. Remember two weeks ago we made the semifinals?"

"Sure I remember. But that's always played on Tuesday evenings."

"You're right, it usually is. But we needed extra ice time for this game and tonight was the only time the arena's free."

"Paul, you know it's my class night. Before I started this workshop, we discussed it together. We sat down and went over every detail. We had a firm arrangement. You told me I could count on you. You said this time was inviolate."

"It is, generally."

"Generally?"

"Yes. But this is an exception."

"What do you expect me to do?"

"Miss the class."

"Miss the class?" Making her miss her workshop must mean nothing to him, she thought.

"You don't have to go tonight."

"I can't do that. Every class builds on the other."

"Look, Barbara, I'm not happy about this. You, of all people, should know that. But what can I do? It's a big game for the firm and I play right wing. If I skip, the partners will be sore. You know how they get. I'd be like that student who didn't show up for the football game—the guy Benton kept going on about when he was here for dinner. The last dinner you invited the partners over for."

Paul never missed an opportunity to remind her of her neglected obligations.

"Lou Higgins could play for you. He's an excellent right wing," she said calmly, referring to the lawyer who had been chosen the league's star player last season, but had since left to become in-house counsel for a major corporation. "He'd come back. I saw his wife last month at the parent-teacher night. She told me what Lou misses most about his old job are the hockey games."

"He can't play. He's no longer with the firm."

"Paul, you know there's no such rule. Even former title searchers played this year."

"Barbara, forget it."

"What do you mean, forget it?"

"Forget it! I'm playing my own right wing."

Why couldn't he realize showing up for the game wasn't going to get him a partnership? The partners would never accept Paul. They didn't care who played right wing as long as someone did. But he had broken his commitment to her over this. Before she began at NYU, he had promised her that he would tell Wayne Collins he was unavailable on Thursday evenings just to ensure a situation like this would never arise.

"Paul, what did Wayne say in September when you told him you wouldn't be able to play on Thursdays?"

"Nothing."

"Nothing? Nothing at all? That's impossible." This time she asked him pointedly. "Did you tell Wayne when he was arranging the ice time for the semifinals that you couldn't play if it was held on a Thursday?"

"No."

"Why didn't you?" she asked quietly.

"James, Benton and Collins depend on me." Paul had recently developed the irritating habit of referring to the partners in the descending order they appeared on the firm's letterhead. "Anyhow, what would I have told them?"

"The truth. That your wife has a class and you stay home on Thursdays with your daughter."

"I told Benton that once already. I was doing some work for him and he wanted me to stay late one Thursday night to finish it at the office instead of taking it home. When I told him what you so magnanimously called the truth, do you know what he said? He told me Margaret often skips her class and it doesn't bother her. None of that nonsense about 'one class building on another.'"

"I'm not Margaret."

"Perhaps you should be."

"What did you say?"

"Forget it."

"Paul, why didn't you tell me this a few days ago? Surely you must have known."

"Why should I have told you? You would have only gotten upset earlier and, of course, blamed me for ruining your precious writing." She felt the bite of Paul's sarcasm.

"I might have been able to arrange something."

"Arrange what?" Now it was Paul's turn to ask the questions. "We had an understanding when Jenny was born that one of us would always stay with her. I told you how I felt then and I haven't changed my position on this. No babysitters. It's too risky. And that includes that nosy, affection-starved superintendent's wife who's always offering to help with Jenny. Listen, Barbara, I have sat home every Thursday for three and a half months while you went into Manhattan for that class, sometimes not showing up until after midnight. I don't feel it's unreasonable for you to stay home for one Thursday."

"Whenever you want to go out for the evening—hockey games, meetings, the guys—you just go," Barbara said, holding her ground. "You never think twice about it. Now I have something which matters to me and you're refusing to stay home. And you won't even consider having a babysitter. . . . Paul, you're not being fair to me."

"Fair to you?" he asked incredulously. "When have you ever been fair to me? Do you think I enjoy coming home to this place after a tough day at the office to find filthy dishes in the sink, decomposing food, beds unmade, books left all over the apartment . . . I gather this is one of yours." He reached for a book that was on the table in front of him and held the evidence in the air for her to see. Then he let it drop. The clunky sound it made as it met the wood resonated in the apartment.

In a quiet voice, Barbara said, "When we discussed this, I thought we agreed I would do the housework after my writing day was over. Why didn't you tell me then that you felt this way about it?"

Paul did not seem to be listening to her. It was as if finding the mislaid book had justified his criticism of her.

"And my shirts you used to take to the cleaners? I have to do that myself now. And what about the cooking, Barbara? The beef with roast potatoes, the onion soup, the Caesar salad with that special dressing? You used to enjoy making these. Did you forget how or is this just another thing you've given up doing?"

Feeling the sting of that comment, she made no further attempt to apologize.

"And while we're on the topic of arrangements, what happened to the firm's dinners? You do recall, don't you, that we both decided it was the best way for me to make partner, so I'd be able to get out from under, give orders instead of take them? That was something we discussed. You said I could count on you. Now you say it's too much trouble. But back then you agreed it was important to have them, that the principle behind them was . . . wasn't it the same word you just used about your workshop? . . . 'inviolate.' And we both know how precise you are with language."

She put down the workshop papers she had been holding in her hand.

"Barbara, you used to tell me all these things were important to you too," Paul said, as she turned to go out of the room. His voice was calmer now, his outburst seemed to be over. "I thought I had married someone who enjoyed cooking, the home, a solid family life. I thought we wanted the same things. You took pride in your entertaining, your friendships. We grew up in the same neighborhood, with the same background and values. I just don't know what's happening to you. I don't recognize you anymore. I mean the person inside. You've changed so dramatically. I haven't changed. I still want the same things I always have. Someone to love me, look after me and my children. Someone to take pleasure in and share my successes. Since you started going to this workshop, I don't know how to explain it, but you're not the same. Not just your writing, but you, the total individual. Maybe the people who you meet there are influencing you too much. . . . Barbara, I miss what we had before. And the woman I thought I had married." He paused and spoke, his voice low. "I love you. And us together. The way we were before. I just don't understand what's happened."

Throughout his angry tirade, Barbara had remained unmoved; but in response to his soft, gentle words, the words that spoke of love, she felt her eyes fill with tears. Unblotted, they streamed down her cheeks. She did not touch them, hoping he might not notice.

"I'm sorry if I've upset you. But I have to leave now. With the half-hearted review I got last week I can't afford to alienate the partners over the hockey game. Tonight is important to me . . . to us," he corrected. Paul removed his hockey bag from the cupboard and walked out the door, closing it firmly behind him.

Didn't he understand that his bad review was due to his client list and a hockey game wasn't going to change that. She went into Jenny's room. Her daughter had fallen asleep with a pop-up book in her hand. A story of Sleeping Beauty freed from a deep slumber by the kiss of a prince. Barbara removed the book so as not to rouse her daughter. She wondered if the heroine would have been better not to have awoken, but to continue to live in an undisturbed, innocent state.

After she left Jenny's bedroom, she sat at her desk. White spotlights glared on the apartment site to the right of the parking lot. Machinery that day had completed churning the soil, excavating it into an upturned, muddy compost. Snow was tumbling into the open pit. She was not able to write but stared despondently at the white flakes falling into the abyss.

People, unlike the images of a snapshot, cannot be protected from time—captured forever, untarnished, untouched and unaltered. As years weather the external body, exposure to people and ideas transforms the inner being and a good relationship should accommodate these.

Writing had become central to her life; therefore it could not be put aside. She had wanted to tell Paul this and how sorry she felt he was experiencing the confusion that often accompanies change. But she could not revert to the way she was before, not even for him.

"If he loves you . . ." Sharon's words, spoken long ago, returned with poignant clarity. It was now up to Paul. If he loved her he must reach toward her and accept the changes that had taken place within her.

It had taken her years to share with Paul the simple fact of her writing. It was impossible for her to articulate these more intimate thoughts. She knew her words this time would demand a commitment from him—one he might not be able to make. So she let her explanation lie between them, unspoken.

She feigned sleep when Paul hours later got into bed beside her, exuding the distinct smell of scotch from his usual postgame sports-bar reveling.

The next morning, she tried to settle into work, but construction noise exacerbated her frayed emotions and made productive writing impossible. The splintering noise of the pile driving which had begun at dawn jammed her concentration as one iron block rammed against another, pounding into autumn's hardening earth a succession of long steel rods. Above this battering sound came the high-pitched whine of a diesel motor. She put aside her creative work and for the remainder of the day dealt pragmatically with last night's problem to ensure the situation would never repeat itself.

∽

This Saturday she was taking Jenny for a skating lesson, someplace fun for hot chocolate and then to a friend's birthday party.

Barbara laid Jenny on the hallway floor and zipped her into her rabbit-eared snowsuit. Jenny pulled her hands into her mitts, which were attached by elastic to the sleeve of her coat. One yank of the toque and Jenny was ready to go outside.

At the arena, Barbara put on Jenny's skates, lacing them tightly. Barbara always felt uneasy when Jenny paused at the rink's threshold. She wanted to go with her onto the ice and remain there until she steadied herself. But Barbara had learned to resist this urge. She anxiously watched from behind the wire grille. Barbara saw Jenny's eyes beneath her woolen hat, searching along the boards, anxious to locate her mother. Barbara waved to identify where she was standing and smiled encouragingly, the reassurance Jenny needed to take her wobbly steps onto the ice. With snowsuits snugly encasing them from head to toe, hands held rigidly at their sides, the seven-year-olds collectively resembled a colony of penguins, primarily pink, parading on ice.

Barbara's favorite time came at the end of the class. She positioned herself at the gate when the lesson was about to finish. Jenny, with the confidence gained from the session, took a few short steps and glided into her mother's arms.

They went to McDonald's for hot chocolate and chatted together in their booth long after Jenny's fat white marshmallow had melted.

When Barbara returned to the apartment after dropping Jenny off at the birthday party, Paul was already there. He was on the phone in the kitchen. As she placed Jenny's skating bag in the front closet, she overheard "Sure you can count on me. Of course I'll be there. . . . Yes, the Wycliffe matter. The closing's set for Monday."

Before the receiver was safely down, Barbara heard herself ask, "What can they count on you for, Paul?" She felt tense, her hands clammy: involuntary reactions to a confrontation she was about to provoke, but felt powerless to avoid.

"The finals. You heard me tell Jenny we won last week."

"Paul"—her voice hardened—"I presume it's not being held on Thursday?"

"I'm sorry, Barbara, it is. I know you're disappointed. I know how you feel about your workshop, but we could only get ice time at six o'clock next Thursday. I promise you this will be the last time. It's the league's championship."

She heard her voice reply coldly, "You're wrong, Paul. Last Thursday was the last time."

He seemed stung by her retort.

"Barbara, everything I said last week still applies. I have to play. It's even more crucial now. . . . You overheard the conversation. Benton didn't really phone to check on the Wycliffe closing. He's phoning everyone to make sure they'll be there for the game. I'm not going to discuss this further with you. Just accept the fact I'm going out Thursday. And you can't say I haven't given you plenty of notice this time."

"I don't intend to miss another workshop, Paul," Barbara continued matter-of-factly, not letting her anxiety show. "Your only choice is to stay home next Thursday or let me bring in someone to be with Jenny. I spent most of yesterday on the phone checking the agencies for Thursday night availability and contacting the references for the nannies they recommended. But I'd prefer to use Mrs. Duncan. Jenny already knows her and it certainly couldn't be more convenient for us since she lives in the building."

"Barbara, we agreed we would never use a babysitter."

"Jenny's not a baby. She's seven years old and can make herself fully understood. She could even phone us herself if it came down to that. The rationale for not leaving her with a sitter is not valid anymore. Besides, it's about time she got used to being with adults other than us."

"No babysitters, Barbara. And that's final."

∽

"I told you not to get a babysitter and you went and did it anyway," came Paul's slurred reproach when, crossing the threshold of their apartment, she returned after eleven from her creative writing course.

Paul was sitting on the checkered sofa in a darkened living room, a highball in his hand. Images from a muted TV flickered across the screen.

As Barbara moved onto the cream carpet, Paul rose. His face was flushed, eyes glassy and bloodshot. He wore the stale smell of alcohol. She began to take off her heavy coat.

"We talked this out thoroughly and I told you not to get a babysitter. You got a babysitter against my instructions. And I don't like it. Don't ever do it again . . . do you understand me?"

A blow crossed the side of her head. Intense pain pierced her ear. The impact knocked her to the side, and she fell onto the sofa. She clamped the flat of her hand against her left ear.

He loomed over her. "Get up. Come on, get up! Stop playing games with me. There's nothing wrong with you!" Anger dominated his voice.

She remained on her side, her knees locked beneath her, cradling her ear.

"I don't need to put up with this, I'm leaving." The apartment door slammed.

Pain immobilized her. She remained in that position, sobbing uncontrollably, time's passage marked only by the change of silent images upon the screen. She must not let Paul find her like this. She forced herself to her feet.

Her head angled to the side, she cupped her opposite hand tightly over her injured ear and made her way unsteadily past Jenny's closed door and into their bedroom. She toppled onto the daisy-quilted spread. Her head still inclined to the side, she instinctively grabbed for a pillow and wedged it beneath her wounded ear in an effort to halt the searing pain.

She lay in the dark, its covering blackness somehow comforting. Pain numbed thought.

"What are you so upset about?" She had not heard Paul's return.

She jerked her body across the spread, recoiling involuntarily from the voice beside the bed. Horrified at the realization that she was afraid of her husband.

"Why are you holding the side of your face?" He made no attempt to come closer. "Did you hurt yourself when you fell?"

She desperately wanted to deny him the satisfaction of a response.

"Barbara, are you hurt?" he asked coolly.

Her will crumbled, the pain was too severe. She needed help, but could no longer turn to this man who had always been her best friend.

"I'm sorry I hit you," he went on when she did not respond. "I was checked hard against the boards in the third period and got a bad head-ache. I went drinking with the guys to celebrate and I must have had one too many. Things at the office were getting to me. I know that's still no excuse, Barbara . . . you know this isn't like me. In all the years we've been married, I've never laid a hand on you and I swear to you it will never happen again. Please believe me," he said contritely.

She offered no forgiveness.

"If you're really hurt, you should go to the emergency room. I'll drive you."

She considered his suggestion. And protected him. "No. I can't go there . . . they'll ask too many questions."

"What do you mean?"

"They'll want to know how it happened."

"Well, is there anything I can do for you?"

"I just want to be left alone."

"Okay. I understand. I guess you'd prefer that I slept on the pullout. . . . Look, Barbara, I can see you're upset. But I promise you this will never happen again. Let's try to put this behind us. . . . Okay?"

∞

She woke with a throbbing ache in her ear. She was on top of the covers, still clothed in the turtleneck and slacks she had worn to writing class. The yellow mohair afghan from the living room had been placed over her sometime during the night. She got up gingerly and, tilting her head to the side, held the palm of her hand protectively over her hurting ear. The apartment was empty. Paul must have made Jenny breakfast so as not to awaken her.

She looked outside. A fresh sprinkling of snow cloaked the exposed earth of the construction pit, the white disturbed only by the imprint of grooved Caterpillar tracks. The work's progress was mesmerizing—the choreographed ease with which the cabin and arm of the pile driver maneuvered to accommodate the setting of the forged iron spears, drawing each into the shaft of its steel belly, and the precisioned symmetry with which one metal mallet squared against the other until the pole slid into the ground. Effortlessly as a nail through a plank.

This morning for some reason there was no pounding. No battering. No shrill whine. Why couldn't they always operate their machinery like this? Quietly, so she wasn't distracted. The windowpane quivered with impact. They weren't being quiet at all. It was impossible to pile-drive silently. It was because she could no longer hear them. She could barely hear a thing, she realized with anguish. She was deaf.

∽

"You have a hematoma and perforated eardrum with some swelling and bruising on the left side of your face. But there shouldn't be any permanent hearing loss." The specialist scrawled something upon a sturdy, fresh chart.

"The hematoma will gradually resolve and the eardrum will repair itself over the next fourteen to twenty-one days. The severe pain you're experiencing in your inner ear will last longer. Expect it to gradually subside over the course of the next four to six weeks. The impact also caused a concussive injury to the other side of the head which temporarily impaired your hearing in that ear. This problem has corrected itself. . . . You really should be more careful with all this ice getting in and out of your car, Mrs. Sterling," he cautioned as he scripted and tore from his pad two prescriptions—an antibiotic drop and a painkiller. "I always get one or two of these cases every year." Then he abruptly left the examination room for another.

Whether the ENT man believed her story—that she had slipped getting out of her Pinto and hit her ear against the steel edge of the door— was of no consequence. She had forgone instant medical treatment and a familiar, comfortable doctor for the sake of anonymity. This doctor had no connection to Paul or herself, no record of their life together: these were the credentials from the American Medical Association roster that had led her to seek this practitioner, an exhausting hour's cab ride away from her home.

Although over the next few weeks his medical prognosis was on schedule, her emotional recovery proceeded more slowly. The rupture left a minute scar on her eardrum; more damaging was the invisible, untreated wound that had torn her heart. She was despondent, something the person closest to her too readily sensed.

"Why are you so sad, Mommy?"

Barbara was seated beside Jenny on the sofa, sharing a chapter from *Alice in Wonderland*. Her rendering of the classic was devoid of the enthusiasm and dramatization she usually brought to the story. As she was reading the familiar words, her mind was again functioning on another plane. Had she provoked the assault?

Paul had told her of his problems at the office, his fear that he was being passed over, the haphazard way he was being treated by the firm, his bad review. And she had trivialized his concerns. She knew how important it was for him not to have a babysitter for their daughter. It had been the subject of many heated exchanges. She never received his approval to let her hire someone—she just went ahead and did it anyway. She should not have surprised him with something to which he was so vehemently opposed. She hadn't fully realized the extent of the pressure he was under at work and she had pushed him too far.

"I'm just tired, darling," Barbara said. "It's nothing."

"Did I make you tired?"

"No, of course not, darling."

Jenny moved closer to her. She took Barbara's arm and encircled her petite body with it as if needing physical reassurance of her mother's love.

Snuggled in this fashion, she said, "Go on, Mommy. Please read some more."

Barbara forced her voice into the dramatic cadences Jenny enjoyed so much. These ruminations that her daughter had rescued her from were not good either for herself or her family. They served no purpose. She had to put what happened in that unspeakable moment aside. She loved Paul. And what he had said in the aftermath of the incident was true: he had never struck her in all the years they had been married. He would never do it again.

C h a p t e r **22**

*I*n the second semester of her workshop with Dr. Stafford, Barbara involved herself more deeply in her writing and turned with renewed commitment to developing the skills to perfect her stories. It was as if she had lifted an antenna into her surroundings—a device sensitizing her to situations, people and language. Wherever her activities took her—a school meeting, shopping mall, restaurant, or exploring New Rochelle with her daughter—she would observe the pathos, humor, struggles and minute triumphs that went on daily around her, isolating the mannerisms of human uniqueness and noting equally the mundane and heroic in each person: anything she could later use to breathe life into a character.

A novel began to take shape in her mind and she started on it. It was the saga of an immigrant family based on the stories her grandmother had told her long ago.

At the last class, Barbara handed in her portfolio of stories to Dr. Stafford and, in addition, included the first thirty pages of her manuscript. All were returned in a battered, recycled manila envelope. She tore at its cover. A hand-scrawled note fell out. "Shows genuine talent. Tightly crafted work. Interesting content—especially the novel."

Throughout the summer, she maintained contact with Lennie. Writing by its very nature was a solitary, isolating process and she was grateful to have someone with whom to discuss her material. He was instructive and sympathetic. She shared with him the plot line and people that filled her pages. But never, despite his continual offers, would she allow him to read her finished chapters.

Barbara was accepted into Dr. Stafford's advanced workshop. Most of the group from the previous year were there except for John, the Ph.D. candidate, who Barbara gratefully noted had moved on to a doctoral course. The format remained the same, except that this session they were encouraged to submit their writing to Dr. Stafford monthly. He would then take excerpts from these and intersperse them with material from respected authors. The selections were presented anonymously. No name would appear beneath any of the passages, nor would the writer later be required to identify herself.

There was a significant difference in Dr. Stafford's approach. He had become gentler and more constructive in his criticism. His earlier prodding—"Is that a good sentence?," the phrase which he used to unnerve a complacent class—had now been replaced by more encouraging words. Dr. Stafford in any one session could be heard to say, "Idea expressed in an interesting fashion" or "Good character description," before the inevitable "Well? Well?" His accolade at times even extended to admiration for an adjective.

Modeling their remarks on those of their instructor, her colleagues became more charitable toward each other's work. Last year's arbitrary condemnations—"Doesn't work" and "Don't like it"—were replaced by qualifiers and suggestions further softened by "It might work better if . . ."

Barbara saw Rita, Lennie and others submit envelopes to Dr. Stafford, but she did not hand in anything herself.

Sometimes after the workshop Lennie accompanied her to Grand Central. On one such occasion in November, he broached a sensitive topic.

"That last piece was excellent. Do you think it was written by one of us?"

"I don't know. Hard to tell."

"You know, Barbara, I haven't recognized any of the excerpts as being yours." Talking during the summer of their writing, each had become familiar with the content of the other's work.

"You're right. I haven't submitted anything."

"Why not?"

"I just . . ." She forced herself to complete the sentence. "I just can't."

"But why, Barbara? Certainly by now you realize your work is good." He stopped under a streetlamp. "Stafford even wrote you that himself and we both know he's not particularly generous with superlatives. . . . You've got to overcome your fear of sharing your work."

"I can't share it. It's too fragile." She meant her belief in herself was too fragile, too precarious, too liable to be broken forever by some classmate's careless, glib remark. At all costs, she had to protect her confidence in herself. Barbara did not have to articulate the deeper meaning of her words to Lennie. He knew what she meant.

"We're all vulnerable, Barbara."

"Lennie, it's enough for me that I write. I write for myself. I don't want more."

"No, it's not enough. To grow as a writer you must subject yourself to the scrutiny of others."

"Do you really believe that?"

"Yes, I do. It's the main reason I began submitting my work for publication."

He continued with her to Grand Central.

Lennie had given her much to think about on the train ride home. By the time she entered the apartment, she had reached a decision. With her coat still fastened, she went directly to her desk. She did not wish to lose her resolve. She shuffled through her manuscript until she found her favorite section: the emotional turmoil of her heroine as she struggles to maintain her dignity in a new country. She placed it in an unmarked envelope to deliver it to Dr. Stafford the following Thursday.

Two weeks later, Barbara's writing was distributed to her classmates. When introducing it, Dr. Stafford called the passage "part of a germane and vital story, one that is crafted with extraordinary passion and sensitivity." A half-hour discussion ensued. To Barbara's surprise, all comments were complimentary. Then Dr. Stafford broke his own precedent. He stopped pacing and looked directly at her.

"This work should be published. Though it's an excerpt from a novel in progress, this segment is complete in itself. The author may wish to submit it to a magazine."

Encouraged by Dr. Stafford's praise, she fine-tuned some dialogue and placed the submission in an envelope addressed to *The Atlantic Monthly*. To Barbara's amazement, six weeks later a letter of acceptance arrived. Spurred on by this success, she had the second draft of her novel finished by May. She handed the manuscript in at the end of the term for evaluation.

Alone in the apartment on a July afternoon, she paused from her writing to answer the phone.

"Can you come to my home on Tuesday at ten-thirty?" Dr. Stafford asked and, after giving his address, abruptly hung up.

Dr. Stafford inhabited a neglected brownstone on West Twelfth Street. She hesitated before pressing the buzzer. When he opened the door he did not offer pleasantries, but impatiently waved her inside.

The room he brought her into contained only the most basic furniture, a desk and two wooden chairs. A corner of the plate-glass window was shattered, allowing the humid air and the street noise easy access. Depositing himself behind the wobbly table on which she recognized her manuscript, he waved her to sit opposite him. He had separately arranged each chapter there the way a child spreads bubble-gum cards he wants to examine. His shirtsleeves were ringed with the perspiration of enthusiasm.

"There's a book here."

"Do you like it?"

"It's ready for submission. Well? Well?" He had bypassed her inquiry and was pressing her for a response.

"I'm not satisfied with some of the sections yet."

"No good writer ever feels his work is ready. You must believe in the integrity of what you have to say and submit it."

Overwhelmed by his confidence in her work and what he was asking of her, she was speechless.

"Barbara, you possess something very special. . . ." He paused. "An original voice. With perseverance, a person can learn to copy a respected writing style, maybe even that of a great writer—a Virginia Woolf or Hemingway. But it is rare to create an individual style. A fresh voice, Barbara, has to be exposed. Your dialogue is realistic, your narrative poignant yet direct. Your writing will have its adherents and its share, I guarantee, of detractors."

She hung on to each utterance, locking it into memory. Instinctively, she knew these words must be saved to shield her, become in the bleakest times her armor against her own uncertainties, and those which someday might be inflicted upon her by unsympathetic reviewers.

"You asked if I liked the manuscript. I ignored that question before. I ignore it now. You must never give anyone the power to influence how you feel about your own work. A writer's lot is to live with insecurity and self-doubt. Write for the joy and the release it brings your spirit, never for an audience." His voice became conspiratorial.

"If you must listen to the critics, listen only to the true critics—other author-practitioners, those successful and mature in their craft. They can afford the magnanimity of an honest statement. But you must protect yourself from the literary frauds, the philistines and false prophets, those failed writers who have fled to the security and sanctimonious high ground of the press. They wrap themselves in its pages, unimpeachable experts. Wear the shell of the tortoise thick and impregnable so their erudite barbs aimed at a writer's vulnerability cannot reach your creative core. Do not permit them the gloating satisfaction of a mortal blow."

His short body shot up from behind the table. "By the way, I've already spoken to my agent about you. Here's his number." He scribbled on a crumpled piece of paper and, handing it to her, added, "He's expecting your call. . . . Now I must get back to my work," he said, brusquely walking her to the door.

As she went down the steps of the brownstone, she felt confident for the first time in her ability to write. It was only 10:30 of an ordinary Tuesday, yet so much had changed. Dr. Stafford believed in her. Was then not all else possible?

She telephoned Paul at the office. He kept short-circuiting her story with alternating interjections of "Good" and "That's nice, dear." When she started to tell him that Dr. Stafford had given her name to an agent, Paul cut her off with "I'm going into a meeting. We'll talk about it later."

Barbara felt too elated to be dismissed. She wanted to share her news with someone who would appreciate its significance.

Spontaneously, she found herself dialing Lennie. His voice reflected her happiness. When she mentioned the agent's name, he responded, "He's the best in the business. If Ken Jorgen accepts the book, you've got it made. He has the contacts to have your manuscript considered by any house in New York."

When Barbara contacted Ken Jorgen, he set up a lunch date for three weeks hence. She was to come first to his midtown office.

Lennie called as she was leaving the apartment for her train.

"Have fun, Barbara. Enjoy every minute. You deserve it."

Ensuring that she would be punctual, she grabbed a cab as soon as she reached the city. The driver deposited her before a relatively small building squashed between two glistening towers. She noted its weathered exterior was matched by a well-trodden, colorless lobby. The elevator laboriously took Barbara to the third floor. She rang the buzzer of suite 309. A face appeared at the small grille in the door. She identified herself and was let in by a young man in his early twenties. He had a diamond stud in his ear and a champagne glass in his hand.

"Leftovers from yesterday's book launch," he said, indicating a magnum standing on an antique desk in the corner. "Ken brought it back for us. Help yourself, he'll be with you shortly."

Barbara found herself in a waiting room of books. Shelves reached to the ceiling on all four sides. Hardcovers and paperbacks, older titles and newer ones shared equal space.

The place was dimly lit. It enjoyed only the minimal light that filtered through a dust-coated window from the narrow shaft of the neighboring building. Barbara sat on a worn leather chair and enjoyed the room's atmosphere. Somehow the endless sirens, the wail of ambulances and fire engines seemed less threatening here.

In this relaxed state, she heard, "I'm Ken Jorgen. Shall we go?" Before she could assess his appearance, he took her arm and steered her from this venue onto the elevator and into the street.

A swift walker, he was expert at navigating the busy sidewalks that had been made even busier by the advent of the New York summer. She kept up to him with difficulty, trying to avoid the hazards of ripped asphalt and open street grates that seemed to proliferate in her path. Within minutes, she regretted rejecting her usual sneakers in favor of high heels. His pace did not slacken as she caught the aroma from the steaming pretzels of a curbside cart and circumvented the layers of lunchtime watchers surrounding a pantomime act.

They continued at this speed for another six blocks. Then he led her into a residential hotel and made a sharp left into its main-floor bistro. They were shown to an outside table that permitted her to watch the elegant and austere bustle through the marbled lobby. The perimeter of the restaurant was defined by red tulip baskets and volumes of gardenias fragrant with perfume.

A waiter approached. Ken declined drinks. He gave his order without opening the menu, the habit of a regular. Barbara was uncomfortably aware of the waiter hastening to her side. Unable to properly peruse the menu, she self-consciously ordered the first entrée whose extravagant description seemed familiar.

Ken got directly down to business. "I understand you have a manuscript for me."

"Yes." Barbara withdrew her novel from an accordion file and extended it to him.

"No," he said, declining to take it from her. "Don't give it to me. Not now."

She felt awkward, not knowing whether to place her material on the tablecloth or banish it from view. She chose the latter.

"Tell me first what your novel is about."

"Basically, people. Ordinary people, who through their strength of character manage to accomplish the extraordinary."

"Why 'ordinary people'?"

"Because I find them the most interesting."

"Where do you find these 'ordinary people'?"

"Everywhere. I feel an author's job is to plagiarize from life." She found herself opening up her thoughts to him. She explained the people in her book, especially the heroine modeled on her grandmother. Through these characters she also revealed herself.

He continued to question her. His inquiries were provocative, encouraging her to expand on her ideas.

"It's been over a decade since Dave Stafford got in touch with me about one of his students. He gave such an excellent report on your manuscript that I decided not to wait to read it myself before I met with you."

It did not matter what she had ordered. Engrossed in conversation, she ignored the food before her. With the arrival of her coffee, the waiter removed a congealed Florentine omelet.

When Ken had concluded both his queries and his cappuccino, he volunteered, "Barbara, let me tell you what you need to know about me. I'm a native New Yorker. You won't find many people who can boast that in this city," he said pleasantly. "That means I know where to go and who to speak to. If, of course, I decide to represent you. . . . I've been in the business a lot of years. I've put together some of the most exciting book deals in this town."

Now that he was no longer asking her questions, she had time to appraise him. He was between fifty-five and sixty. Short-cropped hair. Sturdy build. Vital.

"I don't need the money anymore." He was talking slower now, as if reasoning it out as he spoke. "It's primarily the challenge I like, and placing the first novel of a relatively unknown writer surely has to be a challenge."

Barbara felt his eyes studying her.

"I'll tell you what. I'll handle your book if it meets one of two conditions." He chose his words precisely. "It's bad writing, but I feel it will make me lots of money. Or . . ." He paused for emphasis. "Or your work is of such high literary merit that someone ought to be compelled to publish it. Based on Dave's enthusiasm, I expect your manuscript will fall into this category. . . . It's going to be a little while until you'll hear back from me, Barbara. I always have one of my staff go through a manuscript before I do, and that takes a few weeks, and I leave for Europe early September. The international rights fair is coming round again and I have my usual pre-Frankfurt meetings."

"The rights fair must be fascinating."

"It's not. It's hard slugging. This year I have eight big books to place."

He motioned for the waiter, instructed for the bill to be put on his account, then escorted her from the restaurant. "You have interesting ideas, Barbara. I'll be in touch after I've read the book."

Barbara felt the lighthearted sensation of someone who has had events taken out of her hands.

*I*t was a late October afternoon. Jenny was standing on a chair, carving out a pumpkin for Halloween under Barbara's supervision. Its mouth, with three uneven, jagged teeth, simulated a broad grin. Eyes were inverted triangles. The nose somehow had been forgotten or not considered necessary. Pits were splattered about the kitchen and the newspaper beneath the pumpkin was soggy with orange pulp. Barbara had just plunged her hands into the center of the vegetable to extract the remaining tentacled ooze when the phone rang. It continued several times before Barbara had found a cloth, wiped the smooth, slimy liquid off her hands and lifted the receiver.

Ken Jorgen did not feel it necessary to identify himself. "Your manuscript meets both my tests—someone ought to be compelled to publish it and it will make lots of money." With that one staccato statement, he terminated the call.

Lennie was ecstatic when Barbara phoned him with her news about the agent's decision. "That's great! Great! I knew he would like the manuscript. . . . I'm on a roll too. I've just sold my second story to *GQ*, and *Esquire* has expressed interest in another."

"That's wonderful, Lennie."

"You know, we should really get together regularly and discuss what we're working on," he suggested. "Sort of a postgraduate Stafford course. To be more accurate, 'A Survivors of Stafford's Course.' You must admit, we're quite an exclusive group. What do you think?"

In the last month, Barbara had begun a sequel to her novel and she missed the contact with other serious writers and the feedback which the workshop had provided. In a flash, she accepted.

Barbara found Paul more pleasant now that she was no longer attending class. He misinterpreted her decision not to take any further English courses as a desire by her to return to the pattern of their earlier life together. Paul read the agent's silence as lack of interest in her novel by publishers and never mentioned the submission envelopes that traveled from their apartment to the editorial offices of *The New Yorker* and *The Atlantic Monthly* and the rejection slips that followed. He tolerated Barbara's biweekly meetings with Lennie as the final chapter, the denouement of a stressful period in both their lives.

"It's too bad you got locked into these luncheons with that fellow from the workshop. When winter hits, I'm sure you can tactfully get out of having to go into the city for those meetings" was the type of comment her husband regularly made whenever he referred to these trips into Manhattan.

✍

One January dawn, as Barbara sat at her desk and was looking out into the lifting darkness before beginning her writing, Paul said from the warmth of their bed, "I've been thinking, we really could use a house."

"We're perfectly happy here, Paul."

"I think we should look. . . . Maybe something in White Plains or Scarsdale."

"Paul, we're settled here. You're relatively close to work where we are now. Jenny's going to school with the same friends she's had since kindergarten. And for my writing I have a terrific view of Travers Island and Glen Island Park from here. Why move?"

"For one thing, you can finally have a separate room to write in. How would you like a place with beautiful old oaks and a great garden? Have you noticed how the trees in the park never appear to move. They look acrylic, like they're painted there. When you're up early like this, wouldn't it be nice to hear wind through the trees, and birds?"

"It's not necessary, I'm fine."

Still in bed, Paul rolled onto his side and, leaning on an elbow, said, "Barbara, I was reading in the *Times* where they interviewed some writers. Did you see the piece?" He now had her full attention. "They officially live in a city but each of them has a place somewhere out in the country where they retreat to write. Regardless of the type of writing they did, they all had that in common."

"Interesting. I would have liked to see that article. Who did they interview?"

"I don't remember."

"Paul, please don't worry about me. I'm fine here. Really."

Three weeks later, when Barbara returned from dropping Jenny at her friend's home where she had gone to spend Saturday afternoon, Paul was in the kitchen making coffee. She hung up her duffel coat and went in to keep him company.

"I've been giving this a lot of thought, Barbara. If we don't move now, we never will."

"There's no urgency for us to move, Paul. We're—"

He spliced her words. "It will be better for Jenny. Large backyard, great for playing in the snow. In the summer she'll have safer streets to go biking."

"She rides her bike now in the park."

"Well, there she'll even be able to ride to school. She's already asking to do that. It will have a large basement. Fully finished," he said, continuing to describe their ideal home. "It will be a great place for her to bring her friends. Besides, an apartment is no place to bring up a child."

"Jenny's perfectly happy, Paul. She brings her friends here."

"Consider today, Barbara. She went to Robin's. I'm sure she'd have her friends over more often if we lived in a house. Gives them more room to play. And privacy. You know how kids this age feel about their privacy. They like their secrets and their secret places."

"If you're serious about this, Paul, we should talk to Jenny. I don't think we should even be considering a move without discussing it with her."

"Barbara, I want you to realize Jenny might be resistant at first. That's normal. We should be prepared for it. Not cave in. It's the best thing for her in the long run."

Paul had astutely anticipated their daughter's response. That evening, when consulted about a possible move, Jenny said adamantly, "I don't care what you say. I'm not going. You can't make me," and refused to discuss the matter further.

A week later at the dinner table, Paul again raised the topic with Jenny.

"Move if you want to. But I'm not leaving. I like it here." She fastened angry eyes defiantly on her parents. "You can't do this to me. . . . It's not fair," she said, dissolving into tears, and ran to the sanctuary of her bedroom.

Barbara felt Jenny's behavior was excessive. Paul went further, telling Barbara their daughter was dramatic, willful and, in the psychological buzzword of the day, "controlling." He said he would not permit an over-wrought child to dictate to him.

Late one February night, snow acting as a buffer around the bedroom window, Paul said, "You remember Steve and John at the office? The fellows who started in the firm after me? Both of them have already bought houses."

"Paul, I don't want a better place to write. Jenny doesn't want to move. A house doesn't make sense for us. . . . It's not necessary."

"It's more than necessary. It's critical for me. A lot of questions are being asked at the office about why we haven't moved into a home yet. It's becoming very embarrassing."

"Embarrassing? I don't understand what you mean."

"Collins has been insinuating it's about time we moved. Even Mr. James has. It's . . . well . . . they expect it. Almost insist on it. Corporate image, they call it." He stopped and looked intently at her. "I need it for my career, Barbara. I mean, I need it if I'm going to have a future with James, Benton & Collins."

"Paul, we don't have the money for the type of home you've been talking about."

"Everyone gets a mortgage, Barbara. Honestly . . . I guess the partners like their juniors to have large mortgages. Keeps them forever bound to the firm." His attempt at humor was an obvious foil to the seriousness of his prior statement. "They expect us to get a home, Barbara. They really do," he said fervently. "I need to do this if I'm ever going to make partner."

Barbara was not familiar enough with the dynamics in her husband's firm to know whether this concern was realistic. Apparently he had to look successful in order to invite success. The firm, with its antiquated ways and built-in rules, had imposed yet another condition to her husband's partnership.

Paul had made concessions to accommodate her career and she must do the same for him. If job advancement underlay Paul's resolve to move, Barbara agreed it was necessary. At the time, she did not consider the move a sacrifice—only inconvenient and dislocating.

✐

It took the better part of a year until they found the place that met their requirements. In White Plains, one of an unobtrusive cluster of new, unfinished homes, set among old family properties, it provided an elite address for Paul and was only a forty-five-minute commute to his office. It was the choicest lot carved out of a small estate. Barbara had been attracted to its siting and aesthetics. The back part of the house—three bedrooms, one of which they intended to convert for her into a study, as well as the family room and kitchen—was designed with picture windows to overlook the terraced garden and century-old oaks. These trees also ensured a private backyard, an ideal place for Jenny to share with new friends. The landscaped grounds came with a modern colonial exterior but, unfortunately for Barbara, little else.

Barbara's creative energies were diverted into the house, something she had not anticipated prior to the purchase. She was overwhelmed with the work required to transform the empty-shell interior into a hospitable home. As Paul was occupied with his law practice, the burden of finding and supervising the trades fell by elimination to Barbara. She cajoled electricians, plasterers, painters and carpenters, the tradespeople required to complete the main section of their residence and, in order to keep their promise to Jenny, turn the roughed-in basement into a recreation area with fluorescent lighting and pressed-veneer paneling. In addition to this was added the responsibility for decorating the house with all the detail work and myriad of decisions it involved. The process seemed endless, consuming all her time to the detriment of her writing. After one year of trying to complete the house, she had made no progress on her sequel.

Barbara was also concerned how Jenny was adapting to her new neighborhood. They had moved to White Plains in late August, thinking that if Jenny was present for the start of the academic year this would make it easier for her to make friends. But their timing made very little difference. Jenny's school district drew primarily from the older established communities. Most of the children in the area had grown up together. Even at the beginning of the school year Jenny was finding it hard to break into such long-standing friendships. Barbara sensed this from her daughter's dejected attitude when she returned home more defeated than when she had left in the morning.

"Why don't you give her riding lessons?" Lennie suggested in late October when, after he had commented on how preoccupied Barbara seemed during lunch, she told him of Jenny's difficulty in making friends in such a tightly knit community.

"You know, your home's not far from Coxwell Equestrian Center.

Before I moved to Manhattan, I used to go there myself regularly. When I went there on Saturdays, I'd see classes of kids about Jenny's age. Mostly girls. It might be a good way for your daughter to be accepted into the group."

"It's a great idea, Lennie. Thank you. By the way, Lennie, you never told me you were into riding."

"You never asked," he replied lightly. "I've always liked to ride and Coxwell's one of the best stables in Westchester. I like it because of its trails. When the weather's nice, I still go up there. If you had to move somewhere, you sure chose a great location." After that, their conversation reverted to literature.

Barbara drove Jenny to look at the equestrian center. There were two rings. The grassier one contained painted jumps; the other was used to exercise the horses who were boarded. A whitewashed arena allowed for riding in inclement weather. Behind the rings and stable complex stretched acres of land. Along the perimeter of one distant field, Barbara noticed a large subdivision was being developed.

After seeing Coxwell's, Jenny was eager to take lessons. Barbara explained the situation to Tom Bryden, the manager of the center. He organized five private lessons to teach Jenny to handle her horse with enough confidence to join a class with others her age. He then placed her in the Saturday noon session which had in it three girls from her grade who had been riding there together for years.

Saturday classes extended into Sundays of riding shows. Like the others, Jenny came early to groom and tack up her horse. She would talk to her three classmates about riding and horses. With proximity and common interests, Jenny became tolerated but not accepted, a distinction that confused and upset her. Barbara concluded that Lennie's idea, which might have been effective in a more mobile community, had little chance of success in this entrenched, affluent neighborhood.

In spite of this, Jenny was drawn to riding; perhaps, Barbara thought, as a refuge. What Barbara had envisioned as a pastime for Jenny to make friends had become for her daughter a passionate commitment. Jenny rode throughout the winter. With thermal gloves, woolen hat under her regulation riding helmet and long underwear beneath her jodhpurs, she did not miss a lesson. As the girls worked out in the arena, pigeons hidden for warmth in the high crossbars would drop at random from the rafters upon the riders, spooking the horses. Jenny grew confident at handling

Snowball, the stable mare she rode regularly. She was nicknamed for her white mane as well as being surefooted in snowy weather.

Barbara would drive Jenny to the stables and remain there throughout the instruction. She saw her progress week by week, month by month, through the paces set for her and her horse. She admired her slender daughter's courage astride the large animal.

As these classes became more advanced and competitive, Barbara's fear for her daughter's safety lay unspoken and persistent within her.

By spring, Jenny preferred to spend all her free time at the stables. Keen to continue to share Saturdays with her daughter and lured by the clusters of daffodils that sprang from secluded spots and the fragrance of the awakening world, Barbara took up riding again. She had enjoyed this sport when she was her daughter's age.

When Jenny's class ended at one o'clock, Barbara would ride with her through the extensive fields and trails on the property. Jenny usually chose their route, sure of her competence and mastery over Snowball. If Lennie was there, he would join them. Barbara realized Paul knew nothing of this informal arrangement and did not feel it necessary to inform him as it had been so haphazard and uneventful.

C h a p t e r **24**

Barbara would later write in a foreword to one of her novels, "There are some days when you remember every pulse, minute and sound. Where you were, what you did, said, even thought. The event that occurred being cataclysmic and irreversible. People can recall the details of the day Kennedy was shot, Neil Armstrong walked on the moon, Martin Luther King died."

October 12 of their second autumn in White Plains became such a day for Barbara. Jenny had concluded her lesson and was walking her horse, a handsome chestnut, from the ring. She had been unable to ride her usual gray mare today. Snowball had stumbled over a jump at a show the previous Saturday and was taking what Tom called "a well-earned rest." The stable manager was cautious in his care of the horses and had not used Snowball in lessons for the entire week. Barbara was already mounted, waiting for Lennie in front of the stable. Lennie had come up from the city. He had arrived an hour before and was exercising a small-boned muscular gelding while he waited to join Barbara and Jenny.

It had not rained now for over two weeks, rare for this season. Barbara gave permission for Jenny to take a more demanding course than usual, one that would provide her daughter with a flat, uninterrupted open space in which to canter her horse on the way back to the stables.

They set off behind the barn, across a field still ablaze with tall clumps of goldenrod. Thick and plentiful, their raised yellow heads stood sharply against the expanse of greenery. Beyond this lay a ridge of birch, flanked by a snow line of pine. The stark white bark towered above the evergreens. Despite winter's approach, the lower branches held their leaves and in the sun the bronzed yellow foliage shimmered, its colors glorious above the emerald triangles. The only sounds came from the brush: the hum of crickets hidden in its thick grass, the scrunch of dried crisp leaves underfoot, from both the heavy tread of hooves and the sprint of squirrels who artfully dodged through their curled tangle. Two of them, a gray one and a brown companion, bobbed unafraid alongside Barbara's mount. Ripe acorns, locked in their mouths, bulged between fat cheek pouches, as they methodically raced about preparing for winter, not lured into frolic by the respite of warmth.

The horses splashed across the brook. Spears of bulrushes laid open their mocha froth. Crimson slivers of sumac brushed against her mount's side. Colonies of birds moved in unison, their formation spread over the blue transparency of sky in their progression southward. From the distance came the pungent sweetness of smoldering leaves. The air held a crinkle of cold, the twinge that precedes a first frost.

They rode without conversation. The day was too perfect. It had to be taken and wintered into memory.

At the clearing, Jenny made her choice of the return route, picking the most open stretch. It adjoined the subdivision property presently under construction. Also prepared for development, the field had been recently bulldozed and the dry spell had turned its barren earth hard and crusted, unlike the soft underbrush they had just gone through. It was the perfect terrain for the run she had earlier discussed with Barbara.

Adjusting to the open field, they now rode three abreast. Barbara noticed Jenny give the chestnut extra rein. The head jerked forward, a mannerism never exhibited by Snowball and one she knew her daughter would not have been anticipating. Jenny pulled in her steed and brought it into a trot. Barbara noted Jenny's apprehension, then saw her do as she had often been instructed: tap her heels into the side of the horse to direct it up one gait into a canter. The horse lunged its head forward and took off into an uncontrolled run with Jenny its hostage. It had bypassed the intermediate gaits of canter and gallop so swiftly as to render them visibly undetectable.

With this sudden motion and momentum, Jenny lost the reins. They hung ominously over the horse's head. Groping to reach them, her daughter pressed her body flat along the chestnut's mane. She strained too far forward in her saddle. Barbara saw the right stirrup snap and fall away. With no reins and only one stirrup, Jenny had no means to bring the runaway under control. The horse must have sensed the rider's fear; it increased its speed to a breakneck velocity. Jenny's hands tore at the mane, her thin arms enveloped the stallion's thick, sweaty neck.

Barbara had to reach her daughter. Simultaneously, she whipped her crop and dug her heels into her mare. Whipped and dug in, again and again. Never a proficient rider, Barbara's knees flapped unconvincingly. Her mount ignored her prodding, refusing to quicken its pace. Barbara fell further and further behind. She knew Jenny's horse might continue like this until it reached the barn or, without warning, stop and vault her daughter over its head and possibly to her death. The fear she had suppressed since Jenny started to ride was about to become a reality before her eyes and she was powerless to stop it. She was confined to the role of spectator in the race to save her daughter's life.

Barbara heard the whoosh of Lennie's crop. Saw his gelding bolt forward in pursuit. He was gaining on Jenny's stallion, closing the distance between them. But Jenny's horse, as if bred to race, seemed to sense the approach and somehow ran even faster.

Jenny's animal was now alongside the construction site, running flat out. Jenny fell to the ground and, tucking her neck and arms close to her body, rolled clear of her horse. She missed the scrap dump of the subdivision development by a mere length—a massive fifty-foot-long debris mound of metal sheeting, iron refuse and jagged glass; refuse that, had she landed there and survived, could have permanently maimed her. Equally fortuitous, the horse had not reared and trampled her. The animal stood nearby, innocent of its part in the drama. Its sides heaved; sweat ran down its legs.

Lennie caught the horse, reset the tack, tightened the girth. Steadying the horse, he encouraged Jenny to remount, explaining to Barbara that if her daughter did not force herself to get back on her horse immediately, she might fear riding forever. He led the horse and a visibly trembling Jenny back to the stables.

It was four o'clock. The air had chilled. Wind spiked cold against the body. It dislodged the foliage; leaves streamed down, like rain, toward a dried hardened earth. The stench of burning rubber from subdivision rubbish nauseously thickened the air.

Barbara took Jenny directly home to bandage her cuts. Paul was in the house. In turtleneck and slacks, he was working at the dining-room table, his real estate closing documents spread before him. He took in Jenny's blood-tangled hair, torn riding clothes and the welts that were rising to the surface of her skin.

"What happened?"

"I'm fine, Daddy. I'm okay." Then Jenny broke into tears and, running over to her father, locked her arms fiercely around his waist.

"Jenny, tell me everything." Paul gently pried her loose, enabling her to speak. "Now start at the beginning, darling."

She gulped down her sobs, swallowed hard, preparing to speak. "I was riding a new horse," she began slowly, then continued breathlessly. "He used to be a racehorse. On a flat stretch, he took off with me on him. I lost my reins, my right stirrup broke. I couldn't stop him. Lennie tried to catch him, but he was too fast, even for Lennie."

"Lennie?"

She seemed not to have heard her father. Reliving that terrible experience, she had become as uncontrollable as the horse, who only a half hour earlier had been her captor.

"I was so scared, Daddy. I hung on to the horse's mane, then its neck, but it kept pulling forward. I couldn't keep my grip, so I jumped off. Lennie caught my horse and brought him to me."

Barbara saw Paul flinch.

"I've never been so scared, Daddy," she repeated. "But I'm okay. I really am," and she added proudly, "I got on my horse again and walked him home to the stables."

Coldly, Paul addressed Barbara. "Why did you let her get back on that animal, Barbara?"

"It wasn't Mommy's idea," Jenny said protectively before Barbara could reply. "It was Lennie's. He said it was important for me to get back on my horse or I might be too afraid to ride again."

Paul's face flushed red. "Jenny darling, you'd better go upstairs now. You've had quite a scare." His words were uncharacteristically stilted, his voice tense. "Clean up and rest."

Jenny did as her father instructed. Paul's words and tone prevented Barbara from following.

"Why did you let this happen to my daughter?"

Now that the crisis at the stables had passed, Barbara felt emotionally spent. Since her arrival home she had not spoken a word. "I didn't let anything happen. It was an accident."

"Why did you let her on that horse, Barbara? You go there every week. You watch her. You must have known it was a different horse. You should never have taken her riding in an open area. She could have been killed."

"Paul, please stop it. I can't take it. I really can't." She had endured the morning's strain and was close to tears. She heard a door shut upstairs, then the tap water run. Jenny must be in the bathroom, washing her cuts. She needed help. She must go to her.

"Who is this Lennie guy that Jenny was talking about? The Lennie from your class?" he demanded.

"Yes."

"Is this the same Lennie you go into Manhattan to meet for lunch, supposedly to discuss writing?" Paul's voice was becoming increasingly hostile and accusatory.

"Yes."

"Why didn't you tell me you were meeting Lennie at the stables?" Like a lawyer in cross-examination, he pressed his advantage, her weakness. "Whose idea was it to meet at riding? What was he doing there with you?"

"Paul, please leave me alone. I just can't take any more," she pleaded. Her legs felt weak, as though they were going to buckle beneath her.

"How long have the two of you been meeting there? Tell me."

"He rides there," she said simply, anxious to defuse the interrogation.

"So that explains why you suddenly insisted on giving Jenny riding lessons. What right do you have to involve my daughter in your relationships?" His anger had reached a new intensity.

"Look, Paul," she said, starting into a fuller explanation. "Sometimes Lennie's at the stable on Saturdays and he joins us riding. And that's it. You're making a big deal out of nothing."

"You just wanted to be with Lennie. And you used my daughter as a cover-up. You didn't care about Jenny—what she rode, where she rode. Just your precious Lennie . . . and yourself."

She had had enough of his anger and caustic tongue. She did not respond to his accusations. She was depleted of words and of energy.

"I bought you this house to settle you down. Stabilize you. Turn your mind from fantasy back to real life, to your responsibilities to me and my career. We've been here over a year and you still haven't had the partners over." So this finally was the real reason for his insistence on their move.

"Is it any wonder I never got the partnership? And if they don't offer it to you after you've been there ten years, they never do." He paused, then said furiously, "You lost me my career, Barbara. You don't care about me, only your writing and Lennie." His mind reconnected to Lennie. "You're having an affair, Barbara. Of course. I've been so stupid. That's why you've never stopped running into the city to be with Lennie. Even after we moved all the way out here. That's the reason you kept it a secret that he rode with you. That explains everything . . . when did it all start? I want to know." His voice hardened. Strips of blood vessels pulsated around his forehead and temples. "Where else have you two been meeting?"

"And you think that I'm the one with the overactive imagination," she said. "Nothing's going on. You're being absurd. And I'm not going to listen to this. I'm going to see how Jenny is." As Barbara turned to leave the room, Paul grabbed one wrist, then another. He yanked her toward him.

"Answer me, Barbara. Now! When did this all start?" Barbara was helpless in his grip. With the advantage and strength of his six-foot frame, he bent her wrists back slowly, torturing her for an answer. Impatient for a reply, he wrenched them back until there was no more resistance.

Pain seared through her wrists, her hands went limp, unable to support themselves. The hands she needed to write with, the adjuncts to her mind.

Barbara fled to her room, fell across their bed and succumbed to tears.

About two hours later, Paul entered the darkened bedroom. He stood next to her. She withdrew her body to the far edge of the bed.

Paul lay down. His words came heavily as if spoken from a hollow deep inside him. They seemed carefully selected. "I'm not going to rationalize my behavior, Barbara. I should never have done it." He turned away from her and in anguish said, "I'm so ashamed, Barbara. So ashamed."

She heard the agony of suppressed sobs, felt the tremor of his body. Weakness he did not want her to see.

She put her hand on his back and, turning him toward her, brought him close. She wanted to soothe him, stop the pain that had taken hold of his body as surely as the pain that throbbed in her wrists.

Why was this happening to them? They had everything. A home. A good income. A healthy daughter. And love. The ingredients for a perfect life together.

She held him until his sobs subsided in sleep. Her arms remained around him, but her heart was numb.

∽

To her family doctor's inquiry of cause the next day, she offered no explanation. She was humiliated. She did not know why, despite his attack, she still felt a need to be loyal to her husband and to protect his reputation. Woven into the complexity and fabric of these emotions ran the thin thread of belief that she might have been responsible. She had brought the attack on herself by deliberately withholding from Paul their weekend rides with Lennie.

The orthopedic surgeon her GP referred her to said she was fortunate her wrists had not been broken, but severely sprained. He prescribed flesh-colored wrist braces—metal bars inside a rigid cloth cast. He told her to wear them at all times, even though they would be limiting and uncomfortable. Barbara tried to make light of these constraints to Jenny, calling them her "brown mitts."

Jenny kept asking why she was wearing the braces. Jenny knew her mother was not a strong rider and accepted her story that she had injured her wrists due to her inability to control her horse when it chased Jenny's runaway.

Barbara shielded her daughter from the truth. That fiction was the only possible explanation she could give her. A less definitive answer would have led to more queries. One question would lead to another, until the truth was unraveled in its nakedness. Paul required respect, the lack of which, Barbara suspected, contributed to his frustration with his stalled career. It was inconceivable Paul would continue to live with them if he thought his daughter knew he had abused her mother. If in a moment of candor, she told Jenny what her father had done, Paul would be humiliated and her marriage would be over. She also was convinced that in the long run this fabrication would be less traumatic for her adolescent daughter.

Barbara felt a profound sadness, one that reached into her innermost core. She took great care to conceal this emotion from her daughter, confining her tears to moments of solitude. Paul's mood swings had become so unpredictable and violent that she hardly knew him anymore. But somehow she had to keep her family together. She locked her unhappiness inside, someplace where she thought it could not harm her.

Barbara noticed Jenny was particularly quiet when Barbara was wearing her wrist braces. In spite of the specialist's instructions, she began to restrict their use to when her daughter was not home or she wanted to write and could be certain Jenny would not see them.

Barbara had to wear the braces for six months. She sensed Paul saw them as a constant reminder of his wife's deception and his failure and shame. For Barbara, their use recalled her husband's erratic, explosive behavior and her emotional and physical pain. For each, they became a symbol of an action impossible to forget and capable in itself of wrenching them further apart.

Despite Paul's contriteness after "the misunderstanding," which was how he referred to the abuse, she was worried that he would hit her again.

"Paul, I think we should go to a marriage counselor," she suggested when he once again sympathetically asked her how she was feeling. Jenny had already left the family room to go to bed.

"There's nothing wrong with me. And I have no intention of speaking to anyone about my private life," he replied tersely, foreclosing this possibility.

With his uncompromising attitude, she felt a sense of helplessness and was afraid to be alone with Paul. She would retreat to her study when she and Paul were home by themselves and began encouraging Jenny not to return to her bedroom after dinner, but to finish her homework in the family room.

Yet Barbara could not consider leaving Paul. Even if she had wanted to do so, she did not have the means. She had always known she was completely reliant on him, but not until the abuse had she realized the ramifications of this dependency. From the beginning of their marriage, he had given her money for the household and her personal expenses. His handling of their finances made her feel secure and protected. But she had no source of income independent of him. And as an English major, with only an undergraduate degree, she did not have sufficient qualifications to support herself and her daughter. She had been raised to consider marriage the ultimate goal, the intellect merely an additional, enhancing, seductive asset.

She was part of the Undervalued Generation—those women born too late to be appreciated for child rearing and volunteer work and too early to reap the benefits of the women's liberation movement. She belonged to that generation on the cusp and as such was not protected or respected by the codes and values of either. She was locked into the marriage tighter than any religious ceremony or secular decree could make her.

A divorce—an alternative she did not really want—would not ensure her economic security. As a lawyer, Paul would know who could best represent him, how to present his case in the most sympathetic light and how court procedures could be manipulated in his favor. And a divorce was too risky. Paul would resist letting her have custody of Jenny. He would twist the facts to present her as an unfit mother—regularly abandoning Jenny to attend her workshop, the near-fatal riding accident that happened under her supervision. And if she were to counter with Paul's physical abuse, who would believe her? There had been no witnesses to his attacks. She had even lied to her own doctors about the origin of her injuries. There would be an ugly custody battle, with Jenny the victim.

She had to make herself financially self-sufficient no matter what might transpire between Paul and her in the future. But how could she achieve this? She did not have a strong enough background in English to get a job as an editor. Maybe something in advertising at the entry level. But Lennie wasn't happy doing that kind of work and he was a creative director. And a radical career change did not make sense now that she was beginning to make some progress with her writing.

She had recently sold a story to *The New Yorker*. Almost two years had elapsed since Ken had become her agent, and when she phoned him on the pretext of telling him about this acceptance, he had said, "I'm delighted to hear you're building up your credentials. Every bit of ammunition helps. . . . Not to worry, I haven't forgotten you. We'll have your novel placed soon. Just today I was speaking to a senior editor about *Sarah from Afar.*"

She had to hope his optimism would eventually translate into a contract. *Sarah from Afar* had to get published and launch her into an economically viable literary career. She knew sudden success in this field was rare, but if her book received even modest recognition it would put her in a position to be hired as a creative writing instructor or writer-in-residence at some college. Such an appointment would allow her the opportunity to continue her own writing and have time to spend with Jenny. Ken Jorgen and *Sarah from Afar* had to succeed.

Barbara was careful not to provoke Paul's anger again. Wishing to give him no further cause for suspicion, she told Paul in advance when she planned to see Lennie. But she increased the frequency of her meetings with her former classmate. Having defined her financial autonomy in terms of her writing, she felt she needed Lennie's help and advice even more.

C h a p t e r **25**

At the beginning of November, Barbara answered the phone in her study to hear Ken Jorgen's voice.

"You're on your way. You've an editor-in-chief who's fully committed to your book. She believes the immigrant experience is more vital than ever in our society and plans to give your novel the full treatment. Listen to this from the senior editor's report: 'The unforgettable journey of the courageous Sarah who fights with the power of her grand dreams, triumphs over war and heartbreak to become the matriarch of her family.' . . . You've got yourself a publisher, Barbara. Happy?"

Those magical words she had wanted to hear for so long. All her years of work. Those long hours uninterrupted by the clock. But it had all happened.

"Barbara, are you there? Did you hear what I said?" and not waiting for a reply, he pressed on. "They intend a late spring pub date. She reasons it this way. You're a first-time novelist, virtually unknown. No guaranteed following. You'd be ignored by the press if you came out with the big books in September. Don't mean to upset you, Barbara, but that's the reality in the trade. That's how she sees it and for what it's worth, I agree with her. . . . You'll be pleased to know a senior editor is working on *Sarah from Afar* already. You should be getting a lengthy report on your manuscript from her next week."

"Ken, I don't know how to thank you."

"Aren't you forgetting something, Barbara? You haven't asked me the size of the advance. Ten thousand against royalties. Small, but respectable. Shows they believe in the project. Being married to an attorney, I guess money isn't as important to you as it is to my other authors."

Barbara was not ready to clarify his misconception of her personal life.

"Is there anything I should be doing in the meantime?" she asked. "I've been working on something new and haven't looked at that manuscript for—"

"Good. They're not interested in one-shot novelists. If this book takes off as we're all expecting it to, then you'll have yourself an established following. . . . Barbara, it's taken a long time, but it has been worth it. I've got you in good hands now. Rest assured, *Sarah from Afar* will be well published."

"Thank you, Ken, thank you for everything."

"And, Barbara, we now have a book launch to think about."

After Ken hung up she felt quiet inside. Quiet and special. A publisher had confidence in her and her work.

> *When it all comes true, just the way you planned,*
> *it's funny, but the bells don't ring. It's a quiet thing.*
> *Happiness comes in on tip-toe. It's a quiet thing.*

The words of a Liza Minelli song spun through her mind.

Without further delay she phoned James, Benton & Collins.

"You'll never guess who just called me," she said excitedly when she was put through to Paul. "Ken Jorgen. It's taken two years but my book is finally going to be published. Isn't that fantastic?"

"I'm pleased for you, Barbara." His tone was indifferent.

"How do you really feel about it?" She wanted to talk more. "Paul, I'm ecstatic!"

"I'm glad one of our careers is going so well," he said, and immediately tempered that comment with "I've really got to go, Barbara. I'm late for a closing."

Stunned by Paul's lack of interest, she made no further calls that day about her good news.

True to Ken's prediction, the publisher gave special consideration to *Sarah from Afar* when, after six months of intensive work, it was off the press with its glossy jacket and photo of her on the back cover. With the thousands of titles being published in New York every season, they deemed it essential that the critics know who she was for the purpose of this book and the others which would follow.

The launch, as the trade affectionately called this tool of promotion, took the form of an intimate lunch in the upstairs private dining room of Lutèce, a chic midtown restaurant, on her novel's publication date of

May 20. The room held only fourteen, the guest list culled to the presiding deans of reviewers. Lured by the reputation of the chef and the opportunity to meet each other in a private setting before the clan scattered for the summer, they all accepted.

For the event, the setting, format and even Barbara's outfit had all been carefully choreographed. The public relations director told her to wear a pastel-colored suit to reflect a vulnerable yet purposeful image. This look, achieved by a cream silk jacket, blouse and flowing skirt, was complemented by a corsage of pinks and baby's breath. During cocktails, Barbara was introduced by the publicity director to each reviewer individually. As they returned her greeting with polite generalities about *Sarah from Afar*, she tried to overcome her awe of these literary giants who shaped the thinking of the public and the future of the authors they wrote about or chose to ignore.

When it came time for the luncheon, she took the chair indicated by a calligraphic place card. Each seat had been strategically assigned, allowing her publisher, editor, public relations director and her agent access to laud *Sarah from Afar* and Barbara to the critics. At the middle of the table, behind an unoffending, small chrysanthemum centerpiece, Barbara was flanked on either side by the critics from *The New York Times* and *The Village Voice*. Opposite her sat representatives of *The Wall Street Journal*, *Publishers Weekly* and *The Washington Post*.

As the four-star chef seduced with soufflé and mousse, Barbara responded to questions about the origin of the characters in her novel.

"It's clear you're drawing from firsthand experience," said the editor of *Publishers Weekly*, whose write-up had already reached the publishing house, providing quotable comments such as: "Innovative writing . . . Beautiful language and authentic detail . . . A gripping read."

But all did not go as planned. In the midst of a lively literary exchange the critic on her right, desirous of better eye contact with his colleague on Barbara's left, suddenly nudged Barbara's head forward, tipping her nose unceremoniously into the salmon mousse. The maître d' hovering nearby did not consider this indentation the preferred design. With exaggerated pomp, he indignantly swept the squashed presentation into the kitchen. Barbara felt her face blush pinker than the departing mousse.

The impact of the event was immediate. Whether in apology for their faux pas or with genuine admiration for her work, both these men wrote long, appreciative reviews, which were run in prominent positions in their pacesetting papers. Barbara's career was launched, even if it had not been achieved exactly in the manner Ken Jorgen or her publisher had predicted.

Other publications added to the praise. "A discovery of brilliant proportions," hailed *Newsday*. "A remarkable storyteller" and "A heartwarming tale from an exciting new voice," lauded *The New Yorker*. The smaller presses outside the city followed suit. This critical acclaim led the publisher to double their promotional budget. No longer was Barbara intimidated by that august company, the literary pundits, whom she had imagined larger than any of her characters. They had provided the momentum necessary to catapult both Barbara and *Sarah from Afar* from obscurity into the limelight.

One communications sector fed off the other. An aggressive broadcast media consumed its print counterpart and, appetite whetted, craved more. Production assistants and researchers of women's shows, morning-magazine segments, author interview features, public television, radio listener call-ins contacted the publisher's understaffed public relations department requesting to interview Barbara.

"Fabulous news, Barbara, what I've been hoping for," Ken enthused over the phone a few weeks after the launch. "Your publisher wants to send you on tour. Seven cities. The book-buying and media capitals of America. It'll be great for sales. . . . Have you ever done TV?"

"No," she replied cautiously.

"You can handle it. We'll get the best in the city to media-train you. I'll organize it myself."

" 'Media-train?' "

"No unexpected questions. You'll be rehearsed so you have your answers down pat to anything an interviewer will ask before you set foot in front of a camera."

A press kit was designed: the best reviews selected, each edited subtly to distill its accolades, and a question-and-answer sheet put together to increase the comfort level of the host, who had no intention of reading the book or even the dust jacket.

The tour started the first week of June. This was the earliest date most major shows were available to be booked and the latest the public relations department was prepared to leave the promotion. It was essential that all be completed before the end of the month to capture a share of the lucrative summer reading audience.

Barbara flew to the targeted cities of Washington, Philadelphia, Boston,

Chicago, Los Angeles and San Francisco. New York, the largest market but also the most competitive for attention, was held for the end, anticipating her appeal in the other cities. Readings and signings at leading bookstores as well as major television there preferred well-known literary personalities.

The cities changed but not the rigor of her schedule or the format of her media appearances. The women's shows placed her after the cooking segment and before "This Week's Doctor" and asked in the allocated ten minutes about the difficulties of juggling career, husband and child. Hour magazine programs in five-minute staccato hyped her as the hottest literary sensation and wanted to know how sudden celebrity had changed her life and how her significant other responded to her success. Entertainment segments of the news spliced an interview into a slick ninety-second clip. Their sleek editing, cutting from close-up of author to host, to lingering shot of book cover with three-sentence voice-over, could sell anything. Hosts of radio listener call-ins were grateful to find a guest who could talk engagingly on a subject that had not been presented in their last two weeks of airtime. The half-hour or hour-long formal author interview features explored the psyche and sensibility of the writer, from early childhood influences to sources drawn upon for the immigrant experience.

The publicity generated sales and that benchmark of success: the second printing. For this edition, the publisher enhanced the dust jacket with the superlatives gleaned from the country's most respected critics. To Barbara's delight, within weeks of the tour, *Sarah from Afar* made *The New York Times* best-seller list and was edging its way toward the top.

✒

After her promotional blitz, Barbara looked forward to rest and time with her family. She planned a week's vacation for them during the interval between the end of Jenny's school year and the start of day camp.

Paul did not join them. He excused himself from the holiday a few days before they were to leave, explaining a land assembly closing had been delayed and he couldn't get away.

Barbara took Jenny to Sanibel, a crescent-shaped shelling island off the west coast of Florida. She wanted to take Jenny to the area where many writers had chosen to live and work. They flew from La Guardia to Fort Myers Regional Airport and rented a car. As they left the mainland and traveled over the causeway, huge snowy pelicans circled the bridge, then plunged into the inland waters, comedic entertainers welcoming them.

They chose an eagle-nest efficiency in a cottage colony. Their unit stood high above the sand upon what Jenny nicknamed "crab stilts." It had a spectacular view of the Gulf of Mexico. They would rise early, watch the sun move out over the water and the flocks of birds descend to feed. Sometimes when the ocean was calm they saw porpoises arc through the water.

They shared their days. They biked on paved paths around the island and explored the "Ding" Darling National Wildlife Refuge, with its myriad variety of wildlife. They often spotted anhingas in their sub-aqua snake dance and roseate spoonbills bobbing in the mud shallows with their fat spatulate clamps. At low tide they joined the shell aficionados on the flats. Some collectors brought hand nets to scoop their find, others resorted to a less dignified posture—buttocks up—to claim their treasures. Jenny usually found a mound of miniature coral shells and, sitting on it as if in a huge sandbox, sifted through them, her face joyous with discovery. Together they visited the rotund fisherlady down the road and purchased stone crabs hidden in the larder of her freezer. They enjoyed her parochial conversation and the sound of her words whistling through her few remaining teeth.

Every day they took a lengthy walk along the extensive, wide mocha sand beside West Gulf Drive. This was Jenny's favorite area for beachcombing: it was less built up than other parts of the island and with more vegetation attracted a greater variety of birds. Hook-beaked white ibises and ospreys abounded. Jenny was especially delighted whenever they came upon a resting flock of royal terns, whose long shock of contrasting black hair, when caught by the wind, ruffled into a brush cut. On one occasion, they saw a great blue heron standing sentry beside a fisherman. It seemed intent, as if relying for its next morsel more on man's generosity than on its own hunting prowess.

In the intimacy of one such ocean walk, Jenny told Barbara hesitantly that it was because of her that her mother had gotten hurt. If she had not wanted to show off how fast she could ride, then lost control, her mother would not have had to pull back on the reins so hard and hurt her wrists. She didn't understand why her mother hadn't punished her for what she had done.

"I know I really hurt you, Mommy. You were just pretending it didn't hurt. I bet you never knew this. But at night I would push open your study door and watch you trying to work. I saw how hard those mitts made it for you to write. I'm sorry, Mommy . . . I'm sorry." Jenny turned her face toward the ocean, attempting to prevent her mother from seeing her tears. "I never meant to hurt you."

"Darling, what happened to my wrists was not your fault," Barbara said, trying to repair the damage of her lies and eliminate her daughter's guilt. "It was my bad riding." She went to Jenny, held her tightly and, when she seemed calm again, resumed their walk, her arm placed reassuringly around her daughter's shoulders.

At sunset the following evening they were lounging on their balcony enjoying the sight of the cormorants resting on the shore silhouetted against the dark translucence of the ocean and the streaks of the disappearing day. The large birds sat with their wings spread wide into the wind, their heavy black feathers hung out to dry like enormous wet sheets.

"I heard Daddy screaming at you," Jenny blurted, once again returning to the traumatic autumn afternoon.

She revealed that when she had been sent upstairs to wash her cuts, she hadn't shut the bathroom door. Even though the tap water was running, she had heard her father shouting at her mother.

"I know it's because of me that Daddy's mad at you. He blames you for what happened to me. I'm the reason for all the trouble between you and Daddy," she added earnestly as a final orange line penciled itself across the horizon, then was erased.

"There's no trouble between Daddy and me," Barbara said. "Daddy was upset because of things at the office and he overreacted. None of it had anything to do with you."

"Are you sure you're not angry with me, Mommy?"

"No, darling. I'm not angry with you," she said, moving over to where Jenny was sitting. She began to stroke her daughter's cascade of auburn hair. "I love you very much. And so does Daddy. You've never done anything but bring us happiness. You're the best thing in our lives."

Too late, she realized the effect her lie had had on Jenny—the blame she had unintentionally placed upon her. She had deprived her daughter of the truth. Perhaps at the time she should have made up a different story, one not involving Jenny, such as an accident in the kitchen. Or told the truth of the attack, presenting it as an after-tag of emotion, an adult temper tantrum not to be condoned, but exorcised; its perpetrator chastised. Or, or . . . the possibilities now seemed endless.

What should she do now? Tell her daughter the truth . . . after so long?

The truth, as an antidote to guilt? But how to explain the reason for the cover-up, that Barbara considered the attack too heinous to tell her daughter? The very act of suppression would magnify the enormity of the abuse and possibly, at her daughter's impressionable age, render such candor unmanageable.

Had she originally told Jenny the truth, its effect might have been contained to fear of her father. Revealed now, it might also undermine her trust in her mother for deceiving her and threaten the closeness of their relationship.

Barbara made her decision. Whenever the topic resurfaced during the remainder of their stay on Sanibel, Barbara reassured her daughter of her love and that she was not responsible for her mother's injury. She reiterated that the tension between her parents had nothing to do with the riding incident. But she never substituted the truth for her fabrication of how she had injured her wrists.

As she was tucking her daughter into bed on the evening before they were to leave Sanibel Island, Jenny seized on a new and more terrifying thought: "You're going to get a divorce because of me, aren't you?"

"No," Barbara said fervently. "Daddy and I love each other. There's nothing for you to be worried about."

"I don't know, Mommy. Sometimes I wish I could just disappear. Then maybe things would be all right again with you and Daddy."

"Darling, don't talk that way. We love you very much. You're everything in the world to us."

∽

Paul met them at La Guardia Airport and during the drive to White Plains said, "By the way, your agent has been phoning. He wants you to give him a call."

"Glad you're back," Ken Jorgen began when she contacted him the next day. "Hope you had a great holiday," and without stopping for a response he said, "I'll be in your area tomorrow or the next day. Will you be in?"

"Sure."

He provided no explanation. "Speak to you then."

She opened the door the following afternoon in worn jeans and frayed sneakers, a pencil clamped between her teeth like a golden retriever, her mind still filled with her characters.

"I see you're finally dressing like a novelist," Ken quipped drolly. He faced her immaculate in his gray suit.

After he had kissed her on both cheeks, she said, "I'm delighted you dropped by, Ken. Please, won't you come in?" She showed him into the family room.

"Last week, your publisher sold the mass-market rights to *Sarah from Afar* for two hundred thousand," he said, appropriating Paul's favorite chair. He leaned foward, assuming the keen posture of someone about to transact business. "That means while you were away holidaying, you made one hundred thousand dollars, less, of course, my well-deserved fifteen percent. Not bad for a week's vacation, is it?"

"You can't be serious, Ken."

"You bet I am."

"I don't know how to begin to thank you."

"The mass-market deal was made by the publisher. You wrote the book. I just brought the two of you together," he responded, obviously pleased with himself. "I've never been wrong about books or people, Barbara," he said, reclining in the chair. "I predicted you would make me lots of money and be artistically successful. And you have. How's the sequel progressing?" he inquired, terminating his reminiscence.

"Slowly," she said. "With all the time I lost on it doing promotion—"

"I understand. But now's a good time to finish it up before the mass-market edition comes out. Try to have something for me soon, will you, Barbara? I'd like to be able to put it out for auction as soon as I possibly can. What's your working title?"

"*A Grandmother's Heart.*"

"Great title for the sequel." He rose. "You'll be hearing from my office as soon as I receive the check from your publisher. By the way," he said as he was heading toward the front door, "I'll be taking your book with me to Frankfurt in the fall. You're one of my big books for this season. . . . Also, you'll be pleased to know we're getting some interest in optioning *Sarah from Afar* for a movie. Looks like I've got myself another successful client. More books like this, Barbara, and your husband may soon be able to retire on your royalties."

"Ken, I can't tell you how much I appreciate everything you've done for me."

"I don't usually make house calls but I couldn't resist the temptation to give you the news in person. I must go. My train leaves on the hour. A two-inch pile of messages awaits at the office." He kissed her on both cheeks, as he had upon entering, and was out the front door before Barbara had remembered to serve the coffee.

While *Sarah from Afar* had been a joy to write, its sequel became unexpectedly arduous. Work on it over the ensuing months was overlaid with the growing fear that she could never live up to her own and other people's expectations for it. And although she had no deadline imposed on her, she knew her agent was right: it should be completed before she was required to promote the mass-market edition. The creation of a novel was a fragile, intricate process and one she had learned to respect and to which she felt subservient—a birth at which she sometimes seemed little more than a midwife. Interrupting it at this point might cause her to permanently lose the subtle weaving of character development and plot. It had been difficult enough for her to pick up these threads after the promotion of *Sarah from Afar*. She could not risk breaking her concentration again before the first draft had fully come together.

Driven by this feeling of time urgency and a desire to repeat the success of her first novel, she became consumed by *A Grandmother's Heart*. She no longer shared Saturdays with Jenny, recycling these hours into work. To assuage her guilt about her writing involvement, she allowed Jenny more freedom than she might otherwise have done and was careful not to criticize her.

Barbara's mind was too distracted to cope with Jenny's disturbed sleep pattern that since November would start on Sunday nights, then continue unabated throughout the week. Nor did she deal with the headaches that preceded Jenny's reluctant exit for school. And when her daughter returned home sullen, she didn't take the time to coax from her what was upsetting her or why she would often barricade herself in her room, only emerging to sit without appetite silently at the dinner table.

She ignored the phone that did not ring for Jenny, the children who no longer came by, Jenny's decision not to hang out with anyone from school. Unquestioningly, Barbara ascribed to diligence the hours her daughter sat alone in her room, her books spread before her, her CD player turned off.

Jenny dropped out of riding lessons and even refused to go to the stable at all the year following the accident. Barbara thought this the delayed reaction to that day, a repercussion Lennie had predicted and tried to prevent.

"Congratulations. You're about to become equally famous on the other side of the Atlantic," Ken said when, near the end of October, he informed her that in Frankfurt he had finalized a deal to sell the U.K. rights to a prestigious London trade house.

"Ken's office couriered these contracts to me today," Barbara told Paul when they had adjourned after dinner into the family room. "They're for the British rights I was telling you about." She extended a file folder to him.

"Why are you giving me these?"

"Ken asked me to get them back to him as soon as possible. I'd appreciate it if you could look them over before I sign them."

"You know I'm not an entertainment lawyer."

"These are just straight contracts, Paul. Like you do in real estate."

"Sorry, Barbara. I'm not in the mood now. I'll get around to them when I have the time."

Following this conversation, she kept from Paul any further evidence of her writing success. Increasingly, they spoke of only superficial things.

Barbara submitted A *Grandmother's Heart* to Ken Jorgen at the end of February and the following week commenced the national mass-market publicity tour for *Sarah from Afar*. The public relations groundwork for the hardcover edition had seeded well, making her schedule within the cities she visited even more demanding than the one undertaken for her previous promotion. Media interest, this time out, focused less on the book itself and more on Barbara as a personality, a much more difficult subject for her to discuss.

Barbara found herself traveling across the country for almost a month. She was driven not by the glamour of publicity, rather by fear of commercial failure, and, as such, felt she had to comply with her publisher's itinerary. If *Sarah from Afar* did not achieve the projected sales volume for the paperback edition, it would jeopardize the prospect for mass-market publication of any of her future work.

Exhausted from the hectic public relations tour and from the months of prodigious work to complete her novel which had preceded this and troubled by her deteriorating relationship with her husband, Barbara craved a holiday with her family.

"Spring's my busiest real estate season," Paul said, declining to leave his practice.

She asked Jenny if she would like to go again to the west coast of Florida for school break or to a different place.

"I don't want to go away with you," Jenny stated flatly.

Barbara stayed in Westchester with her daughter over the break, then organized a brief vacation for herself. Alone for the first time, she chose a spa in northern Italy.

∽

Lying on Itaro's floating dock in the late afternoon sun, Barbara felt the images shatter. They had become fragmented and chaotic: an explosion of circuits, memory gone rampant—like a computer printout whose lines had become scrambled, its characters unintelligible. These recollections had disturbed her rest, made her anxious to shake free of them.

"Imagine you are a painting on a wall," the interviewer droned once more into her subconscious. "Are you a solitary figure on the canvas or are there others with you?"

This time, she wanted to answer these personal, invasive questions and, by so doing, rid herself of indecision.

But the questions came too swiftly for her to resolve them. "Are the other figures proportionately large or diminutive? Proud or humbled? . . . How close does each stand to you? . . . Where is each placed on the canvas? . . . Does one figure dominate? . . . How do the others regard you?"

The voice was relentless in its pursuit of her. She had to put an end to these troubling questions, the questions which had forced her to trace through her past, questions she still could not answer.

She roused herself to full consciousness. She felt more tired than at any time she could recall. It had been a wearing sleep, one that had left her with a residue of haunting uneasiness and apprehension.

Barbara picked up her notepad and towel and left the dock. She felt too distressed to compose even a postcard. She might as well dress for dinner.

She took the promenade to the patio entrance, spun through the circular door and entered Itaro's lobby.

ITARO

"May I allow myself to put you together with other ladies from America who've just arrived to make a nice party out of it?" A gangly captain, who carried himself with the permanent stoop of one used to accommodating himself to the height of those he served, was addressing the stylish woman with exaggerated sunglasses who stood directly ahead of Barbara in the dinner line. Barbara stepped back politely from them, but his eyes swept her into the conversation. The woman hesitated.

"For one night, signora? Restaurant very busy. . . . Tomorrow, we see."

His cordiality and the restricted time frame made the request impossible to refuse. "If the hotel wishes," came the terse reply.

"And you, Signora Sterling?"

"Of course."

His hands invited both to follow him. A guest was already at the table intently looking at the menu decorated with the hotel's gardens. It was to her that he addressed himself.

"Mrs. Kruger, may I introduce to you these two nice ladies I spoke to you about before? *Alora*, here is Mrs. Sterling from New York. Here is Mrs. Talbot from Canada."

He offered Barbara the choice of the remaining chairs.

Glass walls captured an uninterrupted view of the spectacular site. One length of windows overlooked Lake Como and the hills across from the spa which tucked into one another like the crinkled folds of a dress. Another side offered the property's tended stately trees, sculptured hedges, bushes of azaleas and roses, and, in the distance, cut into the cliffs, abandoned Napoleonic era fortifications.

Barbara had not been able to enjoy the beauty of the garden this afternoon, obstructed as it had been by the umbrellas surrounding the pool. Her momentary indecision now allowed her reluctant dinner companion to usurp this view. It was of no consequence to her—the lake, too, was even more compelling at seven-thirty than this afternoon. The evening light cast a translucence on Blevio's painted coral homes.

The captain's eyes fidgeted among the women as if uneasy with his placement. "I hope you are to have a nice evening together." He handed the two he had just seated menus.

"My name's Barbara. . . . They're rather formal here," she said when the captain left. She felt self-conscious to have been the one to have initiated the conversation.

"And I'm Judy. Also from the United States. The Washington area."

The third propped her sunglasses on her head and looked the others over. "Dede," she replied, and promptly turned her attention back to the card. Her face was much younger than the timbre of her voice. Barbara speculated she was around the age of Judy and herself.

In the conversation's hiatus, Barbara groped for activity. She too opened the menu. All was in Italian with no translation. "I'm at a loss here. I'm afraid I don't know Italian."

"I'm sure the waiter can help you" was the woman with the sunglasses' entry into the discussion. "Often, in places like these, they have to deal with some guest who can't handle the language." She snapped her menu closed, telegraphing the international signal for service. Red nails clicked randomly on the card's glossy gardens until the captain reappeared.

The selections were explained. The matter dispatched. Menus were removed. Except for the one Judy retained. Barbara noticed her repetitively rolling its silkened, braided green tassel nervously between her thumb and index finger.

"How long have you been at Itaro?" Barbara asked her.

"I just got in from London today," Judy said.

"Great city," Dede remarked. "What shows did you catch in the West End?"

"None. I was there on business."

"That's too bad" was Dede's retort.

Silence enclosed the table, permitting the clamor from the surrounding parties to intrude. The intimate room was now fully occupied. Above the inevitable clatter from plates, cutlery and glasses being presented and removed were heard French, German and Italian.

"I think we're the only people speaking English here," Barbara said.

"Could be. It's still shoulder season for English-speaking tourists" was Dede's explanation.

"From the chef. A terrine of sea bass," said the curly-haired waiter, placing before each of them a minute portion. His arrival rescued Barbara from the strained conversation. "May I suggest from the region a nice white wine? Clastidio. It is a wine the Romans knew. It grows south of Milan near Pavia." He remained beside the table, awaiting a decision.

Judy looked at Barbara, then toward Dede. To the waiter positioned to her left, Judy said, "None for me, thank you," and to the others, "I better not have any. I'm on the spa program."

"Nonsense," Dede overruled. "Think of wine as a digestive. Like tea to the Chinese. A bottle of your best local wine. Clastidio you said. . . . Are we all in agreement?" She took silence as consent. "Also, we want Pellegrino." With an eye on the waiter, she added, "The vines are wonderful in these areas."

"Isn't this a beautiful room?" Judy said as she parted the flecked pink pâté slice into even smaller sections. "Happy like a circus tent." The content of her words was in contrast to her tense face and the rigidity with which she held herself in her chair.

Barbara had not fully appreciated the room about her, so involved had she become with her dinner partners. A blue-striped awning on a burnished gold background, its edge trimmed with golden fringe, sloped down to meet the three walls of glass. The room's fourth side was an exact silk-toned match to the awning, as were the arm and seat pads on the chairs.

As dusk thickened, a fluorescent rim of light between the awning folds became more pronounced and the hats on the series of candle wall sconces opposite gave the illusion of being in the midst of a much larger dining area. With the base of sconces ribbed in a blue velvet similar to their caps and a carpet of yellow daisies woven into a sea-blue background, the cheery ambiance resembled a festive tent.

"It sure does look like one. A great motif. I really like it," added Barbara.

"It's somewhat overdone for the size of the room. Too much of the same fabric. Might have been more effective if they'd used the same colors in another design. . . . I much prefer the other public rooms of the villa," concluded the authoritative voice.

The entrée replaced the appetizer before them. The wine was uncorked and the bottled water presented with a flourish befitting champagne. With one hand behind his back and chest thrust forward, the steward poured Pellegrino with the concentration of a matador engaging a bull.

With night, lights in Blevio's homes across the water appeared, their flickering dots like swinging lanterns. But Barbara found the scenery across the lake no longer diverting. The awkwardness of the evening was interfering with the magic. "I got in only about three hours ago. Came via Milan from New York. International travel sure is tiring. Don't you agree?" she asked, still trying to encourage conversation.

"It's not a problem when your body gets used to it. The secret to avoiding jet lag is never eat on planes. Just drink. Evian, not alcohol."

This clarification, Barbara thought, qualified Dede's earlier discourse on the merits of wine.

"How long will you be staying, Judy?"

"Till Sunday. . . . I'm on a tight schedule," she added reticently.

"That's a good break," Barbara said.

"Much too short," contradicted Dede. "I couldn't have my bags unpacked by then."

"Sounds like you do a lot of traveling," Barbara said to Dede.

"George and I have always traveled," she replied, at last removing her sunglasses from on top of her head and slipping them into her purse. "France, England—Italy, of course. Asia also. The usual. . . . Where did you winter?" This inquiry was directed at Judy.

"I've only been to England this year," came back Judy's stilted reply. "And you?"

"Being a senior cabinet minister, the Secretary of State portfolio, George travels a lot. George has such a high sense of public service that he never permits anyone to stand in for him, not even on those tedious Asia trips. I admire that sense of responsibility—integrity, really—in someone, don't you?" Assuming they knew the relationship of this man to her, she continued, "And George wouldn't go anywhere without me. Except, of course, if I can't leave the boys."

"Dede, how many boys do you have?" Barbara asked.

"Two. Adam and Michael. They're great kids. And they're both doing well in school."

"Do you have them in private school?"

"I'd never put my boys into boarding. We're much too close for that."

What an odd statement, Barbara considered. When she had tried to enter Jenny's bedroom this past week, she had ordered her out, saying she needed her space. "What are you so upset about?" she had asked Barbara. "No one my age gets along with their parents."

"Dede, you certainly come to Europe a great deal. What would be your favorite place over here?" Why had Judy changed the topic? Barbara wondered.

"Here of course . . . Italy. Especially northern Italy. But that's an unfair question, Judy. There are so many fabulous places in Europe. As I've said, George and I have been everywhere."

Throughout the remainder of the entrée, the dessert of sorbets, and the calorie-reduced selection of local goat cheese, Caprino and Bel Paese, the talk was dominated by Dede and her travels.

When the meal had been completed, the crumbs swept off the damask by the waiter's silver brush sweeper, the crystal tulip sorbet cups removed and the espresso replenished, Dede extracted a gold pen from her Chanel purse and asked for paper, a request easily accommodated by Barbara, who never went anywhere without it. Then Dede began a list of what should be seen in the surrounding area. She elaborated on each Italian town, as well as those in Switzerland, only a short distance away. No place was allowed inclusion until it had been embellished with an appropriate and lengthy anecdote drawn from her personal experience. Her suggestions, although as detailed as a Fodor or a Michelin, were quite different in content. They included what must be avoided: a "Not to Do List" was her heading.

Despite Dede's pretentious manner, Barbara found her stories and unconventional approach to Italy engaging and couldn't help laughing along with her. But she noticed that although Judy too was listening with interest to this travelogue, she remained tense and unnecessarily quiet.

By the time the trio rose from dinner, the staff were preparing the morning's tables, the other guests long ago retired. Waiters were unfolding fresh linen and, upon each, placed the breakfast cutlery. Using a soiled dinner napkin, the captain batted crumbs from the chairs, spanking them immaculate in anticipation of the next day's occupants.

As they walked from the salon, Dede lagged behind and zigzagged her way between the tables.

"Please arrange for the wine to be charged to my bill," Barbara overheard Dede say to the captain.

"*Prego*," came his acknowledgment.

"I really enjoyed having dinner with you, Judy, see you tomorrow," Barbara said, and headed toward the concierge desk to pick up her key. Barbara was aware she had not told the others anything significant about herself. She needed a diversion, an opportunity to forget; the chance to be again without care. She had immersed herself in the superficiality of the table conversation, as tomorrow, with ardor, she intended to abandon herself to the trivia of the spa.

∾

It had hardly been a relaxing evening, Judy thought as she strolled along the terrace beside the breakwall before going to her suite. Her way was lit by coach lamps that hung beneath the villa's trestled arches. How could she possibly be herself here? She felt out of place in these extravagant surroundings and with these women. All that talk of places she had never been. It had been difficult trying to hold her own with them. Barbara had been friendly. She seemed like a nice person. But Dede was rather affected. Dede's world was so uncomplicated. She appeared to have money, a good marriage, a close relationship with her sons.

She wished Shane and she were that close. They used to be. Her divorce hadn't caused the change. The whole time they lived in Alexandria he always told her what he was thinking. But then she was forced to sell the home he had grown up in and he ran away. Waiting for the police to locate him had been the worst three days of her life. When she found him sitting on a cot in the halfway house, his thin arms had fiercely gripped her neck as if he never wanted to be separated from her. She knew having her in law school and moving away from his old neighborhood had been difficult on Shane initially, but after she took the entire summer off to go camping with him, it had seemed they were as close as they ever had been. If only that were true today. She didn't understand him anymore. She had no idea he was on drugs. Or that he would steal. What could he have possibly been thinking when he stole that woman's purse? She never would have believed her son was capable of such a thing. And she couldn't seem to get through to him on any level. Not even when she tried to discuss hiring a lawyer for him after they found marijuana in his wallet at the Detention Center. She wished she understood her son like she used to. Could she have let him down in some way?

Where was that dance music coming from? It sounded like it was from across the lake. The night's stillness made it seem as near as the whispers of conversation and laughter from the patio bar. Everyone seemed to have someone. Everyone, except her.

A rush of hollow emptiness swept over her, its intensity unexpected. She was alone in the world. There really wasn't anyone with whom she could share her worries about Shane. Or who even cared about how well she had handled herself at the closing in London. Because of her need to support herself and her son, she had cut herself off from everyone and everything. There was so much she was missing out on. But if she was ever going to let someone into her life again, she'd have to take a chance and trust. It was about time she stopped feeling every man was going to walk out on her, as her husband had done. From the start, she had handled the situation with Terry badly. She should have told Terry about her son, and her son about Terry. And she should never have pushed Terry out of her life simply because she was afraid of being hurt again.

She looked out over the lake. Before her, the water stretched silent and black.

She couldn't remember ever feeling this lonely. She hoped Shane had got her message that she'd be coming back on the day she had promised. Why hadn't she gone directly home from London?

The church bells in the village sounded. High in Bisbino's cliffs the light from the hazard tower rotated green, red, white; its cycle a mesmerizing blink of color. She scanned the night's sky. From behind the clouds appeared the moon; it was a burnished orange, revealing the profile of a joker's face.

∽

A discreet tap on the door awoke Barbara. Then another. Light filtered through the adjoining planks of the ceiling-to-floor shutters. She should get up. But her body refused to comply. The crisp, uncreased sensation of the sheets encircling her, the deeply carved Empire foot- and headboard, both of which she could reach without stretching, held her momentarily in an idyllic state of awakening.

As from a distance, she heard the tumble and catch of one latch, then another, the jangle of a cart, the return of silence, the uneven scrape of wood being pushed across a metal track. Then she felt the warmth of a wash of sun.

"*Buon giorno, signora,*" her benefactor said, and left unobtrusively.

She remained in bed and rolled toward the light. From between the aperture of the shutters and below the perimeter of the balcony grille, a slice of Como morning awaited her.

The day was pristine. Sun glistened off the water. A narrow boat slid across her landscape; its movement barely disturbing the surface's stillness. Hills rose from the rim of water.

A half stretch brought her again on her back. Robin's-egg blue repeated itself on either side of a carved molding of a deeper hue and with the high ceiling and sloped cornice gave her the illusion of resting beneath a floating canopy of sky.

Barbara did not delay any longer. She pulled the glass-paneled shutters toward her, expanding her horizon, and stepped onto the balcony.

Sun accosted her eyes. Above her was the frame of an awning, and leading down from it, an iron handle. She cranked open its width of orange sheath and sank into the chair that had been placed beside the breakfast trolley. A fat brown bird tugged at the twirl on a croissant that protruded from her bread basket, then rested on the railing, its head tilted inquiringly to the side, and regarded her. This directed her attention to the delicacies beside her: a tureen of yogurt, marmalade thick with rind, crisp croissants and a glass of Sicilian orange juice. She sipped the un-expected sweetness of the crimson juice and glanced in the direction of Como.

Jutting into her foreground was the arc of a bay. Sailboats and small craft were randomly moored in it. A row of trees, whose leaves from this distance appeared like an open umbrella, extended the length of the isth-mus to a sheltered landing dock. A ferry approaching from the direction of Como swept wide and attached itself to its wharf. It stopped only moments, then maneuvered into the center of the lake, edging its way ever so slowly toward Bellagio. Its route took it directly in front of her. She watched its unhurried, mesmerizing progression.

The chime of the bells interrupted her thoughts. They rang from the church steeple in the village directly to the right of her, the one she had noticed yesterday. The church was charming with its silver-domed bell tower and dominated all the structures around it. Sets of thick metal bells swung through each of the four open arched sides. Its spoked rope-wheel rotated with the speed of the bells. The sound was ponderous and measured—very different from the cadence to which Barbara had become accustomed since her arrival.

Barbara looked at her watch. From the number of times the chimes had rung, she realized her watch must not be accurate. She had reset it forward the six hours for local time last night after dinner. But she had been too tired to check the exact time with the desk. She had better hurry or she was going to miss the start of her nine o'clock exercise class. She was glad she had opted for continental breakfast rather than going down to the dining room.

She left the balcony and hurried over to the wall of closets, withdrawing brown pants, a short-sleeved shirt and a gym bag. She hurriedly put on her makeup and fluffed her hair in a mirror encircled with ribbons and cherubic figures, then doubled back to the closet. From a pouch in her suitcase she took a notebook and added this to her gym bag. She only needed her key now, and spotted the heavy metal object, with its weight of hotel crest attached to it, on the inlaid wooden commode. A nineteenth-century lady with bare shoulders and dangling brown curls smiled seductively from a gilt frame above it. She scooped her key and exited her suite, hurrying along the wide hallway toward the lift under the gaze of posed nobility in ruffled finery. A gallery of suitable suitors, she mused, for the lady she had recently left in her room.

Her route through the lobby brought her past the concierge desk.

"*Buon giorno, signora,*" said the elderly attendant stationed there. His eyes, over his thin wire glasses, interlocked with hers; jowls shook from side to side displaying disapproval.

"Signora, you should not make a rush."

"What time is it?"

"Signora, the clock she says eight-forty." The concierge indicated the timepiece on the mantel beside her.

"But the bells, I thought they ring on the hour?"

"Every day, yes. . . . Today, no. The bells they ring in a way you can feel what there is in the air." The creases in his face deepened into a profound sadness. "*Campane a morte.* A person died from the village. A young person. This is the sound from the bells that one can feel the moment. If older person dies, they go sad. They pull in a way, gong . . . gong . . ." He imitated the laborious draw of the bell. "But if a younger person, they go always sad, but longer. They ring tomorrow before the funeral to call the people to approach. . . . Signora, you should not make a rush."

She slowed to a walk and, no longer short of time, headed toward the dining room, curious to see what was being offered on the breakfast buffet. The anteroom held a culinary presentation that left one unaware its contents were spa-related. Facing her as she entered, and against the wall which was common to both it and the dining area, were a series of crystal decanters topped up with the juice of Sicilian oranges. And accompanying it, perspiring in silver wine buckets, Mumm's champagne, an additive for the crimson juice beside it. A festive omelet trolley stood nearby. Its canopy, like everything else in the hotel, held by glittering columns. Presided over by a chef attired in the full regalia of his profession, eggs were not intended to be a trifling matter. Whites only were used, a guest's input restricted to choosing a desired filling from among the brimming ceramic bowls holding choice porcini mushrooms, peppers, peeled tomatoes, carrots, peas and slivered cheese.

Across the expanse of wall opposite these, presented on sheets of fuchsia cloth, display trays were filled with the tasty selections Barbara had already sampled upstairs, with the addition of the most perfect specimens of fruit. Wicker-tiered troughs held peaches, pears, apricots, kiwis, plums and strawberries. Unable to resist her first peach of the season, she put one on a plate and went toward the dining room. She paused between the pillars of daisies that flanked its entrance.

"*Buon giorno, signora,*" greeted the captain, who, spotting her standing there, had moved swiftly across the room. He talked to himself loudly enough for her to overhear, "*Devo ricordarmi tavolo delle signore americane. . . . Alora.*" He escorted her to the same table as the previous evening and into the same company.

Dede and Judy were too engrossed in conversation to notice her arrival.

"Plunk it in like this, Judy," Dede said, dropping an apricot into a glass bowl filled with chunks of ice. "And you remove it with these." She poised a set of silver spoons above it. "Don't leave it too long. It's not intended as a bath." The latter phrase was accompanied by the rescue of the oval fruit.

"Good morning," Judy said, acknowledging Barbara's presence beside her. "Please join us." Judy's words, Barbara could tell, were spoken with some relief.

The unseen recipient of Dede's demonstration, Barbara took her peach and with the silver implements immersed it into the iced water, twirled it around and extracted it.

Dede eyed Barbara's sophistication appreciatively. "Sorry we started without you," she said. "We weren't sure whether you'd make breakfast. You were so tired last evening; well, more quiet really. Don't rush. We'll wait for you and go over to the spa together."

Classes were held every hour. Though Itaro was fully booked, and the expertise of its fitness instructors well known, these sessions were not attended by many of the guests. Most Europeans preferred their own individual programs and the personalized services of mud baths, facials and body massage, or had come only for the purifying water from the nearby sulphur spring. Consequently, Judy, Dede and Barbara were left in their own company.

Water activities were held in the spa facility, as were the warm-ups and the various levels of aerobics. The pool's exterior wall was totally of glass and, with the day splendid, had already been fully opened. Lush vegetation—mammoth green leaves and floral fantasies simulating Paradise—was painted onto stucco walls, transforming this area into a garden setting. As the pool was at ground level, it gave a guest the luxurious sensation of swimming outdoors in a warm lake and looking across and up into runways of layered forest. A circular Jacuzzi was positioned to the left of the pool, just a few feet behind the sliding glass wall, permitting the user a choice, uninterrupted view of the same verdant imagery and, in addition, the wide girth of the property's specimen tree, the *platano* with its scabbed, mottled-beige bark.

This room became the trio's favorite. After the stretch and flex and beginners' aerobic class, which were held in an area with a high-impact floor surface, they spent most of their day there. The heated water proved necessary with the number of stationary exercises they were taught—stretches for various muscle groups done against the pool wall, pressing against the water's resistance with mammoth hand paddles to improve upper-arm strength and balancing balls under each thigh to tighten the less subtle problem areas.

"There's nothing quite as good as water exercises," Judy said confidently near the end of the morning. "There's no weight on you. You're using the force of the water to exercise against. You can't get injured. It's one of the best ways to exercise."

"It also ruins your hair," Dede lamented, struggling to tuck a ball under her thigh.

"True. But it's worth it to me. With all the pressure I'm under, I find it's the only thing that relaxes me." And, Barbara reflected as she watched Judy maneuver in the water, this was the first time she had really seen the strain leave her face.

Despite Judy's assistance, working with inflated objects in a pool was neither Barbara's nor Dede's forte. At the conclusion of the session, yellow balls proliferated on the pool's turquoise surface.

Dede suggested lunch on the patio overlooking the lake. This place,

Barbara remembered from her late afternoon dalliance on its adjoining floating dock, became a cocktail bar by evening.

"If you don't mind, I'm going to skip lunch," said Judy, glancing in the direction of the pool.

"That's a mistake. Food is the best part of being in Italy."

"I don't normally eat lunch. . . . Since I got here, I've been promising myself some laps outside."

Three young men in brightly colored bathing briefs were stretched out on the pool's ledge, their hands synchronized with their conversation. Glistening medallions hung around their necks. Two others—one bald-headed—lazed on blue cots. The pool, mist rising from its surface, was empty except for an older, rotund gentleman in cream trunks. He floated stiffly on his back, his tummy protruding above the water's surface like a pouch of goat cheese.

"It sure looks great. It's pretty quiet in there now. Just one person," Barbara said.

"Of course it's quiet. All the smart money is eating now. Twelve-thirty to two. Lunch. A sacred hour. She's a bear for punishment," Dede said with admiration as Judy walked down the woven-rope ramp joining the patio to the dock. "I'd usually say a glutton for punishment, but that expression doesn't apply in these circumstances." Dede requisitioned from the waiter the closest available table to the pool.

Judy was well into her third length of a well-paced crawl when in tandem both groups of men entered the pool as enthusiastically as if her starting laps had signaled an official sprint. The five set a ferocious clip. Easily overtaken, Judy was enveloped by their wake.

"Seems men see everything as a contest," Barbara commented, remembering Paul's refusal to read the contract for U.K. book rights her agent had sent her to sign.

"Well men come first, don't they?" was Dede's flip response. But Barbara noticed Dede's face tense as she dug aggressively into her radicchio salad.

∞

By four o'clock even Judy had had enough exercise. The Jacuzzi swirled invitingly. Judy and Dede followed Barbara into its warmth. The heat, as warned on the chalkboard, was intense. Reflex caused Judy to draw back onto the top step. She paused as one would upon entry into regular water to allow her body to become acclimatized to the temperature change.

"No good," Dede said, seeing her reaction. "Just plunk down. . . . It's wonderful." She demonstrated this conviction by submerging herself neck high. "We must work Milan into our schedule. I never go away without bringing my two boys back a wardrobe. They're always so appreciative. Men's fashions are fabulous here. . . . Boys are so loving and so possessive of their mothers. . . . My two are really very special."

Flush at water level, the forest was more striking than it had been even yesterday afternoon from the dock. Each of its trees stood in bas-relief with such clarity that Barbara felt as if she could reach into it and scrunch its velvety green texture.

Judy turned toward her. "She's been telling me more about her sons. They sound terrific."

"And they idolize George," Dede interjected, her voice becoming strident. "I really am quite fortunate. Actually, now that I think of it, I've always been quite lucky. . . . Judy, it must really be difficult bringing up a son alone," continued Dede.

This must have been what they were discussing before Barbara arrived at breakfast. No wonder Judy seemed eager to have her join them.

"But then you never did say if you were alone," added Dede.

"I used to be. But recently I've met someone," she answered pensively.

"Seems you're lucky, too," Dede replied.

"Barbara, tell us about your family," Judy said, shifting the conversation to her.

"I've a daughter."

"Must be wonderful having a daughter," Judy continued. "What's she like?"

The whirlpool was beginning to have its desired effect. With the percolating heat of the Jacuzzi, its strategically positioned jets bubbling soothing warmth, massaging away her remaining resistance, Barbara was beginning for the first time since arriving at Itaro to relax. She felt the stress unravel and, coupled with the intimacy imposed on her by being in constant proximity with two other women alone in a foreign country, was more susceptible to the sharing of confidences. The questions seemed blunter, the answers easier to relinquish. She wondered if they, like her, found it easier to fabricate reality than to acknowledge the truth. She did not want to explain her life to anyone, including herself. She had come here to escape. "She's great fun. She's into everything."

"What types of things?"

"Riding. School, of course. But primarily riding." Why had she mentioned riding? Even though Jenny hadn't ridden for over a year now, the incident that had occurred that autumn afternoon and its aftermath always seemed near the surface of her mind.

"Enough of this," Dede cut in. "Leave home at home. We don't come all this distance to discuss children."

"Sometimes that's not so easy to do," Barbara thought she heard Judy say softly.

A hydrofoil clipped through the center of the lake on its late afternoon run, returning to Como, leaving behind it a churning deep wake.

"How do you know so much about swimming?" Dede asked Judy.

"I swim every chance I get."

"But not in winter," Barbara interjected.

"Sure I do. It relieves tension."

"You've mentioned that before. What do you have to be tense about?" Dede asked. "You have a terrific job, a son who's devoted to you. And a boyfriend."

The whirl of hot liquid in the ensuing minutes was the only sound in the spa.

"Do you know that in all these many years I've never been away without George like this? But there always has to be a first time, of course. The exception makes the rule, doesn't it?" she asked.

This was posed with a desperation Barbara had not expected.

"I simply had to get away. George wanted to join me, of course. But ministerial responsibilities . . ." The sentence trailed off. A breeze lifted a filament off the outer skin of the *platano*; it crumbled noiselessly toward the ground.

"How long are you going to stay at Itaro?" Judy asked Dede.

"I'm not sure. . . . It depends."

Barbara thought that an odd answer from someone who was so definite about everything.

"You must have some idea," Judy queried.

"It just . . . depends."

Barbara refrained from questioning Dede. She had learned to respect other people's silences.

After the whirlpool Dede opted for an herbal wrap, Judy to return to her lap swimming, this time in the seclusion of the spa facility, and

Barbara to stroll into the village that had attracted her attention from the balcony. Once outside the resort's grounds, the rush of traffic caused her to step up quickly onto a narrow walkway. This minimal protection ended at the car park located at the juncture of the village's sole commercial street. Shops lined both sides of this winding, single-lane thoroughfare. She hurried along, mindful of traffic, glancing, as she went, into the lovely inset cobble courtyards, the entrance to the upstairs living quarters, their window boxes brimming with flowers. She had to press her body repeatedly against storefront walls as one vehicle, then another, hurled itself along the serpentine corridor, this route through the area being a segment of the much-used Via Regina. Their tires, like a metronome set at high speed, clicked a constant rhythm against the cobblestone surface.

Across from Banco Lariano, the road widened and distinctly curved down toward the lake. She continued along it until, a few minutes later, it brought her into the community's core. The town square flourished with activity.

Everything circled a cherub fountain, including the concentric rings of red cobble. All balconies of the local three-star hotel fronted onto it, as did the sidewalk tables of the pizzeria and *gelateria*. Behind it stretched the arbored promenade which led to the boat landing Barbara had noticed that morning.

The indisputable focal point was the two-tiered fountain. The cherub positioned there looked less than ethereal, as much due to the pandemonium taking place beneath its gaze as to the bawdy, indignant posture it had been allocated in its secular life. Thin spouts of water trickled between its toes into a basin whose wide ledge appeared to be the citizenry's favored gathering spot. Barbara squeezed in beside the others seated there.

A tall man was floating a crudely carved, motorized sailboat in the fountain. With an arm around the shoulders of the adolescent crouched beside him, he instructed how to guide its power-driven direction. His pride in this youth became apparent whenever the latter navigated the homemade boat safely to the other side of the fountain; his affection was equally pronounced whenever, at regular intervals, it collided headlong into the basin's cement buttress and capsized.

A chunky toddler tossed a toy plastic car into its water and, screaming unabashedly, pointed his minute index finger passionately toward the spot where the red object had disappeared. Irate, the mother slipped off her sandals and waded into the pool's shallow depth to pick up the coveted car. She emerged with the prized possession and, before returning it to his outstretched chubby hand, scolded him with a staccato tone and stern visage. He nodded comprehension. Then, with concentration, he squared both feet and deliberately pitched the toy back into the water. This drama recurred a half dozen times before the mother scooped up the child under his belly, smacked a ferocious kiss on the crest of his head and carried him screaming from the square.

The boats Barbara had sighted from her balcony were moored in the bay at the base of the square. She left the fountain and walked behind it along the ridge of pavement beside the lake's edge. Drawn up onto the sloped embankment was a potpourri of dories, sculling shells, dinghies, skiffs, rowboats and an unidentifiable assortment of hulls—all old and in various exigencies of repair. Behind this random grouping, a partially sunken narrow wharf provided home for a ragtag colony of scrawny ducks. As she stood there, a wiry gentleman with weathered features and gray scraggly beard withdrew from his overalls a brown paper bag twisted tightly at the neck. He unwound the sack, parting it with care for its contents, and offered its valuables to a youngster beside him. Together they scattered the dry crusts, one by one, delighting in the birds they attracted and in each other's company.

Barbara remained, sharing their happiness, then, stepping off the concrete onto the stones beside it, resumed walking in the direction of the boat landing dock. Pebbles scrunched beneath her feet as she made her way between the double row of linden trees toward the end of the peninsula.

She chose the bench furthest out on the promontory and sat on its hard, sloped slats. From this jut of land she looked down the length of Como into the foothills of the Alps. Mountains misted into one another. Homes far in the distance were clustered between twin hills. From her sighting, Rovenna and the other towns that surrounded the lake became more immediate and vital. Water tapped into the breakwall in front of her—then fell back to repeat again its continuous lulling motion. The consistency of this sound, like the rhythm of life around her, was healing.

A plunge of bells. Barbara counted them. Seven. She got up and began her walk toward the fountain and the center of the square. It was the hour to return to the hotel for dinner. She realized that she too, like those around her, was letting the bells order her existence.

At the earliest hour permissible, Barbara, Dede and Judy presented themselves as arranged for dinner. This synchronized arrival interpreted by the captain to be a tribute to his previous evening's diplomacy, he bestowed upon the three a greeting of effusive warmth, *"Le nostre tre belle signore americane,"* and escorted them to what had become their regular table. Returning with the menus, he stood near Barbara and explained the selections, then patiently awaited their decisions, their table presently the only one in use. His gaze lay unobtrusively away from them and through the wall of glass which overlooked the lake.

"It is a very strange light. Usually not so clear as today. A bit more haze. . . ." He spoke, as Barbara had heard him do on similar occasions, more to himself. "It is the light of September."

Although the meal in its formality and elegance was a repeat of yesterday's, Barbara was finding it a more relaxing dinner. There was a sense of camaraderie among the women and she was enjoying being with them. The three had been together virtually all day and, Barbara assumed, each had disclosed as much of themselves to the others as they were willing to do, no matter how contrived, erroneous or superficial this might have been. They now had acquired as much insight about one another as they ever would. Either from a need to present themselves in a certain manner or within the confines imposed by their capacity for intimacy, each had erected barriers against the others' entry into her life. These limits were intuitively understood. And it was on these terms that each had accepted the others. The conversation tonight was frivolous and undemanding. As if by agreement, each was respectful of the others' areas of vulnerability.

Barbara did not realize the passage of time until the yellow streetlamps clicked into place in the cliffs of Rovenna above the hotel gardens. She later noticed it when a strong wind took hold of the foliage in front of her. A spotlight silhouetted an aged, massive evergreen. Lit from beneath, the boughs on this tree appeared burdened, as if unable to bear their weight of webbed, interwoven, forest-dark leaves.

Barbara shuddered against the wind's chill as she returned by the outdoor route to her suite after dinner. Above her, the black coach lamps pitched against their tight iron chains. The heavy, sporadic splash of the lake slammed against the concrete breakwall. She went inside, anxious for sleep.

*T*he storm started sometime after midnight. A tear of thunder woke Dede. Another spiked close by. Then a crescendo rumbled and crashed directly overhead. Light flashed through the slit between the shutters, with the harsh intensity of daylight. And there was the erratic churning of water, wild slosh of waves striking against the break-wall.

Dede waited deep beneath her sheets for the fury's cessation and for the restfulness of soft rain. Instead came a ferocity of pellets. They battered against the wooden slats. Rivulets plummeted off the canopy onto the concrete surface of the balcony. Lightning burst outside her window with such impact it seemed as if she were the attracting polarity.

The wood-frame glass shutters flung open into the room and with them came the crack of planks against the wall. And dampness. Then a recurring, jarring thud of wood jamming into each other. The exterior shutters must not have been able to prevent the force of wind and rain from seeping through their horizontal open slats.

Dede left her bed. She pressed her weight against the set of open doors and slotted into place a gray crowbar she found dangling forgotten on the back of one of the panels of wooden shutters, diagonally bolting them and everything in front of them closed. For good measure, she wedged against its protruding brass louver a sturdy-looking Regency chair.

Chills trembled her body when she slid back into bed. What an awful storm. Bad things seemed to happen to her during storms. What was she going to do about her marriage? And her boys? Had George read her letter yet? She wasn't going to think about this. Had George ever loved her? If she were able to do it all over again, she probably wouldn't have married him. What a mess she had made of her life. But she had done one thing she could be proud of. She had raised her sons well. Michael and Adam were fine boys. And George never paid any attention to them. He didn't care how much he was hurting them. How was she going to protect them? To think what almost happened to Adam the day of the blizzard.

When was this rain going to end? She hated storms. But tonight there was no reason for her to be feeling this upset, she concluded as she pulled the covers snugly around her. She was thousands of miles away from anything that could harm her. Then why was she this frightened?

∞

At least this held off until after dinner, Barbara thought as she lay listening in her bed to thunder rumble closer and grow in intensity. Rain gusts sliced against her slatted shutters. Then came the sound of canvas being sheared off metal. Probably the awning she had opened that morning. She heard the thunder recede into the distance. Then an unexpected, volatile random crack.

She'd never experienced a storm quite like this before. Perhaps because its noise was being hurled down the lake and was echoing between the mountains as if in a sound chamber. Or maybe it was the erratic, persistent nature of its thunder which pretended at times to be dormant, then cracked unexpectedly seconds later above her. Or possibly she still felt disoriented in a country whose culture was alien to her own and everything, including the rain, seemed different: a difference no longer diverting, but unsettling.

Was her daughter away from her also lonely? Had the vast distance in miles and the expanse of ocean compounded this loneliness? The six-hour time zone difference had rotated the hours between them from day into night and with Jenny's school schedule made it difficult to find a time when she could be certain to reach her. She wished now she had phoned her before she went to bed. Jenny would have been home then. She had just left Jenny two days ago, but she had forgotten to tell her she wouldn't be calling her as often as she usually did when she was away. She hoped Jenny did not feel she had abandoned her. Or even worse, that she did not care about her anymore. Since that riding incident Jenny had become so unpredictable and acutely sensitive.

More thunder. A staccato of rain. Its cadence and force simulated the gait of a horse on rough terrain. This rhythm catapulted Barbara into a restless dream: a chestnut runaway in a field ablaze with yellow flowers, its rib cavity heaving; its neck sweaty and lunging forward. The rain softened, then grew distant; the horse receded, taking with it and out of Barbara's desperate reach the rider, an auburn-haired young girl. Barbara deepened into a troubled sleep.

Her optimism returned by morning. The sounds of the previous night had abated. A hint of light reached through the long crack adjoining the shutters. Eagerly, she left her bed to open them. After her night of turmoil, she craved the day's affirmation and the beauty she had witnessed from her balcony yesterday.

Instead, she looked out onto a dreary landscape, the air heavy and still. Clouds obliterated the cliffs, erasing the perimeter between earth and sky. All was shrouded in a gray pallor which slid down the crevices of the mountains, drawing over the forest and the homes buried in it a tight, opaque sheet. It was difficult to see the other side of the lake. Only the warning sentinel's harsh flash of light pierced this covering. There was no point in having breakfast on her balcony. She'd go downstairs and join the others.

∽

"Hi."

"What a night."

Judy's and Dede's greetings overlapped when Barbara, her plate already filled with buffet selections, slipped into the remaining seat at the table, the one she had occupied the previous evening.

"Hope you slept better than I did," Dede went on over the low density of chatter around them. "I was up all night." She poured herself tea from a silver pot; its thin neck, an embossed brush of feathers, its spout resembling the eager, open beak of an impatient fledgling.

The tables near them were filled. Their occupants were animated and eating with exuberance. Contentedly, a German lady sampled the spa's offering of low-fat yogurt while her husband opened *Die Welt*, snapped it back and at appropriate intervals read aloud select passages for her benefit. A sturdy, silver-haired Milano matriarch, circled by generations of kinsfolk, enunciated her words slowly. She overtly enjoyed her preeminence, as those seated furthest from her strained forward, attentive to each word.

Staff bantered among themselves as they served the guests at their tables.

"Look what it did out there," said Judy, indicating the garden behind her, the area into which Barbara faced. Limbs, their branches ripe with leaves, lay upon the grass. Two workers were gathering the debris, carting it from view.

"And it hardly looks more promising today," Dede concluded.

Barbara looked up toward the cliffs with their mock-medieval battlements. The sentry tower, with its twin symmetrical holes at each side of its cornice, gaped vacant like two emptied eyes.

"The storm must have kept a lot of other people awake too. Seems pretty busy here," said Judy.

"Well, I'm going to get another yogurt before everything's gone," Dede said, getting up from the table. "Anybody want anything while I'm up?"

"No, thanks," Judy said.

"I've more than enough here," Barbara replied.

"Prego, fax per le signore americane."

Judy turned toward the bellman. He took an envelope on which was written "Tavolo No. 5" off the silver service tray he was carrying and set it into the middle of the circular table under last evening's arrangement of yellow flowers.

"Either of you expecting a fax?" asked Judy.

"Not me," Dede replied.

Barbara shook her head.

"Probably my office," said Judy, reaching for the envelope.

"Well, then I'll be back in a moment." Dede moved off toward the buffet.

"This fax looks awfully blurred. No wonder they weren't sure who it was for," Judy said to Barbara as she began to unfold the one-page communication.

"Could have been the storm," Barbara suggested.

"Doubt it. A lot of the faxed documents for the deal I just closed in London came through like this. . . . Sorry about the intrusion," Judy added, then started to read the fax.

Barbara saw Judy's face instantly turn ashen. Her eyes traveled back and forth across the letter, pupils dilated. And the hand which held its tag of corner trembled. The fingers of her other hand pressed her temple with intensity, as if by so doing they could reinstate calm.

01:01   3:05am   30.4.0i   Police Comm

Metro Police

Dear Madam,

Metro Police request that you contact them
immediately in regard to a drug-related fall
of your child. The subject's emotional state
is currently under investigation.

Please contact

Detective Fitzpatrick #7180
Homicide

Three lines were unreadable. The ones which identified the city and the address of the police station. There wasn't even a covering page. But it had still found her. Thousands of miles away from where she should have been: at home, in Washington with Shane. She had no business leaving Shane at this critical time, not even to close the deal in London. And certainly, she should never have given in to Mr. Lewis' persuasion to remain away longer and holiday in Italy.

She didn't think her son was emotionally upset. Apprehensive about his trial, but that was all. That's not true. Of course she knew he was upset. Who wouldn't be if they were seventeen years old and awaiting trial on purse snatching? What the police called the felony of robbery.

And convinced, despite what she and his lawyer had told him, that the police, at the eleventh hour, would lay an extra charge—the more threatening citation—of possession of illegal drugs. The trial and its consequences had been the only thing on Shane's mind when she told him she had to go to London the following evening on business. The conversation came back in vivid recall: "No one's insisting you go anywhere. You asked Lewis to send you to London, didn't you? You don't really have to go. You want to go. You want to get as far away from me as possible. And away from the trial."

When she told him she would be back in one week, arriving three weeks before the court date, he had said, "Why can't you be honest with me, just this one time like you're always telling me to be? You don't want to be here when the shit hits the fan. Having a son brought up on charges of robbery and possession isn't going to help your high-powered career any, is it?" And then his conclusion: "All I am to you is one big problem. You really don't want me hanging around here anymore." She didn't think he really believed the hurtful things he was saying and felt he would settle down once she had left. She hadn't tried to reason with him. There hadn't been enough time. She had to make the six o'clock flight.

And then she did exactly what Shane had predicted: she didn't come directly home. She could have been back with her son within seventy-two hours, but, no, she didn't return. She felt burnt out and knew she would require all her energy to deal with Shane's problem. And Mr. Lewis offered her a holiday gratis, her first vacation in years, and she grabbed it.

She had made Shane's nightmare a reality. He must have felt she had deserted him, as his father had years before. And she had done so when he needed her desperately. Going to Italy must have been his proof that she didn't love him anymore. His words, while he waited with her for the airport limousine, refused to lie dormant; they returned afresh in harsh, poignant detail: "All I am to you is one big problem. You really don't want me hanging around here anymore." It had all been there for her to see. The heaviness in his voice, the moistness that filled his eyes, the wounded look that momentarily eliminated the defiance. She had not paid attention to his anguish, not listened to the terrible agony behind those words.

She thought she had been making the sacrifices all these years. But she had been wrong. Shane had been the one to give up the most. She had become too caught up in their financial struggles to be aware of what

Shane was going through. And even now when it wasn't as necessary for her to do so, she still continued to put work ahead of her son. She didn't realize that Shane was suffering. If only she had realized this earlier. Her poor, sweet unhappy son. . . . Her beautiful Shane. Her . . .

"Judy, what's wrong?" Barbara said softly, her tone sensitive to the transformation she had observed. Judy did not respond, her grip tight on the page. "Judy, may I see the fax?" Barbara removed it gently, coaxing it from her hand. And read its contents.

It was from the police. Homicide division. She read it again: "fall of your child," "emotional state under investigation," "drug related," "homicide." The location from where it came was garbled.

Her eyes strained into each drawn-out oblique letter. It was impossible to decipher. The fax had no city, no address, no phone number. Nothing to tell her it wasn't Jenny. Pain knifed her stomach. Her body flushed and weakened.

Life in that room fell away from her. Its sound, texture and animation. She had no further relationship in time or space with it. The paper she held, once dormant and inert, livened; it became her sole reality. "Fall of your child," "emotional state under investigation," "drug related," "homicide." The words spun around. Again and again. And that dream? The young rider being taken away from her, the features she could not see.

A fall? Jenny hated heights. Always did. She had been terrified to mount Snowball that first time. Jenny wouldn't climb up anywhere. Not unless she had a purpose. "Emotional state under investigation" . . . Jenny had become unusually moody recently. Withdrawn almost, spending hours by herself isolated in her room every day, her door shut.

But this behavior wasn't anything serious. Girls her age were often like that. It was transitory and would pass.

Why couldn't it have been drugs? Drugs were everywhere today. Even the good kids, they said, tried them. Could that be the reason she spent so much time in her room alone? She hadn't considered this before. She hadn't even thought of drugs.

Of course, something was wrong last night. She had felt Jenny needed her. She knew she shouldn't have been so far away from her. The storm. Her thoughts. That dream. She had been given a warning and she hadn't paid any attention. Why hadn't she telephoned then? The time on the fax read 3:05 a.m.—then whatever happened must have occurred around midnight. And the storm—that storm—was around four. That was 10 p.m.

New York time. At that hour, nothing had happened. And her daughter would have been at home. Why hadn't she telephoned? If only she had spoken to Jenny, she would have known she was upset and could have helped her. If she pressed, Jenny would have told her what was wrong. She could have saved her daughter. She could read everything in Jenny's voice. It had always been like that ever since she was little. This incredible and extraordinary symbiotic bond between them. As if they were a single entity: two parts of the same whole. Jenny needed her last night and she didn't even lift the receiver.

She had been careless with her daughter—the person she loved the most. Too confident in Jenny's well-being. Too certain that Jenny would always come to her with anything she couldn't handle herself. Too smug in their special relationship. She believed it to be indestructible; unwittingly, she tested it with neglect.

But Jenny had come to her. When they went to Sanibel without Paul, she realized that Jenny was preoccupied with the tension between her parents, blaming herself for everything and anything that had gone wrong in the family. And despite everything she had done and said, she had been unable to relieve Jenny's anxiety. As she tucked her into bed the last night they would be alone together, Jenny told her exactly what was going on in her mind: "I don't know, Mommy. Sometimes I wish I could just disappear. Then maybe things would be all right again with you and Daddy."

A spasm constricted her chest. Her breath came in quick, short stabs.

It had happened around midnight. Somewhere around then. Where was Paul at that time? She really hadn't thought of him since her first day here. And she didn't want to speak to him now. She couldn't talk to him about her daughter. Jenny was her child, her life, and she did not want to share her grief with him. She would not allow him to intrude into the intimacy of her anguish. She did not want his words of comfort; nor to console him. She felt no compassion toward him for his loss—or even pity. Her capacity to care about him was gone. It must have ceased when he had abused her that last time. He meant nothing to her anymore. Nothing. There was no point in staying with him.

All that they really had in common was Jenny. She must have always known this, but had not wanted to admit it to herself. She had not wanted a divorce, for Jenny's sake and her own convenience. She lacked the courage to leave. But no more. If she had the strength to get through this, she could survive anything. She would no longer endure the pretense of a marriage. If by some miracle Jenny survived, she would do everything in her power to ensure a happier life for the two of them.

But that could never happen. The fax originated from homicide. Clear, unequivocal. And final. She had to get home. She must ask the concierge to book her on the first flight back to New York. She must—

"The two of you seem upset. Is there something wrong?" Like an automaton, she extended the sheet to Dede.

What could be in this fax to have so affected her two companions? As she sat down, Dede scanned the page. "A drug related fall of a child." No wonder they're so quiet. Where was it sent from? It was impossible to figure out. How could she read anything through these blurred lines? Michael and Adam. Her body tensed. It could be one of them.

Her eyes fixed on the page. She reread the fax, trying to clarify its meaning. "Subject's emotional state is currently under investigation." It couldn't be Michael. He's never had any emotional problems, except for that one episode after the ski overnight, years ago. The incessant scrubbing he did for weeks, not able to stop until his poor little body became red and sore. And how he moaned in his sleep, his night's rest disturbed for months. That education student she had brought into their house. He might have molested Michael that day. Maybe Adam too. Other than that, nothing had ever seemed to upset Michael. He's always been a happy child. So easy and well adjusted. This couldn't have anything to do with him. But Adam. Her eldest. It could be Adam.

A sinking sensation seized her stomach in cycles of deepening waves. Her extremities went rigid.

Memories flooded her mind. Adam's obsession for the musty, peculiar-shaped rooms of the attic. It had become his private place although he had his own room that she had designed and decorated just for him. The day she found him there barricaded behind boxes hiding from the house-keeper, frustrated by Maria's inability to speak English and to understand his requests. Whenever he was upset, he went to that solitary place. The third floor gave him access to the roof. She could still see him there in that awful crouched position—legs tucked up beneath him, hands gripping the shingles. Did he intend to throw himself off the roof? Had only her arrival home at that critical instant prevented him? She had tried to tell herself that it was an attention-grabbing gesture designed to bring his father home—a youthful act of defiance. But it might have been more than that. The paper dropped stiffly from her hand. Her eyes followed it down to the table. She stared intently into the cloth's blank flecked surface, as if invisibly written on it was her answer.

Could he have been planning to kill himself? She hadn't discussed this with him when they were in Palm Beach together. She never considered asking him. She had wanted to put that horrible day behind them. But whatever his reason, Adam would never harm himself. To speculate whether he intended to commit suicide was ridiculous. He had no reason to do that. She had always been devoted to him. From the moment Adam was born, she had never left his side. She was always home. Of course, she had help in the house, but she was always there too. Except for that morning a month ago after George canceled out of their holiday to Palm Beach and she had to go out to complete the things made necessary by his withdrawal: the morning Adam flung open the trapdoor from the attic and went onto the roof. The fist of her right hand clenched and unclenched—a reflex synchronized with her mind.

It was a fall. That's what the fax said. An accident. And that's what it was. Last night was Friday night. The fax was sent at 3:05; so the accident must have happened in the evening, sometime after eleven. She concentrated intently, struggling to reconstruct Adam's day. He must have had some kids over. Hadn't it been just last Wednesday in Palm Beach that he had told her all his friends were having parties and that the best time to have one was when your parents were out of town? No restrictions, less supervision. She presumed he had said those things to shock her. But that could have been what occurred. A party would explain the time of the accident. He went to show them his favorite room. And someone asked him about the suspension ladder. He showed them how it pulled down from the ceiling and demonstrated how he used it to get out onto the roof. He'd done this before and he hadn't gotten hurt. He was just showing off like all boys that age do. And he fell . . . he didn't intend to; it just happened. It was an accident. It stormed the March night before Adam went onto that roof, as it had on the night that he was born. Then last evening, the eerie violence of that rain. Upheavals of nature seemed to coincide with danger for her eldest.

Friday night at eleven. Where was George? He promised he'd be home by eight o'clock every Friday once he got back from Nigeria. And this was the first of those Friday nights. But why should she have expected George to be home? He was forever promising things to her and the boys that he had no intention of doing. He said whatever was expedient and would get him what he wanted.

She had raised the boys alone, with no help from George. He had given nothing of himself—neither to her, nor her sons. They could never rely on George for anything. He was absorbed with his own ambition, mesmerized with his own career. It allowed room for nothing else—not even his family. He never considered them. Not even the day their first child was born. He left them both to go to Ottawa before she was out of the anesthetic. And he had not even bothered to fly back for Michael's birth. Yesterday had George found another excuse not to return to Toronto? During those last few days in Palm Beach before their vacation ended, Adam talked of nothing else except seeing his father again. Did George once more disappoint Adam and in a desperate bid to get his father to come home, had Adam climbed onto the roof again?

Only this time she was not there to save him. And he fell. An accident. A horrible, senseless accident. There never was a party. Adam wouldn't have had a party without her being there. He must have meant to do this to himself.

Tears blurred her vision, stung as she struggled to deny them release. She lowered her eyes, fixed them unseeing in front of her. She did not want the others to see her crying.

Who was with Michael now? Had he been told what had happened? Adam was so good to Michael, so protective of his younger brother. And Michael idolized Adam. He must be devastated. She had to protect her surviving son. Michael had lost his brother, she couldn't take his father away from him too—no matter how poor a parent he might be. Michael needed a family now. He needed an anchor, something to hang on to. Stability. Some semblance of permanence. He needed it desperately. She had to think of Michael. How could she handle the loss of her child together with the loss of her marriage? This wasn't the time to think about leaving George.

She picked up the fax from where it had fallen. Spent from her emotions, she read it again more carefully, calmer in the aftermath of shock.

What had gotten into her? Why was she even thinking like this? It says the fall was "drug related." She was living in the same house as Adam. She was there when he left for school in the morning, when he came home and up until the time he went to sleep. She would have known if he was on drugs. She would have suspected something. So it couldn't have been Adam. Adam never touched drugs. He was forever going on about the danger of drugs and what losers the boys were who took them.

This fax wasn't about her son. The circumstances surrounding the accident didn't relate to him, that was obvious. The muscles in her stomach relaxed. Warmth began to surge into her hands. She looked at the other two women around the table. Judy kept rubbing her forefinger across her lips. Barbara's face was ashen. Her eyes moved back and forth between them. Of course. They both have children. It must be one of theirs. She pulled her chair snugly into the table.

Should she say anything now? Or wait until she was told whose child it was?

What could she say that would be of comfort? What could she do to make things easier?

George would never have permitted anyone to send her such horrid news. He would have phoned her himself. She folded the paper in half. Tossed it into the center of the circular table and between the two women. It sat there, untouched, beneath the petals of last night's flowers. Unclaimed by anyone.

The bells began their draw. A steady, dreadful toll. The concierge was hurrying toward them. His approach suspended everything else. "Signora," he began as he neared their table, "there is a telephone call for you. It is urgent. May I show you the way to the telephone office, Mrs. Talbot?"

The vacuum of the still morning made the bells from the village seem closer. Gong . . . Gong . . . Gong . . . Gong . . . Gong. A slow, powerful pull, sorrowful and profound. Barbara recognized the timbre of the bells, the lament the concierge had spoken of yesterday. The dirge for the young man. And she knew it would toll this morning, as if without end.

Acknowledgments

I have always felt that, despite the lonely, exhilarating hours of writing, no one who creates a book does it alone.

Thank you John and Brian for your insight, Lily, Kay and Nicole for your encouragement, Lynda, Ann and Jennifer for your skill in production, and Max for your patience.